Threshold of Deceit

A Blackwell and Watson
Time-Travel Mystery

THRESHOLD OF DECEIT

A Blackwell and Watson Time-Travel Mystery

by Carol Pouliot

LEVEL
BEST BOOKS

To my sister Jan Luca with love.

Contents

Praise for Threshold of Deceit

How can a police procedural be so much fun? Clever and compelling, this intriguing time-traveling puzzle will keep you guessing, keep you turning pages, and have you applauding the talented Carol Pouliot's juggling skills! Nick & Nora meet Timeless in this entertaining mystery. — Hank Philippi Ryan, nationally best-selling author of *The Murder List*

Plenty of authors create a clever premise, but few create a world so crystal clear that we feel as if we're a part of it. With a cast of well-crafted characters and a protagonist that charms on every page, Pouliot accomplishes just that in this compelling time-travel mystery that traverses seamlessly between 1934 and the present day. — Judy Penz Sheluk, author of the Glass Dolphin and Marketville Mystery series

Present-day Olivia Watson and Detective Sergeant Steven Blackwell from 1934 have one thing in common. The house they live in is a time portal, allowing either of them to step forward or back into each other's era. What is at first an experiment in time travel, however, becomes a more serious matter when Olivia inadvertently becomes involved in the case Steven is investigating – the murder of a known philanderer. With delightful twists and turns, Carol Pouliot serves up a delicious tale that is easily devoured. One hopes it is just the start of a long-running series! — Michelle Cox, author of the Henrietta and

Inspector Howard series

A charming mystery with an intriguing premise. Can't wait for the next installment. — Eleanor Kuhns, award-winning author of the Will Rees series and *The Shaker Murders*

A well written and cleverly plotted mystery with a historical twist. — Bruce Robert Coffin, best-selling author of the Detective Byron Mysteries

Carol Pouliot has done it again with her captivating detective duo Steven and Olivia. She's from the 21st century, he's from 1934. Together they solve an intriguing murder in 1930's Central New York. — Rick A. Allen, author of the Star Riders series

Threshold of Deceit takes you on an unforgettable journey merging the present with the past. You are immediately drawn in to the engaging characters and complicated relationships that keep you turning the pages to find out who did it, and what the future might hold for two people from different eras. — Nikki Bonanni, The Killer Coffee Club

No more tears now; I will think upon revenge.

—Mary Queen of Scots

Love bites.
—Def Leppard

Chapter 1

Sunday — April 22, 1934

She sat across from him on the red-and-blue plaid blanket, legs stretched out and ankles crossed. It was a glorious day and the sun felt delicious on her skin. The wide-brimmed hat shaded her face, but already her arms were growing pink. She smiled, watching cardinals swoop back and forth in the lush meadow around them. She closed her eyes and listened—the air hummed with birdsong.

Today was their first picnic of the season. He had carried the wicker basket packed with all his favorites—ham sandwiches and garlicky pickles, potato salad, and apple muffins with chopped walnuts.

He'd finished eating first and was lounging on his back, elbows bent, hands locked together behind his head. He squinted in the bright light as he gazed sleepily at a flock of Canada geese flying high above in a V-formation.

She sat quietly, watching, waiting for the poison to take effect.

As she popped the last bite of oatmeal raisin cookie into her mouth and was brushing the crumbs off the skirt of her new dress, Frankie Russo began to choke. It was clear that, at first, he thought nothing of it. He sat up and took two long pulls on his beer.

"Gee," he laughed, "something must have gone down the wrong way."

A minute passed. She sighed contentedly and sipped her iced tea.

He pressed a hand to his chest as if trying to force in air. The deep breath defeated him and his face contorted as a ripple of coughs rumbled through his lungs. "I can't breathe." He groaned and reached for his belly. "I feel sick to my stomach." He pitched toward the side of the blanket and vomited onto the grass.

"It feels like I swallowed broken glass," he croaked, falling back to the ground.

His companion tilted her head toward the sun. A small smile crept onto her face. She said nothing.

"What's going on?" Frankie asked, his eyes growing large and wild.

She heard the fear in his voice. She savored the warmth of the day and the fresh-smelling air. She savored the moment. She gave no reply.

"You found out," he said, panicking. "You did this."

Frankie Russo rolled to the side and brought his knees up to his chest. A crimson wave washed over his distorted features. He tried to sit up but had already lost control of his arms and legs. Struggling to breathe, he drilled her with red eyes. He moaned then was silent.

She got to her knees and looked around. Still all alone. This had been the perfect day to choose. She knew the whole town would be down on Victoria Avenue for the Little League Parade. Good. She packed the picnic basket and set it on the grass, then rose to her feet and walked around behind Frankie. She put her shoe on his back and shoved hard. He barely budged. She kept pushing until he rolled to the center of the blanket. She bent down and got a tight grasp of the two corners nearest her. Holding on, she stepped over him and grabbed the two far corners. Frankie was now a lump in the middle.

Little by little, tugging and pulling, Frankie Russo's killer dragged him across the short expanse of field to the thick woods beyond. After stopping to get a firmer grip on the blanket, a corner of which had slipped out of her hand while hauling him over a rock, she entered the forest. She yanked and pulled as she strained to get the dead weight through low-hanging branches, around the end of a mossy log crawling with insects, and over some fallen limbs.

At last, she reached the top of the slope that led to a deep gully. She positioned her cargo on the edge, let go of the two far corners, and pulled hard on the blanket, jerking it forcibly upward. The body rolled over and tumbled down into the ravine.

Phew. She stood with one hand on her hip panting, trying to catch her breath. She turned to leave.

What was that?

Was that a groan?

No. It couldn't possibly be. She'd put enough poison in those muffins to kill a horse.

She craned her neck to peer down to the bottom. She stood still as death. She squinted and strained to pick up the tiniest sign of movement, the slightest stirring or shift in his position. Frankie lay immobile. She squeezed her eyes shut to block out any distraction and listened hard. Birds. The chirp of a chipmunk. Rustling in a pile of dried leaves, a snake maybe or a squirrel in search of an acorn. Nothing more. She let out a deep breath, so relieved that she felt dizzy. She swayed then caught herself.

Time to finish and get out of here.

Frankie Russo's killer gave the blanket one strong shake, so violent that the edge snapped harshly. The crack broke the quiet of the woods and a murmuration of starlings flew out of the trees—for a moment the sky was black with them.

She folded the blanket neatly into quarters and returned to the picnic site. Then she calmly made her way down the hill to join everyone at the parade.

Chapter 2

For once in his life Detective Sergeant Steven Blackwell felt like a regular fella, strolling among the crowds along Victoria Avenue with his family, happy to be off duty on this beautiful day.

Earlier he'd enjoyed the rare treat of Sunday dinner with his aunt and uncle, cousin Jim, and Jim's wife Martha. After the meal, the women had caught up on village gossip while they washed and dried the dishes. The men had retired to the porch with a second cup of coffee where they fell into a lively discussion on the massive manhunt for the outlaw John Dillinger, "Public Enemy Number One" according to the posters. Shortly before two o'clock, they headed up the Mohawk River Road to the parade.

The small New York town of Knightsbridge exploded in red, white, and blue. Streamers fluttered from the doors and windows of shops open especially for the festivities. A gust of wind caught a large American flag and forty-eight stars snapped to attention as Steven and his family passed below. And when Uncle Mike entered Sal's News to buy the latest issue of *Field and Stream*, he had to duck under the bunting draped in the doorway. All along the avenue vendors hawked treats, walking among the crowds, their goods on trays held up by leather straps around their neck. The air smelled of popcorn and cotton candy and crackled with excitement. Families squeezed together at the curb, eager to grab the perfect spot to glimpse the boys marching in their new team shirts. The annual Little League Parade had arrived. Today was the official start of spring and the baseball season.

"Hey!"

Steven spun around and peered over his cousin's shoulder. His best friend Artie Sinclair strode toward him, closely followed by his wife Helen and her sister Lucy. Helen had their daughter Annie's hand in a tight grip and the two women were fighting the crowd so as not to get separated.

"Quite a turn out," said Steven, as the men shook hands.

"Best one yet!" Artie exclaimed.

"It should be starting soon," said Aunt Jenny, a thrill in her voice.

"Let's find a good spot before they're all gone," suggested Uncle Mike.

The two families made their way to a place near the corner, stopping to buy ice cream cones en route. Steven thought of Olivia and wished she'd been able to come. Then, he remembered their plans for tonight and a river of excitement coursed through him. He was taking her out for the first time. *Okay, so it's only a part of our experiments, but still.*

"Jim, there's Hannah," said Martha. "I want to go talk to her."

Across the street, Martha's best friend Hannah Grantham was holding on to her straw hat, yelling and waving.

"Sure, honey, go ahead. But don't take too long."

Helen turned to Lucy. "I just realized…where's Frankie?"

"He went back to Syracuse this morning. It's his week at the brewery." Lucy licked her ice cream, getting some of the chocolate and strawberry together. "Mmm, this is good. I tried talking him into taking a later bus, but he said he had to get back early."

Helen spun her ice cream around her tongue to catch a drip before it landed on her Sunday dress. "Well, too bad for him. He's missing all the fun."

Chapter 3

Sunday — Present Day

"You'll never get away with it," said Liz, peering through the steam of her cappuccino.

"Sure I will," said Olivia.

"What makes you think you can do this?" Sophie asked, her eyebrows drawing together.

"Why do you think I can't?" Olivia replied gently.

"What if you get trapped there and you can't get back?" Sophie said in a strained voice.

"I won't get trapped. I've always been able to get back okay." Olivia wanted her two best friends to share in her excitement but she could see they were worried. Sophie's pale face was even whiter than usual and Liz, normally stoic, looked concerned.

"Sophie, you know she's going to do it. No matter what we say," Liz said.

"I'm scared," Sophie whispered.

Olivia took another bite of croissant, wondering if she'd ever get used to the extraordinary new life she'd been thrust into.

It had started out as the most terrifying week of her life. One night last winter, when she'd been deep asleep, warning bells rang out in her unconscious mind. She sprang awake and faced her worst fear. A strange man stood at her bedroom door. Her heart pounded. Her mind screamed. She tried to move but panic had paralyzed her. Trapped and vulnerable, Olivia searched frantically for an escape. The man leaned into the doorway, craning his neck to peer in at her. Then he jerked back, shook his head as though confused, and walked through the wall.

That first night, Olivia thought she must have been dreaming. What else could it be? But her visitor came back every night for an entire week. The terror of being physically harmed became the horror that she was losing her mind. Eager to come up with an alternate explanation, she considered the possibility that he was a ghost. Perhaps she was a medium and he a departed soul. Finally, although she couldn't say what made her do it, Olivia spoke to him.

And he answered.

He said his name was Steven Blackwell and he was a cop...in 1934.

Once they began to talk, they couldn't stop. They were determined to figure out what was happening. They concluded it was Einstein's theory: all time happens simultaneously, there is no past, present, or future, and time can fold over itself. They discovered they could plan to meet and, at the appointed time, each saw the other appear at the threshold of Olivia's bedroom door. Steven and Olivia had learned to time travel.

Now two months later, Olivia and her lifelong friends, Liz and Sophie, were on the patio behind Sophie's *Pâtisserie-Café* debating Olivia's latest adventure over breakfast.

Liz picked up the conversation. "Okay, putting aside the danger of leaving the house. Let's see if I've got this straight." She leaned forward. "You're going out to dinner with Steven...in a public place...in 1934."

"Yep," Olivia grinned.

"Where you're bound to run into people...," said Sophie.

"…who'll want to know who you are…," said Liz.

"…and where you're from." Sophie finished.

"That about sums it up." Olivia grabbed the French press and poured herself more coffee. "Anyone else want some?" She held up the pot.

"Don't try to change the subject," said Liz. "Olivia, there's no way you look like you live in 1934. People didn't look anything like us back then. They dressed differently. They moved differently. You'll never pull it off."

Sophie piped up. "Ohmygod! Olivia, they'll know! They'll know you're from…*now*," she whispered, blue eyes as wide as dessert plates.

"No. They won't. People see what they expect to see." Olivia shaded her eyes as the sun moved from behind a tree. "If I look odd to them, they'll just think I'm eccentric. Or from New York or L.A. But," she laughed, "there's *no way* that someone is going to say, 'Gee look at her. She must be from eighty years in the future.' Think about it."

Sophie's face was pinched. Liz frowned and shook her head. Her razor-cut blonde layers floated out, reminding Olivia of a Japanese paper fan.

"I know we should be used to your escapades by now," Liz said. "But a trip back in time outside the safety of the house…it's a lot to take in."

Olivia knew they were all thinking the same thing. Would she be able to get back? What if she had to live out her life in another time? Would she ever see them again? Would she be the same if she did get back? What if the time shift somehow affected her DNA? Or her mind?

So much could happen. So many things might go wrong.

Olivia waited.

A fat bumblebee buzzed by the table on his way to some luscious lilac blooms. A chocolate-colored puppy raced over the lawn toward the swiftly-moving river, his leash flying, his owner chasing after him.

The couple at a nearby table leaned over for a kiss then got up and walked away hand-in-hand.

Liz broke the silence. "You *have* already spent a lot of time there and you've always been able to get back. I guess you should be okay," she said reluctantly.

"I think you're taking a big risk, Olivia. You've never left the house before. This is different from sitting in Steven's kitchen drinking tea and eating Fig Newtons," Sophie said. "This is dangerous."

"Come on, you guys. It's gonna be fun. Besides I'll be with Steven. He's my connection to the house. We know I'm safe there. Plus," Olivia went on, "we're going to the pub. That's like my home away from home. *And* it's a place that spans both times."

"Just when I think we've seen it all," Liz sighed, "you come up with this. Well, your life certainly isn't boring. I'll give you that."

"I want you guys to be excited with me. Wait until you see what I'm going to wear!" Olivia exclaimed.

Momentarily distracted by one of her favorite topics, Sophie leaned forward. "Ooh, that's right. You've got all of his mother's gorgeous outfits to pick from. What *are* you going to wear?"

"A black-and-white silk dress. It fits like it was tailor-made for me."

"It's weird how you and his mother are exactly the same size. Don't you think?" asked Liz. "Almost like this was meant to be."

"Don't start on that again. You know I can't think about Steven like that."

"Get back to your outfit," Sophie said.

"Well, it's formfitting. The skirt flares out a little on the bottom, down by my calves. It has short sleeves and a black patent leather belt."

"What are you going to do for shoes?" Sophie asked.

"Remember those open-toed white pumps that I never want to throw away?" Sophie nodded. "I think they'll pass for 1934."

Sophie nodded again. "Cool."

"So, is this a date then?" Liz persisted. "How did it come about? When did he ask you out?"

"No, it's not a date." Olivia took another drink of her coffee and popped the last flakey, buttery bit of croissant in her mouth. "We've been talking about the next phase of this time-travel stuff and we want to find out if I have to stay in the house in order to stay in 1934."

"Ohmygod!" Sophie was back to worrying again. "You mean this is an *experiment*? You're putting yourself out there like a guinea pig? Are you kidding me?"

"Oh, Sophie. Please, don't worry. I promise you I'll be safe. Nothing is going to happen. I'll be back later tonight. And I'll text you *immediately*."

Sophie said she didn't want to think about it anymore. "Here," she muttered, passing the basket around the table, "there're a couple of croissants and a brioche left. I'll have Luc bring us more coffee."

"You just want an excuse to see your new boyfriend. Who are you trying to kid?"

"Mmm," said Olivia, tilting her face toward the sun. "I agree with Liz. But who cares? Luc's always easy on the eyes."

"So true," commented Liz.

"Shh, someone's going to hear you." Sophie blushed, glancing around.

The conversation picked up again. Luc Dupont, barista extraordinaire, set another foamy cappuccino in front of Liz, winked at Sophie then replaced the empty coffee pot with a fresh one. All three women appreciated the view as he walked away.

Chapter 4

Sunday — April 22, 1934

Olivia looked in the mirror and tried to get used to her modern self in clothes that belonged to another time. She felt like she was playing dress-up and had to keep reminding herself it was real. She smoothed her hands over the chic silk dress that hugged her slender curves and floated several inches above her ankles. Olivia had hesitated when Steven had offered his mother's closet full of beautiful outfits. Wouldn't it be weird for him to see her in Evangeline's clothing? It had only been four months since her devastating death. Steven had quickly put her at ease, saying that everything would look different on Olivia. It also made sense, since she could hardly wear her own clothes. Amazingly Evangeline's clothes fit perfectly.

Olivia turned away from her reflection and went into the bathroom to coax her dark bob into a style that wouldn't look out of place. Last week, she'd gone online and researched women's hair styles of the early 1930s. This afternoon, she'd spent what seemed like ages trying to wrap sections of damp hair around her finger and pinning little circles with the awkward and unfamiliar bobby pins. *Damn! I should have practiced more. It'll have to do.*

Olivia took out her selfie stick and snapped a picture. She almost sent it to Liz and Sophie. Then she stopped, remembering Sophie's distress earlier that morning. She didn't want to worry her friend any more. She could show them any time.

The phone rang.

"Hey, Olivia, I want to wish you good luck and a wonderful time tonight."

"Thanks, Liz."

"I hope we didn't upset you this morning."

"No, I know you guys worry. Actually, I'm kind of nervous."

"About what? Dinner with Steven or the experiment part of it?"

"Both. I know it's not a real date but even so."

"As soon as you see him, you'll relax. You've gotten to know him really well."

"Yeah, you're right. I guess it's because we're going out. Not just hanging out in the kitchen talking about his investigations. I've got butterflies."

Liz laughed. "You're going to be so busy looking around, the butterflies'll vanish. To be honest," she confessed, "I'm a little jealous. I'd kill to see all those clothes and hair styles. And the decorating. And how Knightsbridge looked back then." She sighed. As curator for the local history museum, Liz loved all things vintage.

"I'll sneak some pictures." Olivia turned at the sound of a deep voice behind her. "Steven's here. I've got to go."

"Okay, have fun."

"Thanks. I'll text you later."

Olivia slipped on her shoes and met Steven at the doorway.

"You look swell." He stood in his hallway, surrounded by navy wallpaper splashed with white hydrangea blooms.

"Thank you." Olivia noticed that he'd put on his Sunday suit—a gray double-breasted jacket and full-cut, cuffed trousers; white shirt; and burgundy tie. He'd slicked his hair back and put on freshly polished dress shoes. His ever-present fedora hung from his hand.

"You look great, Steven."

"Thanks." He smiled down at her and held out his free hand. "Are you ready?" he asked.

Olivia's face lit up and she nodded. The light caught flecks of gold in her hazel eyes and auburn highlights in her shiny hair. "Hey! You did something different with your hair."

"I tried copying a 1930s style. What do you think?"

"Looks aces."

Olivia took his hand. They gazed at each other for a moment. Then, Steven gave her hand a squeeze and took a step back. Olivia stepped over the threshold into the past.

Steven had forgotten his watch and ran back upstairs to fetch it. Olivia waited on the front porch, sensing she was on the cusp of something epic. The enormity of what she was doing made her a bit light-headed and her heart beat faster from the fear of the unknown. She wondered if she was the first person to ever time travel. No matter. She was determined to soak up every detail, in case this was her first *and last* foray into the Knightsbridge of 1934.

It was her neighborhood, but it wasn't her neighborhood. It looked familiar and foreign. Neighbors—lots of neighbors—visited on porches and in front yards, all looking at each other and actively, genuinely involved in conversation. Not a cell phone in sight. The women looked like those she had seen in her great-grandmother's photo albums. All wore housedresses and stockings. *Stockings! Good grief! Hanging out around the house and on such a warm day.* And there was something else. They looked a bit...stiff. What was it? *Oh, my God! Girdles!* These poor women were all stuffed into girdles. *Remember that, Olivia, if you start liking it here too much.*

15

Most of the men were smoking. They wore baggy trousers held up with suspenders stretched over short-sleeved, cotton shirts. Squeals of happy children filled the street. Three little boys were playing with their dogs, running, laughing, jumping in the air for the pure joy of it. A couple of girls were doing cartwheels and somersaults. Two older girls wearing old-fashioned roller skates whizzed by on the sidewalk. Olivia had never seen so much activity on her street.

When Steven and Olivia stepped off the porch, Olivia experienced a flutter of panic. She imagined movie stuntmen felt like this when jumping from the roof of one tall building to another. Steven answered familiar greetings of Hello and How are you but didn't stop to visit with anyone. Nor did he take her arm as they turned down the street. Their story was that she was a family friend visiting from out of town. They walked slowly, tentatively at first, each step taking Olivia further and further away from safe ground. Steven didn't take his eyes off her.

"Are you alright? Do you feel anything?" he asked.

"Besides my heart in my throat, you mean?" She laughed. "So far so good."

Olivia wanted to see what the stores looked like and by the time they reached Victoria both had relaxed somewhat and had begun to enjoy the evening.

They rounded the corner. Olivia gasped in delight. Three mannequins stood in the window of Grace's Dress Shop, smiling falsely, wearing the new spring fashions—a colorful cotton shirt and wide-legged, white trousers; a twin sweater set and matching hip-hugging skirt that flared out at the calf; a cotton dress with thin diagonal stripes in red and cream.

"I *have* to get pictures of this!" She snuck a couple of shots before they moved on.

Steven didn't hurry her. Olivia knew by the look on his face that he was enjoying her gleeful reactions to everything she saw. They passed a tiny shop and she breathed in the earthy tobacco scent that leaked out the door and windows.

"This is where I buy my Christmas cigar every year," Steven told her. "A *Partagas Corona Grande*."

Olivia peered in the window where heavy glass jars filled with loose tobacco occupied every square inch of the display shelves. The shop was old—dark and full of character. It reminded her of places she'd seen in London.

They walked past Bailey's Diner, looking much the same now as it did in her time; the very narrow Sal's News, *I have to go there!*; Mo's Barber Shop, identified by the brightly striped pole; the Village Drugstore, whose window revealed things belonging in a museum. They reached the corner where she saw a familiar sight. Across the street The Three Lords took up nearly half the block. Olivia smiled at Steven as they stepped off the curb.

The Three Lords was an authentic English pub, founded by British settlers more than 200 years ago. Steven opened the door and ushered her into the dimly lit room. A cloud of smoke hit them and Olivia experienced a fit of coughing.

"Yikes, the smoking! So, this is what it was like."

"What do you mean? People don't smoke anymore?" Steven exclaimed.

"Not in public. It's against the law." She gazed around the crowded tavern. "It looks the same," she whispered.

Eight decades seemed to have had little or no effect on the pub. The long, wide mirror—dotted with bare spots where the silver backing had worn off—reflected a dozen or so men with slicked-back hair standing and sitting at the polished wooden bar. Many wore fedora-style hats. Several sported pencil-thin moustaches. A

17

portly barman held a pint glass under one of the taps, tilted it expertly then pulled back on the pump. Throughout the room, thick dark columns supported the low ceiling that was crisscrossed with heavy wooden beams.

Steven placed his hand on the small of Olivia's back and steered her toward an empty booth in the back. As they wove their way across the room—stepping around tiny upholstered stools that circled small tables packed closely together—a buzz zipped around the pub.

Olivia's stomach was doing somersaults. Her heart was racing and her mouth was as dry as the Sahara. She felt lightheaded and prayed she wouldn't pass out. She concentrated on gripping her phone so she wouldn't drop it, thereby initiating a flurry of questions.

What am I doing here? What is wrong with me? Why can't I be satisfied with a normal life like everybody else? Time travel? Really?

And, *what* had they been thinking? Naturally, she and Steven would be an object of interest and gossip—he was a prominent figure in town. When several women glared at Olivia, she realized he was probably one of Knightsbridge's most eligible bachelors.

Everyone seemed to know Steven. People turned to stare, halting their conversations in mid-sentence and craning their necks to get a good look. Some shouted greetings. A couple of men shook Steven's hand, getting an eyeful of Olivia as they tipped their hats. Steven did not introduce her but was friendly and polite to everyone. They reached the booth and sat across from each other.

Olivia leaned over and hissed in a low voice, "I thought you said it'd be empty tonight!"

"Sorry." He winced. "I guess a lot of people are making a day of it after the parade this afternoon. I should have known we'd cause a stir. This is such a small community."

"They're curious because they all know you. At least I *hope* it's not because of the way I look."

"No, you look fine. Listen, Olivia, all we have to do is stick to our story. It'll be okay. There's no way somebody's going to say 'Hey, I think she's visiting from the future.'"

Olivia made a face and they both laughed.

"Come on. Let's enjoy ourselves," he said, removing his hat and settling against the wooden back.

A short balding man approached the table. "Steven! It's nice to see you take a break from that job of yours once in a while. And who is the lovely lady?" he asked, boldly scrutinizing Olivia.

"Olivia, I'd like you to meet Cooper Lewis, one of the owners of The Three Lords. Coop, this is Olivia Watson, a family friend."

"Nice to meet you, Mr. Lewis."

"My pleasure, Miss Watson."

"How is your cousin Theresa doing, Coop? And her beautiful new daughter?"

"Isabel's a good baby," Cooper exclaimed. "I hardly ever hear her fussing. I thought she'd be keeping us up at night but she sleeps better than I do." He chuckled. "She's a little trouper, that one. Theresa has her propped up in her basket in a corner of the kitchen while she's working and you never hear a peep out of her. Every time I walk by, those big blue eyes of hers follow me around. Never thought I'd enjoy having a baby around, but she's a peach."

"I'm glad to hear it. She ought to be a couple of months old now, right?" Steven said.

"Yeah, about that. So, what can I get for you folks tonight?"

Steven ordered for both of them and the innkeeper left.

"Oh my goodness!" Olivia exclaimed. "I think you were talking about Isabel." She leaned across the table and whispered, "My *eighty-year-old* friend Isabel."

"The white-haired lady."

"Yeah. How many baby girls named Isabel were born in Knightsbridge two months ago? Wow, this is surreal." She laughed. "Well," she exhaled forcibly and calmed down. "I guess that's my first hurdle. Okay. I can do this."

For the next hour, Olivia paid little attention to her food. She couldn't stop watching people. She noticed how they stood and the way they moved, the gestures they made and their facial expressions. She delighted in the clothes they wore and the ubiquitous hats on the men. Hiding her phone in the palm of her hand, she managed to sneak a dozen pictures.

"Olivia, although I admire your determination, your food is getting cold." Steven looked up as a couple approached their table. "Artie! Helen!"

Steven stood and the men shook hands. He gave Helen a hug. Olivia knew who these people were—Artie Sinclair was Steven's childhood friend. Steven performed the introductions and invited the couple to join them. He slipped back into the booth and Artie sat next to him. Olivia moved over to make room for Helen.

For a while, the conversation rolled along touching on everyday topics—the weather, Artie's job, their daughter Annie, the parade. At the mention of baseball, the men fell into an animated discussion about their favorite teams—Steven's New York Yankees and Artie's Brooklyn Dodgers—and Olivia was forced to have an actual conversation with Helen.

Uh oh, she thought, *show time.* But, before she had the chance to control where it might lead, Helen asked, "So, Olivia, where are you visiting from?"

"I've been living in Syracuse the past few years. I found a job with *The Syracuse Journal* after college."

When discussing their strategy, Steven and Olivia had decided it would be best to tell as much of the truth as possible. They could fudge the details to suit life in 1934, but telling the truth would be easier than trying to remember stories they'd made up.

Olivia had graduated from Syracuse University then stayed on at Newhouse to get her Masters degree in journalism. After a summer in Europe, she'd returned and spent several years working as a reporter for *The Syracuse Post Standard*.

"Oh, that sounds exciting. My sister works, too, but I don't. All I ever wanted was to marry Artie, be a housewife, and have children." Helen gave a contented sigh and looked fondly at her husband.

What should she say? *Quick, Olivia, think.*

You work around the house all day and that counts.

You could do both.

You seem very happy together.

Olivia was saved from having to find an appropriate reply when Helen asked, *"The Syracuse Journal?* The newspaper?" She whispered in awe, "You're not a reporter, are you?"

"I was but I quit and started my own agency a few years ago."

Helen's eyes popped. "You own a business? Doing what?"

"Research. I find information for writers and college professors. Usually background material. Sometimes lists or a survey."

"Are you here in Knightsbridge for work?"

"Sort of. I'm starting a research project of my own."

"About what?" The look on Helen's face said that she was finding this friend of Steven's fascinating.

"I'm preparing a series of articles about how women are living during these hard times. I'll write about some famous people like Amelia Earhart and Mrs. Roosevelt. And maybe a writer or an actress. But mostly I'm interested in ordinary people like you and me."

"I'd rather read about somebody who does more than wash clothes, iron, and clean the house." Helen scrunched up her face and gazed off in the distance. "How about Katharine Hepburn?" she suggested. "I always go see her pictures. She's swell."

"I like her, too. Thanks, Helen. That's a great idea."

Helen beamed as she took a drink of the shandy her husband had ordered for her. "Are you going to interview people in Knightsbridge?"

"Yes, but I just got here. I don't know anyone yet."

Helen hesitated, then said, "Olivia, I'm not really this bold—blame it on the shandy." She gave a nervous laugh. "Or maybe it's spring in the air. But, I'd love to do something different. It was hard being cooped up in the house all winter."

Olivia nodded encouragingly.

"Is there something I could do to help you?" Helen leaned closer. "Your project sounds exciting."

"Thank you, Helen. I'll need to meet some local women and get them to trust me enough to talk about their lives. It would help a lot if one of their friends introduced me."

Helen broke out in a huge smile. "I'm going to help a real writer with research," she exclaimed. She called across the table. "Artie! You're not going to believe what I'm going to do with Olivia!"

Chapter 5

Monday — April 23, 1934

Steven swung around the curve that Chiltington Road made as it hugged the small park the locals called The Green. There was a spring in his step as he thought of last night with Olivia—he couldn't remember the last time he'd stepped out with a girl. Then he reminded himself it wasn't a date. Olivia had called it "Phase I" of their next group of experiments. Even so, it had felt like more than that.

Earlier in the evening when he'd been getting ready, he'd been excited and nervous. Would he get tongue-tied and not be able to think of anything to say? Would she think he was too old-fashioned and boring? Would she enjoy herself? Would anyone suspect that she was masquerading as someone who lived in 1934?

But, it had turned out aces. The best part was that Olivia was okay. She'd experienced no side effects and had walked back into her own time as easily as she always did. His only disappointment was that he hadn't been able to take her arm or hold her hand. It would have been inappropriate because of their family friend story. He grinned to himself. Even if he had decided to ignore that, Olivia had been distracted by everything she saw, running off to peer in yet another store window and talking non-stop all the way home.

Steven delighted in Olivia's company. She was easy to talk to and one of the most interesting women he'd ever met. Because his job required him to work long hours, often six days a week, he had little time for socializing. Steven's daily confidante had been his mother until her unexpected and shattering death in early January. His father worked for the Navy in Washington, D.C. The demands of his job had increased as of late, so they didn't see each other as often as Steven would have liked. Although Admiral Blackwell was unable to share any details with Steven, he had hinted at something. *Pay attention to the news, son. There's something dangerous brewing in Europe.* When Steven had pressed his father, he'd added some disturbing comments. *It has to do with this upstart in Germany. Dangerous fella. And while we're at it, watch out for some of our own. Mr. Henry Ford and that flier Charles Lindbergh are going to have some things to answer for one day.* His father's tone had chilled Steven to the bone. But, Europe was far away and everyone said the Great War was the war to end all wars. Whatever Hitler was up to, it wouldn't affect him.

"Morning, Steven," a voice called out, breaking his reverie.

He looked up and saw a plump young woman leaning out of a second-floor window at The Three Lords. "Morning, Theresa. How are you? How's the baby?"

"She's wonderful but I'm rushed off my feet," said the new mother, brushing a wisp of light brown hair from her forehead.

Steven noticed a haunted quality on her face and put it down to fatigue. Maybe the baby wasn't sleeping as well as Cooper had said. Maybe Coop was simply taken with Isabel.

"She'll be sleeping through the night before you know it," he said encouragingly.

"I sure hope so." Theresa Covington waved and disappeared back into the room.

Steven made it a habit to walk to work at least once a week. He liked being out on the streets and thought it was important for his job. If the police stayed in touch with the community and knew people well, solving crime would be easier. People had a tendency to lie when questioned by an officer of the law. Whether the lies were relevant or not, they clouded the case and made the truth harder to get at. They wasted valuable police time and energy. But on the street, people talked. Casual conversations revealed details of private family life and past histories. Secrets leaked out.

Steven reached the corner and crossed the Margate Road to the one-story brick building that housed the Knightsbridge Police Department. He climbed the front steps and entered the quiet station. Looking like somebody's kid brother with his dirty blond hair and bright green eyes, Tommy Forester greeted him from behind a high wooden counter that served as the front desk.

"Morning, Tommy. Saw you at the parade yesterday."

"It was a good one, huh, Detective Blackwell?"

Steven headed down the long narrow hallway and entered the CID room. The Criminal Investigation Division was where the detectives worked and where the murder board was set up during an investigation.

Sergeant Will Taylor sat at his desk with *The Gazette* spread out on the uncluttered surface. Every morning, Will read the local paper from cover to cover, leaning forward, his feet planted firmly on the floor, his brawny forearms braced on muscular thighs. Will had been Steven's partner for nearly two months now, ever since he'd earned his sergeant's stripes. Steven had great respect for his skills. Will had a near-photographic memory, could read people like they were wearing signs, and possessed tracking skills like nobody else. He was invaluable on a case. Steven still missed the joking and light-hearted banter he'd had with his former partner, Detective Harry Beckman, but he liked working with Will and, if he really needed a laugh, there was always Jimmy Bou.

Will looked up, said good morning, then returned to his newspaper. Steven pulled out a couple of open files. Over the next half-hour, Steven heard the men arriving, the opening and closing of doors, the sounds of conversation and laughter. He had just decided which of the unsolved cases he wanted to resurrect when he heard a commotion at the main entrance.

"Stop!" Tommy Forester hollered. "You have to wait here."

Steven hurried out into the hall. Further down, he saw Jimmy Bou poking his head out of the patrol room and Chief Thompson entering the building.

"What's going on, Tommy?" Steven asked, approaching the young officer.

Two teenaged boys paced back and forth near the front desk, gesturing wildly, and talking over each other. They saw Steven.

"Dead body," one of them shouted.

"We found a dead guy in the woods," his friend yelled.

"You'll let me know, Detective Blackwell," said Chief Andy Thompson, raising bushy eyebrows and jerking his head toward the boys.

Steven nodded as his boss skirted the group and continued to his office at the back of the building. His burly shape took up half of the hallway and his orangey-red hair shone like a torch in a dim tunnel.

"Well, boys, you'd better follow me," Steven said. "Jimmy, come and take notes."

Steven dragged two wooden chairs over to his desk, invited the boys to sit, and regained his seat. Officer Jimmy Bourgogne took out his notebook and pencil and stood to the side. Will rose and leaned against the edge of his desk, arms folded, studying the youngsters.

"I'm Detective Sergeant Blackwell." Steven nodded to the blond boy. "I recognize you. Aren't you Connor MacIntyre's son?"

"Yes, sir. Kevin." He pointed to his friend. "This is Joey Renard."

"Okay, Kevin, tell me what happened."

"Joey and me always meet up for a smoke before school. We was there on top of the hill behind the high school and Joey looks down toward the gully and sees something."

"I thought it was a tramp or somebody sleeping it off, ya know?"

Steven nodded encouragingly.

"We climbed down to see who it was."

Probably hoping the fella's bottle or cigarettes were on the ground nearby, thought Steven. Both boys were clean and presentable—no doubt they'd had their weekly bath last night in preparation for school. But, like so many others during the Depression, their clothes were worn and patched. Joey's pants were too short and Kevin's shirtsleeves didn't make it to his wrists. Neither, Steven was sure, had any money to waste on cigarettes. And if their parents found out they *were* spending money on cigarettes—a pack cost fourteen cents these days—they'd probably skin them alive.

"When we got to him, his arms and legs looked all funny," Kevin went on.

"Yeah, sort of sticking out and bent in the wrong way." Joey made a face and imitated the dead man's arms. "We figured somethin' ain't right."

"I grabbed his shoulder and rolled him onto his back," Kevin said.

"How was he lying when you first saw him?" Steven asked, frustrated that the boys had moved the man.

"Kind of on his side and his stomach at the same time. He was leaning up against a big rock."

"You shoulda seen his face," exclaimed Joey.

"Yeah, purple! And his eyes were bulging out. Awful!"

But Kevin's own face betrayed this statement. Clearly, both boys thought this was a great adventure and relished every minute they were spending in the police station as the center of attention.

"Well, gentlemen, we'd better go see then, hadn't we? You did the right thing, coming here. Good for you."

Kevin and Joey beamed.

"Officer Bourgogne, tell Tommy to call Doc and Gray."

"Right, Detective Blackwell." Jimmy tucked his notebook and pencil in the pocket of his new dark blue uniform.

"Have them meet us down in the ravine," added Steven.

"Jimmy, tell them to go 'round the hill and behind the school grounds along Route 13," suggested Will. "From what it sounds like, I think we'll be able to get closer to the body …"

Kevin and Joey leered at each other at the sound of the word *body*.

"… if we go that way," he finished.

"Jimmy, get Ralph and Pete, too," Steven said.

"I'll let the chief know, Steven," said Will. "I'll grab the keys to the cars."

Chapter 6

Moments later two black Ford sedans pulled out of the parking lot behind the station. In the back seat of the lead car, Kevin and Joey, thrilled to bursting, had all they could do not to open the windows and yell at everyone they saw.

The cars sped across town, turned up the Mohawk River Road, and made a right on Victoria. After two blocks, they veered onto County Route 13 then circled around the bottom of the hill behind high school. Will had been right, from that vantage point they managed to get the cars close to the ravine.

Steven parked next to an old black Ford. The Oneida County Medical Examiner, "Doc" Elliott, leaned against a dented fender smoking and coughing. Thinning gray hair spoke of his age and a sagging colorless face reflected the corpses he examined. Doc's eight year-old suit was rumpled and his tie was crooked but his white shirt was clean and pressed. "Hell of a place to be looking at a body," he grumbled, heaving himself away from the motor car.

Gray Wilson balanced against his blue Chrysler B-70 roadster, pulling on a pair of rubber boots. Today, the dapper photographer sported a Glen plaid worsted wool suit in navy with a thin red line running through the fabric and scarlet tie tucked beneath the matching waistcoat. He reached around the spare tire that sat in a space in the rear bumper, stowed his dress shoes in the trunk, and grabbed his gear.

Before entering the woods, Steven had Kevin and Joey sit on a nearby log. "Stay still. You're going to get your picture taken." He turned to Gray. "Would you photograph the bottom of their shoes? And Pete, measure both boys' feet."

The woods were vibrant with new life. The group of men hiked past bud-heavy saplings, forsythia bushes bursting with yellow flowers, and fragile white trillium. They tried not to trip on wild raspberry vines that snaked across the forest floor. Steven led the way, trailed closely by Kevin and Joey, who couldn't believe the morning they were having. This sure beat the hell out of going to school. They couldn't wait to tell their friends, especially Petey, who was going to be royally pissed when he heard. Petey Ferguson was always up on the hill with them every morning smoking. This week he was quarantined with the mumps and was missing out on everything.

"There he is!" Joey shouted, as he and Kevin ran toward the dead man.

"Whoa, boys. Not so fast." Steven made a grab for them. "We don't want you destroying any more evidence."

The crime scene was a mess. It was hard to miss evidence that deer, raccoons, and coyotes had traipsed through the area. There was scat from a fox not far from the body. Steven observed a spot where someone had shuffled through the dried leaves to the right of the remains. Kevin and Joey? A killer?

"Ralph, mark off the area. Give us a radius of fifty feet," Steven said.

The stocky blond officer paced off the distance then moved from tree to tree, wrapping rope around oak, maple, and beech trunks.

Steven made the boys stand well outside the perimeter. "You two, wait here. Don't move!"

The dead man lay on his back, partly covered in leaves, bits of twigs clinging to his clothes. A painful death had obscured his once handsome features. His generous mouth was stretched from side to side and blood-red sclera surrounded the once luminous brown eyes. His face was covered in scratches.

"Oh!" said Jimmy Bou. "It's Frankie Russo. I saw him in church yesterday."

"When was that?" asked Steven.

"Eight o'clock Mass."

"Did you see him leave?"

"Yeah, I walked out behind him. A few minutes after nine."

"I remember Frankie. He was in my class at school," said Will.

"I wonder whose husband he crossed now," said Ralph, scowling.

"What do you mean?" asked Jimmy Bou.

"Frankie Russo had a reputation for chasing anything in a skirt. Whether she was married or not," Ralph explained.

"*He's* married," said Will. "His wife's name is Lucy. Nice girl. She's an English teacher at the high school."

"I hope for her sake, he reformed," said Ralph.

Steven was well aware of Frankie Russo's reputation. Several years ago, Artie had told him he was concerned for his sister-in-law, who had announced her engagement to the local ladies' man. Helen had tried to dissuade her younger sibling but when Lucy set her mind on something, there was no talking her out of it.

Lucy and Frankie had been married for some time now and it appeared Frankie had settled down. Steven had seen him with an old girlfriend a while back, but he hadn't heard any rumors of a recent affair. Knightsbridge was a small town. There would be whispers if Frankie were cheating.

While Gray photographed the body and surrounding area, Steven stood aside and sketched the scene in the notebook he always carried. Something caught Will's attention and he walked to the base of the hill. Ralph and Pete prowled the area outside the rope, examining the ground. As the photographer worked, the sun rose in the sky. The shadow cast by a towering blue spruce traveled with it and the light filtering through nearby branches shifted. Gray Wilson checked the light exposure, adjusted the shutter speed and aperture on his Speed Graphic press camera then took his final shots.

"Okay, fellas. Let me get started." Doc Elliott pushed past Jimmy Bou, who was keeping an eye on Kevin and Joey. "The quicker I look him over here, the quicker I can get him to the morgue and find some answers for you."

The ME struggled to kneel next to the body. He hummed as he donned a pair of gloves and scanned his mental catalog of popular tunes—Doc was known for singing to the victim. Conventional wisdom said it hid a sensitive soul. Perhaps. Or maybe he just liked singing.

On this bright morning, accompanied by the chirping and twitter-ing of a forest full of birds, Doc chose "Let's All Sing Like the Birdies Sing," a tune by Ben Bernie, famous for his hit "Ain't She Sweet." The medical examiner's baritone rang out.

"This birdie's not singing, Doc," said Jimmy Bou. "Steven, look." A dead robin lay on its side a couple of feet away.

"That's a bit strange. Wait until Gray gets a close-up, then bag that bird carefully." Steven called to his partner. "Will, would you see if you can figure out how Frankie got here?"

"I've already got an idea. Look." Will traced an imaginary line from the body up the slope to the top of the hill. "See all those broken branches? And look there to the left, those two big rocks have been disturbed."

"An animal couldn't do that," said Jimmy Bou, screwing up his face as he followed Will's pointing finger.

"Frankie might have rolled down here from the field." Will walked back over to Steven.

"That could account for the scratches on his face," said Steven.

"I'll wait for Gray to get shots of that trail then I'll mark it off as I go up."

"Good." Steven turned to Ralph and Pete. "Have Kevin and Joey show you where they were when they saw the body then secure the spot. Pete, walk 'em over to school and explain why they're late. We don't want them getting in trouble after all the help they've given us." Steven knew full well that Kevin and Joey would give their eye teeth to stand here and watch all day long.

"That's okay, Detective Blackwell," Joey rushed in. "There's nothing important going on today. We can miss school."

"Yeah," agreed Kevin. "You might need more help from us."

"You know, that's true," Steven said. "Get the boys' addresses and telephone numbers, if their families have a phone. We might need to contact them again later."

The boys sagged like deflated balloons then set off behind the patrolmen, dragging their feet like they were heading to the gallows.

"Pete, while you're at the school," Steven added, "call the chief and let him know what we've got here. Ask him to get one of the fellas to write up a warrant to search Frankie's house and his work area at the mill. There's probably a desk, maybe a filing cabinet and a shelf. Then, help Will and Ralph up in the field." He turned to the medical examiner, who was cradling Frankie's head in his hands. "What can you tell me, Doc?"

"Not a whole lot. I don't feel anything that indicates a blow to the head." He unbuttoned the victim's shirt and pulled it open to the waist, exposing Frankie's lean chest. "There's no blood from a knife or a gunshot wound." He leaned back on his heels. "You'll have to wait until I get him up on the table, Steven. He's stiff but, because of the condition of the body, I'll go out on a limb and say I don't think he's been here that long. But that's it for now. Do you want the stuff out of his pockets?"

"Yes, thanks."

Doc extracted a crumpled red pack of Pall Mall cigarettes from Frankie Russo's shirt pocket and dropped it into the brown paper evidence bag that Steven held out. He reached into the pants pocket and pulled out a worn leather wallet. "Here," he said, adding it to the bag. The ME groaned as he got to his feet. "I'll call you this afternoon. I'll start as soon as I get back." He grabbed his black bag.

"Thanks, Doc."

The mortuary assistants placed Frankie Russo's body on a canvas stretcher and carried it to the van. After stowing the corpse in the back, they slammed the doors shut and left, followed by Doc in his sputtering motor car.

The scene settled back into silence. Steven and Jimmy Bou combed through the area one more time. Except for the broken path that Will had pointed out, neither found anything else that appeared disturbed by humans. The thick bed of dried leaves prevented the possibility of foot prints. There were no scraps of paper littered about.

Steven reached into the evidence bag and took out Frankie's billfold. Frankie had carried no identification, which wasn't uncommon. Apart from a couple of dollar bills shoved deep in a separate space, the wallet was empty. He checked the pack of cigarettes. A half dozen smokes remained in the packet. Except for the dead robin, there was nothing.

"Let's go up top, Jimmy, and see what they've got."

LUCY

Another Monday morning. Lucy Russo sighed as she reached up and slid the apron over her neatly coiffed head. She pulled the ties behind her, knotting them securely at her waist. Meticulous about her appearance, she spent hours spot cleaning, washing, and ironing her clothes. She'd chosen a favorite outfit today—a sleeveless white blouse, navy skirt with polka dots and a matching unconstructed jacket.

The kettle whistled. Lucy poured boiling water into a delicate tea cup. She tipped one perfectly poached egg onto her plate, spread strawberry jam on a slice of toasted homemade bread, and sat down to eat. The house was peaceful without Frankie. And neat. Lucy looked around her—everything was in its place. It was like being on vacation not to be constantly picking up after him. There was no trail of discarded clothing. The living room floor wasn't littered with newspapers. And when she set something down, it stayed there. She didn't have to go looking all over the house because he'd left something where it wasn't supposed to be.

There was also no wondering when he'd be home. She hated it when Frankie didn't show up for supper. Lucy was a planner. She liked knowing what she was doing.

Lucy savored her breakfast. This was the last jar of jam. Before she knew it, she'd be making this year's batch. That was always her first project after school got out for the summer. She'd stand in her kitchen slicing plump juicy strawberries, while on the windowsill pots of rosemary, lemon balm, and basil soaked up the sunlight and perfumed the air.

She finished eating and drank the last of her tea. Better get going or she'd have to walk fast—she was never late. She washed and dried the dishes then returned them to their places in the cupboard. She gathered up her lunch and book bag and, as she was slipping on her jacket, remembered she was giving a test to her seniors this morning. That would make a nice break, but it also meant a night of grading essays. At least with Frankie gone, the house would be quiet and she'd be able to concentrate. Maybe it would go quickly and she'd be able to listen to the George Gershwin program on the radio.

Lucy loved Mr. Gershwin. Several years ago—right before her wedding, in fact—she had done something bold. She'd bought a phonograph, all for her very own and despite the fact she was still living with her parents. Her father had made her keep it in her bedroom, grumbling that he didn't want it competing with his radio in the living room. Her mother had gaped at her in shock. Why hadn't she spent the money on her going-away dress and trousseau? But, Lucy was adamant. She didn't care whether they understood or not.

Lucy had found the Fairfax phonograph—one of the Tru-Phonic Silvertone collection—in the Sears catalog. Although it was a splurge, it was a price she could afford on her teaching salary. She paid the four dollars down, filled out the Time Payment Order Blank in the catalog, and sent the Sears Roebuck Company three dollars a month for the next thirteen months.

Over the years, her collection of phonograph records grew. She had Stravinsky's "Rite of Spring," Holst's "Planets," and of course, all of Mr. Gershwin's recordings. Lucy listened to "Rhapsody in Blue" over and over again, never tiring of it. The music worked its way inside her, filling her up and expanding until she thought she'd drift away with the notes. It stirred the wild side in her, making her wonder what it would be like to simply walk away from her life and go live in Paris or some other exotic place.

Lucy caught sight of the kitchen clock. Time to leave. Dreams of Paris would have to wait. She closed and locked the front door behind her. As she headed up the Mohawk River Road, thoughts of Frankie invaded her mind and she shuddered. *How had it all gone so wrong?*

Chapter 7

When Steven and Jimmy Bou crested the hill, they saw Pete McGrath placing something in a bag.

"What've you got there, Pete?"

"Another dead bird, Steven. It was right here." The wiry patrolman pointed to a cascade of purple and yellow crocus along the edge of the woods. "I nearly stepped on the poor thing."

"Two dead birds that close to a body," said Jimmy Bou. "That's gotta mean something."

"Is this where the boys were when they saw Frankie?" Steven pointed to a pile of cigarette butts within a small area that had been cordoned off.

"Yeah, that's it. I asked them again about seeing anyone else this morning but they still say they were alone," said Pete. "There's usually another kid with them but he's home sick."

"Steven, I found some fibers caught on a branch over there," said Ralph, pointing to a bush inside the tree line, near the path Will had marked off. "No telling how long they were there but Gray took pictures and I've got them." He held up a small envelope.

"They couldn't have been there too long," Jimmy observed.

"What do you mean?" asked Pete.

"It's nesting season. A bird would have grabbed those for sure."

"Good observation," said Steven.

Jimmy beamed.

Several feet away, Will Taylor finished pounding four wooden pegs into the ground, creating an area roughly the size of a double bed. He looked up and saw Steven. "What did Doc say?"

"The usual. Wouldn't commit to anything. Said he'll call later. What's this?"

"I noticed a pool of vomit," Will answered, pointing to a spot marked with a small flag. "So I stepped back and laid down to see if there was anything nearby." He handed Steven his magnifying glass. "See this section of grass? Look at it up close."

Steven crouched down and examined the spot from various angles. "It looks flattened down."

"Right, see all the broken blades of grass? I wonder if something covered this area."

Jimmy Bou, Ralph, and Pete walked over to join Steven and Will.

"Did you see his face?" Ralph was saying.

"What do you think made him look like that?" Jimmy said.

"Steven," said Pete, "remember that accidental poisoning we had about two years ago? I think Frankie Russo's face looked a lot like that fella."

"I thought of that, too, Pete, but let's not jump to conclusions," Steven said. "We'll wait for Doc's report."

Eager to discover what Steven and Will had been discussing, Jimmy Bou lay down in the field. Steven handed him his magnifying glass. "Look carefully. See all those broken blades of grass?"

Jimmy pressed his nose to the ground. "Yeah," he exclaimed. "Something was covering this spot, right? Maybe a blanket?" He crawled to the far edge of the area and looked in the direction of the woods. "Hey, it keeps on going. Look." Jimmy Bou, magnifying glass in hand, slithered snake-like to the edge of the meadow. "It goes all the way into the woods here."

Will grabbed more pegs and, with Jimmy's help, hammered them into the ground. When they'd finished, it was clear that a path of broken blades of grass about four feet wide led directly from the square space in the meadow to the woods. While Steven was sketching this new discovery, Ralph and Pete were speculating.

"So, let's say it was a blanket here," said Pete.

"We know what kind of fella Frankie was. He was making time with a dame," Ralph stated.

"What? Then all of a sudden he drops dead?" said Pete, making a face.

"Maybe he had a heart attack. That could explain his face, couldn't it?" said Jimmy Bou.

"The past couple of days were really nice. What if Frankie and the girl were having a picnic and he choked on something?" Pete said.

"You mean poisoned food?" said Jimmy Bou.

"Maybe. Or he was allergic to something they ate. Or he just choked. You know like something got stuck and he couldn't breathe," Pete explained.

Steven had been listening to his team as he sketched. Speculation was all well and good, often one of the men hit upon something useful, but it was time to finish here and work the evidence they had.

"Those are all interesting thoughts, fellas, but we don't know much of anything for a fact yet. If Kevin and Joey were telling the truth, and I think they were, Frankie was found at the bottom of the hill. The path Will discovered seems to be a direct line from this spot in the field down to the ravine where the body was. It would appear that Frankie was here recently. But remember, he could have died of natural causes and fallen into the gully."

"He might have been poisoned, Steven," Ralph said. "Remember the dead birds."

"You think the birds were poisoned, too?" asked Jimmy Bou.

"Why not? What if Frankie and the girl ate something that was poisoned?"

"So, where's her dead body?" said Jimmy.

"Could be alive and well if she was the one who poisoned his food. Or they might not have eaten the same things." Ralph raised his eyebrows and let the thought sink in.

Steven turned to his partner. "Will, would you organize a grid search of the field? Ralph and Pete, stay here and work with Will. Mark off any other spots that look like they might have been involved. I'll send over some extra men."

"Thanks, that'll help."

"I'll take Jimmy with me. We'll notify Lucy and get a preliminary interview. In case it is foul play, we'll find out where she was yesterday." He consulted his watch, a beautiful gold-filled timepiece his parents had given him when he'd made detective. "It's nearly eleven. They eat lunch early in schools. Maybe we can catch Lucy out of class." He picked up the evidence bags. "We'll drop off the birds and fibers on the way so Hank can get started."

Steven scanned the scene one last time. Clusters of daffodils dotted the lush green grass. Sunbeams pierced the surrounding woods, creating a misty, magical feeling. A young man had died close by. Had it been an accident? Had Frankie succumbed to a heart attack or a stroke? Had he been ill? Or was he murdered?

Chapter 8

Monday — Present Day

Early Monday morning, Olivia threw on a pair of leggings, t-shirt, and hoodie and went for her daily run. Thirty minutes later, feeling energized and righteous, she made her way to Sophie's *Pâtisserie-Café*, located in the century-old house Sophie had inherited from her grandparents several years ago. Last night, as soon as Olivia had slipped back into her own time, she'd texted her BFFs. *It was awesome! Cant wait 2 tell u.* Sophie had responded with *Saving our table 7am.*

When Olivia entered the French-inspired, cream-and-black *pâtisserie-café*, Sophie's passion was evident. Black-and-white portraits of her favorite writers—Balzac, Baudelaire, and Camus, among others—graced the walls and famous quotes had been written in script under the glass table-tops. Sophie always saved the Descartes table for the threesome. Olivia grabbed an Americano and joined her friends.

"You came back!" Sophie cried, jumping up and giving Olivia a big hug.

"I'm so relieved," sighed Liz, reaching out to squeeze Olivia's hand.

"How was it?" said Sophie. "Did anybody look at you funny?"

"How did it feel?" Liz asked. "Did you have any problems?"

"Yikes! Hang on, you guys," Olivia laughed. "First of all, I feel great. Nothing bad happened. No headache, no weird creepy feelings, nothing. And before you ask, my brain feels totally fine."

"Phew!" they chorused.

"You look normal," observed Sophie.

"You sound okay," said Liz. "What was it like?"

"I have to admit I was scared. When I was about to take that first step off the porch it was like my heart clenched. I thought of you guys." Her eyes filled up and she swallowed hard. Liz and Sophie both reached over to hold her hands. No words were necessary. They all knew their lives would never be the same without one of the three. Olivia wiped her eyes. "Anyway, it was like being in an old black-and-white movie. Only it was in color. And it was real. I had to keep reminding myself that these people were real not actors playing a part. They had no idea who I was."

"Good," pronounced Sophie. "What was it like being out with Steven?"

"It felt like it always does. Comfortable, like we were home. But," she hesitated, "there were a couple of times when I wasn't sure what to do."

"What do you mean?" asked Liz.

"I thought he was going to take my arm or grab my hand but he didn't."

"He didn't make any moves?" Sophie said, looking disappointed.

Olivia shook her head.

"Did you meet anybody?" Liz asked.

"The guy who owned The Three Lords and Steven's friends Artie and Helen."

"How did he introduce you?" said Liz.

"As a family friend."

"That's not very good," said Sophie, ever the romantic.

"Sophie, you know we're just friends. Besides, this was an experiment to see if I could leave the house and not get jerked back, remember? Anyway, a relationship with Steven would be insane."

"No, it wouldn't. You've spent almost every evening together for the past two months," said Liz. "That's more than I see Joe some weeks." Liz's doctor husband worked long hours at the hospital.

"I can't let myself go there," said Olivia. "It's an impossible situation."

"Well, maybe," Liz commented mysteriously.

"Listen, I want to ask you guys something. Especially you, Sophie."

"What?"

"You know I never want to worry you. Would be better if I didn't tell you when I was going to spend a chunk of time in 1934? I could let you know when I get back that I'd been there."

"No," said Liz.

"Absolutely not," Sophie replied.

"We're not going to start keeping things from each other now. Not after all these years of telling in each other everything."

"I appreciate what you're trying to do, Olivia, but I'd rather know," said Sophie. "And now that you've done it with no problem, I don't think I'll worry so much any more."

"All right. I kind of thought that's what you'd say. So, I'll tell you I'm going to spend all day tomorrow alone in Steven's house."

Liz and Sophie looked at each other and shook their heads.

"So, is this going to be a regular thing now?" asked Liz.

"What do you mean *alone*?" Sophie asked, frowning.

"Steven's going to pick me up for breakfast then he'll leave for work. We want to see if I can stay in the house without him. I'll bring work to do so I can get something accomplished." Olivia looked from one to the other. "It's the next logical step. We really want to see how far we can push this."

"That's exactly what I'm afraid of," Sophie said sadly.

"Hey, let's change the subject. What about pictures?" Liz asked. "Did you get any?"

Olivia's face lit up. "Did I ever," she exclaimed. "Look."

They spent the next half hour poring over the photographs and dishing about all the clothes and hair styles until Liz had to leave for work, Olivia's daring plan temporarily forgotten.

Olivia took a long steaming shower then spent the rest of the morning writing in her journal. She felt it was important to record everything and wanted to keep a detailed log of her trips into 1934. Who knew how long she'd be able to do this? The thought that some day she wouldn't be able to see Steven through the doorway or slide over the threshold with him into the past chilled her. Could her ability to time travel be temporary?

Olivia began with how she'd felt while waiting for Steven to get his watch—the fear and excitement, the feeling that it was a dream and couldn't possibly be happening, the sense of amazement that it was happening to her. She wrote about the moment of panic when she'd stepped off the porch feeling like she'd flung herself off a cliff. She described her pounding heart, accelerated breathing, and sweaty palms. She wrote about the fear when it hit her that she might never come back to her life. Images of the people she loved most in the world flew through her mind's eye. What if she never saw her mom and dad again? She thought they would understand what drove her to explore something like this, but they'd probably think she'd been reckless with the life they had given her. And she couldn't even begin to imagine her life without Liz and Sophie. Their friendship had been her most treasured possession since she'd been six years old.

Olivia moved on to a detailed description of the people, places, and things she'd witnessed and how she'd had to keep reminding herself it was real. She made note of the triumph she'd felt at the end of the evening after not being detected as an imposter. Satisfied that she had written everything she could think of about that first incredible night, she tucked it away in a dresser drawer.

At twelve o'clock, Olivia's elderly neighbor, Isabel Covington, arrived for lunch.

"How about minestrone soup and a PBJ?" Olivia asked, jumping as a crack of thunder shook the house and the kitchen lights flickered. It had been pouring since she'd returned from the *pâtisserie*. The sky looked like pewter and the temperature felt like November.

"Perfect on a day like this." Isabel pulled her cardigan tighter. "I can't wait to invite *you* for lunch. You've been so sweet helping me out."

"When does the cast come off?"

"Friday. And not a minute too soon. Oh!" Isabel exclaimed as a bolt of lightning lit up the room. "Boy, this is some storm!"

When Olivia was five and her beloved grandmother had succumbed to Alzheimer's disease, Isabel had stepped in to become her honorary grandmother. Over the years, the two women had created a strong bond, confiding in one another and sharing hopes and dreams. Olivia thought she knew everything about Isabel. How wrong she was.

Isabel glanced past the red-and-white polka dot curtains as sheets of rain lashed the window pane. "Where's our beautiful spring weather?"

"I bet you can't wait to get out in your garden," Olivia commented.

"Oh, yes. You know how much I love it. I have my mother to thank for that. During the Depression, everyone grew as much of their food as possible. If you had a patch of soil, even a small one, in went the potatoes, onions, tomatoes. I remember weeding a tiny patch of garden when I was probably four years old. My mother taught me early on how to care for plants. Even now, I can smell that loamy richness of the earth."

"Those pots of herbs on the sill are my first attempt at gardening," Olivia chuckled. "But, I've loved having fresh basil and thyme to throw in a recipe. I'm going to do that from now on."

"You might want to try some lemon thyme. It's heavenly. Add rosemary, too. That'll grow well in a small pot."

Isabel popped the last bite of sandwich into her mouth and drank the rest of her milk—Olivia insisted she needed calcium. "Thank you. Food always tastes better when you're sharing it, doesn't it?"

Olivia was about to get up and make coffee, when Isabel grabbed her hand. "Wait. I need to talk to you about something."

"What's the matter? Are you okay?" Olivia leaned closer.

"I'm fine. Listen, Olivia, how busy are you with work right now?"

"Not bad. I e-mailed the *salt* research Friday. I'll finish the travel piece on the eagle's nest villages today or tomorrow."

Although only in her early thirties, Olivia had solved a puzzle many adults never conquer in a lifetime. She'd figured out how to earn a living doing the two things she loved most—finding things out and traveling. Five years ago, she established The Watson Agency, a small research enterprise. The business flourished and her client list now extended along the entire East Coast. Olivia also worked as a freelance writer, penning travel articles which she sold to a variety of magazines.

"Why?" she asked Isabel.

"I'd like to ask you a favor if I could."

"Of course. What is it?"

"I need you to find someone," Isabel said.

"What do you mean?" Olivia thought Isabel looked uneasy.

"I have a twin, Olivia. A brother named Alex. We've never met."

"Oh, my goodness!" Her jaw dropped. "How do you know this?

When did you find out?" She stared at Isabel.

"My mother told me shortly before she died."

"That was years ago," Olivia exclaimed. She felt hurt, like she'd been left out of a secret. Why had Isabel kept something this important from her?

"I know. I tried to find him on my own but I never got anywhere. I thought with all the internet stuff you can do, maybe you'd have more luck."

"Wow, Isabel, a twin! It's hard to take in." She got up from the table. "We definitely need that coffee now. *And* some dessert. It looks like we're going to be here awhile."

A memory rushed back making Olivia wince. Unbeknownst to Isabel, Olivia had been instrumental in the loss of Isabel's husband and daughter. The guilt of her involvement still crushed her in unexpected moments. *Talk about keeping secrets*, she chided herself.

Olivia moved quietly about the kitchen. She was determined to find Isabel's twin, determined to make up for what she had done to this woman whom she adored. She made a pot of coffee, took some mini cream puffs from the freezer, and warmed them in the microwave. She set everything on the table and grabbed her laptop.

"Okay, let's start at the beginning," said Olivia.

Isabel came around the table and gave her a big hug. "Thank you! It's all I can think of lately. We turned 80 in February. For all I know, he could be dead. This has haunted me since my mother told me. I *have* to find out what happened to him." She brightened. "I might have nieces and nephews I don't even know anything about."

"Yeah, you probably do. All right, Isabel, what did your mother tell you?"

Chapter 9

Monday — April 23, 1934

S teven pulled the police car up to the sidewalk and parked at an angle next to a dark blue Chevy smelling of spilled gasoline. He and Jimmy Bou mounted the wide concrete steps and entered the two-story school. In the main office, Mrs. Betty Stoner, a plump woman with gray-brown hair, stood behind the counter arguing with a tall skinny girl.

"No, Molly. I've already told you a dozen times. You cannot take part in the school play unless *all* your grades are passing. There's no point in talking with Mr. Kennington. He'll just tell you the same thing."

The woman huffed. The girl rolled her eyes and whined. Steven thought this looked like something of a ritual.

"Now, look," continued Betty Stoner, pushing her glasses back up on her nose and placing her hands flat on the wooden counter separating them. "It would be a better use of your time studying for your history test. Miss Grantham said if you pass the test, your grades will make the cut-off and you can work on the sets. Now, go!"

The girl slouched out. As Steven approached the secretary, he wondered how long the woman had worked here. He remembered her from when he was in school.

"Good morning, Mrs. Stoner."

"Ah, Steven." She patted her hair in place and straightened her dress. "Or should I say Detective Sergeant Blackwell?" She smiled warmly at the officers. "And Jimmy Bourgogne. I heard you were a policeman," she said proudly, nodding at his uniform. Betty had always felt a certain responsibility for the character of the students who went through her school—and it really was her school. After all, it was she who kept the place running.

"Yes, ma'am," Jimmy Bou answered.

"How nice to see you both."

Her face fell as she realized this was a visit from the police, not two former students stopping by for a chat.

"Oh, dear. I thought I saw Pete McGrath marching Joey and Kevin down the hall a while ago," she said, looking only mildly concerned. Betty Stoner had spent her entire life working in the high school and there wasn't much she hadn't seen or heard. Thirty-plus years working with kids will leave even the most sentimental of souls a bit jaded, and Betty had never had a sentimental moment in her life. "I assumed he was taking them to the truant officer. So, what have they done this time?"

"You haven't heard?" Steven was amazed the news wasn't all around the school by now. The Knightsbridge grapevine was surpassed only by the thick vines of gossip snaking through the hallways of the high school. It was unbelievable that no one knew yet.

"Heard what? I've been so busy this morning I haven't even been able to take my coffee break." She sighed heavily. "And now it's lunch already. So, what's happened?" She looked from one police officer to the other with a matter-of-fact expression.

"Is Mr. Kennington here?"

"Yes." She made it sound like a question and glared at Steven with raised eyebrows and a steady stare. Clearly, she felt she should be informed first. When Steven said nothing, she gave in. "I'll get him."

A tall, broad-shouldered man with dark blond hair came striding to the front counter.

"Good morning, Steven, Jimmy." The principal reached over the counter and shook their hands. "What can I do for you?"

"We need to speak in private," Steven said.

"Of course. Come in." He swung open a small gate admitting the two policemen into the restricted section of the main office. "No interruptions, Betty. And don't say a word to anyone until we know what's going on." Betty Stoner was an active participant in the grapevine.

Tim Kennington ushered Steven and Jimmy into his office, closed the door, and indicated chairs as he settled behind his huge desk.

"So, what's this all about?"

Steven felt the best way to divulge bad news was like tearing a bandage off—the slower you did it and the longer it took, the more it hurt. He got right to the point.

"Lucy Russo's husband Frankie was found dead this morning."

"Oh, my word," Kennington exclaimed, shooting forward. Whatever he had been thinking, it had been nothing like this. "Where? What happened?" He exhaled deeply and leaned back. "Poor Lucy. Does she know yet? She's here today. I saw her come in this morning."

"That's why we're here, Mr. Kennington. We have to tell her."

"She's in class right now but the period ends in a few minutes. It'll be lunchtime." The principal stood up then, realizing there was nothing for him to do, sat back down. "Breaking the news to loved ones must be the worst part of your job."

"It's never easy." Steven shook his head. "We'd like to speak with her alone, please."

"Yes, of course. Use my office. Shall I send someone to get her?"

"Yes, but no mention of the police."

"Right." The principal left the room. Steven could hear him instructing Betty Stoner.

A shrill bell clanged throughout the building. Doors hit the walls as students poured out of their classrooms, anxious to get to the lunchroom or home to eat. No one wanted to waste a precious moment of the hour-long break. Excited chatter, laughter, and shouts filled the corridors as students stowed books, notebooks, paper, and pencils in wooden lockers, grabbed brown bags holding homemade sandwiches, and headed to lunch.

There was a light knock and a throat being cleared. Betty Stoner, accompanied by a cheerful Lucy Russo, opened Kennington's office door.

"I have Mrs. Russo for you."

The three men rose.

"Thank you, Mrs. Stoner. Let's give the detectives and Mrs. Russo some privacy," said the principal, firmly steering his secretary out of the room.

"Hello, Lucy," said Steven. "Come in and have a seat."

Her smile faded. "Steven! What are you doing here?" She stared at Jimmy's uniform. "Oh, no. Something's happened. Is it Frankie? Is it Helen?"

Steven guided her onto a chair, pulled his close, and faced her. Jimmy Bou stood to the side where he could study her reactions. He'd make brief notes now and elaborate later when he wrote his report.

"Lucy." Steven leaned forward and softly said, "I'm sorry, but there's no easy way to say this. Frankie's dead."

She looked at him as if he'd spoken Chinese.

"What? No, Frankie's in Syracuse."

"Why would he be in Syracuse, Mrs. Russo?" Jimmy asked.

"Who are you?"

"Officer Jimmy Bourgogne." Jimmy straightened up and asked again, "Why do you think your husband is in Syracuse?"

"This is his week at the brewery."

"I'm sorry, ma'am, I don't follow."

"He works one week here at the mill and one week in Syracuse at a brewery."

"That's kind of unusual, isn't it?"

Her eyes narrowed as her face tightened. "Times are tough, Officer. People take what they can get."

"Lucy, when was the last time you saw Frankie?" Steven asked.

At this, her composure broke. Tears trickled down her face. "It's really true? You're sure it's him?" She blinked, as if struggling to focus. "Was it an accident?"

"We're not sure yet. Doc Elliott will have to do an autopsy."

"You're bringing him back here?"

"He's here, Lucy. Doc's got him now."

"You brought him back already?"

"We're not sure he ever left."

"Yes, he did. He took the bus." Lucy stared at Steven. She'd stopped crying but hadn't wiped away the tears. Her dark eyelashes glittered.

"When was that, Lucy?"

"Yesterday afternoon. One o'clock. Maybe one-thirty."

"Was that the last time you saw him?"

"No, it was earlier. Before lunch."

"Frankie was found here in Knightsbridge early this morning."

"That can't be right. He left the house yesterday morning. Around eleven, I think. He was on his way to the bus station."

"He was found here, Lucy. Behind the school."

"The school?" she choked. "You're saying he was…"Her gaze drifted toward the window, then back at him. Her breaths were short and shallow. She cleared her throat. "You're telling me Frankie was here...dead...behind the school?" The tears returned.

Steven watched while Lucy Russo wept. She slumped on the hard wooden chair and made no sound, but her shoulders shook. She took a hankie from her jacket pocket. He watched her make several attempts to swallow. Thinking she might be sick, he pulled a wastebasket closer. She wiped her eyes and blew her nose. Her hands trembled.

Flooded with emotion, Lucy flashed back to the moment she had met Frankie.

Lucy and Helen bundled up against the cold, grabbed their skates, and set out for the rink. The snow crunched under their boots and the icy air scorched their throats. A crescent moon shimmered in the starlit sky, making it easy to find their way.

They'd only been skating fifteen minutes, when Frankie Russo raced past, spun around, and slowed then skated backwards directly in front of Lucy.

"Get out of my way," she growled.

"That's not very nice," he said, smiling broadly.

Helen took that very minute to skate off with a couple of friends, leaving Lucy annoyed and on her own. Frankie still blocked her path.

"Come on. There's plenty of space here. You don't need to be in my way." Lucy tried again.

"We could skate together," he said lazily.

"Why would I want to do that?"

"I can be good company."

"I'm sure there are lots of girls who agree with that. I'm not one of them. Please leave me alone." Lucy knew that Frankie Russo stepped out with more girls than all the fellas put together. He spent about two weeks with each one then dumped them. She had no intention of giving him the time of day.

Lucy had never cared about stepping out with a fella, getting married, and having kids. She loved her job and the fact that she was in charge of her life. Why would she want to give control to someone else? The mere thought gave her sleepless nights.

But Frankie Russo persisted. He wooed her, courted her, charmed her, and after three whirlwind months, he won her like a carnival prize.

Steven waited. *Is she playing for time,* he wondered. *Or is this real?* He had the feeling something wasn't right but couldn't put his finger on it. Steven knew the sound of heartache and he knew Lucy, but, at this moment, he wasn't sure what he was witnessing. It appeared to be grief. But what was Lucy grieving? Was it the loss of the man she loved? Or did she have something to do with his death?

Steven had seen cases where a person killed a loved one then genuinely grieved that death. Maybe Frankie had been up to his old cheating habits and she'd had enough. Maybe she'd put a stop to it...for good. He leaned over and tried to see into her eyes. *Bam!* He felt like a door had slammed in his face. Her head snapped to the side. She glared at him and sat up straight. A transformation had taken place before his eyes.

"Tell me about yesterday morning, Lucy."

"It was a normal Sunday morning. We walked to early Mass like we always do. Frankie doesn't—sorry, *didn't*—drive but St. Joseph's is only a block away so it's fine. We came home and had breakfast...pancakes...I made pancakes. We looked at the paper. I helped him pack his clothes for the week."

Steven interrupted. "You packed clothes? In what, Lucy? Did Frankie use a valise? A duffel bag? What?"

"A small suitcase. Why?"

Steven shot a look at Jimmy Bou, who wrote something in his notebook. He ignored her question. "Okay. Go on. After you helped him pack, then what?"

"I wanted him to go to the parade with me but he wasn't interested.

I asked him a couple of times. He said he had to get back to Syracuse before suppertime." She pursed her lips and hesitated.

Steven waited quietly—a lot of interviewing was giving the person time to tell the truth.

"We argued over it. But you know Frankie. Once he makes up his mind about something there's no talking him out of it. So, he left. I don't know where he went before he caught the bus. Maybe just sat at the station. I don't know. Steven, what happened?"

"I don't know yet, Lucy, but we'll find out. What did you do after he left?"

"I cleaned up the kitchen and wrote out my lesson plans for the week. After that, I went over to my sister's. We had a sandwich then we all walked to the parade."

"What time did you leave for Helen's house?"

"Around twelve, maybe quarter after. I wasn't paying attention to the time. Can I see him?"

"Not today, Lucy." Steven rose from his chair. "You should lie down and rest. Maybe call Helen or ask a friend to stay with you for a while."

"Maybe. I don't know. I can't think." She stood up but swayed to the side.

Steven made a grab for her and eased her back down on the chair. "Easy, Lucy. We'd better drive you home. This has been a shock."

"My pocketbook and lunch are in my room," she said vaguely.

"Would you like me to get them for you?" Jimmy Bou asked.

"Thank you." She nodded.

"While we're waiting, I have a couple more questions if you think you're up to it," Steven said.

"Okay."

"When Frankie left yesterday, did you walk him to the door? Did you see which way he turned?"

"No, I was in the kitchen. He stuck his head in the door and said he was leaving."

"You're sure you have no idea why he left at eleven when his bus wasn't until one or one thirty?"

"No, I'm sorry, Steven."

"All right. Did Frankie have any health problems that you know of? Did he have a heart condition?"

"No, not that he ever told me."

"Was he taking any medicine?"

"Like what?" Lucy asked.

"A prescription. Anything at all," Steve replied.

"If he had any prescriptions, I probably would have picked them up at the drugstore for him. He took an aspirin once in a while for a headache. But, there's nothing else that I know of."

"Who is your family doctor, Lucy?"

"Dr. Kranken."

Fifteen minutes later, when the front door closed behind Lucy, Steven pulled the police vehicle away from the curb. He looked across the bench seat at Jimmy Bou and asked, "What do you think, Jimmy?"

A few months ago, Steven had taken Officer Jimmy Bourgogne under his wing and was guiding him along the path to detective. Jimmy Bou was doing a good job so far. He was perceptive and decisive. He often blurted out ideas that flew through his mind and, more than once, those ideas had pointed Steven in a direction that paid off. Jimmy was also unassuming, which gave him the advantage in an interview.

Jimmy scrunched up his face and shook his head. "I don't know. Something was off but I can't figure out what it was. Mrs. Russo was all over the place. She was confused and shocked. We expect that. Then she was crying and I thought *Yeah, okay, she loved him*. All of a sudden, she pulls herself together and acts almost *mad* at us for...for

I don't know what." He lifted his hands in exasperation. "I'm sorry, Steven. I don't get her."

"I know what you mean. I agree. Her emotions ran the gamut. She *seemed* shocked."

"She *acted* sad."

"Her story made sense."

"I was wondering," Jimmy Bou hesitated.

"Yeah?"

"I know she's your friend's sister-in-law, but...."

"Spit it out, Jimmy."

"Do you think she's feeling guilty because the last thing she did was fight with him or because she killed him?"

"Good question. So, what do we know about Lucy Russo?"

"I'll start finding out this afternoon, huh, Steven?"

That was another thing about Jimmy Bou. The kid had initiative.

"Yes, you take charge of her background." Steven braked at the corner of Tulip Street, down-shifted, and turned onto the Margate Road. The gravel crunched as the heavy motor car pulled into the small lot behind the station.

When they got out, Jimmy Bou looked at Steven across the hood and added, "I think she loved him. But if it turns out to be murder, that doesn't rule her out, does it?"

"No, Officer Bourgogne, it does not."

Chapter 10

Monday — Present Day

Isabel launched into her story. "You know I was born during the Depression."

"Yes, 1934." Olivia almost smiled remembering Cooper Lewis's comment last night. *Isabel's a good baby. A real peach.*

"That's right. Times were very tough. Money was scarce. My dad was a farmer."

"What were your parents' names?" Olivia's fingers hovered over her laptop, ready to record all the details.

"Theresa Lewis Covington ..."

Theresa. Yes, that was the name of the mother.

"... and Sam Covington. My father was killed in an accident two months before I was born."

"Oh, how awful for your mom. Did she have her family around to help her?"

"Well, yes and no. That's how it all got started. Her father was killed at the Battle of the Somme in 1916 and her mother died two years later during the influenza epidemic."

"Oh, my goodness. How sad."

"Yes, and her brother had left to work for the Civilian Conservation

Corps."

"I've heard of that. Wasn't it part of Roosevelt's New Deal?"

Isabel nodded. "They recruited single young men to work on environmental conservation. Her brother planted trees on Bear Mountain. So, except for a cousin, my mother was all alone. Did you notice her maiden name? Lewis?"

"Oh, the family that owns The Three Lords."

"Right. Her cousin was very good to her. Cooper Lewis gave her a room upstairs in the pub and a job in the kitchen. He said the baby could stay in a basket in a corner of the kitchen as long as it stayed quiet. By then, she suspected she might be having twins."

Olivia could see where this was going. Her heart clenched. *Oh, no.*

"My mother was sobbing when she told me this part, Olivia. She said it was the worst moment in her life, even worse than losing my father. She could only keep one baby—there was no way she could afford to raise two children. She couldn't say no to the job offer because there was no other work and she was desperate for money. When my father died, she lost the right to live on the farm. They gave her a month to find someplace else."

"Isabel, this is heartbreaking. Choosing only one of your babies. God, that poor woman."

"I can't even imagine." Isabel looked on the verge of tears. "Anyway, she accepted her cousin's offer. She decided to keep the first baby that was born and give away the second one for adoption. She told the doctor..."

"Do you know his name?"

"No, she never said. My mother explained her situation to the doctor and asked if he could arrange the adoption of the second baby. But, and here's what makes it hard, she wanted the adoption to take place out of town. She said she couldn't watch her baby grow up with someone else. She'd always want to tell the child she was really the mother."

"It would take extraordinary strength never to say anything," said Olivia. "I can understand that."

"Yes, me too. It turns out the doctor had a brother in Syracuse who was a priest. He knew a family in his congregation who'd been wanting a child and," Isabel sighed, "that's it."

"Wow! That's not a lot but it's something. I've got a place to start." Olivia hit *save*. "Can you think of anything else? Even a tiny detail?"

"Oh my goodness! Where is my brain? Yes. How could I have forgotten?" She took a drink of coffee. "Maybe the caffeine will wake me up. My mother left a valuable clue. She said she always hoped Alex and I would find each other. To make it easier, she gave each of us her maiden name as a middle name. So, I'm Isabel Lewis Covington and he's Alex Lewis Covington."

"That should help. This might not be too hard after all, Isabel. At least your twin is a brother. Imagine if it was a sister! A woman gets married, takes her husband's last name, and *pouf* disappears."

"Olivia, I can't thank you enough. This has really been getting to me. For a long time, I felt like something was missing in my life. Like I was somehow...," Isabel screwed up her face, as if searching for the right word. "I know this is going to sound corny but *incomplete* is the best way to explain it."

"I get that. You hear about twins who were separated at birth. I've heard people use the same word." Olivia sadly remembered the other people who were missing in Isabel's life—the ones Isabel had no memory of. She brutally pushed away the thought.

"Where will you start?" Isabel leaned forward, eager for Olivia to begin.

"I have a couple ideas." A tiny smile escaped Olivia's lips. "And I might have a source."

Chapter 11

Monday — April 23, 1934

S omehow Tommy Forester managed to look efficient as he dusted the front desk with his sleeve.

"Is Will back yet?" Steven asked, as the door closed behind him and Jimmy Bou.

"No, but Chief Thompson said to go see him when you got back."

"Okay, thanks."

Steven poked his head in the chief's office and saw his boss on the phone. Thompson covered the mouthpiece and whispered, "I'll be down in a minute."

Steven returned to his desk in the CID room, glad the chief was occupied for the moment. He hoped to catch Dr. Kranken before the physician went out on afternoon house calls. He consulted a thin telephone directory and found the number he wanted. A receptionist answered on the first ring.

"This is Detective Sergeant Steven Blackwell with the Knightsbridge Police Department. I'd like to speak with Dr. Kranken if possible."

"You just caught him, Detective. One moment, please."

The doctor's reedy voice came on the line. "Hello, Detective. How can I help you?"

Steven explained about finding Frankie's body then asked, "Can you tell me if Frankie Russo was taking any kind of prescription medicine?"

"No, he was a healthy young man."

"So, he didn't have a heart condition or something that might cause him to pass out?"

"No, nothing like that. He was quite fit."

Steven thanked him and hung up. He decided to eat his sandwich then prepare his report on the morning's activities.

Chief Thompson entered and sat at Will's desk. He handed Steven an envelope. "A clerk from Judge Randolph's office brought these over a half hour ago. Your warrants."

"Swell. Thanks, Chief."

"So, what've we got, Steven?"

"Mostly questions right now. Frankie could have died any number of ways: accident, natural causes, murder. Doc said he'd call later this afternoon. After Pete called you, we found something up in the field. A square area of grass about the size of a double bed and a path leading from it into the woods close to where we think Frankie may have fallen over the edge. The grass in both spots had been flattened down and broken like something had covered it. The fellas were speculating that maybe Frankie was up there with a girl on a blanket. It was nice out yesterday."

"Could be. Could be a lot of other things, too."

"True. Will's still there with some of the fellas doing a grid search. I left some fibers and two dead birds with Hank at the lab. We'll see if they have anything to do with this. I notified Frankie's wife Lucy."

"How'd she take it?" The chief lit a cigarette and leaned back in Will's chair.

"Pretty much what you'd expect. Shocked, confused, dazed. She said she thought Frankie was in Syracuse." Steven explained Frankie's job arrangement. "I'm not sure though. Something wasn't right but I couldn't put my finger on it. I'll talk with her again."

"What's your next move?"

Steven explained his plan for the rest of the day. As Chief Thompson headed out of the room, he said, "I want to know as soon as you hear from Doc. Sam Silverstone already called me from *The Gazette*. I've got to give him something to keep the wolves at bay."

An hour later, the telephone on Steven's desk trilled. He picked up the Bakelite receiver.

"Hello, Steven." Doc Elliott's gravelly voice boomed so loudly that Steven pulled the phone away from his ear.

"Hi, Doc. You have news for me?"

"Yes, I'm phoning to tell you that Frankie Russo's stomach was loaded with arsenic. He was poisoned. Hank did a Marsh test this morning that confirmed it."

"Any chance he ingested it accidentally?"

"There's always a chance but I doubt it. He would have had to eat a handful of the stuff."

"I see. What about time of death?"

"Well there, Steven, I'm afraid I have disappointing news. I don't know if Frankie died soon after he ingested it or if he fell into a coma and died some time later. That can happen with arsenic. I can tell you he was completely rigid at the scene but he began loosening up around noon. Some people say the stiffening starts to reverse from 36 to 48 hours after death but I've seen it begin as early as 24 hours."

"Jimmy saw him leaving church yesterday morning around nine. And Lucy says he was home until late morning. She thinks around eleven. Do you think we're looking at lunchtime on Sunday?" Steven asked excitedly.

"Hold your horses. I'm not done. Will just dropped off a sample of vomit. Hank's testing it and I checked the stomach contents earlier. "

Steven grimaced. He'd never gotten comfortable with certain aspects of the post mortem.

"I smelled beer and there was partly digested food. I'm putting it between early Sunday morning—say seven o'clock, although that's unlikely because of the beer—and Sunday afternoon before two, also unlikely because the body's already started loosening up." Steven must have let out a sigh because Doc continued, "I know. I know. That's not much of answer for you and your boys. But, I'm afraid that's the best I can do. You know this isn't an exact science. Certain factors can throw off my calculations.

"But, listen. If people saw him out and walking—and I mean that literally, Steven, not swaying or stumbling around—but walking normally, I'd say you'd be safe in thinking after nine yesterday morning. Arsenic packs a punch and the quantity that we found in his stomach would lead me to believe he either died or fell into a coma pretty soon after he ingested it."

"I understand, Doc. Thanks. It gives us something to start with."

"I'll have my report finished by tomorrow. I'll send it over in the morning."

"Any thoughts on the two birds?"

"Hank's got them. I don't think we've ever tried a Marsh test on tissue samples from birds but I don't see why it wouldn't work. If it doesn't, I'll send them to the Crime Lab in Washington." Doc coughed and cleared his throat. "But, Steven, common sense tells me that if those robins were poisoned, it was probably by whatever killed Frankie since you found them so close to the body. I'd say Frankie ate something and the birds finished off the crumbs."

Steven thanked the ME and hung up. He poured a cup of coffee from his Thermos; the rich steamy aroma cleared his head. Still seated at his desk, he closed his eyes and thought about everything Doc had said. Although they would explore the possibility of an accident, it appeared they had a homicide investigation on their hands. Time to set up the murder board.

Visual organization was one of Detective Sergeant Blackwell's most important investigative tools. Several years ago, he'd commandeered a rickety old blackboard framed in wood and set on wheels. It was large enough to post crime scene photographs, maps, diagrams, and as much information as he needed. He grabbed the board and rolled it away from the wall. He picked up a piece of chalk and wrote:

<u>VICTIM–FRANKIE RUSSO</u>

1st job-Bookkeeper - Kbridge Knitting Mill
2nd job - Brewery - Syracuse
Married to Lucy Russo, teacher. No children.
Found dead in ravine behind HS
  Mon. Apr 23, approx 7.30 am
Body appears to have rolled down hill from field.
  Thrown off edge? Pushed? Fell?
Possibly spent time in field on blanket.
  With who?
COD - poisoned with arsenic
TOD – Sunday 7 am – 2 pm Mid-day likely.
Accident unlikely.

Steven boxed off an area and printed <u>QUESTIONS</u>. Every homicide investigation carried with it some obvious questions related to *Motive, Means,* and *Opportunity.* There were also dozens of questions that led to those answers and ultimately solved the case. Steven listed the ones that flew into his mind right away.

Where did Frankie Russo eat lunch on Sunday?
Who would be able to prepare poisoned food without someone else in the

house knowing about it? Or accidentally eating it?

Does the killer live alone?

Is the killer alone in the house all day while another inhabitant goes to work?

Was the poisoned food prepared in a house? Maybe a workplace? What kind of workplace has a kitchen? What type of employee would have access to this kitchen?

Where are the cooking/baking utensils the killer used to prepare the poisoned food?

Would it be possible to clean them well enough to ever use them again safely?

Did the killer throw out bowls, spoons, and measuring cups? If so, where are they?

Where is Frankie Russo's suitcase?

There were many more he and his team would ask over the coming days—and they would prioritize their importance—but Steven liked to work fast on his initial set-up.

Next, he created a column headed <u>EVIDENCE</u> and noted the vomit, two birds, and fibers. He drew a small diagram representing the square and path of flattened grass and noted the woods at the end of the path. He sketched a small hill and drew arrows showing the trajectory of broken branches and dislodged boulders to the spot where the body was found.

Steven left space for a column headed <u>WITNESSES</u> and hoped they'd be able to fill it. Finally, in the center of the board, he wrote <u>SUSPECTS</u>. Because the spouse is the first person to consider, and because of Frankie's history as a ladies' man, only one name occupied the list—Lucy Russo.

Satisfied with his basic framework, Steven returned to his desk and propped his feet on an open bottom drawer. He poured another cup of coffee and took out his second sandwich. While he ate, Steven remembered the night in The Three Lords when Artie had told him about Lucy's engagement. He'd been worried. Helen's baby sister was going to marry the town Lothario. They had talked about Frankie's one-night stands, flings, and affairs. There had also been a longtime girlfriend with a high-school connection. *Who was it?* Steven raked his memory. *Was it Hannah Grantham?* He'd seen Frankie with so many girls over the years it was hard to keep track. He'd have to ask around.

Steven could not imagine why women were attracted to a fella like Frankie. *What was the appeal?* Maybe he'd ask Olivia. Maybe she could explain how girls thought about fellas. Steven couldn't even imagine being pals with a guy like Frankie.

As he was brushing crumbs from the front of his white shirt and dark vest, Will, Ralph, and Pete came in, followed by Jimmy Bou who never wanted to be left out of anything.

"We're done with the search," said Will.

"That was fast."

"The field's not all that big and with the extra men you sent over, it didn't take long."

"Before you tell me, fellas, Doc called. Frankie *was* poisoned. Doc said his stomach was full of arsenic. He said there was so much it probably wasn't an accident. We're treating this as a suspicious death."

"Wowie," breathed Jimmy Bou.

"Can he tell when Frankie was poisoned?" Will asked.

"Officially, he's saying Sunday from seven a.m. to two p.m. But...," Steven explained why they unofficially thought it was closer to noon. "All right, what have you got there, Ralph?"

"Pete drew us a map," Ralph said, holding up a large piece of paper and waving it like a flag.

"I made a grid of the whole area. With measurements," added Pete.

"We marked everything—where the dead bird was and the spot

where there might have been a blanket," said Ralph, craning his neck to peer in Steven's empty lunch pail. "Mmm, we didn't get a chance to eat yet."

Steven ignored him and stood up. "What did you find?"

"A few things," said Pete. He grabbed the paper from Ralph and, as he leaned over to spread it on Will's desk, his bald pate reflected light from the overhead fluorescent tube. "I found more of those fibers. They were caught in the grass where we think Frankie and the girl might have been sitting."

"So, your blanket and picnic idea is holding water, Pete," Steven nodded. "Interesting."

"There was a bunch of useless stuff scattered around. Trash like you'd expect near a school," said Ralph.

"The only item we think is important is this," said Will, slipping on a cotton glove and carefully extracting a glass bottle from a paper bag."

"It's an Old Crow whiskey bottle." Jimmy Bou peered at the pristine label. "That hasn't been there long."

"We found it on the other side of the field a few feet into the woods," Will said.

Steven bent over the map. "Where exactly?"

Pete pointed to a spot across the meadow from what they now thought of as the crime scene. He had marked an X on the map and labelled it.

"There were cigarette butts, too," said Ralph.

"It looks like someone spent time in that spot smoking and drinking," said Will. "There were four cigarette butts." Then, he said the words Steven longed to hear. "We could have a witness."

Jimmy Bou lit up like a kid on Christmas morning.

"Somebody could have been there at the same time as Frankie and the girlfriend," said Pete. "The woods are thick. Whoever it was would've been hidden."

"Yeah, and if you're schmoozin' a dame you're not gonna notice," added Ralph.

"I'll bet it was a kid who sneaked off with his father's bottle," said Jimmy.

"Or the father hiding it from his wife," commented Will.

"Could be either one," said Steven. "A high school boy would sure be interested in watching a fella making time."

"Yeah," smirked Pete, "picking up on how it's done."

Steven shot him a look. "There are still plenty of people who think President Roosevelt was wrong when he repealed Prohibition last year. A man might feel like he has to sneak out of the house to drink."

"Especially if his wife's a member of the Women's Temperance Union," said Will.

"I bet there'll be some prints on the bottle," exclaimed Jimmy Bou, with his usual optimism. He noticed the murder board. "Ooh, you got started already." Jimmy Bou loved the organization that Steven's murder board offered. He loped to the other side of the room. Ralph and Pete scurried after him.

They read what Steven had posted then Ralph grabbed the chalk and added the new information. Will picked up his sandwich and joined them.

When he was finished studying Pete's map, Steven said, "Fellas, we've got a lot of ground to cover before the end of the day. Let's get started." He turned to Ralph and Pete. "I've got a warrant to search the Russo house. Grab Ray and go over there."

"Are we looking for arsenic?" asked Pete. "They've probably got a can of rat poison stashed somewhere. Everybody does. It's cheap and it works."

"Yes, that's true but we need to check anyway. You're also looking for items that might contain traces of arsenic. The killer had to prepare the poisoned food somewhere. Take your time in the kitchen. We want to know about cooking or baking things that were thrown out or are stored in an odd place, like they won't be used again. Check the garbage in case something's still there. Also, look for anything that might indicate Frankie was cheating again. Maybe he kept a note or a Valentine card from a girlfriend."

Ralph scribbled in his notebook. "Do you think he'd be stupid enough to keep something like that in his house?"

"Nah," piped up Pete. "Lucy could come across it any time."

"Probably not, but be thorough," Steven said. "Jimmy, you're on Lucy's background like we agreed before. And put Frankie's together while you're at it." He turned to his partner. "Will, before we leave for the mill, would you get five or six patrolmen? Have them spend the rest of the day out on the streets asking questions. Split them up. I want a couple of fellas in Lucy and Frankie's neighborhood tracing Frankie's movements from when he left the house yesterday morning. Lucy says it was around eleven. The rest can focus on the parade route and the area near the school. We need a picture of Sunday. Who was at the parade? Did anyone see a couple having a picnic up in the meadow? Did anybody notice someone coming down the hill, especially carrying a blanket? You know the routine."

"The whole town was at the parade," said Jimmy Bou. "Somebody must've seen something."

"I hope so."

"I'll make sure they understand we need to know if Frankie was back to his old cheating habits, too," added Will. "This is one time we want to listen to gossip."

"Good point," said Steven. "Tell them to get people talking about Frankie. And about Lucy, too. Let's find out more about the widow."

ADONA

"Adona! Hey! Wait for me!"

A shapely woman with shining, jet black hair stopped, turned to scan the parking lot, and saw Joanie hurrying as fast as her short legs would allow and blowing goodbye kisses to her husband, who was pulling away from the curb.

"Gee, Dona, I called a couple of times. You're miles away."

Adona Russo bent and gave her best friend a warm hug.

"Sorry. I didn't hear you."

"Are you okay? You don't look so good."

"Yes." She attempted a laugh but what came out was thin and unconvincing. "I'm fine."

Her chum wrinkled her nose, narrowed her eyes, and peered at Adona's unusually pale face for a sign of the truth. "No, you're not. And you haven't been for a week. But that's all right. I'll wait. You'll tell me when you're ready." Joanie Bishop tucked her hand in Adona's curved arm and together they marched into the Knightsbridge Knitting Mill.

Inside the factory entrance, they pulled their time cards from the thin metal slots and inserted them in the clock, which stamped *6:45 a.m.* next to today's date. They entered the locker room where they stowed their lunches and put on their aprons. All mill seamstresses were required to buy and wear simple, gray cotton uniforms, which hung straight and shapeless. They topped these off with crisp white aprons, light-colored stockings, and plain black shoes.

The small vestibule next to the bathroom was crowded and noisy. A few women were changing into their uniforms. Some were straightening the seams on their stockings. Others were puckering up in the mirror putting on lipstick or wrapping a kerchief around their hair.

Joanie leaned against her locker and lit her last cigarette until lunchtime. She inhaled deeply and blew smoke upward. "So, Adona, how was the birthday party Saturday?"

"It was good."

"What'd you give him?"

"A dump truck. They love cars and trucks at that age."

Joanie nodded and took another long drag. "Did Connie make a meal? Was there cake?" she asked excitedly.

"The usual. Spaghetti and meatballs."

"Jeez, it's like pulling teeth with you this morning. What's wrong?"

"Nothing, I'm fine. Really."

"So...?"

"What?"

"So, did you have birthday cake? I don't remember the last time I splurged on ingredients for a cake," Joanie said dreamily. "My Johnny's birthday is next month and I've been saving up. I'm going to make him the biggest, fanciest cake he ever saw!"

Adona smiled at her friend, always so easily distracted. "Yes, Maria made one. It was lovely."

"So, who was there?"

"The family—Nick and me, Maria and Vito, Lucy and Frankie."

The factory siren exploded and the shrill sound vibrated off the walls in the small room. The blast was blinding.

"I *hate* that thing," growled Joanie, pinching the end of her cigarette. She rubbed the butt over her shoe bottom and slipped it in her pocket to save for later. "I'm deaf for half-an-hour after it goes off." She sighed. "Well, here goes another Monday. Another week of the same old thing. Nothing ever happens around this place."

They joined several dozen women, then folded in with a large group of men and entered the cavernous work area. The men veered to the right and began turning on equipment. The roar rendered conversation impossible. The women headed to the left to row upon row of industrial sewing machines. Each found her place, sat down, and picked up where she'd left off on Friday.

The morning dragged on. The huge room was dusty and loud. The work demanded the women's full attention—if anyone ruined a garment, the cost was taken from her pay packet. No one could afford that.

At long last, the siren sounded for the noon break. As the men powered down the giant machines, the noise level dropped. The seamstresses stopped sewing and pushed back from their machines, their chairs scraping over the rough concrete floor. The women crowded into the vestibule once again to use the restroom, repair their lipstick, comb their hair, and grab lunches.

As soon as Adona and Joanie were seated at their usual table in the back of the cafeteria, before they had even unwrapped their sandwiches, they knew something was up. Whispers rushed around the room and people turned in their seats to stare at their table. No one needed to say a word. Adona knew it was about her.

And Frankie.

Every moment for the past week, Adona had battled a guilt that was suffocating her. At night after slipping into bed alongside Nick, she would toss and turn until around midnight, when she'd get up and go downstairs for a glass of water. She'd sit at the kitchen table gazing at the framed picture of the Virgin Mary on the wall, praying. Adona had no idea how to cope with the shame that had come to live inside of her.

She had to protect Nick. He could never know.

I have committed a sin.

She should have fought harder.

I have broken a commandment.

What should she do?

Confession. I will go to confession on Saturday.

If she could only get through the week.

Adona choked on her food. She coughed and took a long drink of water.

"Dona, are you all right?"

"Sure, just went down the wrong way. Thank you."

One of the office secretaries came over to their table. "Adona," said the matronly woman, "I'm so sorry. You must be in shock." She reached out and patted her on the shoulder.

Adona Russo stopped breathing and her eyes grew wide. "What?" she squeaked.

"Haven't you heard? Nick's cousin Frankie was found this morning in the gully behind the high school. He's dead."

"*Dio mio.*" She sucked in breath, crossed herself, and toppled off her chair in a dead faint.

Chapter 12

Eager to get the investigation under way, Steven left skid marks in the stones as he peeled out of the driveway alongside the station. He took the corner too fast then slammed on his brakes at the first stop sign. Grinding the gears, he shifted into first and turned onto Oak Street. Will glanced over but said nothing as they sped to the next intersection. Finally, Steven slowed down and drove the short distance along the river at a safer speed. As he pulled into the parking area, a towering smoke stack, nearly lost a gray haze, loomed over the police vehicle. The emissions blended seamlessly with clouds coming in from the west.

The Knightsbridge Knitting Mill sat on the banks of the Mohawk River as it had for decades. The building was an odd conglomeration of square- and rectangular-shaped blocks that had been added one at a time, years apart. The original three floors were constructed with local stone and connected to a two-story, shed-like box that held the enormous chimney. A long brick addition was attached perpendicular to the mid-section. Steven imagined it would take a while to find your way around.

They got out of the car and chose a door at random. Inside, they stepped toward a pair of heavy swinging doors and pushed into a wall of noise. The sound was so deafening that Steven shook his head as if he were getting water out of his ears. Will looked like he'd been slapped.

They found themselves in a vast machine-filled room whose ceiling soared three stories high. Stretching in front of them were rows of giant spools being wrapped with knitted textiles. There were more than fifty men working on these complex machines. On the other side of the cavernous space, dozens of industrial sewing machines manned by seamstresses reached to the back wall. Steven noticed the smell of industrial oil and imagined they used a lot of it here.

"Detective Sergeant Steven Blackwell and Sergeant Will Taylor," Steven shouted to a man at a wooden sentry station keeping an eye on the room. They flipped open small leather folders and showed their badges and IDs. Steven asked where they could find the office manager, Len McMillan. The foreman understood right away.

"Russo. Yeah, we heard," he yelled back.

Steven imagined the town's few dozen telephones had been ringing all morning. He pictured housewives gossiping in the aisles of the A & P Market or talking to each other in backyards, while they hung their washing on clotheslines. He knew they would be spreading a mix of facts and rumors about Frankie Russo's death.

"McMillan's office is in the other building." The foreman jerked his thumb to the right. "Upstairs. The far end."

He gave a shrill whistle and a gawky teenager ran down one of the aisles where he'd been sweeping the floor. The boy screeched to a halt when he caught sight of the policemen.

"I...I...didn't do anything," he stammered nervously and took a step back.

"Get a hold of yourself, boy. Nobody said you did." The foreman impatiently shook his head in disgust. "Take these detectives over to the offices. And stop acting stupid."

Steven and Will followed a twitchy Dickie Hughes through a maze of narrow corridors, over creaking oaken floors, up rickety stairs, and into the mill offices. Work stopped abruptly when they entered. Four women and two men, seated at desks arranged in the center of the cluttered space, froze. The feeling of apprehension and disquiet was so thick Steven thought he could wrap his fist around it. It wasn't every day that a man you worked with was found dead and the police came calling.

A barrel-chested man approached them with long strides, thrust out a hand, and said in a deep voice, "I'm Len McMillan. How can I help you?"

Steven and Will introduced themselves and showed their IDs again.

"I imagine you heard about Frankie Russo?" Steven began.

"Yeah, a while ago. What a thing, huh? Somebody said he was poisoned."

"Mr. McMillan, I'd like to speak with you while Sergeant Taylor takes a look at Frankie's desk. Which one is his?"

"Sure. It's that one over there." McMillan took the warrant Will held out and pointed to a battered wooden desk.

Steven followed Frankie's boss to a corner office and shut the door behind them. "Mr. McMillan, what can you tell me about Frankie Russo?"

"Like what?"

"We need to find out as much as we can about a murder victim. His habits. The kind of worker he was. Who his friends were. Anything, because we never know what will be important in the end." Steven leaned back in the chair and propped his foot on his knee.

"I see. He was a very good bookkeeper. Accurate, paid attention to details. A crackerjack mathematician. Almost never made a mistake in his calculations."

"Why was he reduced to half-time?"

"After the Crash, we had to make some changes. In January of '31, we decided to get along with two full-time bookkeepers and one part-time."

"How did you choose Russo to be half-time?"

"Two reasons really. First, he was the last man hired."

Steven nodded—he understood the business practice of last man hired, first man fired.

"And second, because…well…Frankie was distracted by the office girls. I didn't always get a full eight hours out of him."

"Can you be more specific?"

"When one of the girls got up or went back to her desk, he'd ogle her or make a comment. Sometimes he'd go over to one of them and whisper. I don't know what he said but it sure wasn't about work."

"Do you think he was stepping out with one of them?" Steven asked.

"No idea. But the behavior was inappropriate for the office. I had to speak to him a number of times."

"How did he react when you did?"

"Very casual. Like it was nothing. Once or twice he even acted indignant and said 'I'm a married man.' He didn't seem to care." McMillan leaned back in his chair. "Truth be told, I thought it was bullshit. Excuse my French. I've heard the rumors about his reputation. Although I have to say, I had hoped he'd settle down when he married Lucy. Nice girl. Anyway, I was glad when we had to cut his hours. I was thinking of canning him altogether."

Steven thought that Frankie's behavior must have been really bad for his boss to consider firing a man who did his job so well.

McMillan stood and turned on an overhead light. Ever thickening clouds were drifting past the high windows and the room had darkened. They were in for a storm. Steven tried to remember if he'd closed the windows of his beloved Chevy parked in the driveway at home. It was nearly four thirty. He hoped the rain would hold off a few hours.

The manager returned to his seat and lit a cigarette. "To be fair, I should say he *used to* behave like that. I noticed a while back that he seemed different."

"How?"

"He stopped flirting. Settled down and did his work. Maybe he knew I was thinking of firing him." He tilted his head back and blew smoke toward the ceiling.

"Do you remember when that was?"

"I couldn't say for sure but I think it was after I made him half-time."

"That would be sometime in 1931?"

The manager nodded.

Steven made a note. "Can you be more specific?"

"Sorry," said McMillan.

"Who were his friends here?"

"He ate lunch with Carl Eastwood, one of the other bookkeepers. Beyond that, I don't know."

"Thank you, Mr. McMillan. Now, I need to talk with the girls in the office."

When Steven and McMillan went to the manager's office, Will headed straight to Frankie's work area. In the middle of the desk was a blotter that had seen better days. It was full of random numbers, calculations, and doodles, as well as stains from spilled coffee and cigarette ashes. On the left corner under an electric lamp with a flexible arm sat a pile of dog-eared catalogs. On the opposite corner, next to an overflowing ashtray, a stack of stuffed file folders tilted dangerously close to the edge. Will sat down. He flipped through the files, looked inside a ledger, and confirmed that both contained nothing but mill business. He went through every other item on the desk, then pushed back and opened the center drawer. After a thorough examination of invoices, orders, telephone messages, paper clips, erasers, pens, and pencils, he was sure there was no information of a personal nature. He moved to the side drawers.

He found it in the back of the bottom drawer on the left.

The tiny notebook was cheap and tattered. The thin cover—the color of manila file folders—was stained and creased. Will opened it and discovered page after page of penciled notations written in Frankie's small cramped hand. Each page was divided into four neat columns—there were dates, amounts of money, a capital letter, and groups of letters and abbreviations in small case.

The first page began:

```
Jul. 16    $ .50    H    mov/popc
Jul. 22    $ .75    J    pub
Jul. 30    $1.00    H    b'day pres
```

Will noted the year at the top of the page—1925, the year they'd both graduated from high school. He wondered if Frankie had found a job right away and had money to spend, possibly for the first time in his life. He made a note to find out when he'd started working here, or where his first job had been.

Will thumbed through the next couple of pages.

```
Oct. 13    $ .80    B    pub
Oct. 20    $ 1.25   C    supper
Oct. 31    $.45     H    Hallow. party
```

The dates continued through the next several years. The amounts of money varied, but all were well under three dollars. In addition to H, J, B, and C, there were L, E, K, M, V, R, and many more. Some letters repeated over months and years, others were noted once or twice and disappeared. One letter was noticeable because it didn't follow the format. It was the only one with a notation beside it. The note said *Working on A*. There were more than twenty-five pages crammed full of these notations. Frankie Russo had been a busy man.

A busy cheater, Will thought as he stared at the book. It never ceased to amaze him how people thought their personal belongings were secure. Certainly, Frankie had never expected to be murdered. Nevertheless, the mere idea of writing down such intimate information and leaving it in a place where anyone could discover it was incomprehensible to the very private policeman.

Will flipped to December 1931. The list had dwindled to L, H, and a new one—S. He turned one more page and found something unexpected: in January 1932, there were only two notations, both involving L and S. The final pages were empty. Something had happened to Frankie Russo two years ago. And Will bet her name began with S.

This did not look good for the widow. If ever a woman had a motive, here it was in black and white.

Will pocketed the notebook. He rose and approached a slender young man with bright green eyes, who, although he had tried not to, had watched the policeman search Frankie's desk.

"Jake, I'm Sergeant Will Taylor. I think we met once or twice."

"We did. My brother Charlie introduced us one night in The Three Lords."

"I need to ask you some questions about Frankie Russo."

"Sure. We heard about it this morning. It's awful."

"There's an empty office," said Will, pointing to a doorway. "Let's have some privacy."

"What can you tell me about Frankie?" Will asked, when he'd turned on a light and they'd been seated.

"Not much. I didn't know him outside work."

"Okay, then how did he act when he was here? Was he friendly? Was he a conscientious worker?"

"I think he did a good job. He was careful, paid attention to details.

He worked hard to make sure his accounts always balanced." Jake hesitated.

"Frankie's dead, Jake. You can't hurt him. Whatever you say can only help us find the person who killed him."

"Something happened a while ago. I don't know if it's important."

"Don't worry about that. We'll figure out what's important," Will said.

The bookkeeper nodded. "It was between him and Adona."

"Adona?"

"Adona Russo. She works in the factory. She's married to Frankie's cousin Nick."

"Tell me what happened," Will said.

"It was in the lunchroom. Everybody was done eating. People were sitting around having coffee and a cigarette. We had maybe ten, fifteen minutes before we had to go back to work. Adona was at her usual table in the back with some of the girls. Frankie left where he was sitting and went to talk with her. All of a sudden, she jumped up and slapped him. Then she rushed out."

"What did he say?"

"I don't know. I couldn't hear. The only reason I noticed was because I was facing them. You could ask the girls she was with. Or maybe she'll tell you."

Will wrote down the names of Adona's lunch companions.

"Do you remember when this happened?"

Jake shook his head. "All I can say for sure is that it was a Friday. I remember I was glad it was the end of the week. And it wasn't last Friday. Maybe the one before that?"

"All right, Jake. Is there anything else?"

"No, like I said, I didn't really know Frankie," he hesitated again. "To be honest, I didn't like him much."

To Will's final question, the bookkeeper said that Frankie had been rude and disrespectful toward the girls in the office.

Will made one final note in his book: Is A Adona?

It was after five when Steven and Will finished at the knitting mill. Rain bucketed down and Steven engaged the heavy wipers. They clicked slowly back and forth, leaving a greasy film on the windshield. He wished they worked better. The roads were slick and it was hard to see.

"What did McMillan have to say?" Will asked, his breath fogging up a portion of the windshield.

"Frankie was an excellent worker but he was thinking of canning him because he was always going after the secretaries in the office."

Will pursed his lips and shook his head. "I don't understand some people."

"Until a few years ago, that is. Sometime in 1931, his behavior took an about-face and he stopped harassing the girls," Steven added.

"That might go along with something I found, Steven. What about your interviews with the secretaries?"

"They all said pretty much the same thing. He put the moves on them. They resisted. Said they weren't interested."

"Did you believe them?"

"Yeah, I think so. There seems to have been an attraction with one of them at first, but she found out what he was really like and ignored him after that."

"Good for her. I talked with Charlie's brother Jake."

"I noticed him. I forgot he worked at the mill," said Steven.

"He told me about an incident between Frankie and his cousin Nick's wife Adona."

"What happened?" Steven asked.

"One day recently, *possibly* a week ago last Friday, Frankie approached Adona in the lunchroom and said something. She got up and slapped him. Hard."

"What did Frankie say to her?"

"Jake didn't know, but he gave me the names of the girls she eats with. If Adona doesn't tell us, we can ask them." Will reached into a pocket and pulled out a tattered notebook.

"What's that?" Steven glanced at the little book, momentarily taking his eyes off the wet road.

"A lot of motive for Lucy Russo." Will explained what was written inside.

"He kept track of the girls he was stepping out with and the money he spent on them? Why would he do something like that?"

"That's what it looks like. I think we can forget about most of the initials at the beginning."

"Right, that's too long ago." said Steven.

"There are four letters that seem significant," Will continued. "L, H, A, and S."

"L's probably Lucy."

"I thought that, too. I'll check to be sure the dates work out."

Steven nodded. "What about the other three?"

"There was an H on almost every page from the beginning in 1925 until the fall of '31." Will looked over at Steven. "Granted, the H in '25 might be a different person but let's assume it's the same girl."

"All right."

"From September 1931through the end of the year, H appears less and less. By January of '32, H is gone for good."

"Something happened in 1931. You hit pay dirt, Will." Steven experienced a rush of excitement. "I think Hannah Grantham was a girlfriend of Frankie's at one time. H could be Hannah."

"You're right. They were a couple in high school but that's ten years ago."

"True, and she's been stepping out with Ben Maxwell for quite

84

awhile. Hannah might be the H in 1925, but it probably refers to somebody else in the later years." Steven downshifted and turned a corner. "Remind me to ask the team during the briefing tomorrow if anybody knows another H. A more recent one. So, what about the other two—S and A?"

"S, I don't have any idea. But, there's something special about A. It appears differently in the notebook," Will said.

"What do you mean?"

"It's one of the last notations before the list dries up. It said 'Working on A.'"

"Working on A? None of the others are like that?" Steven asked.

"No, just initials, the amount of money, and evidently what he spent it on." Will sighed.

"What? You know who A is?"

"No, but what about that incident in the lunchroom when Adona slapped Frankie?"

"But her husband is Frankie's cousin," Steven exclaimed. "Frankie was a lowlife but he wouldn't have gone after someone in his own family. Would he?"

Will shrugged. "Who knows?"

Lightning split the sky as Steven pulled in behind the station. He swung the motor car around so they faced the street in case he had to take off fast. He left the gearshift in first and cut the engine, but made no move to get out. After a few seconds, he turned to his partner and said, "What I want to know is what happened to Frankie Russo in 1931? And who is S?"

Chapter 13

Monday — Present Day

After Isabel had left, Olivia went upstairs to her exercise room. She loved the Zen-like transformation from what used to be Steven's bedroom. She'd painted the walls a pale celery green and left the room empty and the wood floor bare, with one exception. In the far corner, she'd placed a basket with her yoga mat, weights, and Thera-bands. This was where she practiced her kickboxing exercises, stretched, and worked on muscle building.

Olivia worked out for forty minutes then returned to the kitchen with her endorphins popping. She took a bottle of water from the fridge and settled at the kitchen table. She had plenty of time before meeting Steven and wanted to make a good start in her search for Isabel's long-lost twin brother.

Whenever she tackled a research project, the first thing Olivia did was figure out her strategy. What was the best way to get the information she was tasked to find? The internet was usually her first choice. Would an online search be the most efficient and least time-consuming approach? Should she go to the library for a particular book or DVD? Was there someone she could consult or a place she should visit? What kind of specialized assistance did she need and did she know anyone who could help?

This project was different from anything she'd taken on before. This time Olivia had an ace in the hole—her new-found ability to time travel. She could go right to the original sources. The thought was mind-blowing. She cautioned herself not to get over-confident. After all, this week was the first time she'd be spending a significant amount of time in 1934. What if their time-travel experiments didn't work? Then what?

That stormy night back in February when they had seen each other for the first time was crystal clear in Olivia's mind. Since then, she and Steven had learned a lot. They knew the house played a role in their ability to move across time. And the doorway to Olivia's bedroom was the key. At first, it was the only way they'd been able to enter each other's time. But, after spending many evenings together in his kitchen or hers, they discovered the connection they'd made and the bond they were creating also played a part. Once, Steven had been shocked to see Olivia and her friends in his kitchen as he'd been leaving the pantry. Olivia had been stunned to hear Steven slam the front door when he returned home one night. They realized that their desire to be together influenced their ability to see each other. At one point, Olivia was actually running into Steven too often. They had discussed this new phenomenon and had agreed to try to control things better. Olivia valued her privacy and didn't want to run into Steven unannounced.

Now, they had more questions and planned new experiments. The first test of going out to dinner at the pub had worked perfectly. Although Steven and Olivia hadn't made physical contact as they'd left the house—he didn't take her hand the way he always did when bringing her across the threshold of her bedroom doorway—she had not faded away when they'd stepped off the front porch. As they'd walked farther and farther away, Olivia stayed in 1934. They concluded that the connection with the house was not essential to her being able to stay in the past.

Aside from her initial nerves and sweaty palms, Olivia had felt no adverse affects to her body or mind. She'd had no trouble returning to her own time. And, to her delight, no one had suspected she was time-traveling from 80 years in the future. The next question she and Steven had discussed was Did Olivia have to physically be with Steven to stay in his time? This test was happening tomorrow morning.

A crash of thunder rattled the dishes and lightning lit up the kitchen, rousing Olivia from her reverie. Rain beat down on the roof. Only three in the afternoon and it was dark as night. She felt the temperature drop again. She turned on another light and went upstairs for a hoodie and pair of socks.

Okay, Olivia, let's get cracking. She stared at the blank computer screen. Mr. Moto jumped up onto her lap, startling her—her kitten was afraid of thunderstorms. He turned around twice, found his spot, and settled in, purring softly. She stroked his silky black fur and he promptly fell asleep.

With the kitten's soft snores in the background, Olivia focused on her search for Alex. She made a simple chart with a list of questions on the left and two columns to the right—one labelled *1934* and the other designated *the present day*. The questions that needed answering right away were: *What was the name of the doctor who delivered the twins? What was the name of his brother, the priest? What was the church in Syracuse where the priest was assigned?* Lastly, Olivia listed the sources she planned to check for each question in both time periods.

Olivia imagined the adopting family would have followed Catholic practices at the time and had the baby baptized right away. When she discovered which church was instrumental in the adoption, she'd check their baptismal records from late February through the end of May, 1934. Here, she fully expected to discover little Alex's new name. Once she had the family name, she was sure the internet would reveal Alex's current whereabouts.

Chapter 14

Monday — April 23, 1934

L ucy watched Steven pull away from the curb. She moved from behind the curtain, stumbled backwards, and dropped onto the sofa. She closed her eyes and let her mind drift.

Lucy had imagined the moment when she'd be free of Frankie for good, but she never thought it would feel like this. How many times had she searched for ways to be rid of him? Divorce was not an option in her family. So, that took care of that. For a while, she considered leaving him. She dreamed of packing a bag while he was at work and simply disappearing. There were plenty of girls living on their own nowadays. Lucy was a modern woman, too, with a college degree and a profession she could rely on. She possessed the skills and confidence to live independently. But, she loved her house and her garden. She liked her job. And she couldn't walk out on her sister—Helen would worry like mad.

Thoughts of being free of Frankie reminded Lucy of what had pushed her over the edge.

Lucy rode a roller coaster from the moment she said "I do." Frankie was attentive and loving during the year he courted her and during the first three months of their marriage. Then she began hearing rumors, whispers that he'd been seen with his old girlfriend Hannah Grantham. At first, she refused to believe it. Some people didn't like seeing others happy. So-and-so was jealous. It was a case of mistaken identity. Lucy came up with all kinds of excuses.

But she couldn't hide from the truth when it stared her in the face. She cringed and hastily turned away when she came upon him and Rita together while out shopping, when she saw him kiss Virginia on the village green, and when she heard him cooing on the telephone to someone named Edith.

When Frankie's job was cut to half-time and he found a second part-time job in Syracuse, Lucy clung to the hope that life would improve. During that summer, it seemed her prayers had been answered. She noticed a gradual transformation in his behavior. He was coming home from work earlier and staying home in the evenings. He actually listened when she talked to him. Although she was afraid to let down her guard and open herself up to the pain that used to rip through her every time she'd discovered he was cheating, Lucy allowed herself to think he might be hers again.

Things drifted along for a couple of years. Then a week ago she saw him with her.

And that did it. He had crossed a line.

She was done. Lucy Russo had finally had enough of Frankie Russo. She was sick of his cheating and tired of her own humiliation. She couldn't stand any more whispering behind her back. She would no longer pretend to ignore conversations that stopped abruptly when she entered a room. Lucy Russo had reached her threshold of deceit.

Now, only a short time after Steven Blackwell told her the police had found Frankie's body, Lucy felt the healing process take hold. An incredible, magical peace was washing over her. She knew she'd have moments when the memory of the love she once knew would ambush her and she would mourn what might have been. But at this very moment, Lucy Russo knew she was going to be fine. Maybe even better than fine.

Lucy pulled herself up off the couch and went into her sanctuary. She was always happy working in the kitchen—cooking, baking, or even cleaning. She decided to bake a pie. She'd enjoy kneading the dough and the aroma of baking apples and cinnamon would be heavenly. She knew the apples she'd picked last fall needed to be used up. Lucy set her bowls, measuring cups, utensils, rolling pin, waxed paper, and pie plate on the table then went downstairs to her fruit cellar.

Lucy loved growing things. She'd always planted a garden, even before the Depression. She grew a variety of vegetables in nice straight rows and harvested berries as they ripened throughout the summer months. She spent weeks canning and preserving. Year after year, her fruit cellar was stocked with heavy glass jars on rough wooden shelves. One shelf held all the berry jams as well as pie-fillings, mostly pumpkin. She stored preserved tomatoes and sauces on a separate shelf. Canned root vegetables and beans were arranged on the lowest plank, and on the uneven floor wooden bins held potatoes, onions, and apples. A braid of garlic hung on a nail to the side. Sometimes in the winter Lucy would go into the cellar, lift the metal latch on the rustic door, and pull the string dangling from the bulb in the low ceiling. In the shadowy light, she would stand in her fruit cellar admiring the neat and orderly display.

Now, she opened the heavy oak door. The musty smell of the dirt floor mingled with the sweet and sharp scents of fruits and vegetables. Lucy closed her eyes and breathed in the aromas. Her body relaxed. Her mind calmed.

She reached up to pull on the light, then bent over and examined the bin of apples. They were perfect. She slipped a wicker basket from a nearby hook and filled it with a dozen Red Delicious.

Lucy had just slid the pie from the oven and was picking up a mixing bowl, when there was a loud banging at the front of the house. Startled, she dropped the ceramic bowl, which hit the floor and broke in a dozen pieces.

Officer Ralph Hiller yelled through the screen door into the silence. "Mrs. Russo! Lucy, are you home?" He heard a crash at the rear of the house. "Mrs. Russo! Are you all right?"

Lucy hurried to the front door, wiping her hands on her apron. "Officer Hiller, what is it? Have you found out what happened to Frankie?"

"No, ma'am, not quite. This is Officer Ray Monroe. I think you know Pete McGrath." Pete and Ray respectfully doffed their hats. "We have a warrant to search your house."

Lucy paled. "What?" She stared at him. "Why would you do that?"

"It's a part of our investigation, Mrs. Russo."

"I don't understand."

"We believe Frankie was poisoned. May we come in, please?" Ralph said.

Lucy gasped. "Poisoned?" she whispered, then held open the flimsy door.

"Mrs. Russo, I know this is hard. We'll be as quick as we can. But we gotta do our job," said Ralph, noticing that she'd crossed her arms over her chest in a protective way and that her relaxed manner of moment ago had disappeared.

"I suppose there's nothing I can say." She frowned and pursed her lips.

Ralph turned to the other officers and said, "Pete, take the bedroom. Search Frankie's belongings. Check all his pockets, under the bed, in the back of dresser drawers, and inside any boxes. Like shoe boxes on a closet shelf."

93

"Gotcha." Pete climbed the stairs and disappeared from view.

"Ray, look for poisons, in pure form or mixed in with something else. You know the usual places." He turned to Lucy. "I noticed a shed in the back. Do you have a key?"

"Yes."

Ralph and Ray followed Lucy to the kitchen. They stepped over the chunks of broken crockery scattered on the floor. *Hmm. Was she getting ready to throw out the bowl that she made the poisoned food in? She hears banging on the door and doesn't know what to do with it so she throws it on the floor? She can never use it again so no loss. But, why was it still here? She should have gotten rid of it before now. What if she made a mistake and used it again?*

Lucy reached a hook in the tiny back hall. "Here you are, Officer," she said, handing a key to Ray Monröe. "Be sure you lock up when you're finished. There's rat poison in the shed." She held his gaze. "Everyone's got some. You know that."

"Yes, ma'am."

"What about you, Officer Hiller?" Lucy turned to Ralph. "What's left for you to search?"

"The kitchen, Mrs. Russo. We think Frankie ate something that was loaded with arsenic."

"I see."

"Now about these broken dishes, ma'am. Can you tell me what happened here?"

Chapter 15

Monday — Present Day

After searching the internet and coming up with nothing, Olivia picked up her phone and called Liz. Maybe the Knightsbridge History Museum would have records or phone books to get her started on the search for Alex.

Liz answered after two rings. "Hey, Olivia. What's up?"

"I've got a new research project and I need your help. Can I come over?"

"Sure, if you really want to venture out in this deluge. I just got back from a meeting. It felt like I walked through a car wash."

"That's okay. I need to get started."

"What's the project?"

"Actually it's a favor for Isabel. I'll tell you when I get there."

Olivia found Liz in her crowded office. She hung her rain-soaked jacket on a hook behind the door and gratefully accepted the steaming mug of tea. The scent of chamomile tickled her nose as she inhaled.

"Mmm. Thanks."

"What's going on with Isabel?" Liz asked.

When they were six years old, Olivia, Liz, and Sophie had found themselves in Isabel's first-grade class. There, Miss Covington introduced the three little girls and made them study partners. This simple action began a friendship that would last a lifetime. Like Olivia, Liz and Sophie loved their former teacher and considered her family.

"Have you noticed how she hasn't been her usual self lately?" Olivia asked.

"Yeah, she's been a bit down. I figured it was the broken arm. Isabel doesn't like limitations."

"I had her over for lunch today and she told me something."

"What?"

"Basically on her deathbed, Isabel's mother told her she was a twin."

"What? Are you kidding me?"

"Amazing, huh? Her mother was a widow. She couldn't afford to keep both babies so she gave up Isabel's twin brother for adoption."

"Holy cow!" Liz was stunned.

"It's been bothering her a long time. She wants me to find her twin. His name is Alex."

"I can't imagine how that must feel," Liz said.

"Isabel said she's sensed something was missing all these years. Now that she's getting older, she wants to find him before it's too late."

"I can understand that. She's getting up there. Who knows how much time she has left? Where are you going to start?" Liz asked.

Olivia explained the arrangements Isabel's mother had made and the plan she'd formulated. "So, if I can get the name of the doctor who delivered the babies, I'll have the last name of the priest, too. Then, I can locate the church where he arranged the adoption. After that, it shouldn't be too hard to find out the name of the family."

"What can I do? Are you looking for old hospital records?"

"No, Isabel and her twin were born upstairs in the pub."

"The pub?"

"I know, right? The owner—I actually met him last night, by the way...,"

"This is getting weird," Liz mumbled.

"Yeah, well, he was Isabel's mother's cousin. Her husband had died and she didn't have any family around. He let her move in upstairs and gave her a job cooking. So, basically it was a home birth. I'm hoping you have a phone directory from 1934. Even the year before or after would probably do it. That'd give me a starting point."

"Well," Liz said, hitting some keys on her laptop, "let's see what we've got." She leaned forward and ran her finger down the screen. "It looks like we've got about a dozen old phone books and…there's one from 1934. Boy, you lucked out."

"Yay." Olivia waved her hands in the air.

"It's in storage. Let's go get it."

Olivia and Liz stood next to the open file cabinet drawer flipping through a thin directory for Knightsbridge 1934 to 1935. They were astonished to find more than a dozen physicians.

"Who would've thought there'd be so many doctors back then? I suppose some had private practices and some probably worked at the hospital, right?" Liz said.

"I guess so." Olivia snapped a photo with her cell. "It looks like I'm going to have to depend on Steven after all. Darn. I thought I could do this on my own."

"Be glad you've got Steven. A private adoption, 80 years ago. Even with his help you might not be able to find this doctor."

Olivia returned home eager to get ready for tomorrow's adventure into the past. Steven was going to meet her at her bedroom door and bring her into 1934, where they'd have their first breakfast together. Then, he would go to work leaving Olivia alone for the day. They wanted to know if Olivia had to be with him or physically near him to make the time travel stick, so to speak. When Steven left, would she still be in his house or would she be transported back to her own time? Olivia briefly envisioned herself as a marionette, controlled by strings, jerked back and forth in time. Not a pretty picture.

Olivia had decided that when she was in Steven's time, she would live the way women lived in 1934. If she were going to write believable articles about how real women coped with the Depression years, she needed her experiences to be authentic. This meant wearing clothes from that time and getting ready in the morning the way they did—no blow dryer, no hair iron. She also needed to scrutinize every item she used in her daily life and decide whether it could go with her into the past or not.

Olivia had shared her concerns with Liz and Sophie. "The hardest thing will be not having my laptop. I'm leaving it here."

"You're kidding!" Sophie had sounded horrified. "What are you going to do? Write by hand? With paper and pencil?"

Liz was intrigued by the idea. "It's romantic. Makes me think of you writing away in an attic someplace with a kerosene lamp or by candlelight."

"Yeah, that's me, Jane Austen. Haha."

Olivia knew Steven got up early every morning so he could be at the station by seven. He liked the time alone at his desk to get his thoughts together, especially when he was working on a case. She wanted to get everything ready ahead of time so she wouldn't hold him up. Last night after they'd returned from dinner at the pub, she had gone into Evangeline's bedroom to select the outfit she'd wear for her first entire day in 1934. Upon returning to the present, she'd hung the two pieces on her closet door. Now, she double-checked everything. She grabbed a sharpened pencil and one of the notebooks with the black-and-white covers that Steven had purchased for her the other day. This one was dedicated to the Women-in-the-Depression project. The other was the journal, where she'd already begun to chronicle her trips into the past. She curled up on the love seat in her reading nook to transfer the remainder of the notes from her laptop into the project notebook.

As Olivia was finishing hand-copying the final note, her cell rang. It was Liz. She smiled to herself remembering a comment her mother had made when she was in 8th grade. "What in heaven's name can you two have to talk about now?" Mom had exclaimed. "You walked to school together this morning, you spent the entire day together, then you talked all the way home." She had shaken her head in bewilderment. Neither Olivia nor Liz thought this was strange. Best friends never ran out of things to say. She chuckled at the thought.

"Hey, Olivia, I want to wish you luck tomorrow. I'm still a little nervous about you spending the day there all alone."

"Thanks, but I'll be fine. What's the worst that can happen? All of a sudden I'm sitting in *my* kitchen instead of Steven's?"

"Yeah, I suppose so. At least you'll be in the house. That's safe. You can always run up to your bedroom door and come home."

"You know, we were so caught up in looking for the doctor's name I forgot to ask. Are you excited about renewing your vows this weekend?" Olivia asked.

"I will be. Right now, I've got all the arrangements on my mind. I'm glad we decided to limit the guests to a small group."

"And it helps that you've got a built-in pastry chef."

"Yes, it was really nice of Sophie to make all the pastries. To say nothing about using your backyard. I don't know how to thank you."

"What are friends for? It'll be fun."

They chatted until Olivia said, "Hey, I just noticed the time. Steven'll be home soon. I want to get dinner started."

"Text me tomorrow as soon as you get back, okay?"

Olivia added the notebook to the items she'd set aside for Tuesday morning. As she turned to leave, she saw her hallway transform into the 1934 garden-like hall that was Steven's. She watched him exit his bedroom. She liked the way he looked—a bit taller than average, good build, dark hair and eyes. He had changed the suit he'd worn to work for a comfortable pair of pants and shirt, and was wearing his slippers. He stopped abruptly, gazing at the floor but apparently not seeing. After several seconds, he turned and headed toward her bedroom doorway.

"Hey, are you okay?" she asked.

He looked up.

Steven watched as the sleek, modern double bed and dresser with round mirror in his mother's room were replaced by Olivia's queen-sized sleigh bed. White walls turned pale blue and satiny blue drapes became billowing white curtains. It hadn't escaped either of them how similar the two versions of this bedroom were. Evangeline had arranged a small sitting area—a chair with a tufted back resembling a clam shell, upholstered in midnight blue; a caramel-colored, leather, and brass-studded Moroccan pouf used as a footstool; and a floor lamp. In Olivia's room, a small couch fronted the bow window where wall sconces were attached to the frame and a long coffee table piled with books and magazines sometimes doubled as a footstool.

"Oh, Olivia." He had an odd look on his face.

"Steven, what's wrong? Did something happen at work?" Olivia guessed that was where the answer lay. It probably meant someone was dead.

"Helen's brother-in-law was murdered yesterday."

"Oh, my goodness! How is she? How is her sister taking it? Do you have any clues? Do you have a suspect?"

His face relaxed and he chuckled. That was Olivia, always asking lots of questions, still acting like the reporter she once was.

"Jimmy and I broke the news to Lucy this morning."

"I can't imagine how awful that must have been for her."

"She's...," he paused, "... *dazed* I guess is the best way to put it."

"She probably hasn't taken it in yet."

He nodded. "It takes time when someone dies violently."

"Are Lucy and Helen close? Hopefully she'll be able to help her."

"Yeah, they are. Helen's a brick. She'll get her sister through it." He gave Olivia a smile that lit up his face. "So, what's for supper? I'm starved."

Olivia's stomach did a little somersault every time those velvety brown eyes held her gaze. She grinned. "I was just about to go down to the kitchen and start things. Good timing." She reached out into the middle of the doorway and took his hand. It felt warm and his grip was strong. She took a step back, guiding Steven over the threshold into her time.

They stood in her bedroom for a moment then turned around. Still holding his hand, Olivia led him through the doorway into the 21st century. They walked down *her* hall and descended the stairs.

Olivia stood at the kitchen sink washing lettuce while the chicken sizzled on the grill outside. Steven relaxed as he leaned against the counter, a glass of wine in hand. He had asked if he could help and her answer had been to hand him the bottle of Chardonnay, the corkscrew, and two glasses.

"Steven, does this murder affect my visit tomorrow? Maybe I shouldn't come. I don't want to get in the way. Besides, you'll probably be working late, right?"

"I never know how late I'll be." He took a sip of his wine. "But, you should come. We still want to find out if you can stay in my time without me. That hasn't changed. And it would look strange if all of a sudden you were gone, especially after hitting it off with Helen last night. She thinks you're staying at the boarding house in Rome, right?"

"Yes, but I told her I'd be spending the day here while you're at work. Maybe I could call her in the morning to offer my condolences. Do they have a phone?"

"I think she'd like that. It'll help take her mind off things." He snuck a piece of celery and crunched. "I'll write down the number for you later."

"Steven, you know I watch a lot of police shows on TV, right?"

Steven had been stunned when he first came into Olivia's time and discovered TV. Used to listening on the radio, he'd been thrilled to be able to *watch* the Yankee games. "Yes…?"

"They say the spouse is always the main suspect." Olivia hesitated. "Do you think Lucy killed her husband?"

Chapter 16

Tuesday — April 24, 1934

Olivia jumped out of bed the next morning more excited than she'd been in ages. She was spending the day in 1934! Even though two months had passed since she'd begun visiting Steven's Depression-era world, she'd never spent more than a few hours there at one time. She couldn't wait to read the paper and listen to the radio. Maybe she'd be able to visit with Helen, too. That'd be cool.

Olivia was careful to do only what she imagined 1934 women would do to get ready in the morning: brush her teeth and wash her face at the sink, and fluff up her now wavy hair (She'd washed and styled it late last night). She cut off the tags on a new camisole she'd found in one of Evangeline's dresser drawers and slipped it over her head. The silky fabric flowed over her skin. Suddenly, she had never felt sexier. *Ooh!* Maybe there was something to living like 1934. She slipped on a pair of wide-leg, cuffed trousers and buttoned a fitted, V-neck top. *Katharine Hepburn, eat your heart out.* She added a thin gold chain with a medallion and a gold bracelet. She surveyed herself in the mirror and was happy. She looked appropriate and would be comfortable hanging around the house all day. She would have liked to put on some make-up but thought most women wouldn't, so she pinched her cheeks and contented herself with a neutral lipstick.

She took a second selfie to document her adventure and, this time, sent it to Liz and Sophie. She attached it to a text and wrote *Here I go!*

Steven approached her bedroom door as the carriage clock in Olivia's living room struck six.

"You look swell." He gave her a big smile. "Like a real thirties girl."

Olivia laughed. "Thanks. I have to tell you, Steven, I love your mother's clothes. Are you sure it doesn't bother you seeing me in them? If you change your mind, I hope you'll tell me."

"Of course, I will. But like I said before, they don't look at all the same on you. Ready?"

Olivia grabbed a cream-colored leather bag of Evangeline's that she'd filled with her supplies for the day. She had the idea that it was a precursor of modern-day tote bags. It was roomy and serviceable but too boxy and awkward for her taste. She moved to the doorway and held out her hand.

Steven wrapped his hand around hers and stepped back into the hallway, bringing her into the past.

"I hope you're hungry," he said. "I've got breakfast all set out on the table."

The aroma of percolating coffee hit her when they entered the kitchen. Steven removed the pot from the burner and poured their coffee. He waved Olivia to a chair. "Help yourself," he said, indicating the box of cereal, milk, sugar, bowls, and spoons.

"Mmm. You make a good pot of coffee, Steven Blackwell." She grinned at him across the table as she sipped the rich dark brew.

Steven poured whole milk and added a generous spoonful of sugar on his daily bowl of Wheaties. "Are you sure you don't want more sugar?"

"No, thanks. I don't eat much sugar. This is good." She accented her statement with a crunch. "So, what are you doing for your investigation today?"

"I'll update my team at the morning briefing and send everybody out with an assignment. Then, I need to interview Frankie's cousin's wife Adona." He explained the notation in Frankie's little book and the altercation in the lunch room. "I also have to talk with his sister Connie. I have a lot of questions for her." He took a drink of his coffee. "The rest of the day will depend on what I find out from my men and those interviews."

"I wish you luck. I hope you get close to solving it."

"Thanks. What about you? I hope you won't be bored here by yourself."

Olivia explained that she'd be working on her Women-in-the-Depression project. "After I read the paper, of course."

He grinned at her. "Of course." *You can take the reporter out of the newsroom, but...*

At six thirty, Steven left Olivia in his kitchen with a second cup of coffee and her notebook. He fervently hoped she'd still be there when he returned home.

Knightsbridge was peaceful early in the morning. He rolled down the car windows and listened to the concert orchestrated by dozens of invisible birds in the treetops along the way. He passed the paperboy zipping along on his bike and heard the rhythmic *thud* as each tightly bound edition landed on someone's porch.

The drive to the station took no time. Steven left his motor car in the postage-stamp sized lot and walked around to the front of the building. As he climbed the steps, a breeze blew a string of wispy clouds aside, revealing a horizon washed in gold.

The station appeared empty when Steven let himself in. He was surprised Tommy Forester hadn't arrived yet. That kid was so full of enthusiasm for his job they never saw the front desk unmanned. As he walked down the hall to the room where he and his partner had their desks, Steven smelled coffee. Ah, that explained it. Tommy liked using the new electric percolator the chief had bought for the department. He'd gotten into the habit of making a pot as soon as he arrived. Steven still preferred the coffee he made at home but occasionally drank the station brew.

As he entered his office, Steven hit the wall switch flooding the CID room with light. *Criminal Investigation Division* was a grand-sounding name for such a small police force but it was the center of every investigation. The men working the case came and went freely. They stood at the murder board checking developments and discussing their progress. More than once, someone had noticed a new connection or interpreted a clue in a different way that led to solving the case.

Steven stowed his lunch and settled at his desk to prepare for one of his favorite parts of the day—the morning briefing. This daily meeting was a chance for him to update his team and for the men to share what they knew about the people involved in the case. All the officers who worked with Detective Sergeant Blackwell understood that they could offer up any bit of gossip or rumor they'd heard going around town without fear of ridicule or disdain. The team would openly discuss the item and someone would be assigned to find out if there was any truth to the matter.

Since Knightsbridge was a small town, at least one police officer usually knew, or was related, to someone involved in a case. Although personal connections often made the job more difficult, they also provided valuable insight and information. The Frankie Russo case was new, still full of the promise of discovery. Steven was excited to talk with his team today.

He pulled a pad of lined paper toward him and grabbed a pencil. He went over everything they had done since the body'd been discovered yesterday morning. He organized his thoughts and planned his strategy for the day. He got up and studied the murder board. Who had hated Frankie Russo so much that they had cut his young life short? What had the victim done to trigger such an irrevocable action? Once you took a life, it could not be undone. In Steven's experience, the very act of killing took a piece of the killer's life as well. His—or her—existence would never be the same.

At seven, the station came to life. Down in the CID room, Steven continued to focus on his notes, but the sounds of his colleagues arriving and settling in for the day registered in the back of his mind.

"Hey, Ralphie. I got a new one for ya."

Steven's subconscious identified Pete McGrath, the station comedian.

Lumbering footsteps in the hall, accompanied by a rumbling cough deep in his chest.

That was Chief Andy Thompson.

"Did you fellas see today's paper?" asked Jimmy Bou, his voice louder than usual and filled with excitement. "The Feds put more men on."

"They're bringing them in from all over! Philadelphia and Washington, D.C.," exclaimed Ray.

"Baby Face Nelson was with him last weekend. The dirty bum killed an FBI agent up at that lodge in Wisconsin. Boy, I'd like to get my hands on those two," muttered Ralph.

"The Feds issued the shoot-to-kill order," said Pete.

"I hope they get him before somebody else gets hurt," added Jimmy.

The manhunt for John Dillinger had grabbed everyone's interest and occupied conversations for days now. You couldn't go anywhere—Bailey's Diner, Pinky's Bar and Grill, The Three Lords, even the YMCA and the gas station—without hearing people talking about Public Enemy Number One. Everyone had an opinion. Some said they'd bring him in alive. Others were positive the killer himself would be shot down in cold blood—a lesson that crime didn't pay. Still others were sure the gangster would get away and never be found. Steven idly wondered if the Feds would get him this time.

Will entered the detectives' room and sat down to read today's *Gazette,* memorizing a variety of items for future reference. Steven couldn't imagine what it must be like to have a memory like that. Didn't your head get to a point where it felt impossibly stuffed? The innate talent was probably as much of a curse as a blessing. Maybe more so.

Jimmy Bou stuck his head in. "What time do you want to start, Steven?"

"Five minutes."

Steven entered the crowded patrol room. All the chairs were occupied and a few officers leaned against the wall. Most of the men held a small notebook and pen or pencil. The room smelled of coffee and yesterday's sweat. Though someone had opened the windows, the air was thick with cigarette smoke. It clung to the ceiling and walls. As Steven walked to the front, he noticed some sneezing going on, par for the course in the spring when everything was budding. The chief entered the room. One of the younger patrolmen jumped up and ceded his chair.

"Good morning, men. As you've probably heard by now, we found Frankie Russo's body yesterday morning in the ravine behind the high school. Based on an examination of the slope that goes up to the field, we think he rolled down the hill. Maybe he fell or was pushed. The body showed the classic signs of poisoning. Doc called and confirmed it was arsenic. According to his findings, Frankie ingested the poison sometime between seven Sunday morning and two in the afternoon. Seven is unlikely because Doc found beer in his stomach, but that's our window, fellas."

Most of Steven's team leaned forward listening, many jotted down notes. The beginning of a murder case created a buzz around the station, sending everyone's adrenalin racing.

Steven continued. "We don't know for sure if Frankie was killed where he was found but we suspect so." He told them about the vomit, the birds, and the flattened grass then explained their preliminary conclusions. "We think he might have been poisoned during a picnic."

"That's harsh," commented one of the patrolmen who was hearing this for the first time.

"It is. And it brings us to the usual question. Who hated Frankie Russo or was angry enough to murder him?" Steven turned to Will and said, "Tell them about the notebook."

This sounded intriguing. Everyone sharpened his attention.

Will described the log and their interpretation of it. "There are four initials I want to identify right away: H and L, the two that appear over the years; the one that was written differently, that's A; and the new one, S. The others are important but they can wait.

"We think H refers to Hannah Grantham. I seem to remember Frankie and Hannah stepping out when we were in school. Can anybody confirm that?" Will looked around the room. He saw Jimmy Bou scrunch up his face and cock his head to the side as if trying to recall something. The light bulb must have gone on because Jimmy Bou shouted out, "Yeah! You're right. Hannah and Frankie were high school sweethearts. I saw them next door at her friend's house all the time."

"Swell. That's one letter down. The initial H appears on almost every page but we can't assume it always refers to Hannah. Can anybody think of another girl whose name starts with H that Frankie was seen with in the past few years?" Will waited but no one spoke. A couple fellas shook their heads. "No? Well, if you think of someone, be sure to tell me or Steven." Will asked about the other three initials. The men agreed L was probably Lucy. No one could think of an S. They all thought that, although Frankie had been a womanizer, it was unlikely he'd been stupid enough to think he could get away with fooling around with his cousin's wife. The letter A remained a mystery.

"I'll post a list of the initials for the past five years, going back to '29. I'll write a question mark next to the names we think we know. I'll keep it updated and erase the question mark when we confirm each identity. Be sure that you look at the board at least once or twice a day. Let us know if you have any information on these girls."

Lastly, Will talked about the change in the list. "In 1931, the letter S appeared for the first time and all the other initials except L, H, and A disappeared for good. Steven and I think something happened that changed Frankie's behavior. We need to find out what it was."

"Remember," Steven added, "that was the year Frankie began his second part-time job in Syracuse. We need to find out if something happened in Syracuse."

Everyone made a note of this point. Will stood aside for Steven to continue.

Steven told his team the results of the grid search then he turned the briefing over to Jimmy Bou. "I asked Jimmy to put together Frankie and Lucy Russo's backgrounds. Jimmy, what have you got?"

The tall, lanky patrolman stood and opened a notebook filled with detailed information. "Well, we already talked about some of the stuff I have on Lucy. Other than that, she graduated from the Oswego Normal School in 1929. That's for teachers," he added. "She's been teaching here at the high school ever since.

"Frankie was born Francis Russo in August nineteen-oh-six. One sister, Connie. She's married to Lucio Morelli. They run a dairy farm out on Route 5. Three kids. Both parents are deceased. There are a bunch of cousins all over the place."

"I remember a lot of Russo kids when we were in school," said Will.

"Yeah, I do, too," said Pete.

Charlie spoke up for the first time. "My girlfriend Ava's family lives next door to some Russos."

"You sly dog, you," oozed Ralph, wiggling his thick eyebrows. "A girlfriend."

"Yeah, you've been holding out on us," crooned Pete.

"Stop," interrupted Steven with a faint smile, "You can grill the new man later. Where do they live, Charlie? And what's Ava's last name?"

"Baker. She lives with her parents and brothers on Warwick."

"Do you know the first names of these Russos that you mentioned?"

"The ones we just talked about, Frankie's cousin Nick and his wife Adona."

Jimmy Bou glanced at his notes and continued. "Frankie had a funny job arrangement. He worked here at the knitting mill for a week then went to Syracuse and worked at a brewery for a week."

"So, two half-time jobs," said Ralph.

"Maybe the motive is at one of his jobs. Look at all the men out of work. And here's a fella that's got two. Maybe somebody resented that," suggested Ray.

"We're not discounting anything right now. I'll have one of you fellas look into that," said Steven. "But, for the time being, we're leaning toward a female killer. The flattened area in the field suggests a picnic or maybe Frankie making time with a girlfriend on a blanket. Both ideas point to a woman." Steven looked at Jimmy Bou. "That it, Jimmy?"

His protégé nodded.

"All right. Before I give out assignments for the day, we want to hear from Ralph. He took a team to Frankie and Lucy's house yesterday afternoon." Steven turned to the patrolman. "I saw your report on my desk this morning. Tell the fellas what you found."

"Maybe we got something, maybe we don't," Ralph began.

Several officers groaned.

"Get on with it, Hiller. We've got things to do," someone shouted.

"Yeah, places to go, people to meet," chortled his pal Pete.

"Okay, okay," Ralph went on. "Pete searched through Frankie's stuff and didn't find anything. I guess that little book Will's got has all our clues. Ray looked for poison. Like everybody else in town, there was a can of rat poison in the backyard shed. The thing is," Ralph paused for effect, "it was half gone. We figured it was worth bringing it in. The can looks new and we haven't had a plague or anything." A couple of people chuckled. "So anyway, it's Berger's Pure Paris Green pesticide. Comes in a one-pound can with a lid that's so tight you need a screwdriver to get it open. It's *loaded* with arsenic."

"We'll get a sample to the lab," said Steven. "I don't know if they can tell if it's from the same can as the poison that killed Frankie but we've got to check. Now, the kitchen, Ralph. Tell them about the dishes."

A few men elbowed each other and raised brows. This sounded like it might be good.

"Steven figures whoever made the poisoned food had to destroy the dishes. They couldn't take a chance that all the poison was washed out. When I went into the kitchen, there were broken dishes on the floor. We've got the pieces. Looks like it was a bowl. We took it to the lab. I wondered if Lucy was going to throw it out but we got there before she had the chance. I asked her. She said she dropped it but I don't know if I believe her. She was acting kind of funny. Steven, I know you're friends with Artie," Ralph added. "I think you should ask Helen about Lucy. When she came to the door and saw us, she acted friendly. She probably thought we had new information about

Frankie. But, when I told her we were going to search her house, she turned cold. She did *not* want us looking around her house. I don't know if it means anything. But, I think you oughta talk with her sister."

"I will, Ralph, thanks. I'm planning on it." Steven looked down at his notes. "One more quick item, fellas, then you're on your way. Will and I talked with the people who work in Frankie's office at the mill. General consensus confirms what we already know—he was always on the lookout for a new girlfriend. That is until the fall of 1931. Frankie's boss said he noticed a change about that time, too. He stopped bothering the women in the office and just did his job. I spoke with all four secretaries. Every one insisted she had nothing to do with him. We'll check, of course, but it sounded like the truth. His pal Carl Eastwood swears Frankie was a stand-up guy, as he put it, but I didn't believe a word."

"Steven, if Frankie was chasing that many girls, there must be a lot of husbands and boyfriends who had it in for him," said Ray.

"And fathers and brothers," said Charlie.

"Yeah, but poison is a woman's weapon," Jimmy Bou piped up. "And remember the picnic."

"It looks like we have plenty of potential suspects. We've got our work cut out for us," said Steven. He ended the meeting with the day's assignments. "I want Ralph and Pete to concentrate on Frankie's movements. Pick up where the team left off yesterday. We have to know where Frankie went when he left his house Sunday morning. Get over to the bus depot, too. See if Frankie's suitcase is there."

"You got it," they chorused.

"Ray, I'd like you to work on the Old Crow bottle. Find out who drinks the stuff and especially who buys it. You know the drill."

"I'm on it."

"Charlie and Jerry, I want you to question all the Russo cousins. Call

Connie Morelli and get names and addresses. Find out everybody's whereabouts from seven Sunday morning until about five o'clock. I know Doc said probably no later than two, but I'd like you to cover the whole afternoon.

"The rest of you, get back out there on the streets. Try to find out if anybody saw a woman coming down that hill with a blanket or a picnic basket early Sunday afternoon."

Chief Thompson caught Steven and Will on their way out. "Did you see *The Gazette* this morning? It made us look bad." He scowled. "We've gotta do better today, fellas. I'm counting on you."

Chapter 17

O livia left the kitchen and stepped out onto the front porch. As she watched Steven drive up the street, she gripped the railing and willed herself not to disappear back to the future. *I'm still here. I'm staying here. I'm not going back home. Yet.* Nothing happened. She smiled to herself. Steven was gone. She was still here. *Yay!*

It was a beautiful morning. She took a deep breath. The air was clean and fresh, like being deep in the woods or at the ocean. It made her sad when she realized the damage that had been done to the earth in a handful of decades. She gazed around. A young boy rode by on a bicycle, moving with a distinctive rhythm as he pedaled. As he approached each house, he reached behind him into a canvas bag and threw rolled-up newspapers on lawns and porches. One of them thudded onto their front steps. The milk truck slowly made its way down the block. *Wait. Milk truck?* Olivia watched the white-uniformed man climb down from the open-sided truck, grab glass bottles from a crate in the open back, and hand-deliver them to the front door of house after house. *This is nice. Surreal, but nice.*

After waving to the milkman and picking up Steven's copy of *The Gazette*, Olivia went back inside. She opened the kitchen window and back door to let in the soft breeze then settled comfortably at the kitchen table with the newspaper. As a former reporter, Olivia was addicted to the news. She read *The Gazette* and *The New York Times* every day, in addition to checking several online news sites.

Savoring the moment, she unfurled the large black-and-white sheets and opened to the front page. The headlines proclaimed *Hunt for Dillinger Gang Continues in Several States, Many Clues Found.* A shiver ran through her. *Dillinger. As in John Dillinger, Public Enemy Number One. Oh, my God, this is so cool.* She read every word, tracking the end of the article to page eight. Federal agents were hot on the trail of the mobster. She turned back to the front page and, after devouring two more pieces on Dillinger from different angles, she read what the League of Nations was doing in response to an action Japan had taken, an article on the price of milk, and finally, what she had been looking forward to most—the article on Steven's case.

STILL NO ANSWERS IN RUSSO MURDER

It's been twenty-four hours since two boys discovered Frankie Russo's body lying in the gully behind the Knightsbridge High School and notified the police. When asked what progress the police have made, Chief Andy Thompson said, "Veteran officer Detective Sergeant Steven Blackwell is heading up the investigation. Blackwell has a stellar record. I promise you he will get results. We have every available man working with Detective Blackwell on the Russo case."

When asked for specifics, Thompson reported, "Evidence shows that Mr. Russo was poisoned some time on Sunday. We are conducting interviews and gathering information at this time. For the moment, that is all I can say. The public will be informed when we have more information."

Chief Thompson praised the two boys who found the murdered Russo and immediately reported their discovery. "Kevin MacIntyre and Joey Renard are to be commended for their clear thinking and brave actions. I'm proud to call them Knightsbridge folk."

Olivia chuckled at the hometown spin. The chief had answered the reporter's questions giving no answers at all. She recognized the stonewalling technique and admired his ability to keep sensitive information private. Praising the boys was a good PR move.

Olivia poured another cup of coffee and savored reading every word of every article, front to back. At last, she set it aside, saving the crossword puzzle for later, and took out her notebooks and sharpened pencils. She soon got lost in her plans.

When Olivia had first thought of the project on Depression-era women, it had been nothing more than an excuse to justify the time she'd be spending at Steven's. Then one day, while she was working on her initial outline, she realized she'd become genuinely interested in the research. She'd decided to take it seriously and sell it as a series of magazine articles.

Late last night before leaving the internet for twenty-four hours (*OMG!*), Olivia had expanded the list of the women she planned to research. It included Amelia Earhart, the most famous female aviator in the world at the time, and first lady Eleanor Roosevelt. She decided to keep Margaret "Molly" Brown on the list although the renowned *Titanic* survivor had died in 1932. Brown had been an early feminist who ran for the Senate years before women had the vote. Olivia also considered including the author Pearl Buck, artist Georgia O'Keefe, actress Katharine Hepburn, and photographer Margaret Bourke-White. Those women were easy to research. The challenge would be the ordinary women she hoped to meet this week.

Steven had told Olivia she could telephone Helen early, since Artie started work at seven. Time to make a connection. Olivia rose from her chair and went into the hallway. On a small table near the front door attached to the wall with a thick black cord sat a chunky black telephone with *a dial*. Steven had left a scrap of paper with KB56 written on it. *Is that a phone number?* She picked up the receiver—it felt awkward and heavy. She stuck her finger in a hole and dialed the first letter. She waited. The disk slowly returned to its original position. *Good grief. This could take all day. What if it was an emergency? What* do *they do in an emergency?* Finally, Olivia managed to dial all four numbers and heard ringing on the other end.

"Hello. KB56. This is Helen Sinclair."

"Good morning, Helen. It's Steven's friend Olivia. We met the other night in the pub."

"Of course. I remember, Olivia. How are you?"

"I'm fine, thanks. I wanted to express my condolences. Steven told me about your brother-in-law. I'm sorry for your loss."

"That's really nice of you, Olivia. Thank you."

"How are you holding up, Helen? Are you okay?"

Helen sighed. "Yes. No. I don't know."

"Listen, I don't mean to bother you," Olivia quickly added. "I just wanted to let you know I'm here if there's anything I can do to help."

"Thank you," Helen said again, then paused. "Actually, Olivia, I'm glad you called. I need to take my mind off this for a while."

"Would you like to come over for a cup of coffee or tea, Helen? I'm at Steven's."

"I don't know. Maybe I should stay home in case my sister calls. Why don't you come here?"

And there it was. In less than two minutes, Olivia had to decide. Should she take the sensible route and stay in the house like she and Steven planned and, more importantly, agreed on? Or should she take a chance and go?

Chapter 18

By nine o'clock, Steven was speeding along Brighton Road in his shiny green Chevy, on his way to the Knightsbridge Knitting Mill with Jimmy Bou riding shotgun. Jimmy sat straight as a poker, clearly thrilled to a part of the investigation and eager for the next step.

"Is there anything special you want me to do, Steven? Do we have an angle on this interview?"

"I want to find out if Adona is the 'A' in Frankie's notebook. We'll play it by ear, Jimmy. You never know what else we might discover. Stay sharp. Take notes. And watch her carefully."

Steven pulled up to what he now knew was the factory entrance and they entered the cavernous room. The plant foreman stood at his station, alert as before. Steven showed his badge and ID in case the man had forgotten and told him he needed to speak with Adona Russo.

"She's not here," the foreman shouted over the noise. "Called in sick this morning."

"Right. Thank you," Steven yelled back, nodding. He turned and exited the deafening factory with Jimmy Bou on his heels.

"Warwick Avenue. On the corner of Second Street," volunteered Jimmy, palming his notebook and sliding it back in his pocket. At Steven's look, he added, "I asked Charlie what Ava's address was. I wrote it down."

Steven grinned appreciatively. That Jimmy Bou was a go-getter.

It took no more than five minutes to arrive back in town and even less to find the Russo house.

It was a two-story, shingled home built in the early years of the century. The wide front steps were partially covered with a makeshift wooden ramp.

"I forgot he was in a wheelchair," observed Jimmy. "I think he was in the war."

"If he's here," Steven whispered, "we'll split them up."

He knocked on the flimsy screen door.

"ADONA!" a voice bellowed from a few feet away. "Somebody at the door."

The woman who hurried to the door was a knock-out. She had curves in all the right places, jet black hair pulled back in a loose chignon at the nape of her neck, and emerald green eyes that Steven thought would sparkle on another, better day. She wore a simple housedress and was wiping her hands on a kitchen towel.

"Hello. Can I help you?" The color drained from her face at the sight of Jimmy Bou's uniform.

"Detective Sergeant Steven Blackwell and Officer James Bourgogne." Steven produced his badge and ID.

"Let'em in," a gruff voice snapped.

They entered a crowded living room. Steven's first thought was to wonder how Nick Russo managed to manoeuver his wheelchair in such a cramped space.

"This is my husband, Nick," Adona said quietly.

"They know that, woman. Go get us a drink."

"We need to speak with you, Mr. Russo, about your cousin Frankie."

"Hell of a thing," Nick said with obvious regret. "He was too young."

"Officer Bourgogne, why don't you see if you can help Mrs. Russo?

I'll get started here."

"Yes, sir," said Jimmy Bou, and trotted off to the kitchen to question Adona.

Nick Russo swung his chair around and rolled to a tufted plum sofa.

"Have a seat, Detective." He leaned forward and pulled a white ceramic ashtray—*Souvenir da Napoli*—toward him. He took a partly smoked cigar from the dish, lit a match, and puffed until he got it going again. "So, what do you want to know?"

The change in the man was startling. Less than two minutes ago, he was rudely yelling at his wife, now he was calm and polite. Steven wondered how ill this man was—and what he suffered from.

"I need to know about Frankie. It helps us find the killer if we know what the victim was like."

"It's true then. He was murdered?"

"Yes, I'm sorry for your loss."

Nick Russo shook his head, frowning. "What can I tell you?" he said, more to himself than to Steven. "Frankie was younger than me. Ten, twelve years. He was a normal kid. Played ball. Got into scuffles with kids who called him names. You know, in those days, some of the boys thought it was funny to insult our parents. They were new here. Their English wasn't too good."

Steven nodded. He knew that a wave of Italian immigrants had arrived in the Northeast in the late 1890s.

Like thousands of others, the Russo family had sailed past the Statue of Liberty full of hope and faith in God. The three brothers passed through the port of New York with their wives then settled in the upstate area. The young men found work and were proud not be *ritornati*, those who returned to the old country. They were even more proud to be able to send money back to their parents.

Nick sat lost in the past for a minute. Steven let him be, then prompted, "So, Mr. Russo, what about Frankie as a man? Were you close?"

"Of course, we were close! We're family," he said, as though this was the most obvious thing in the world. "When I came back from the war, lookin' like this," he indicated the useless legs and two long scars on his face—one across his right eyebrow that looked like the man had been lucky not to lose his eye and the other a wide slash on his right cheek, "Frankie was here for me. Him and Vito—that's my brother—they built the ramp out front and fixed up some things in the house. To make it easier to get around, you see? They put raised beds out back so I can keep my garden. I got roses," he said proudly. "And I still work my grapevines."

"My goodness." Steven was impressed by the man's effort. "Now, there's a question I have to ask."

A surly expression appeared on Russo's damaged face and he muttered, "Women. You're gonna ask me about his women."

"Yes."

"What a man does behind closed doors is nobody else's business, Detective. Sometimes a man needs a bit more, if you catch my meaning. Frankie went to work every day, brought money home. He was good to his wife. Never hit her. I got nothin' more to say about that." He stuck the cigar in the side of his mouth and jammed his powerful hands on the wheels of his chair. Then he swiveled around and propelled himself toward the front door.

Steven had learned long ago that when people clammed up there was no point in trying to browbeat them into giving up more information. Much better to let it go and talk to them another time. He followed Nick into the hall.

However, Russo did have one more thing to *say about that*. He spun the chair around and spat, "Detective, when you end up like me, you learn what's important in life and what isn't. You learn who your friends are, who you can count on. Frankie was *always* here for me, so I'll tell you somethin' for nothin'. I didn't give a damn about his women."

His cigar had gone out. He set it on a small entry table and yelled, "Dona, you can forget about those drinks. The police are leavin'."

Nick Russo was back to shouting.

When Steven had begun his interview with Nick, Jimmy Bou trailed Adona Russo into the kitchen at the rear of the house. Although she was older, he thought she was a real looker. Her backside swayed slowly left and right in a sultry rhythmic manner as he followed her down the long hallway. *Phew! This is some dame!*

Politely, he asked, "Mrs. Russo, can I help you?"

She jumped at the sound of his voice. "Oh! I didn't know you were behind me." She crossed the room, stood on her toes to reach into a top cupboard, and took out two tall glasses. "You can get the lemonade. It's in the icebox."

"Sure thing." He handed her the pitcher. "My condolences, ma'am, on the loss of your cousin."

Her arm jerked up. Lemonade splashed over the tabletop. She grabbed a towel.

"Thank you." She swallowed hard.

"Were you close to Frankie, Mrs. Russo?"

She stopped and gaped at him wide-eyed, like a deer in the headlights. "Why do you ask that?"

"Nothing, ma'am. I'm just making conversation. I'm sorry if I upset you." He arranged his face into an innocent expression.

Adona sat down heavily. She rested her elbow on the table and cradled her face in the palm of her hand. Jimmy wondered if she was crying. He wished she would start talking. This little routine of his usually worked but he wasn't at all sure it was going to succeed this time.

"I'm sorry, Officer…what did you say your name was?"

He told her.

"I'm sorry, Officer Bourgogne. I know you're only trying to be nice."

Ignoring the fact that the drinks were intended for Steven and her husband, Jimmy handed her a glass of lemonade, took one for himself, and sat companionably next to her. "What was he like, Frankie?

"He was my husband's cousin."

"I know that. I meant his personality. It helps if we feel like we knew the victim."

She winced.

"You want us to find whoever killed him, I'm sure." Jimmy smacked his lips. "Mmmm! This is delicious." He smiled gently at her.

"He helped my husband after the war."

"That was nice. I'm sorry to see your husband got hurt."

"*Grazie*. It has been very hard for him. For us. But I work. He has his garden. Frankie did that for Nick. Whatever else he did, at least he did that."

"It sounds like Frankie had a good side…," Jimmy watched her as he let a full four seconds pass before finishing his sentence, "… and a not-so-good side."

He tried to read her reaction, but she rose and turned her back on him, pretending to be busy at the sink.

"I'm sorry to have to ask you this, Mrs. Russo, but can you tell me where you were on Sunday?"

"What?" She spun around and stared, her hands dripping water on the cracked linoleum.

"We have to ask everyone. I'm sure you realize that. Say early Sunday morning until later in the afternoon," Jimmy prompted as he stood and insinuated himself in the narrow space next to her.

"How could you think I would have anything to do with this? I'm a

Catholic!"

"Unfortunately that doesn't seem to stop anybody," he said wryly. Then his voice lost its amiable quality. "Where were you the day Frankie was killed, Mrs. Russo?"

Her eyes grew as hard as gemstones but without the sparkle. "Where do you think I would be on a Sunday? *In la chiesa*. We attend Mass every Sunday morning." Her chest heaved in indignation. "At one o'clock, we had our dinner like always. Then, Nico spent time in his garden and I cleaned the house. I work at the mill during the week. I work here on the weekends."

She faced him, hands on her hips and back ramrod straight. "I will tell you something. I do not care about Frankie," she said, green eyes flashing. "The only thing I care is how this upsets Nico. He feels real bad. He has been through too much. I don't want him hurt no more." She held Jimmy's gaze and continued unflinchingly. "I do anything for my husband. Anything."

Adona felt proud for having spoken up. She never spoke up for herself and it felt good. Just one mistake. One horrible mistake should not be allowed to change her whole life. And Nico *was* her life. Standing up to the policeman made her feel powerful. For the first time since that horrible day, she felt strong and optimistic about the future. Standing here in her kitchen, in the warmth of the home she and Nico had built with love, Adona knew nothing mattered more than protecting the life they shared.

There was a shout from the front parlor.

Adona stretched out her hand and pointed to the door. "I think you're leaving now."

Steven had one foot in his motor car when he said, "Hang on, Jimmy. I'll be right back." He hurried to the porch, flew up the steps, and quietly slid to the side of the screen door where, unseen, he peered in.

Adona Russo was curled up on her husband's lap in the wheelchair. His face was buried in her breasts, her arms wrapped around him. She gently stroked him and murmured softly, *"Sta bene, vita mia.* It's all right, my love."

Nick Russo's shoulders shook as he repeated over and over, *"Adona mia. Cara."*

Chapter 19

"So what do you think, Olivia?" Helen's voice echoed over the phone line. "Would you like to come over? I'll put the kettle on."

Olivia had always been a lone wolf, answering to no one. She did what she wanted, when and how she wanted. Right now, she ached to walk out the front door and explore 1934. But, she and Steven had discussed this. They had agreed. She had promised to stay in the house until they had more information. She could not go back on that promise. Helen was waiting for an answer.

"Where does Lucy live, Helen?" Olivia asked. "Is Steven's house on the way?"

"Sort of. She's over on the Mohawk River Road. Why?"

"How about you come here and visit? You could walk over to see your sister after."

"Oh, that's a good idea. I wasn't thinking. You're not familiar with Knightsbridge. You wouldn't know how to get to my house. Give me a few minutes to make myself presentable."

Olivia and Helen sat at Steven's kitchen table, cups of tea in front of them. Helen was chattering away in a state of nervous energy.

"I can't think of what to do this morning. I want to call Lucy but I'm afraid to wake her. I don't know if she slept last night. What if she was awake all night and only fell asleep a couple of hours ago? She'd be mad plus she needs her sleep now."

"When you leave here, you'll be able to see if she's up. If the blinds are down or the curtains are drawn, you'll know."

"Oh, that's right. Olivia, I just can't think." Helen's face was pinched.

"Are you and Lucy close?" Olivia asked.

Helen sighed. "I don't know. We love each other, of course. She's my baby sister. I always seem to want to protect her. But, to tell you the truth, I don't understand how she thinks."

"What do you mean?" said Olivia, hoping to discover something Steven could use.

"She spent a lot of time on her own when we were growing up. She wasn't interested in playing together. I'd want to play house or dress up our dolls but she'd take her toys and go off somewhere alone. When we got older, she'd take a book and hide away by herself."

"Is she shy?"

"Not really. I think it was more that she didn't want me playing with her things. When we visited our cousins, she'd play in a group. But, it was with their toys so it was different. She can be possessive."

"Sharing is hard for some kids." Olivia didn't know how to say what she was thinking without insulting Helen's parents, in case they'd been poor. "Especially if she was afraid the toy would get broken and couldn't be replaced."

"Yes, that's true. But our parents were generous with us. We always had plenty of everything."

Olivia nodded and they drank their tea. "You mentioned the other night that your sister works?"

"She teaches English at the high school. See, that's another thing. I know there are girls who work nowadays. But Lucy is *so* independent. She never wants any help from anybody. Never did." Helen pushed a strand of hair from her forehead. "I was surprised when she got

129

serious with Frankie. I thought for sure she was going to be an old maid. Perfect for it really." She drifted away for a moment.

"She must have loved him very much," Olivia said softly.

"I suppose so. I mean yes, of course she did." Helen held Olivia's gaze. Her voice was tinged with sadness when she said, "You're not from around here, so you won't know."

"Know what?"

"Frankie had a reputation for being a flirt. My sister swears he stopped fooling around when they got married but…," she hesitated. "Olivia, I know we just met but I feel like I can talk to you. Please, don't think I'm gossiping."

"No, of course not." Olivia reached across the table and gently patted the other woman's arm. "Helen, I can't imagine what you're going through right now. I'm an only child but I have two best friends that I've known my whole life. If something like this happened to one of them my heart would break for them. I'd be going through all kinds of emotions." She gave another pat then withdrew her hand. "I think it helps to talk. Don't worry, I'm not going to make any judgments. If you need to say something, go ahead." She smiled reassuringly. "I'll let it go in one ear and out the other. How's that?"

Helen visibly relaxed. "No wonder Steven likes you so much."

Olivia nearly choked on a mouthful of hot tea. "He does?"

"Of course. You must know that. I've never heard him talk about anyone the way he talks about you."

"Wow."

They sat quietly for a moment, the only sound was the ticking of the clock on the wall.

Olivia spoke first. "What were you going to say about Frankie? It sounded like you didn't trust him…although your sister did."

Helen looked around the kitchen as if someone might be lurking around the corner, behind the door or the icebox. She said in a near whisper, "I saw Frankie having coffee in Bailey's with Hannah Grantham only a few months after he and Lucy got married. He explained it away the next time I saw him. Said he ran into her by accident." She made a noise that sounded something like *tsk*. "I don't know if I believed him or not. But even so...." She caught her new friend's gaze for a second time and held it. "Olivia, he was a creep! There's just no other way to say it."

"Oh, dear," Olivia said in an understanding tone.

Helen noticed the clock. "Ooh! It's almost nine. Are you sure you don't want to walk over to Lucy's with me? Maybe she's up by now."

Olivia thought of her promise and reluctantly said, "I can't intrude on Lucy today, Helen. It wouldn't be right. How about the next time? I'll go with you another day, okay?"

Helen pushed her chair back. "All right, sure."

After Helen had left, Olivia realized she'd passed her second test. She'd had a normal conversation with a real woman who lived in 1934 and Helen hadn't suspected a thing. Of course, she reminded herself, Helen was so distracted this morning she probably wouldn't have noticed if Olivia had danced naked on the kitchen table. But even so, it felt good to be accepted. Olivia felt as though she'd made a new friend.

Chapter 20

"We could haul her in, Steven, and grill her until she talks." Steven and Jimmy Bou were discussing Adona Russo on the way to Frankie's sister's house.

"You've been reading *The Black Mask* again." Steven grinned, referring to a popular pulp magazine crammed with tough-guy detective stories.

"Well..."

"Remember, Jimmy, Frankie's notebook said *Working on A.* That doesn't sound like an affair."

"Maybe he was putting the moves on her. Trying to get her...you know." Jimmy blushed. "Maybe that's why she slapped him in the lunchroom."

"What I saw and heard when I snuck up on the porch tells me Nick and Adona Russo have a good marriage. But, we don't know how extensive his war injuries are. Maybe she needs physical comfort that Nick can't give her anymore."

"Oh, I didn't think of that." Jimmy turned a deeper shade of red and cleared his throat.

"If she loves him but cheated anyway, especially with his cousin, she'd be feeling guilty. She'd certainly want to keep it secret. Who knows what she'd do to keep Nick from finding out?" Steven downshifted and turned left on the Mohawk River Road.

"Frankie Russo sounds like a real louse. Maybe he threatened to tell Nick," Jimmy suggested.

"That's an idea. *Working on A* could mean blackmail."

"Or, what if she wanted to stop the affair and Frankie didn't? *Working on A* could mean he was trying to convince her to keep cheating with him," Jimmy suggested.

"Too many possibilities right now. We'll question her again as soon as we can," Steven said.

Jimmy Bou scowled, growling like James Cagney.

Steven laughed. "We're only going to talk, Jimmy, not beat it out of her. She might let her guard down a little if her husband's not in the next room."

Steven pulled into a long dirt driveway leading to a white clapboard farmhouse. Behind the home and to the left were a red barn and tall silo. Dairy cows grazed lazily in a field. A piece of farm equipment sat near an older model truck. It was an impressive operation, given the difficulties farmers were enduring. Many dairymen were forced to pour their milk into the streets because they couldn't afford to ship it to a city. Steven couldn't imagine how devastating that must be. How were those families surviving?

He knocked on the screen door. A child playing on the living room floor made car noises and a dog barked in the distance. Connie Morelli came to the door.

"Steven, I've been expecting you. Come in." She held the door open. "How are you, Jimmy?"

"I'm truly sorry about Frankie," Steven said.

"I know you are. Thanks."

Connie was a lovely, down-to-earth woman who put her family first. She had filled out since the birth of her three children but was still an attractive woman who seemed unaware of it, which in Steven's opinion made her even more attractive. Dark brown hair and eyes set off a clear olive complexion.

"You know this is an official visit, Connie," Steven said.

"Yes. Listen, Steven, would you mind if we talked in the back yard? I need to get my clothes off the line."

"Sure."

They followed her out a side door. Steven chatted with Connie as she took down her washing.

"My brother and I weren't close, Steven. But I loved him. He was just Frankie. Same now as he was when we were kids. He liked to have a good time. He loved his family." She stopped abruptly. A shadow crossed her face. Her eyes filled up and she dabbed them with a man-sized cotton handkerchief that she pulled out of her apron pocket. "He was a good boy. Thank the Lord Mama and Papa are gone and don't have to see this. It would kill them."

"Can you tell me anything about his marriage?" Steven asked.

Connie Morelli frowned. "I know he wasn't much of a husband. God knows Lucy put up with a lot. But, he provided for her."

"What about his relationship with Hannah Grantham?"

Connie's lip curled. "Don't talk to me about her," she said. "That girl would *not* leave Frankie alone. I even saw them together after he married Lucy. Talk about nerve! She wouldn't accept it was over between them."

"What ever happened between Frankie and Hannah? Do you know why they never got married?"

"I think it was because she went off to college. I'm only guessing, of course. It's not the sort of thing Frankie would have discussed with me. But, Frankie was never the kind of fella to sit around and wait for someone. During the four years Hannah was in Oswego, they grew apart. Well, it was more his feelings that changed. Whatever he felt when they were in school, it lost its intensity while she was gone."

"But they did see each other when she got back, right?"

"Yes, but it wasn't serious anymore. At least not for Frankie."

Connie set the wicker basket of clothes on a tree stump, grabbed a pair of scissors and glass canning jar sitting on a nearby crate then wandered to a lilac bush. She snipped a handful of lush blooms, stuck them the impromptu vase, and worked the iron pump to splash enough water to cover the bottom. Connie buried her face in the bouquet. "My favorite part of spring," she sighed. "Let's sit over here." She led them to a grouping of chairs in the shade.

Steven asked about Sunday while Jimmy continued to make notes.

"We always go to eight-o'clock Mass. We sit together up front—the whole family. Father can tell you we were all there. We take turns driving Nick and Adona so they don't miss. Sunday was our turn."

"And after church, Connie?"

"Sometimes there's a big family dinner around one or two o'clock."

"What time was it this week?" Steven asked.

"We didn't have one because they were all here Saturday for Tonio's birthday party. Everybody went home on their own."

"Who were Frankie's friends, Connie?"

She shook her head. "I'm sorry, Steven, I don't have any idea. I already regret not spending more time with him." Her face crumbled. "Why didn't I know him better? I can't even tell you who his best friend was."

They left her crying softly under the maple tree.

"Jimmy, we've got enough time to accomplish two more things before lunch if we split up," said Steven, once they were in the Chevy heading back to town. "I'm going to the high school and talk with Hannah Grantham. I'll drop you off at the corner of Victoria and the Mohawk River Road. I want you to go over to St. Joe's and talk to Father Seraphino. Verify what Connie told us. I know you said you saw

Frankie at church yesterday but it doesn't hurt to have an extra confirmation from somebody not on the force. When you've finished, go back to the station. You can work on your report."

"Sure thing, Steven," said Jimmy, pleased to have this responsibility.

HANNAH

Steven headed to Hannah Grantham's classroom tucked away in a corner of an upstairs wing. He saw lights on through the transom window and knocked as he pushed open the heavy wooden door.

Hannah was seated at her desk, red pen in hand poised over a pile of homework papers, luxuriant honey blonde hair falling to her shoulders, looking like Rita Hayworth. She glanced up at the sound, her dark blue eyes clear and bright.

"Steven, what are you doing here?"

"I need to talk with you about Frankie, Hannah. It's an official visit," he said.

"Good heavens, you don't have to say that. How long have I been friends with your cousin? Ask me anything you want." She indicated a student's desk. "Have a seat."

Steven considered the wooden chair, decided he would fit, and slid in. The desks ran in pairs from the front of the room to the back, like seats in a motor coach. There were three such rows with aisles in between. Each desk-and-chair unit was bolted to the floor by means of a decorative iron frame.

Steven pretended to consult his notebook. He'd nearly reached the last page and would have to purchase a new one soon. The dark brown leather cover was creased, there was a smudge where he'd put a greasy finger one day. The small notebook had been a gift from his dad last fall. For no reason at all. Just to say *I'm proud of you.* The best kind of gift. Despite the type of notes that filled the book, Steven felt good every time he took it out. "Let's see, Hannah. First, I need to know where you were from early Sunday morning until later in the afternoon."

"Oh, my goodness. Let's see. In the morning I was at home with my mother. I helped her fold some of the clothes she does."

"What do you mean?"

"She takes in washing for some of the out-of-town men working on the bridge project. They don't have any facilities. And for that matter, I've never heard of a man who washed his own clothes."

"I see. Then what?"

"I got ready to leave. Ben picked me up and we went to the parade. You saw me. You were with Martha and Jim. Remember?"

"Yes, I do. What time did you leave the house?"

"Oh, dear, I don't know. Mother might remember. I fixed her some lunch. Maybe one o'clock? Sorry, Steven. I'm not sure."

"That's fine. Tell me about the rest of the day."

"Ben and I watched the parade until it was over then we took a drive in his motor car. We went to Sylvan Beach. It was lovely." She smiled at the recollection. "The amusement park's not open yet but the hotels and restaurants are. We walked on the pier and the beach. We had supper in a place that just opened up, it's called Eddie's. Then, we drove home. It was getting dark when Ben dropped me off. I guess it was around eight."

Steven made notes while Hannah talked. She stopped at one point and waited while he caught up. When he nodded and raised his eyebrows, she went on. "I made myself a cup of tea and read the Sunday paper. A few minutes before nine, I turned on the radio. My mother and I listen to 'Manhattan Merry-Go-Round' on Sunday nights. It's a half-hour program. After that, I went to bed."

Steven continued to scribble, turned a page in his notebook, and regarded her. "Good. Now, Hannah, I need to know about your relationship with Frankie."

She frowned at him. "Steven, that was years ago."

"You know I have to ask."

"Fine." Her face lost a bit of its friendliness and she held herself more stiffly. "Go ahead."

"When was the last time you saw Frankie?"

"I don't know. I've seen him around but that's not what you mean, is it?"

"No."

She looked off in the distance as if trying to pinpoint a date. "I'm sorry. I don't have any idea when it was."

"Maybe you saw him for coffee once or twice...just as old friends?"

"No." She shook her head. "You know we were an item once. But, that was a long time ago. We were kids." She shrugged casually then held his gaze. "Steven, that was over long before he married Lucy."

And that was the moment he knew she was lying.

Chapter 21

When Steven returned from the high school, it was after one. He entered the CID room, trailed by Jimmy Bou, who'd noticed him walk past the door to the patrol room. Ralph and Pete were deep in discussion at Will's desk. Pete broke off the conversation and said excitedly, "Steven, Will was just telling us we might have a witness."

"Yeah, you know Mrs. Sweeney, the history teacher?" Ralph said. "She called this morning."

"She saw one of her students coming out of the woods near the school Sunday," Pete leap-frogged over Ralph. "After lunch. Maybe twelve thirty, one o'clock."

"It was Dickie Hughes," said Ralph.

"Steven and I saw Dickie Hughes at the mill yesterday," Will told Ralph, Pete, and Jimmy Bou. "He was acting jumpy. And as soon as he saw us he said something like 'I didn't do anything.' But we never asked a question."

"This could be our big break! A witness!" cried Jimmy Bou.

"How sure was she? Mrs. Sweeney's getting on. How reliable is her eyesight?" Steven asked.

"She doesn't wear glasses," Ralph said.

"I asked her how she could be so sure," said Will. "She said it was the way he walked. But, she saw his face, too."

"That's swell." Steven turned to Ralph and Pete. "Go to the high school and bring him here. I'll question him away from the other kids. By the way, how'd you make out this morning on Frankie's movements Sunday? Have you found anybody who saw him?"

"No, we finished his street and part of the neighborhood where he should have walked if he actually went to the bus depot but so far no luck."

"Well, police work takes a lot of shoe leather. After you drop off Dickie Hughes, go over to the bus station. Maybe that'll save you some time."

Ralph and Pete took off, chatting like magpies about the possible end of the case.

After they'd left, Will spoke. "I went to Lucy's, Steven, but there was no answer. I'll go back later."

Steven told Will about his and Jimmy's morning. "We think Adona Russo is hiding something. But, there are a lot of possibilities as to what that is and whether or not it has anything to do with Frankie's murder." Steven shared the ideas he and Jimmy Bou had discussed. "I'd like you to take a crack at her. But, let's give her a chance to relax a bit first."

"I'll go to the mill tomorrow," said Will. "Hopefully by then, I'll have talked with Lucy and I'll know more about the change in Frankie's behavior. It might help when I talk with Adona."

"Speaking of odd behavior," Steven said, "Nick Russo was yelling and acting angry one minute. Then, he was sweet and docile the next. Could that be a result of the war, do you think?"

"Could be. But, I've also read about people who go back and forth between extremes in emotion. Maybe he's one of them," said Will.

"One thing's for sure. They're devoted to each other. I think she'd do anything to protect him. She's wife and mother all wrapped into one," Steven observed.

"Because of the wheelchair, I suppose."

"Maybe. But the question is…," Steven began.

"Why would she *need* to protect him?" said Will.

"Exactly."

"There's one more thing. I talked with Hannah." Steven paused, holding his partner's attention. "She lied."

"No kidding. About what?"

"She said her affair with Frankie was over before he married Lucy. That's not true. His sister Connie mentioned it earlier this morning. She knew they were still stepping out after Frankie and Lucy got married. And it reminded me that I saw them together, too."

"Why would she lie about a thing like that when it's so easy for us to check?" mused Jimmy Bou.

An hour later, Sergeant Will Taylor rang the bell at 114 Mohawk River Road. He heard the chime echo through the quiet house then someone clearing her throat. Lucy Russo had obviously just awoken from a nap—there was a pillow crease on her cheek and her hair was mussed. Will formally identified himself and showed his badge and ID.

"I remember you from school, Will. Is there news?" she asked, opening the door and inviting him into the neat living room.

"Not yet. I have some questions if you're feeling up to it."

They sat across from each other—Lucy in a chair upholstered in a leaf pattern, Will on a couch covered in a soothing forest green. He noticed the walls were painted a pale green. It felt like he was outside. He liked it.

"Just two questions really. First, could you tell me when you and Frankie met?"

Whatever it was Lucy thought he was going to ask, this definitely was not it. "When we met? Why is that important?"

Will watched carefully as he told her about Frankie's little book. Lucy deflated. Her shoulders sagged and her head dropped.

"I suspected," she whispered. "I ignored the rumors. I didn't want them to be true."

Will had a way about him. People felt they could trust him, confide in him. Even very private people like Lucy Russo told him things.

"When you met...?" Will prompted.

"Oh." The shadow of a smile fluttered across her face. "It was the winter of 1929. March. We met at the skating rink. It was wonderful in the beginning. During the first few months of our marriage, I thought he had changed. He came home after work. We did things together. Then...." The smile vanished.

"What about a few years ago, Mrs. Russo? The summer and fall of 1931?"

"That would have been after he got the job at the brewery. When he started spending every other week in Syracuse," Lucy said.

"Did you notice a change in Frankie's behavior towards the end of the year?"

She looked surprised. "Yes, I did. I couldn't believe he was finally going to be faithful to me. It seemed like he was done with his old ways. I thought maybe the separation was what he had needed all along. Some men feel suffocated, you know. Things were better between us then."

"Did you ever visit him in Syracuse?"

"No, he said the work was tiring. When he got back from the brewery, all he wanted to do was eat supper and sleep."

"Do you know where he was living?"

"A rooming house. It must have been close to the brewery because he walked to work. I don't know the address. If I needed to get a hold of him, I had the telephone number at his office."

"Did you ever call him there?"

"No, it was never necessary."

"What about weekends?"

"He worked on Saturdays and came home on Sundays."

"You didn't have a phone number at the boarding house?"

Lucy shook her head.

While Steven waited for Ralph and Pete to return with their possible witness, he updated the murder board. Under WITNESSES he wrote *Dickie Hughes (Seen by Mrs. Sweeney)*. He forced himself not to get excited. Wouldn't it be swell if Dickie had seen everything and they could wrap up this case today? He could spend more time with Olivia this week. There were so many things he wanted to show her, things he wanted to do with her.

In the top right corner of the chalkboard, Steven drew a box for information connected to Frankie's little book. He wrote:

FRANKIE'S NOTEBOOK

```
L Lucy Russo?            H Hannah Grantham?
"Working on A" meaning?  Is A Adona Russo?
Who is S ?               Is anyone else impt??
```

Below the box, he began a timeline. So far there were five items:

```
January 1931      FR's job at mill cut to ½ time
May 1931          FR starts work ½ time at
                      Haberle's,Syracuse
Summer/fall 1931  FR's behavior changes
December 1931     H disappearing from log
January 1932      H gone from log
```

Steven created a new section and labeled it SUSPECTS. For each name listed, he tackled three key elements.

In order to make an accusation stick, the police had to prove the accused had the motive, means, and opportunity to commit the crime. Reluctantly, Steven considered number one on the list—Lucy Russo, the widow. Lucy had plenty of reasons for wanting her husband dead. The notebook proved that beyond a doubt. Frankie Russo had been a lifelong cheater.

What about the means to pull off the murder? Everyone in town knew Lucy was a wonderful baker. She could have baked any number of delicious desserts or breads hiding the taste of arsenic. Frankie would have gobbled them down without hesitating.

Opportunity was going to be the problem for every one of their suspects. If they could only narrow down the time of death. Could Lucy have poisoned Frankie before joining them at the parade? Why not? But, was she really that cool, that self-contained? Could she have acted in such a normal, ordinary way right after killing her husband? Would she have been able to talk and laugh and eat an ice cream cone so soon after poisoning the man she had loved? If so, then Lucy Russo was an extraordinary actress who hid more secrets than Steven could imagine.

Adona Russo went in the number two slot. Did Frankie's cousin's wife have the means and opportunity to kill him? Like Lucy, Adona was a good baker, but how would she have been able to prepare poisoned baked goods with Nick in the house? Unless she'd done it in the middle of the night while he slept. No. Steven shook his head. He couldn't see her taking a chance that Nick might eat some of the food. He decided *maybe* was the better answer to the question of *means*.

As for whether or not Adona had the opportunity, the police didn't know exactly when Frankie was poisoned. It could have been after Adona had gone to Mass with her family. Steven wrote *yes* on the board next to *opportunity*.

That left *motive*. The key here was the way in which Frankie had written the note *Working on A*. To Steven, it sounded as though he were trying to put the moves on her but she hadn't given in yet.

Steven worked through the implications of the phrase. Frankie was a cheat and a liar. He could have threatened Adona, saying he was going to tell Nick he'd had his way with her even though he hadn't. Adona would have believed him more than capable of lying to her husband. Or, Frankie managed to seduce Adona after he'd written the note in his book. He threatened to tell Nick the truth. Or, Frankie seduced Adona after the note was written but the affair was still going on. Adona wanted to break it off but Frankie refused to let her go. Frankie could have threatened to tell Nick any number of things.

In less than a minute, Steven had easily come up with several possible motives for Adona to want Frankie dead. She remained on the list.

The last thing he did was add Hannah Grantham's name to the list and make a note that she had lied about her relationship with Frankie. He wanted to think about that before he spoke with her again.

Steven returned to his desk and picked up Ray's report on the Old Crow whiskey bottle. There were seven men who usually purchased that brand. Ray had eliminated four names. Dickie Hughes's father Marvin was one of the three remaining possibilities.

Ralph and Pete hurried in.

"Dickie Hughes wasn't at the high school," said Ralph.

"We checked the mill to see if he was working. He's not due back until tomorrow morning," said Pete.

"The Hugheses don't have a phone so we're going to his house and see if he's there," said Ralph.

Steven's work day ended the way it began—sitting alone at his desk in the silent station. The members of his team were either still out on the streets, quietly writing their reports in the patrol room, or already home enjoying the evening with their families. He settled in to write his report to the chief. It had been a busy day, but had they really accomplished anything? Ralph and Pete hadn't been able to confirm Frankie's movements yet. They hadn't talked with Dickie Hughes. Hannah had lied. Lucy was acting strangely. Forty-eight hours and Steven felt no closer to identifying Frankie Russo's killer.

STELLA

Stella looked up at the kitchen clock—nearly four. She wiped her chapped hands on the cotton dish towel and turned back to the table where she was preparing the evening meal for the house. *The house,* that's how Stella thought of her boarders—three girls and a fella.

When Stella married her first husband, she never imagined she would end up a widow at twenty-three and that, in order to survive, she'd have to turn their home into a business. She wouldn't have guessed she'd even be capable of running a business by herself. Then, after years of being alone, Tony—her wonderful, loving, gentle Tony—knocked on the door looking for a place to stay. Love blossomed and they'd been happily married for nearly two years now. Three feet away Charlotte gurgled in her high-chair, her teddy bear and doll in lively conversation. Charlotte had turned eleven months old yesterday.

Stella frowned. That's what made it even more puzzling. Tony had been looking forward to their birthday celebration last night. She'd planned an extra nice supper and baked a cake, practically unheard of these days. Now, here it was Tuesday and he still hadn't come home. He hadn't called either.

This had never happened before. Stella was worried.

The screen door clattered shut and Mabel entered the cheerful kitchen. She walked over to Charlotte and gave her a big kiss.

"How's my beautiful girl?"

The baby cooed, waved her chubby arms, and kicked her plump

legs.

"What's for supper, Stella?"

"Pork chops, potatoes, and carrots in the oven. And red cabbage."

"Mmm. Sounds good. Any word from Tony yet?"

"No, and I can't understand it. He always calls if he's going to be late. Actually he's only been late once. I'm afraid something's wrong."

"It's been two days. You have to call the police."

Stella squeezed her eyes shut and swallowed hard. "Oh, Mabel! That makes it real."

"It's already real, my friend. Do you want me to dial?"

"No, I'll do it."

Lieutenant Fred Schultz picked up the clamoring phone at the Syracuse Police Department and boomed, "Schultz here."

Stella identified herself and explained her situation.

Fifteen minutes later, there was a banging on the front door. Stella gazed up at the policeman filling the doorway and invited him in. While Mabel watched over Charlotte, Stella poured her heart out.

"Where did your husband go, Mrs. Russo?"

"He works part-time with his cousin near Utica."

"When was he supposed to come home?"

"Sunday."

"Don't you have a telephone number where you can reach him?"

"No, Tony always calls every couple of days. He never wants me to worry or feel cut off from him."

Privately Fred thought if this Tony was so concerned about his wife's feelings, he would have given her a telephone number. "Where does your husband stay when he's away?" he asked.

"At his cousin's house."

"Do you know the name of this cousin? We can look up the phone number in a directory."

"Yes, it's Frankie. Frankie Russo."

Chapter 22

Steven had been so busy at work that he'd only thought of Olivia once all day. Now, as he drove the short distance home, he became increasingly anxious. Would she still be there, in his house, in 1934? Would she be all right? Steven hoped that spending the day in his time had had no adverse effects on her. He made a quick turn into his driveway, slammed his foot down on the clutch, and, throwing the gearshift into first, cut the engine. He took two steps at a time and flung open the front door, calling as he entered, "Olivia. Olivia, are you here?" Relief flooded over him when he heard her voice.

"I'm in the kitchen, Steven."

He hurried down the hall and was delighted by what he saw.

Olivia was leaning back in a chair, legs bent, bare feet on another chair with a notebook in her lap. She'd obviously been working on her writing project.

"Well," he exclaimed. "You're a sight for sore eyes." He grinned. "So, you're still here." He breathed another sigh of relief.

"Yes, I am," she replied, "but only because I promised you I wouldn't leave the house."

"What do you mean?"

"Helen asked me—twice, no less—to go out. The first time, when I called to offer my condolences, she invited me over for coffee. I made up an excuse and asked her to come here, which she did. Later, when she was leaving to go to Lucy's house, she asked me to go with her. I made up another excuse." Olivia set her notebook and pencil on the table and stood to face Steven. "I was dying to go. I felt totally fine. No problems at all. And I was just *itching* to get out of the house. I never spend a whole day without going out. It was driving me nuts!"

Steven laughed. "Well, I'd say we have the answer to Phase II of our experiments. You don't need me to stay with you."

"I agree. And later this week I'm going for broke," she exclaimed.

"What does that mean?"

"It means that I'm coming here Thursday morning then I'm going out." She raised her eyebrows and stared up at him as if to say *I dare you to stop me.*

"Okay, okay. I'm not going to argue. We'll talk about it later. Right now, I'm hungry."

"What are you making for dinner?" Olivia grinned. "After all, I'm still your guest, right?"

Steven smiled back at her. "Of course, you are. I'll put a meatloaf and potatoes in the oven. It won't take long."

"Sounds great. I need to go for a run. I've got loads of energy to burn off after sitting here all day. I'm going back to my time, get my run in, and take a shower. And I want to check my messages in case a client tried to reach me while I was here."

"I'll come up to the doorway and get you at seven. How's that?"

After a second helping of Steven's delicious meal, they sat at his kitchen table talking and savoring the wine Olivia had brought.

"Tell me how the case went today," she said.

Steven looked at the ceiling and rolled his eyes. "The bad news is that I still don't know who did it. By now, I should have some idea but we've got too many suspects, too many alibis, and no definite time of death. So," he made a face, "I'm not happy about any of that."

Olivia mirrored his disappointment. "Aww."

"But, having said that, the good news is I think we have a witness."

"Oh, that'd be great."

"It sure would. He's a high school kid, maybe fifteen or sixteen. One of the teachers saw him leave the woods around the time of the murder."

"Which woods? Next to the field or at the bottom of the hill behind the school? For that matter, what was she doing in school on the weekend?"

"She wasn't at school. She lives across from the field where we think Frankie and his killer had the picnic. She was looking out her front window and saw one of her students walking out of the woods. My team found a spot where we think he witnessed the murder. There were cigarette butts and a whisky bottle on the ground. We found out today the boy's father drinks the same brand of whiskey."

"Wow. So, you think the kid stood there watching what happened, smoking, and drinking." Olivia leaned closer. "What does he have to say about it?"

"I haven't had a chance to question him yet. Two of the fellas went to school to get him but he wasn't there. They hiked back across town to the mill where he works a few hours a week. He wasn't there either. Or at his house. He's probably down by the river with his friends. A lot of the boys go fishing after school. We'll catch him first thing tomorrow and bring him in."

"Aren't you worried that something will happen?"

"No. He would have been well hidden in the trees. I'm sure nobody knows he was there except for me and my team. We'll get him in the morning." Steven sipped his wine. "Tell me about your visit with Helen. How did it go? Were you nervous like the other night?"

"No, even if I'd been wearing a sign that said 'visitor from another time,' she wouldn't have noticed. She was upset about her brother-in-law's death. I did learn something about Lucy that you might not know." Olivia raised her eyebrows twice in quick succession and grinned in what she thought was an enticing manner.

Steven laughed and said, "Okay, I'll bite. What did you learn, my intrepid reporter?"

"Ha! Good one. Helen told me Lucy's possessive about everything that belongs to her." Olivia repeated Helen's story about Lucy not wanting to share her toys. "Maybe she was possessive about Frankie, too. Didn't you tell me he cheated on her?"

"Yes, for years." Steven explained Frankie's notebook.

"Eww! What a creep." Olivia had always thought cheating was despicable but after her ex-fiancé had cheated on her, she felt even stronger about it.

"I agree." He poured more wine into their glasses. He stretched then leaned back in his chair. "So, what are you planning to do Thursday on your trip outside the house?"

"I want to go shopping. I'm psyched to see Woolworth's. Isabel used to talk about going there when she was a kid. We don't have 'em anymore. They sound cool."

"That'll be fun. I'll give you some money."

"I appreciate it, Steven, thank you. But I have a couple thoughts on how I can use my own money."

"We already talked about this, Olivia. We said we'd use my money to pay for things here and when I come into your time, we'll use yours."

"I don't think it's right for you to spend money on presents I want to buy for my friends. I'd like to spend freely. I have an idea how I can buy stuff on my own."

He grinned. "Of course you do. All right, let's hear it." But, his grin turned grim. "Why do I get the feeling I'm not going to like this?"

"Now, wait and see," she said in a soothing tone. "It's two ideas really. First of all, over the past two months I've collected a lot of change...."

"Oh, so you've been planning this, huh?" he kidded.

She made a face. "... nickels and old quarters and dimes because there's a new style of those. I think we can mix some of mine and yours, if it's okay with you. They'll all look the same except for the date. And no one in a store is going to peer down at the date."

"So, I'm going to be passing counterfeit money now? You're starting me, a policeman, on a life of crime?" He stared at her.

"Come on. I know you're kidding." She paused. "Right? You *are* kidding, aren't you?"

"I don't know. Wouldn't it be cheating?" Steven frowned. All his life, he'd faithfully stuck to the letter of the law. He was cautious while Olivia tended to rush headlong into whatever took her fancy. He was circumspect, she sometimes acted without thinking.

But, was his way really better? This was an unexpected dilemma.

Olivia watched Steven wrestle with the issue. It hadn't occurred to her that using her perfectly good 21st-century money might cause a problem between them. Why did she never take that one extra step to *think* before she spoke or acted? Was she asking him to do something shady? Did her plan straddle the line between legal and criminal? She hoped she hadn't insulted him. It was true they had talked about the issue of money but the discussion had centered more on groceries than gift buying. In addition to presents for Liz and Sophie, Olivia wanted to buy whatever took her fancy for herself. She knew there'd be a lot of interesting things. The reporter in her was dying to buy newspapers and magazines. The kid in her wanted comic books.

Steven took his time to study all the angles of her idea. At first, it had sounded dishonest. But after careful reflection, he decided what she was suggesting wasn't actually illegal. Her coins had value. Her money was American money. The United States government had minted them. *Just not yet*, he thought wryly. And anyway, her money might even be more valuable than his. Why not?

"All right, Olivia, I agree. We'll mix our coins together so you'll feel free to buy what you want. What's the rest of the plan?"

"This is a bit trickier."

"I'm all ears."

Olivia hesitated then jumped in. "One day last week I went to a coin shop in Syracuse. The guy helped me compare bills from the twenties and thirties with the ones in the nineties. I found out the mint changed the style in the early 2000s. Saturday, I inked over the date on an older twenty-dollar bill. I made sort of a blob so it would look accidental. Then, I put it in the pocket of an old pair of jeans and threw them in the wash."

Olivia took out a faded, partially torn banknote and handed it to Steven. "This is how it came out."

"Hmm. Wait a minute."

He went upstairs then returned with a twenty-dollar bill in his hand. "Let's compare them."

They put the two pieces of currency on the table and examined them closely.

"Wow, this could really work," Olivia declared. "It's better than I expected.

He smiled at her. "You did a good job. How'd you think of this? No, don't answer that. I know you."

Olivia blushed and cleared her throat.

"There is one thing, Olivia. Twenty dollars is a lot of money. That's more than a full week's wages for most people. You can't go into Woolworth's and buy only a few things with this much money."

"Oh, I didn't think of that."

He waited and, a moment later, saw the light bulb go on. "Okay, Sherlock, what's the plan?"

"We tell the truth."

He gave her a puzzled look.

"We go to the bank and explain that the bill went through the wash and we're afraid it might rip even more if we try to use it. We ask if they'd exchange it for us," she finished triumphantly.

"You're going to get me dismissed from the force," he exclaimed, his voice louder than usual.

"No, I'm not. It's real money. It's not like we're printing it up in the cellar."

"That's true." He sighed. "What am I going to do with you?"

Olivia blushed again.

Steven pretended not to notice and continued. "All right. I'll take it to the bank when I have a chance. In the meantime, I'll loan you five dollars. How's that?"

"Thank you. Steven, you know I would never ask you to compromise your principles. I really do think this is okay. And legal. My money is real money exactly like yours is."

"That's why I said yes. It feels odd, that's all. And, Olivia," he gave her a penetrating stare, "no matter what the situation, I would never do anything I thought was illegal. Not even for you."

Chapter 23

She saw him walking down the path, framed by hanging branches and backlit by the moon rising high in the inky sky. She heard the river murmur, and the whisper of a splash as a fish jumped out of the water then dove back in. She stepped from behind the bush where she'd been waiting onto the walkway to greet him. He had lost the swagger she'd noticed yesterday. She watched him hurry the final few steps. Then they were inches apart, face to face in the shadowy night.

"Thank you. I'm sorry." He bent over to catch his breath. "I'm glad you came." The words tumbled out of his mouth.

"You thought I wouldn't?"

"I didn't know. I *really* don't want to do this," he pleaded. He scrunched up his face. "But I need the money. I *have* to get out of town."

"Sure."

"You'll never see me again. I *promise*. This'll see me right. When I get someplace else, I'll get a job. I just have to *get* there."

"What's that?" She craned her neck and peered over his shoulder at the silhouetted trees.

As he turned to look, she withdrew something from her purse, moved to the side, and swung with all her might. The brick connected with his temple and he dropped to the ground.

"Try and blackmail me," she hissed in a whisper. She took a couple of steps and heaved the makeshift weapon into the center of the river, where it quickly sank.

Dickie Hughes's killer took a small mirror from her bag and held it in front of his mouth. In the moonlight, she could see no sign of breath. Satisfied, she grabbed his feet and dragged him down the small embankment. At the water's edge, she swung him around until a thin shoulder met the river. She yanked and pushed until his upper body was submerged face down in the cold water.

There she left him, the current lapping over his head, his hair waving like seaweed.

Chapter 24

Wednesday — April 25, 1934

As Steven entered the police station early Wednesday morning, Ralph and Pete were walking out.

"We're going to the mill to get Dickie Hughes," said Ralph. "Today's his day to work."

"He goes over for a couple of hours before school," Pete added.

"He sounds like an ambitious kid," Steven commented. "Hand him off to Will when you get back. I'm leaving for Syracuse in a few minutes. I'm taking Jimmy with me."

"Okay, when we drop him off, we'll get back to our canvas for Frankie's movements," said Ralph.

Will was at his desk reading the morning paper, filing away information as usual. Steven briefed him on Dickie Hughes.

"And after you interview him, Will, keep him here. I want to talk with him, too."

"Okay. I'm going to question Adona Russo this morning. By the way, my report from yesterday is on your desk."

"Swell. What did you find out at Lucy's?"

"She's definitely the L in Frankie's book. The dates match. They met in the winter of 1929. Got married the following June. She said he was faithful in the beginning but after a few months he went back to his old habit of staying out late every night. You should have seen her when I mentioned Frankie's notebook. The life went out of her."

"What do you mean? Was this the first she's heard of it or did she know about his cheating?"

"I got her to admit she suspected it. She said she couldn't face it. She didn't want to know." Will stood and stretched, muscles rippled across his chest and tightened in his arms.

"I was talking with someone last night who had information on Lucy's personality. Helen said Lucy was possessive about her things when they were growing up."

"That's interesting," Will said. "As far as I could tell when I was there, Lucy has her routine and provided Frankie didn't upset it or the house—you should see that house, Steven, immaculate. Everything perfectly in its place. It looked like she lived alone." He caught his breath. "Anyway, I got the impression that as long as Frankie didn't upset her routine or leave his dirty socks on the floor, things rolled along okay. Somehow she managed to look the other way and ignore his cheating. Maybe she didn't love him anymore."

"I'm going to talk with Helen, see if she can shed some light on her sister. What about the change in Frankie's behavior? Was Lucy aware of it?"

"Yes, she said she couldn't help but notice. It was a few months after he got the job in Syracuse. She said he seemed different. It reminded her of when they first got married. He was home more often, didn't go out at night. He seemed more interested in her. She said that, at the time, she thought maybe he'd finally grown up and outgrown his running around."

"What do you think, Will? Could she have done it?"

"She's certainly capable of it. We know jealousy can be a strong motive. If we throw in the idea of her being possessive about the things she considers hers, we've got obsession as well. I think that would be a deadly combination. Yes, Lucy could be our killer."

Steven slowly shook his head. He didn't want it to be his best friend's sister-in-law. "I'd better get moving. I want to get to the brewery before it's too late. On the way back, I'm going to stop at the high school. I want to talk with Hannah again."

"We need to know why she lied." Will nodded.

"According to Frankie's little book, their affair was over two years ago."

"Two years seems like a long time to hold onto resentment over an affair gone wrong. She knew Frankie was married. What did she think was going to happen? And if it *was* Hannah, why did she wait so long to kill him?" Will frowned and shook his head. "No. Killing him because he didn't leave his wife two years ago doesn't seem right. It's too strong a reaction and she waited too long," said Will.

"I agree. But, we've got to be sure it really was over two years ago. I'd like to rule her out and focus on somebody more recent," Steven added optimistically.

"That'd be nice."

It was after nine by the time Steven and Jimmy Bou pulled up in front of the Haberle Congress Brewing Company on Butternut Street on Syracuse's North Side. During the drive, both had donned sunglasses and opened the car windows.

"What a swell day to be out on the road," Jimmy had enthused.

"You have the search warrant?" Steven asked.

"Yup. Right here in my pocket." Jimmy Bou patted his chest.

Yesterday Steven had telephoned his friend Lieutenant Fred Schultz at the Syracuse Police Department and filled him in on the case. Fred had offered to have one of his officers meet Steven at the brewery.

The young SPD officer was waiting when Steven killed the engine and got out of the car. Syracuse policemen wore navy blue uniforms and caps with a visor. Steven approached the young man and offered his hand.

"Hello, I'm Detective Sergeant Steven Blackwell. Thanks for meeting us."

"Yes, sir. It's my pleasure. I'll stay a step behind you and let you do what you need to but just say the word and I'll help any way I can."

The receptionist at the entrance told Steven the offices were on the second floor and that a Mr. Mort Ingersall was in charge of the bookkeepers. When he knocked on the frame of the open door and entered, Steven came face to face with a man who looked like he sampled too much of the company's product. Thin red veins crisscrossed Ingersall's cheeks and his belly hung over his belt.

Steven identified himself and Jimmy, showing his badge and ID. "Mr. Ingersall, we're here about your bookkeeper...."

"Russo! Yeah, he hasn't shown up all week," the manager exclaimed.

"Is this normal behavior for him?"

"No, not at all. He's a good worker. Very reliable. Always on time."

"Have you had any problems with him bothering the girls in the office?" Steven asked.

"There aren't any girls up here. We're all men in this office."

"Who does he pal around with?"

"No one special. A group of us eats lunch together."

"What does he have to say for himself?"

"Not a lot. He's pleasant, friendly, but he doesn't talk much about himself. I know he's married. That's about it."

"Can you tell me where he stays when he's in Syracuse?"

"One of the boarding houses on Park Street. I don't know which one. What's going on? What do the police have to do with it?"

"I'm sorry to have to tell you he's dead. He was killed Sunday."

Ingersall's jaw dropped. "Killed? Was he in an accident?"

"No, sir. We're treating his death as a homicide."

"Good God!"

As Will Taylor had done two days ago at the knitting mill, Jimmy Bou handed the warrant to the office manager then went to search Frankie's desk at the brewery. While Jimmy looked for information that might help with the investigation, Steven questioned Frankie's co-workers. Sadly, both policemen came away with nothing. There was no little book in Syracuse. Worse, no one knew which rooming house was Frankie's home away from home.

"What do we do now, Steven?"

They had returned to the car, where Steven was consulting a street map of the area.

The Syracuse police officer pointed out Park Street. "It's a long street but the boarding houses ought to have a sign out front."

"Right," said Steven. "Let's divide it up but stay within sight of each other. If we leap frog over each other, we can cover several blocks pretty quickly. We'll see what we find."

For the next hour, the three officers knocked on doors and spoke to a dozen landladies. No one knew Frankie Russo.

Chapter 25

"What do you mean he's not here? Isn't he supposed to be working this morning?" Pete had to yell over the clamor of the textile-making machines.

"Yeah," Dickie Hughes's boss shouted back, "but he didn't show." The supervisor shrugged. "Kids these days."

"Does this happen often then?" asked Ralph.

"Well, no," McMillan had the grace to look embarrassed. "No, Dickie's a good worker. Always here on time. Maybe he had something at school this morning."

"What's that all about—school and his job here?"

"It's a work-experience program for his business class. He comes here three days a week for a couple of hours."

"What's the schedule?"

"Monday's a split-shift. He's here an hour early in the morning and an hour after lunch. It's not ideal but he's gotta work around his classes. Wednesdays and Fridays are better. He's here a couple of hours in the morning then he goes to school."

"We'll check the school and see if he's there. Call the station if he shows up."

McMillan nodded. Ralph and Pete were happy to leave the cavernous, noise-filled workplace.

"No, Ralph, it's Wednesday. He's not supposed to be here until eleven-thirty," Mrs. Stoner answered the patrolman's question. "And believe me, Dickie Hughes would never be early for school. You've checked the mill, I suppose?"

"He's not there. We'll go to his house. Maybe he's sick or overslept or something."

"I'm sure that's it, Pete." The high school secretary patted him on the hand. "It's so nice to see you boys once in a while. You made good, after all," she said, admiring their uniforms.

Ralph and Pete looked at each other and smirked.

The two police officers trekked to the opposite side of town and, after twenty minutes, arrived at a weathered clapboard house on the corner of Oak and Second Streets across from the railroad station. They stepped over a broken board in the front steps and climbed to the dilapidated porch. The sounds of a shouting match blew through the screen door.

"Where the hell is he, woman? I swear to God that brat is going to get the beating of his life. I'll kill him!"

A whimpering voice pleaded, "Marvin, please. Maybe you finished the bottle and just forgot."

A resounding smack echoed through the house as a palm hit flesh. "I know when the hell I finish a bottle of booze. Mind your business and get me some breakfast."

Ralph and Pete looked at each other with silent understanding. Domestic disputes were the most dangerous incidents to take on. When a police officer interrupted a fight between family members—especially an abusive husband—you never knew how volatile or potentially fatal it could become. Both officers fingered their nightsticks as Ralph knocked loudly on the doorframe.

The disheveled man who came to the door was smaller than he had sounded but muscles bulged out of a white sleeveless undershirt. He needed a shave and a haircut and had the unlit end of a cigar between his teeth.

"Who the hell are you?" he asked belligerently, hooking a thumb behind his suspenders.

"Police, Mr. Hughes," answered Ralph, who was a head taller and much beefier than this man. He and Pete showed their IDs and badges. "We're looking for your son Dickie."

"Get in line. Whadda ya want him for?"

"We think he may have witnessed something. We want to ask him some questions."

"He ain't here."

"When was the last time you saw him?"

"How the hell should I know? He comes and goes when he likes. You'd think *he* was the one puttin' food on the table." Marvin Hughes coughed up a wad of phlegm and swallowed.

"Do you have any idea where he is? He's not at work or in school."

"Naw. Probably ran away again."

"He's run away before?"

"Yeah, couple a times. I don't know where the hell he goes."

"Is your wife here, Mr. Hughes? Can we talk with her?"

"She's fixin' my breakfast."

"It'll only take a minute, sir." Ralph thought his face was going to break from the fake smile he had plastered on.

Reluctantly, Hughes turned and ambled into the depths of the house. They heard him yelling at his wife to hurry up and get back to the kitchen before his eggs were ruined.

Mrs. Hughes rushed to the screen door. "Is he in trouble?" she asked, wiping her hands on her apron. Her face was strained with worry. She looked as if she might cry. Ralph noticed the red mark on her cheek from the slap they'd heard. He felt a deep sorrow for this woman. It made him furious to see how some men treated their wives. For the life of him, he could not understand it.

165

"No, ma'am," he answered quickly. "We think Dickie saw something that would help us in an investigation. We just want to talk with him."

"I haven't seen him since yesterday. Usually when," she paused and glanced back into the house, then whispered, "things are difficult here he goes to Billy's house for a few days."

"Who's that?"

"His best friend Billy Burton. Lives at the other end of Second, down by the river. He'll be in school though." She brushed a wisp of gray-brown hair out of her eyes.

"Thank you, Mrs. Hughes. And," Ralph whispered, "if you ever need help…" He raised his eyebrows and nodded toward the back of the house. "…we can protect you. You can come to the station day or night. Someone will always be there."

"Shh," she said in a panicked voice, her eyes as wide as saucers. "I'm fine. Everything's fine. I must get back to my husband's breakfast. Let me know when you find Dickie, please. Tell him to come home."

Shaking their heads in frustration, Ralph and Pete hiked the three blocks back to the station.

"I'd like to get my hands on that bastard," Ralph growled. "Catch him alone in a dark alley some night." He slammed a fist into the palm of his hand.

"He'll get his. You can't go through life doing shit like that and get away with it. Don't worry, Ralphie, he's got it comin'. Hey," Pete added, "did you hear what he was yelling about the bottle?"

"Sure did," Ralph said excitedly. "That's two things pointing to Dickie Hughes in those woods. I think we got our witness, Pete!"

The morning was flying by and Ralph and Pete still hadn't brought Dickie Hughes to the station. Will finished the work he was doing and decided to interview Adona. Dickie could wait here until he returned.

"Tommy, I'll be at the knitting mill," Will told the front desk officer.

"When Ralph and Pete come back with Dickie Hughes, make sure they keep an eye on him until I get here. We don't want him sneaking out. He could be our only witness to Frankie Russo's murder."

"Sure thing, Will."

The room that the mill supervisor let Will use was dismal: one small grimy window high on the wall, a bare low-wattage bulb hanging from the ceiling, a wooden table and two hard chairs. Will had a passing acquaintance with Adona Russo. Now, he would use it to his advantage.

She entered with obvious trepidation. Adona Russo did not want to be there.

"Take a seat, Mrs. Russo." Will motioned for her to sit across the table. "Do you remember me from church? I'm Sergeant Will Taylor."

She nodded, eyeing him warily.

"You should know this is an official interview. We need to talk about your relationship with Frankie."

"I did not have a relationship with him. He was my husband's cousin. That's all." She looked everywhere but at him and spoke in a hushed voice. Will had to strain to hear her.

He caught her gaze and saw the fear in her eyes. "Can tell me why you slapped him in the cafeteria the other day? What did he say to you?"

"Nothing. Frankie was always flirting."

"Are you sure it wasn't more than that?" he asked gently.

"Isn't that enough? I'm married."

"Did he threaten you?"

"What could he threaten me about? I didn't do anything."

"We found something that belonged to Frankie, Mrs. Russo. It was a little book where he wrote down the names of his girlfriends." Will explained how the log was set up. "The initial A was in it."

"It's not me!"

"The letter A was written differently than all the others. It said 'Working on A.'"

"I can't listen to this. I won't!"

"I need you to tell me the truth, Adona." Will softened his voice and relaxed his face. "I see you at Mass every Sunday. I know you're a good person. You always do the right thing. Anything you tell me here is exactly like talking with Father Seraphino in confession. As long as it has nothing to do with Frankie's murder, I promise you *nothing* will leave this room. Whatever you say to me, I'll forget I ever heard it. And, Adona, I'm not here to judge you. Your private life is your own. I need to find Frankie's killer."

"I didn't kill him."

"I don't believe you did. But I have to know what happened between you."

Adona Russo was shaking. "Please don't do this. I can't talk about it," she begged, her eyes filling up.

"Then, tell me the truth."

"How do I know I can trust you?"

"You know you can, Adona. You're like me. We sense things about other people. You know you can believe me. You just know it."

Will watched her struggle with the decision. She slumped in her chair as resignation settled over her. He gave her the silence and the space to fully embrace her choice.

"You *swear* no one will ever know. Nick can never know."

"If it has nothing to do with the murder, you have my word."

"It doesn't."

Will saw her steel herself. She gazed at the ceiling, took a deep breath then looked straight at him. He knew how much this was costing her.

"All right."

And she confessed what Will already knew.

"Frankie was always flirting with me. When Nico came back from the war in the wheelchair it got worse. It was easier for Frankie to catch me alone, away from the family. One day in the cafeteria, he said I should give in. He threatened me. He said if I didn't...," She swallowed hard. "...you know, he would tell Nick that we did anyway. That's when I slapped him. The Sunday after that he trapped me in the pantry when we were all at Maria and Vito's house. He tried to force me. I pushed him away. I hit him. I made him stop. But," her face crumbled, "he put his hands on me."

Will thought he had never seen such destruction on anyone's face. *That miserable bastard.*

Adona was openly crying now. Tears dripped onto her gray uniform. She gulped for air. "Frankie was a pig. *Un animale!*" she spat. "I wished him dead." Adona Russo took one more deep breath, nailed him with her emerald eyes, and said, "But I didn't do it."

"Do you think Nick had any idea what Frankie did to you?" Will asked gently.

"No, Frankie acted exactly the same as before." She sobbed quietly, making no attempt to wipe away her tears. "He ruined my life and he acted like nothing happened."

"Did anyone see the two of you together?"

She hung her head as the tears cascaded. "Lucy."

"Lucy?" Will's heart skipped a beat. "Did she say something? What did she do?"

"She was walking into the kitchen when I was coming out of the pantry. She turned around real fast and left. Frankie was behind me. Maybe she didn't see him. Maybe she didn't know," Adona said with some hope in her voice.

"Did she say anything about it to you?"

"No."

"Did Frankie say anything to you in the pantry...afterwards?"

169

"He whispered something but I didn't understand what he was talking about."

"What did he say, Adona?"

"He said *I can stop now*. What is that supposed to mean? *È pazzo!* He's crazy!"

It was the confirmation Will wanted. He believed that Frankie Russo had fallen in love for the first time in his life—with a woman in Syracuse. But for some strange reason, because of a peculiar flaw in his make-up, he needed to fulfill a kind of depraved wish list. A catalog of girls that he had to conquer. And Adona Russo was the last one on that list. That's why there were no more letters in his little book.

Except L—his wife—and S—the love of his life.

Chapter 26

Wednesday – Present Day

Olivia woke Wednesday morning to birds singing and the sun shining. She jumped out of bed, her mind still full of yesterday's adventure in Steven's time. She ate a light breakfast, played with her kitten, and, after reading her newspapers with a second cup of coffee, went into her office to work. A little after nine, she headed out to the YMCA for her kickboxing class.

Liz and Sophie arrived at noon for lunch and, what Liz called, a debriefing.

"Well, it looks like you had another successful experiment," Liz said, opening a bottle of sparkling water and handing it to Sophie who poured three glasses.

"It was awesome."

Olivia set a salad and a baguette on the table and they each picked a chair.

"I decided something yesterday," Sophie said, tearing off a hunk of French bread. "I trust you, Olivia. And I'm happy you've found someone you like so much and get along with. *And* who likes adventures the way you do. I'm not going to worry any more."

Liz and Olivia raised their eyebrows. "Wow!"

Olivia rose, ran around the table, and gave Sophie a big hug.

"Thank you. I really appreciate that, Soph. I'm having so much fun with this, I want to share everything with you guys."

"I agree with Sophie," said Liz, as Olivia regained her chair. "No more worrying." She tasted her salad. "Mmm, this is good. Did you do something different today?"

"I threw in some arugula."

"I like it, too," said Sophie.

Liz paused with her fork in the air, as if a thought had struck her. "Olivia, how come you never googled Steven? It seems like something you'd do."

Olivia nodded. "Yeah, it is. I thought about it when we first met but, by the time I got around to it, I changed my mind."

"Why?" said Sophie.

"I was getting to know him in the normal way, over time. And I was starting to like him. I was afraid I'd find his obituary."

Liz and Sophie shuddered.

"Oh, that would've been awful," Sophie exclaimed.

"I couldn't have taken that. I realized I didn't want to know anything in advance."

"I totally get that," Liz said.

"I don't even want to *think* about it," Olivia said. "Let's talk about something else."

"Clothes!" Sophie exclaimed. "All those beautiful clothes you get to wear now."

"I have to confess," Liz went on. "I'm a bit envious. I'd love to go with you to see what people are wearing."

"I've got an idea," Olivia said. "Why don't I bring some of Steven's mother's clothes here to my house? I'm going to need more outfits and I always get dressed in my room anyway. It would save me from bringing one outfit at a time the night before."

"That'd be so much fun!" said Sophie.

"I've died and gone to heaven," swooned Liz. "What about Friday for our girls' night? We can come back here after the pub."

"Perfect," said the other two.

"Do you think Steven will mind you taking his mother's clothes?" Liz asked.

"I doubt it but I'll ask him first."

"Tell us about yesterday," Sophie asked excitedly.

"Did you meet anybody or talk to anyone?" Liz added.

"I don't know where to begin." Olivia thought back to the moment when Steven's car disappeared up the street. "When Steven left, I went out on the porch to take in the neighborhood. I've gotten so used to being in his house it doesn't seem all that different anymore." She sipped her Perrier. "But, when I'm outside I feel the impact again. The best way I can think to describe it is things today seem glossier, more polished. Back then, even though most of the houses on my street were pretty new, everything seemed rougher. Does that make any sense?"

"I think so," Sophie said.

"What was it like early in the morning?" Liz asked.

Olivia described the paperboy on his bike and the milk man.

"Milk man," Sophie exclaimed. "I heard my grandparents talk about those days. How funny. There's a sort of disconnect going on here."

"I'm glad you said that, Sophie. That's exactly the way I feel sometimes when I'm there. Like I slipped and the whole world flipped upside down in that second."

"So, did you meet anybody?" Liz asked again.

Olivia told them about Frankie Russo's murder. "I called Helen to offer my condolences. It's her sister who was married to him. She came over and we had tea and talked."

"What's it like talking with a woman from that time?" Liz asked.

173

"Our conversation was all about family stuff because of the murder. She talked about her sister Lucy and how she loves to work but Helen likes to be home." Olivia chewed some salad. "That reminds me, I forgot to tell you something she said Sunday night in the pub."

"What's that?" Sophie asked.

"She called herself a *housewife*."

"A what?" Both Liz and Sophie gaped.

"A housewife. She said she didn't understand how her sister was so passionate about working when all she'd ever wanted was to marry her husband—that's Steven's friend Artie—have children, and be a housewife."

"Well, it was that generation, I suppose. That's the way they thought," Liz commented.

"That's the way things were back then," Sophie agreed.

"I'm glad we live now. I'll always respect a woman's choice but that's the point. We have *choices*," Olivia said.

"When are you going back next?" Liz asked.

"Tomorrow. I told Steven I want to wander around town and explore Woolworth's. I'm going to buy some things for us."

"Ooh, I'm going to get a present from 1934?" Sophie sparkled. "Thanks, Olivia."

"You sure know the way to my heart," said Liz, the vintage enthusiast.

Chapter 27

Wednesday – April 25, 1934

Since the trip to Syracuse had taken longer than Steven had anticipated, he decided to interview Dickie Hughes first and speak with Hannah later. When he and Jimmy Bou entered the station, Tommy Forester informed him that Ralph and Pete were still out looking for Dickie Hughes.

"What? Are you saying they've been looking for him since this morning?" Steven exclaimed, consulting his watch. "That's more than five hours, Tommy. Have they reported in?"

"Yes, Detective Blackwell. Once. They stopped on their way to the high school. They said he never showed up for his job at the mill. I don't know where they are now."

Steven frowned. He did not like the sound of this at all. He regretted not looking harder for the boy last night. *Damn. Don't let this happen.*

"What about Sergeant Taylor, Tommy?" he asked.

"He's gone to the knitting mill. Oh! I almost forgot. Gray Wilson dropped off the crime scene photos a while ago. I put them on your desk," Tommy said, efficient as ever. "And you got a telephone call from a…," he picked up a piece of paper and read, "Lieutenant Fred Schultz at the Syracuse Police Department. He wants you to call him

175

back as soon as you can."

Steven spread the stack of black-and-white, eight-by-ten photographs across the surface of his desk. He ate his first sandwich standing up while he looked through them. As always, the pictures were sharp and clear. Steven sorted them into four piles—one of the victim, one of the area surrounding Frankie Russo, a third that showed the path up to the field, and finally, the field itself. Steven scrutinized each photograph. He grabbed his magnifying glass to check a detail here and there. Nothing jumped out at him. He had seen everything there was to see when he'd actually been at the scene two days ago.

As he was tacking the best shots to the wooden frame surrounding the murder board, Tommy came in with a large envelope in his hand. "Doc Elliott sent his autopsy report over. Hank's report from the lab's in here, too."

"Swell, Tommy. Thanks. Leave it on my desk," Steven replied, as he pinned up the final photograph. While he was standing there, he decided to update the information with notes from this morning's work in Syracuse. Sadly, there wasn't much to write and he finished in a couple minutes.

Steven returned to his desk and sat down, poured the rest of the coffee from his thermos, and pulled a half-dozen pages from the manila envelope. The first thing he saw was a small handwritten note attached to the top page with a paper clip. It said:

Sorry for the delay, Steven. We had a bit of a
problem during the Marsh test yesterday when
we were analyzing the tissue samples of the two
birds. A minor explosion with one of the glass vials.
Not to worry though. We got it done in the end.
  Doc

Steven marveled at the mysteries of the forensics lab and what

Hank was able to accomplish, often assisted by the ME. He thanked his lucky stars they even *had* a lab. Mr. Hoover had established the federal crime lab at the Bureau of Investigation in Washington, D.C. a mere two years ago and that was the first one Steven had heard of. Although maybe in big cities they already had them. He had no idea. He considered himself lucky that Oneida County had seen fit to follow suit last year.

Steven extracted Hank's lab report first. Most of it was mumbo jumbo. He had no background in chemistry. He skimmed the details: *...sample containing arsenic, sulphuric acid, arsenic-free zinc...results showed arsine gas...ignited...transformed into pure metallic arsenic.* He jumped to Hank's conclusion at the bottom of the page—the birds were poisoned with arsenic.

Steven considered the implications of this. The most important thing was they now had proof that the field was the scene of the crime. In order for the two birds to have been poisoned, Frankie must have also been poisoned in the meadow. That seemed to be the only way for the birds to have ingested it. This also lent credibility to the picnic theory. Both Frankie and the birds ate something loaded with arsenic.

While his mind was on poison, Steven put aside the rest of Hank's report and skipped to Doc's conclusions. Much of it was what the ME had told him on the phone Monday afternoon. Frankie had ingested a large quantity of arsenic. The time of death had not changed. Steven continued reading. When he came to the last item in the report, excitement surged through him. Doc had found some crumbs in Frankie's shirt pocket and speculated that they came from something Frankie had eaten Sunday. Tests showed they held traces of arsenic and came from a item prepared with apples. Doc had written "most likely bread, cake, or muffins." *I bet a lot of people around town have apples left from last fall,* Steven thought. *Maybe not much of a clue after all.*

Having learned everything he could from Doc, Steven flipped back to the remainder of Hank's forensic report. His breath caught when he read what Hank had discovered about the fibers found on a bush near the crime scene. They were 100% wool. They'd been dyed red and blue. Hank had written that whatever they came from probably had some sort of pattern on it. Steven immediately knew that this information would be crucial if the police came across a red-and-blue wool blanket. Was this case finally taking on momentum? He hoped so.

Steven went back to the murder board, grabbed the chalk, and added the autopsy and forensics results. The lists of facts and evidence were growing. He stared at the board and let the information settle into the compartments of his mind. Then, he returned to his desk to write up his report on the Syracuse trip. *Syracuse. Oh no!* He had forgotten to telephone Fred Schultz. He grabbed the receiver and dialed the Syracuse Police Department. A desk sergeant informed him that his friend was out. He didn't know when he was expected to return. Steven left a message for Lieutenant Schultz to call him back.

Ralph, Pete, and Will all returned to the station at the same time. Ralph and Pete grabbed their lunches and followed Will to the CID room, trailed by Jimmy Bou, always eager to be in on the action. Steven was on the telephone, so the four officers headed straight for the murder board, eager to see what was new. Munching their sandwiches, they read Steven's updates.

"Something with apples," Ralph said. "Everybody's got apples in the cellar. That's not gonna get us anywhere."

"At least we know the birds ate it, too. That's something," commented Jimmy Bou, always full of optimism.

Ray, Charlie, and Jerry walked in and joined the team for what was turning into an impromptu briefing.

"Red-and-blue wool fibers," read Charlie. "I bet Frankie Russo *was* having a picnic with a girl on a blanket. That sounds like a blanket, doesn't it?" The newest officer did not hesitate to voice his opinion.

"I think so," said Will. "It makes sense."

"Will, how did you make out with Adona this morning?" Steven asked, putting down the receiver and joining the group.

"She's the A in Frankie's notebook. It seems that Frankie had been after her for some time. He finally cornered her in the pantry when the whole Russo clan was at Maria and Vito's house a week ago Sunday—Vito's Nick's brother. Adona said she fought him off but during the struggle he managed to get his hands on her."

Jimmy Bou gasped looking horrified.

"Bastard," spat Ralph.

"If there ever was a guilt-ridden, tortured soul, Adona Russo is it. I felt sorry for her. But I don't think she had anything to do with killing him."

"That's another one off our list," enthused Pete. "We're getting there."

"Here's the crucial bit," said Will. "Lucy saw them."

The entire team gasped this time.

"Her motive just got stronger," said Ray.

All seven men nodded.

"Okay, Adona Russo is off our list," said Steven, erasing her name from the murder board. He looked at Ralph and Pete. "It looks like you struck out with Dickie Hughes. You haven't found him yet?"

"No, we went to the mill, the school, and his house. His mother said that some nights he stays at his pal Billy Burton's house. He doesn't let her know because they don't have a telephone," said Ralph.

"When we showed up, she thought he was in trouble," said Pete. "She took one look at our uniforms and got upset. She wanted to know why the police were looking for him, what he did."

"We calmed her down as much as we could," added Ralph. "But I don't know if it did any good. She was pretty jumpy when we left."

"All right," Steven said. "After you're done eating, I want you to find Billy Burton and bring him in. Maybe he knows where Dickie is. I'll send a few more men out to look, too. We need to find this kid."

Ralph told Steven and the team about Dickie Hughes's father—what he'd said, how he'd acted toward his son, and the way he had treated his wife. Everyone in the group reacted strongly. Frowns, shaking of heads, and Ray Monroe punched a fist into the palm of his hand.

"I learned a thing or two during my stint in the Army during the war. I'd like to get my hands on that bastard. I'll show him what it feels like to be slapped around."

Understanding that the men had to blow off steam every once in a while, and that Ray's comment had been only talk, Steven said nothing. He popped the last bite of his second sandwich in his mouth and followed it with a swig of coffee. "Ray, now that we know for sure Frankie was poisoned with arsenic, I'd like you to work on that. Check the people on our suspect list." Steven nodded in the direction of the murder board. "Find out who has poison at home—in a carriage house, shed, cellar, wherever—and who recently bought some. Go back about six months for purchases."

"You got it, Steven."

Tommy Forester rushed in, panting. "Detective...Blackwell." He took a deep breath. "They found Dickie Hughes. He's dead."

"Nooo." Steven cried. He spun around to face Ralph and Pete. "Find Billy Burton *now!*"

When Steven arrived at the scene with Will, Jimmy Bou, Charlie and Jerry, he was surprised to see Doc and Gray already there. They stood about thirty feet apart on a path that ran along the river, waving away a few curious onlookers, protecting the area.

"How'd you two get here so fast?" he asked.

"We were at Mother's eating lunch. Herb Steadman ran in shouting he'd found a body in the river," said Doc.

"Where is Mr. Steadman?"

"He was real shook up, Steven. I told him to stay there, have a cup of tea, and try to calm down. I said one of your officers would be over to interview him."

"Will, would you?"

"Got him."

While Jimmy Bou secured the scene and Gray took photographs, Steven sketched the hard-packed dirt path, chest-high bushes, and sweeping drag marks leading to the victim. He drew the inert body of Dickie Hughes, face down on the river's edge, his shoulders and head in the water. Lastly, he added the willow branches that gently skimmed ripples on the surface on either side of the victim.

"Are you ready, Steven? We'll turn him over," asked the ME, when the photographer had finished.

Doc enlisted Charlie's help and they carefully rolled the body face-up.

Dickie Hughes's unseeing eyes looked up at them.

"This is heartbreaking," commented Gray Wilson, as he took his final shots of the boy. "Hasn't even had a chance at life yet."

Steven shook his head, not trusting himself to speak. He was furious at himself for not following up properly last night. He should have told Ralph and Pete to keep looking until they found the kid. It was basic police work. What had he been thinking? Now, he'd lost his only eye-witness. He ignored the embarrassing realization that his first thought had been that of Dickie Hughes as their witness to a murder rather than Dickie, a boy whose short life had been snuffed out. Was he becoming jaded? At only 33?

"Jimmy, we're going to need to search Dickie Hughes's bedroom.

Get back to the station and talk to the chief. Let him know what we've got here and ask him if he'll get us a search warrant. There's a new form that we're using now. It should go fast if he can catch Judge Randolph. I want you to wait at the station then find me. If we're lucky, I'll still be at the Hughes's house."

Steven turned to the MD. "What do you think, Doc?"

"It looks like he was hit on the side of the head with something heavy. Here, see by his temple? It was rough, too. Notice these scratches."

"Was that what killed him, Doc? A blow to the head?"

"I won't know until I check his lungs for water. He might have been knocked unconscious then drowned. I can tell you it was probably late last night though. I'll get you the results soon as I can."

As the coroner's van removed the body and Doc and Gray left the scene, Steven saw Will striding down the path. He was eager to hear what his partner had learned from Herb Steadman.

"Herb Steadman was walking his dog," said Will. "Georgie—that's the dog, a cocker spaniel—took off so fast that he pulled the leash out of Herb's hand. Herb followed him down to the water. Said Georgie was barking up a storm. Herb grabbed the dog and hurried to Mother's where he knew there'd be a telephone. That's when he called us. He said that Doc and Gray rushed out when he told them what he'd found. Was it Dickie, Steven?"

Steven nodded.

"Poor kid. Did you find anything?"

Steven pointed to the ground. "We've got these drag marks down to where the body was. It looked like the killer held him by his feet and his torso made the impressions in the dirt." Steven looked grim. "I didn't see any footprints. There were no scraps of paper, nothing on the body. If there *was* anything on his upper body, it got washed away by the river."

Steven bent his head and ran his fingers through his hair. "I'll bet it was Dickie drinking and smoking in that spot near the field. The killer saw him. She had to protect herself so he had to go."

"I hope we don't have two killers out there, Steven. What if this has nothing to do with Frankie's death?" Charlie asked, sounding worried.

Steven shook his head. "I don't think so."

Steven and his team returned to the motor car.

"Will, would you handle the canvas? Maybe Dickie or the killer left something behind. Maybe you'll find a witness." He turned to Charlie and Jerry. "You fellas work with Will."

As Steven climbed in his motor car, he said to his partner, "I'll notify Mr. and Mrs. Hughes. I sent Jimmy to get a warrant for Dickie's room. I'll see you back at the station later." Steven frowned and shook his head in sorrow. "I hope Ralph and Pete found Billy Burton and have him at the station right now. Because if Dickie Hughes told his friend what he saw, that boy's life is in danger, too."

Chapter 28

Steven left the river to perform the most difficult duty in police work—informing Dickie Hughes's parents that their son was dead. He berated himself all the way to the house. He should have known better. He should have found the boy. He'd have to live with this guilt for the rest of his life. He vowed never to make the same mistake again.

Steven knocked on the frame of a flimsy door. From somewhere deep in the house, a man yelled, "Get the damn door, woman!"

A middle-aged woman in a faded housedress appeared on the other side of the screen. Steven showed his badge and ID and identified himself.

"Have you found him? He still hasn't come home." Mrs. Hughes's face was creased with deep worry lines.

"Can I come in, ma'am?"

She led him to a sagging sofa in the sparsely furnished front room.

"Would you get your husband, please? He needs to be here."

Dickie Hughes's mother whimpered and fingered the edges of her apron but said nothing. She left then returned with her husband. After they were seated, Steven broke the news.

"I'm very sorry for your loss."

Mrs. Hughes let out a wail. "Nooooo." She sobbed. "Not my baby. Not Dickie." Her hands shook as she wiped the flood of tears. Her jaw trembled so badly she could barely speak. "What...what...." She sucked in a breath. "What happened?"

Marvin Hughes sat in stony silence staring at Steven, his mouth clamped shut.

"We don't know yet. We found him down by the river. It appears he was hit on the head. It would have been very quick, Mrs. Hughes. I don't think he knew what happened," Steven added hurriedly, as Dickie's mother tensed in a transferal of pain for her son. "We'll know more tomorrow."

Steven made an effort to learn something of the victim's life, routine, and friends but soon realized Dickie Hughes had not had a close relationship with either of his parents. They could tell him nothing he didn't already know.

There was a knock on the front door. Mrs. Hughes left the parlor and returned with Jimmy Bou.

"Detective Sergeant Blackwell, I have your warrant." Jimmy handed the paperwork to Steven.

"Warrant?" Marvin Hughes scowled. "What the hell for?"

"I need to search Dickie's room. It may help us find out who did this to your son," Steven answered, his voice brooking no argument. He handed the warrant to Mrs. Hughes, who passed it to her husband.

"Where is his room, please?"

Mrs. Hughes pointed to a hallway on the left.

"Thank you. While I'm gone, Officer Bourgogne has some questions about your missing whiskey bottle, Mr. Hughes. If you don't mind."

Marvin Hughes grunted.

Steven took Jimmy aside, whispered something, then headed down the hall to Dickie's bedroom. Poor Jimmy Bou. This was going to be a difficult interview.

A half hour later, Steven and Jimmy climbed into Steven's Chevy and headed back to the station.

"What did you find out, Jimmy?"

"I think the Old Crow bottle is his. Mr. Hughes said there was a half-bottle left after he had a few drinks Saturday night. When he went to pour his Sunday drinks, the bottle was gone. He said Dickie took it before. Wouldn't be surprised if he'd done it again. He was real mad."

"Did he say anything about his son's murder?"

"Nope, not a thing. Dickie was our witness, wasn't he, Steven?"

"Everything points to it so far. Let's hope he told Billy Burton what he saw and Ralph and Pete have him back at the station."

"Did you find anything in Dickie's room?" Jimmy asked eagerly.

"Nothing. And I think that'll turn out to be important, Jimmy. When I say *nothing*, that's exactly what I mean. Dickie's closet and dresser had been cleaned out. They were empty. No shirts, no pants, no underclothes, or socks. I have a feeling Dickie Hughes was running away for good this time."

"I bet he got scared when he heard Frankie was murdered. Maybe he thought the killer saw him."

"If we can talk with Billy Burton, we might find out."

Steven got his wish. As soon as they entered the police station lobby, Tommy Forester blurted out the good news.

"We've got Billy!" he said excitedly. "Ralph and Pete brought him in a while ago. Nobody said anything about Dickie."

"Thanks, Tommy. Where is he?"

"One of the patrolmen is babysitting him in Interview 1," Tommy said, then added, "Ralph and Pete went out again. They said they were going to the bus depot."

Steven poked his head in the interview room. "Bring Billy to CID."

Dickie Hughes's best friend was tall and had a head full of coarse, dark brown curls. He dropped into the chair Steven indicated. "I didn't do anything. Why'd ya have to send your goons after me at school?" He tapped his heel repeatedly.

"You're not here because you did anything wrong, Billy," Steven said. "We need your help with an investigation."

"Frankie Russo."

"That's right. We need to know what Dickie told you."

"Why don't you ask him?"

"We're asking you, Billy. Dickie saw it, didn't he?"

"Yeah," he frowned at his shoes. "He said at first he didn't know she killed him. When we heard they found the body, he figured it out."

"Who, Billy?"

"I don't know. He wouldn't tell me." Billy continued staring at his shoes, only glancing up to make eye contact for fleeting moments.

"What did he tell you?"

"He was up in the woods smokin' and drinkin' his old man's whiskey when he saw 'em. Frankie Russo and some dame."

"Did he say who she was?"

"No, I asked him but he wouldn't tell me."

"Okay, so Dickie saw Frankie Russo and a woman up in the field," Steven prompted.

"Yeah, Frankie carried a picnic basket. She had a blanket. They sat down on the blanket and ate lunch. Dickie said it was a real feast." Billy's stomach growled as if to punctuate the idea. "They had beer, too."

"What time was it, Billy?"

"Around noon."

"All right, go on."

"That's it. He watched 'em for a while. Then, Frankie got sick. Dickie said he puked all over the grass. The girl wrapped him in the blanket and dragged him over to the woods—you know, the other side of the field?"

"I understand. Then what?"

"She dumped him over the hill. Dickie said that was it. She took her stuff and left."

"Any idea what time she left?"

"No. Dickie swore he didn't know Frankie was dead. Thought maybe they had a fight and…." He screwed up his face as if struggling to make sense of it.

"That's all right, Billy. You did swell. Would you like a soda pop?" Steven asked.

"No, why? Where's Dickie?" Worry and confusion invaded his face. The tapping got louder.

"Just another minute, Billy. Tell me about Dickie and his father."

"What's that got to do with anything?"

"Are they close?"

Billy snorted. "Only when Mr. Hughes beats the crap out of him. The rest of the time Dickie stays as far away from his old man as he can. Guy's a bastard."

"He comes to stay at your house when that happens, right?"

"Yeah, he's at my house most of the time lately."

"When's the last time you saw Dickie, Billy?"

"Yesterday afternoon at school."

"Tell me what else he told you. About his plans, I mean."

Billy Burton gave a deep sigh. "He was leavin'. He couldn't take it anymore. Said he screwed up his courage and asked her for some money. Enough so he could get out of town and never come back."

"He told the killer what he saw?" Steven's breath caught. *Dickie Hughes signed his death warrant when he tried to blackmail the killer. That poor kid.*

"Yeah, said he'd make sure she knew she could trust him, see? He was gonna tell her that he'd *never* tell. *Ever!* He was goin' far away. He was gonna tell her she'd never hear from him again. He just had to get out of that house before his old man killed him."

"When did he talk to the killer? Where?"

"I don't know. Must'a been after Monday though, right? Everybody was talkin' about Frankie bein' dead behind the school. Dickie said he was gonna pack his stuff and come over to my house Tuesday night after he got the money from her." Billy Burton drooped in his seat. "He didn't come," he whispered in a thin voice filled with sadness. He stopped tapping the floor. "Is Dickie in trouble? You're makin' me scared."

Steven told him as gently as he could. A moan escaped from deep in Billy's throat. Tears flowed freely, covering his crumbled face. His jaw quivered. "Who's going to be my friend now?" He bent over with his head in his hands and sobbed like a baby.

Chapter 29

"Jimmy, I want to see this all laid out. I need a timeline."

Steven and Jimmy Bou were alone in the CID room. Will hadn't returned from the canvas at the river. He hoped Ralph and Pete were making progress tracing Frankie's movements on Sunday and that they'd found his suitcase. He'd sent a patrolman to escort Billy Burton home, armed with a warning and instructions for his parents to keep him in the house until the police told them otherwise. They could not know for sure how much danger the boy was in and, until the killer was caught and behind bars, they couldn't take any chances with his safety.

Steven moved to the murder board and spun it to the flip side. With Jimmy Bou looking over his shoulder, he grabbed a piece of chalk and logged what Billy Burton had told them, then stepped back to assess the information.

```
                   DICKIE HUGHES — TIMELINE
Sunday lunchtime   Smoking, drinking in woods near field
                   Witnesses Frankie Russo having picnic
                   with female
                   Watches her drag FR to edge and dump
                   into ravine
                   Doesn't realize FR is dead
```

```
Monday morning        FR's body discovered
                      Kids at school learn FR's dead, body
                      behind school
                      DH realizes he saw a murder--and the
                      killer
Monday afternoon      DH working at mill
        Dickie Hughes blackmails - killer WHEN???WHERE???
Tuesday afternoon
                      Tells BB he's leaving town with money
                      from the killer

Tuesday night         DH murdered
```

"Okay, Jimmy, sometime between lunchtime Monday and Tuesday afternoon, Dickie blackmailed the killer. Who would he have seen and talked to during that time?"

"He'd want to talk in private. Do you think he saw the killer in person or did he call?"

"There was no phone at the Hughes's house. And money in that family is tight. He wouldn't have the extra nickel to use a public telephone. Let's say he spoke to the person face to face," said Steven. "When Will and I saw him at the mill Monday afternoon, he was already acting nervous and jumpy."

"So, Dickie heard at school Frankie was murdered and realized what he saw."

"Right. The question is when did he decide on blackmail? If it was right away, then he had time to find the killer either at school or at the mill on Monday. Maybe he was jumpy because he already talked with her," Steven said.

"Or, maybe he was getting up his nerve and he was scared."

"He had every reason to be afraid, Jimmy. The kid must have been desperate to go through with that harebrained plan."

Steven turned back to the board. To the right of his timeline, he made two columns. He wrote *Knightsbridge Knitting Mill* atop the first one and listed the secretaries in Frankie's office. The second column was headed *Knightsbridge High School.*

"Steven, hang on a minute." Jimmy grabbed the telephone. "Hello, Mrs. Stoner, this is Officer Jimmy Bourgogne...I'm fine, ma'am. Thank you...How are you?...Mrs. Stoner, can you tell me who Dickie Hughes's teachers are this year, please?...Sure, I'll wait." A moment later, he put down the receiver and told Steven, "He's got Mrs. Sweeney for history, Mrs. Russo—English, Mr. Howard's mathematics, and his business teacher is Mr. Cartwright."

Steven wrote the names of the two women. "Mrs. Sweeney isn't our killer. And unless he went to the Russos' house, Lucy's out. She's on bereavement leave this week." Steven narrowed his eyes and frowned. Then it occurred to him. "Jimmy, he could have talked to *any* of the high school teachers or staff. A guidance counselor, a physical education teacher, a secretary. Anybody."

Jimmy's face fell. They were swimming with potential suspects.

A noise behind him caused Steven to turn around. Ray had returned from visiting suppliers of rat poison and items containing arsenic. Will entered on his heels, trailed by Charlie and Jerry, back from their canvas at the river. Will set a dirty white duffle bag on his desk.

"We found this tucked under the brush near the base of a tree, Steven. It's Dickie Hughes's."

Will opened the draw string and extracted a pair of pants, two shirts, some underwear, socks, a photograph of Mrs. Hughes, and a bus schedule."

"It looks like he was planning to leave town," said Charlie. "The schedule lists buses to Albany, New York City, Syracuse, Buffalo, and a few out of state."

Steven told them about his interview with Billy Burton and explained what he and Jimmy Bou had been discussing. "I think

Dickie Hughes was killed because he witnessed the murder and tried to blackmail the killer. We've got two homicides, now, but we also have a whole new set of circumstances that might help solve them." Steven turned. "Charlie and Jerry, how are you fellas coming along with the Russo family interviews?"

"We're almost done," Charlie answered. "We can prove what everyone's told us. The family always goes to St. Joe's for eight-o'clock Mass Sunday mornings—they take turns driving Nick and Adona. He can't drive anymore and Adona doesn't know how. That's all been verified. And we've got a lot of people who saw them all at church."

"And, we've got independent sources who can vouch for everybody's movements in the afternoon and evening," said Jerry.

"It looks like they're all clear, Steven," added Charlie.

"All right, finish up and get your reports in today before you leave." Both officers nodded and headed to the patrol room. Steven heard them discussing how they were going to tackle their final interview.

"Ray, write your report on the arsenic and rat poison purchases before you do anything else. Then, I want you to find out what kind of beer Frankie Russo drank and who bought some of that brand last week."

"Sure thing, Steven."

"I know it's getting late but get as much done as you can before you leave. Maybe the killer slipped up and didn't buy the beer until a day or two before the picnic. Maybe she couldn't have it sitting around the house for some reason."

"But, Steven," interrupted Jimmy Bou. "What if it was Lucy Russo? She could have had it in her icebox for a while."

"That's a fair point." Steven thought a moment. "Jimmy, prepare a warrant to search for any kind of beer at Lucy and Frankie's house. Be sure you include empty beer bottles. I want Ray to be able to search the house, outside in the shed, and in the garbage. You'll need to list all those places so he can look everywhere on the property."

Jimmy Bou looked wide-eyed at this responsibility. He said with a hitch in his voice, "Steven, I've only done a couple of warrants so far."

"I know but it's part of your training. Don't worry. You're going to have the chief look at it before you take it to Judge Randolph. I'll have a word with Chief Thompson before I leave. You'll be fine. Just take your time."

Steven and Will returned to their desks. "Will, I need to get to the high school before the teachers leave. I want to talk with Hannah Grantham about that lie of hers." He pursed his lips. "I want to see what our suspect list looks like by the end of the day. Are we seriously considering Hannah? Isn't the mysterious S or a recent girlfriend more likely?"

"Or is Lucy still our number one choice?" Will added.

"Right," Steven said. "As much as I hate to say it, it looks bad for her." He turned to leave. "While I'm at the school, I'll talk with Mrs. Sweeney, too. Maybe she saw Dickie Hughes with one of the female staff Monday afternoon. Maybe she noticed something out of the ordinary that'll point us in a direction."

"What do you want me to do?"

"Trace Dickie Hughes's movements in as much detail as possible. From Monday morning when he left his house until he was killed Tuesday night. We need to know where he went, what he did, who he saw, who he talked to. Especially any women he talked with from early afternoon Monday until late Tuesday afternoon. That's the only time he could have spoken to the killer to try out his blackmail scheme."

"You got it. I'll work later tonight."

"Thanks." Steven added, "Maybe I'll have something for you, too. If Mrs. Sweeney or someone else at the school noticed him...you never know."

By the time Steven arrived at Knightsbridge High School and pulled open the heavy front door, he could tell classes had ended for the day. The building had that empty feeling. He headed upstairs and, as he rounded a corner, barreled into Mrs. Sweeney.

"Oh, Mrs. Sweeney, I'm sorry. Are you all right? I'm in too much of a hurry."

The short stout teacher laughed. "It'll take more than a little bump to knock me off my feet, Steven. No harm done."

"Can I talk to you for a few minutes? Are you leaving?"

"Unfortunately not. I've still got at least a half-hour of grading papers. You're here about that poor boy Dickie Hughes, I bet."

"Yes, ma'am."

"Let's go down to my room," she suggested.

Steven trailed her down the long unlit hallway into a large room with sunshine pouring through an entire wall of windows. "Wow, what a difference," he exclaimed.

"Yes, I asked for this classroom when I came here. It's a happy place." She sat behind her battered wooden desk. Maps of the United States and Europe covered one wall. Tacked on another were posters of famous American landmarks in major cities—New York's brand new Empire State Building and the Statue of Liberty, the Capital Building and Washington Monument in Washington, D.C., and a cable car climbing a hill in San Francisco with a bridge under construction in the background. "How can I help you?"

Steven pulled his notebook and a pencil from his pocket. "First of all, when is Dickie's class with you?"

"It's the last one of the day. Starts at one thirty and ends at two twelve. He was here Monday and Tuesday."

"Did you by any chance see him hanging around after school on

Monday?"

She gazed off and murmured, "Monday." Her face brightened. "Yes, as a matter of fact I did. He was going down the front steps when I left. That was unusual because Dickie's normally out the door when the final bell rings."

"What time was that?"

"My work was caught up so I left after my tutoring session. It would have been three fifteen or a little after."

"Do you have any idea why Dickie would have stayed late? Was he involved in a student organization? A club? Sports team?"

"Dickie?" she laughed wryly. "Let me tell you about Dickie Hughes. I'm guessing you want to know what he was like," she said with raised brows.

Steven grinned and nodded. He had always believed his former second-grade teacher could read people's minds. He had adored Mrs. Sweeney with the blind love of a child. She still held a special place in his heart after all these years. Despite the sad circumstances, he was happy to see her.

"Dickie was a misfit, Steven. He didn't belong anywhere, not in any of the groups that kids gravitate to. You know what I mean. There are the sports-minded kids, the so-called smart kids, the kids who are put on a pedestal and labeled *popular* for some unfathomable reason. He had one friend," she said sadly.

"Yes, I spoke with Billy Burton a little while ago."

She nodded. "He'll be devastated of course. Those two were joined at the hip. Dickie had a terrible time at home. I always suspected his father beat him. I've no proof, of course, or I would have done something. It seemed like no matter what he did, that child could *not* get a break at home or in school. I remember when he was seven—that's before I switched to teaching high school, of course—he was in my class. Such a sweet child. And smart, too. But, he was troubled even then. He struggled every day. A child shouldn't have to live like that." She spat the last sentence out. Steven couldn't remember ever seeing her angry. The smile lines at her mouth turned down. "Nothing ever went his way. He got blamed for things he didn't do or that were out of his control. Eventually he filled up with anger. Such potential. All gone." Her normally sparkling blue eyes deadened and she pronounced, "It's an unspeakable waste of a life."

Steven's interview with Mrs. Sweeney had produced one of those moments in police work that he tried to guard against—too much sympathy for the victim. He couldn't let his emotions distract him from concentrating all his energy and thoughts on solving the case. Nevertheless, at this moment Steven felt a profound sense of loss and outrage at the murder of Dickie Hughes. This poor boy who had struggled so with life no longer had a chance to turn things around for himself. Mrs. Sweeney's words echoed in his mind. It *was* an unspeakable waste.

He shoved his feelings out of the way and doubled his determination to find Dickie's killer. Then, he would put that person behind bars for as long as possible. For life, if there was any justice in the world.

Steven left Mrs. Sweeney grading her stack of papers and strode down the hall toward Hannah Grantham's classroom.

"Hi, Hannah. Still hard at work I see," Steven said entering the bright room.

"Steven," she exclaimed. "What are you doing here?"

"I want to know why you lied to me the other day."

"About what?" she asked.

"Your relationship with Frankie. I know you were seeing him after he married Lucy."

She cast her eyes down. "Yes, you're right. I'm sorry. I was embarrassed. Stepping out with a married man." She looked up and gave him a steady gaze. "It doesn't have anything to do with your case, Steven. I didn't want you to think badly of me."

"All right. Don't lie to me again, Hannah," he said. "Now, I have some more questions for you. Where were you last night?"

"Last night? Why?" Hannah frowned.

He told her about Dickie Hughes.

"Oh, yes." Her brows drew together and she winced. "That poor boy." She looked genuinely sorry. "I heard it was an accident. He drowned or fell into the river."

"No, Hannah, he was murdered."

She gasped. "No! He was a nice kid—bit of a misfit—but a nice boy. I had him in class last year. What time do you need to know about?"

"Why don't you tell me from the end of the school day until you went to bed?"

"Okay," she said. "After school, I had play practice. I'm holding rehearsals from three to five, Monday through Thursday now. We're working extra because opening night's next week." She rose and went to open a window. "I love the breeze I get in this room. Heavenly." She turned back to Steven. "Let's see…I got home around five thirty. I fixed supper for Mother and me. Ben arrived after I had finished the dishes. We sat on the porch and had coffee." She grinned slyly. "Do you want to know what happened then?"

Steven knew what was coming—the grapevine hadn't disappointed the citizens of Knightsbridge on that juicy piece of news this morning—but he let her have the thrill of telling him anyway. "Of course. What happened?"

"Ben proposed again and I said yes!" She held out her left hand where a small diamond sparkled.

Steven opened his eyes wide as if he were hearing this for the first time. "Congratulations, Hannah," he said warmly. "I hope you'll be very happy together."

"Thank you."

"What time did Ben leave?"

"Around nine. I went to bed early because I was tired. Play practice makes for a long day."

Chapter 30

After supper Wednesday night, Steven and Olivia moved outside to the porch. This had become a treasured evening ritual since the end of winter, when they'd still had to bundle up in jackets—their noses cold and fingers tingling. They would drift to the wooden Adirondack chairs and talk about their lives, their dreams for the future, and Steven's investigations.

Tonight, he told her about Dickie Hughes and his attempt at blackmail. "Even after thirteen years on the force, I still struggle with the murder of a child," Steven confessed.

"Steven, there would be something seriously wrong with you if you didn't. Obviously, a sudden and violent death would be hard to take, but somehow when it's an older person, you figure at least they've had a chance at life," Olivia said.

"That's it exactly." He reached over and squeezed her arm. "I feel doubly sorry for this boy, Dickie Hughes. His father abused him. The kids at school shunned him. He was always getting into trouble through no fault of his own. It was like trouble found the poor kid. At least he had a best friend."

"It is sad, but what was he thinking trying to blackmail a killer?"

"Kids don't think. He was desperate to get away from his old man," Steven said.

"I suppose I can see that. What kind of horrible person are you dealing with?" she said rhetorically. "Do you think it's the same woman who killed Frankie?"

"I do. We know Dickie watched them having their picnic. On Monday, he finds out what he saw was murder. The kid'll do anything to get out of town. He tries to blackmail her so she arranges to meet him late at night in a secluded spot by the river. She pretends it's to give him the money but...."

"That poor boy. He didn't have a chance."

Steven was quiet a moment. "Olivia, this was so cold blooded. It takes a lot to hit someone on the head hard enough to kill him or at least leave him unconscious—we don't know which yet. I'm waiting to find out if he drowned or if the blow to the head killed him."

"So, to make sure he was dead, she dragged him into the river. You said face down?" Olivia shivered as Steven nodded. "What a psychopath!"

"You hit the nail on the head, Olivia. I've done some reading on sociopathy...."

"Wow, you're up to date."

"Hey, just because you're 80 years ahead of us...."

"Yeah, yeah, okay. So, teach me about sociopathic behavior, Doctor Freud."

"We're looking for someone who is nothing like what she seems. The killer only cares for herself although she might pretend to be kind and concerned for others. She's a good liar and a good actress." Steven tilted his glass, finishing his wine. "Thanks for listening, Olivia, especially to something like this. Talking with you always helps me think. Sometimes I see things that I missed during the day." He stood and began walking back and forth the length of the porch. A couple of loose boards creaked as he trod on them.

"Our killer needed to get rid of Dickie to save herself. You can never trust a blackmailer. No matter how much they protest that it's 'only going to be this one time', they always come back for more. I'm sure that's what the killer was afraid of."

"I vote for one of his teachers. He probably saw the people at school more than anyone."

"That's true."

"Go through the list of all the faculty and staff and pick out the women who are the right age and who Frankie would have been interested in. There can't be that many."

Steven stopped pacing, stretched, and sat down. "You're right. So far, we've eliminated Dickie's mother, the secretaries at the mill—that's his part-time job, and Adona Russo."

"She's the cousin's wife, right?" Olivia interrupted.

Steven couldn't bring himself to tell Olivia about Frankie's assault on Adona. "Yes."

"Is Lucy still a suspect?"

Steven frowned. "Yeah."

"Steven!" A voice called out and a striking young woman came walking up the sidewalk.

"Lucy!"

"Damn," Olivia whispered. "I hope she didn't hear us."

Lucy Russo climbed the front steps. "Steven, I'm sorry. I forgot you had company."

"That's okay. Lucy, this is my friend Olivia. Olivia, this is Helen's sister Lucy."

Without thinking Olivia stood and held out her hand for Lucy to shake. When the other woman looked confused, she quickly made a gesture toward her chair and said, "Here, Lucy. You can take my seat." She slid by Lucy and perched on the porch railing.

"Steven, I didn't really mean to come over here," Lucy began. "I couldn't settle down tonight so I thought I'd go for a walk. Somehow I ended up here. Have you found out anything yet?" Her voice sounded strained. Her face seemed drawn and Olivia noticed dark patches under her eyes.

"I'm sorry, Lucy. You know I can't talk about the case."

"Do you think it's almost over? Do you at least know when we can plan Frankie's funeral?"

"I'm pretty sure Doc's releasing his body tomorrow. He'll call you."

"Well, I guess that's something. I'm starting to go a little crazy at home. Tim gave me some time off from school." She stopped abruptly and turned to Olivia. "I heard you were a reporter. Is that true?"

"Yes, I was. I'm not doing that right now but...,"

Lucy interrupted. "The thing is I can't *stand* someone else trying to teach my classes. My principal hired somebody to come in for me this week but there's only so much I can give him for the kids to do on their own. Would you be interested in talking to my classes about being a reporter? Do you have a degree? Did you go to college?" She spoke fast, firing the questions out at warp speed.

"Yes. Yes. And yes," Olivia smiled at her. "I'd love to talk with your students, Lucy. I could go in for you on Friday."

Lucy heaved a deep sigh. "Thank you," she breathed. "That's one thing I won't have to think about. I'll tell Mr. Kennington. My first class starts at eight. You should get there at seven thirty. Check in with the secretary in the main office. Thank you, Olivia," she repeated, slowing down. "I appreciate it."

Lucy stood up and crossed the porch. She paused at the top of the stairs. "Please, let me know something as soon as you can, Steven. You *are* making progress, aren't you?" Her face was pinched. She turned abruptly and walked off into the night before he could answer.

"Wow!" Steven and Olivia whispered, staring at each other.

"I've had my fill of murder tonight, Olivia."

"Me, too. Hey, I almost forgot. There's something I want to ask you."

"Sure. What is it?"

"It's about my friend Isabel."

"The baby in the pub." He grinned.

"Yes." She grimaced. "I'm on a mission for her." Olivia told him about Isabel's missing twin brother Alex.

"Wowie! They kept that quiet! I haven't heard a whisper about two babies. What do you need from me?"

"I tried to get information online—you know, using my computer?"

Steven grinned and nodded. He'd learned a lot about the future in the past two months.

"But, I couldn't find anything," Olivia finished.

"That must be a first."

"Yeah, well…I need to know the name of the doctor who delivered Theresa's twins." Olivia explained her plan.

"I see. There're two doctors who usually deliver babies at home. So, it would've been Dr. Summerwood—his first name is James—or Dr. Kranken, William Kranken."

"Thanks. That should get me to the next step. You don't happen to know which of them has a brother who's a Catholic priest, do you?"

"No, but neither of them go to my church. So, either one could be Catholic."

"Or something else."

"Or nothing at all," Steven reminded her.

Olivia rose and leaned against the railing. The sun was slowly sinking below the horizon. In the distance, tree silhouettes etched a cobalt sky. "It's a Maxfield Parrish night," she said.

Steven left his seat and stood close to her, their hands nearly touching. "Mmm. It's beautiful."

"Have you heard of Maxfield Parrish? Do people know him yet?"

"I've met him. He was one of my mother's artist friends. And you're right. Parrish blue. With that house across the street, it looks like one of his paintings." He turned and looked down at Olivia. "How about a stroll around the neighborhood?"

"I thought you'd never ask."

They had barely gone the distance of three houses when they heard shouting.

"What's going on?" Olivia exclaimed.

"Probably a baseball game but they ought to be finished by now. Maybe they're in extra innings."

Steven guessed right. When they reached the corner, they saw a Little League game in progress.

"Want to stop and watch?" Steven asked.

"Sure."

They crossed the street and joined a crowd of enthusiastic onlookers. A wooden board showed the game was tied at 3 runs.

"Hey, Steven," called a voice to their left.

"Hi, Jim." Steven led Olivia to a young man in the company of two women. "Olivia, this is my cousin Jim, his wife Martha, and her friend Hannah," he said. "This is my friend Olivia."

They all said hello. Steven got into a conversation with his cousin about a recent Yankees game. Martha turned back to the match, yelling, "Run, Bobby. Run." Hannah stepped closer to Olivia.

"We heard Steven had someone visiting. Where do you live, Olivia?"

"Syracuse."

"What do you do all day when Steven's at work? You must be bored."

"Not at all," Olivia smiled. "I brought some work with me."

"What kind of work?"

"I'm doing research for a magazine article." Olivia explained her project about women during the Depression.

Hannah looked impressed.

"Do you work?" Olivia asked.

"I teach social studies at the high school. And I direct the school play."

"Oh, I love theater," enthused Olivia. "What play are you doing this year?"

"*Little Women*."

Olivia looked confused. "I didn't know that had been made into a play."

"I think it's based on the movie from last year. You know, with Katharine Hepburn?"

"Oh, right. I like her." Olivia was glad she'd already talked with Helen a couple of times. It had been good practice. Not knowing where a conversation could lead, she had to be quick on her feet. "When's opening night?"

"Next week. And there's still a lot to do." Hannah laughed. "Let me know if you get bored while you're here."

"I'd be happy to help, Hannah. Actually, I'm going to be at school Friday. Lucy asked me to talk with her students about being a reporter."

"Olivia, are you ready to go?" Steven joined them.

"Whenever you are. I'll see you Friday, Hannah. It was nice meeting you."

Chapter 31

Thursday — April 26, 1934

S teven sprang awake before his alarm clock rang at five thirty. It took him a couple of seconds to realize why he was so excited. Olivia was spending the day in 1934 again. He closed his eyes and said a prayer that nothing would happen to her and she'd be able to return to her time as easily as always. He rose and made his bed right away, as he did every day. Steven had inherited his father's love of routine and discipline. The familiarity of daily rituals always gave him a sense of comfort.

After getting dressed, he walked to the bedroom window and snapped up the shade. A wall of gray loomed before him, blocking his view. It was a dreary rainy day. The temperature had plummeted and the air felt clammy. He shivered and added a sweater under his suit jacket then went downstairs to fix breakfast.

Olivia groaned as her phone alarm sounded at five thirty. Sprawled on her stomach with her face buried in her pillow, hair covering her eyes, she reached over to her bedside table groping to turn it off. She lay there wondering why she'd set the alarm so early. Then it hit her. She twisted around and sprang up into a sitting position. *It's today!*

I'm going to Steven's for the whole day. By myself. And I'm going shopping. Woo hoo! She jumped out of bed and headed for the shower.

Last night before returning to her own time, Olivia had selected another outfit from Evangeline's well-stocked closet. Now, she buttoned the short-sleeved white blouse and tucked it into a pair of high-waist, wide-leg cotton trousers in a pale blue. She picked up the cropped navy jacket she'd discovered in the fabulous closet and smiled, remembering how her jaw had dropped when she'd read the tag—*Chanel.* She grabbed the straw bag that had been tucked away on a top shelf and stowed her belongings and the money Steven had loaned her. She hoped five dollars would be enough for everything she wanted to buy.

As she was slipping on a pair of sandals, she thought she smelled coffee. She looked toward the doorway and saw Steven appear on the other side of the threshold.

"Good morning," Olivia grinned. "I'm almost ready." She took a quick selfie and met him at the door.

"Good morning to you, too. You look swell." He gave her an admiring look, gazing from her still damp waves down to her painted toenails. "What was that you were doing?"

She explained the selfie stick.

The heavenly aroma of percolating coffee was unmistakable now. "Mmm, you've got coffee on the stove. Let's go!" Olivia was a coffee snob—she used a finely ground imported espresso in her French press every morning. She'd been thrilled last winter to discover that Steven's coffee—boiled in a pot called a percolator—was delicious.

Steven reached into the doorway and took her hand, then backed up slowly. Olivia stepped over the threshold into the past.

It was always a bit disconcerting for Olivia to walk through her house in Steven's time, although his mother did have spectacular taste. The Art Deco living room delighted her. The couch and two upholstered chairs were sleek and streamlined, in tones of cream and taupe. Original paintings by Steven's mother and some of her artist friends hung on the walls. In contrast, the kitchen was sparse by present-day standards—a free-standing enamel cupboard unit with built-in sections for coffee, tea, spices, and flour, a tiny sink, and a small combination stove-heater. The only counter space was a porcelain worktop in the cupboard unit.

Steven had already set cereal bowls, spoons, the sugar bowl, a glass bottle of whole milk, cups and saucers, and a box of *Wheaties* on the table. Pictured on the front of the orange box was a woman decked out in a leather bomber jacket, aviator helmet, and goggles. She stood on the wing of an airplane waving at the camera. Assuming it was Amelia Earhart, Olivia was surprised to read a name she'd never heard—Elinor Smith. Later, when she googled the aviatrix, she would learn that Smith had been the first woman on a Wheaties box.

"This is great, Steven," she said. "What can I do to help?"

"Just sit down and fix your cereal."

Steven set a steaming cup of coffee in front of Olivia and joined her at the table. They ate in silence for several minutes, enjoying the quiet and each other's company. Then Olivia asked what time the stores opened.

"Ten o'clock. What are you going to do until then?" Steven asked.

"I think I'll stay here and have some more coffee. I want to get used to being here before I leave the house. I might sit on the porch a while."

"Are you scared?"

"A little," she admitted. Then, she sparkled as she added, "But mostly I'm excited."

Steven rose from the table and went into the pantry. He took a loaf of Wonder bread from the metal bread box and stepped to the small countertop on the odd cupboard where he made a couple of sandwiches for his lunch. While he was spreading peanut butter and grape jelly on slices of white bread, he told Olivia that if she needed or wanted anything she should either telephone the station or stop by. "Any time, Olivia. You won't be bothering me. If you need me, I want you to come over."

"I won't embarrass you if I show up at your work?"

"No, the whole town's going to know you're here in five minutes anyway."

"Good point."

Steven closed his lunch box. "If you do go over and I'm not there, Tommy at the front desk will know where I am and how to get ahold of me." He reached into his trouser pocket and extracted a small handful of coins. "Here's a nickel in case you have to use a public telephone. The number at the station is KB10. There are umbrellas in the hall closet. And I think you're going to be glad to have that jacket. It's supposed to warm up but it's pretty chilly this morning."

She trailed him down the hallway toward the front door. "Steven, wait. I don't have a key. The lock on my door is new. My key won't fit yours."

"What do you need a key for?"

Her eyebrows drew in as she frowned. "To lock the house when I leave."

He laughed. "You don't need to lock anything. No one does."

"People don't lock their doors?"

"No."

"Wow. Okay, if you're sure. It feels weird though."

They reached the entry. Steven grabbed his fedora from the hall tree and opened the door.

"Have a good day. Find lots of clues," Olivia said, holding up crossed fingers.

"Thanks. I hope so. I keep dreaming of the case where the murderer walks into the station and gives himself up."

"Yeah, like that's going to happen," she smirked. "See you tonight."

"You have a good day, too, Olivia. I can't wait to hear all about it."

She gave him a big smile and hunched up her shoulders. She punctuated each word with a light hand clap and punched the air on the final one. "I. Am. So. Excited!"

He reached over and smiled, letting his fingertips drift across her cheek. "Have fun. See you later."

Yesterday had been difficult. A pall had hung over the station and all the men had been quieter than usual. The death of a child was heartbreaking. The murder of one was unspeakable.

Steven and his team now had a second homicide to solve. Resources were stretched thin. His men were working as hard as they could, but there was a lot of ground to cover and leads to follow up on. Nearly 72 hours had passed since Frankie's body had been discovered. In an investigation, the more time that passed, the greater the odds the killer would never be found. Steven could not let that happen. He owed justice to Frankie. And he owed it to Dickie Hughes.

The telephone in the CID room rang as Steven bent to stow his lunch box.

"Steven, finally!" Lieutenant Fred Schultz's baritone voice boomed over the phone line. "I was starting to think I'd have to come to Knightsbridge and track you down. Haha."

"I know the feeling, Fred. It's been busy. We've had a second murder."

"Oh! Is it connected to your first victim?"

"I think so. It's the witness to Frankie Russo's murder. A young boy."

"Ah, that always makes it worse."

"What can I do for you, Fred?"

"I've got a missing person who's connected to your Frankie Russo."

"No kidding. Who is it?"

"Fella named Tony Russo. He was due home Sunday. His wife called us late Tuesday afternoon, said she hadn't heard from him. Turns out he went to Knightsbridge to work with his cousin Frankie Russo. The wife thinks he was staying with him, too."

"I haven't seen or heard of a cousin called Tony. What kind of job were they supposed to be doing? Frankie worked part-time in the knitting mill office. I can't see how this Tony could get in on that. I went to the mill and talked with his supervisor. There was no mention of hiring an extra guy."

"Was he moonlighting on the side?"

"Not that I know of. He worked a week here and a week at the brewery like I told you the other day."

"I hate to ask but have you heard of any recent mob activity in your area? One fella dead, another missing, both Italian. Utica's not far from Knightsbridge," said Fred Schultz.

"Don't even think it." Steven shuddered. If Frankie's murder were mob-related, he'd never get the killer. Those fellas covered their tracks and protected their own. "No, I haven't heard of anything. Not even a whisper. If Roosevelt hadn't repealed Prohibition last winter, I'd say maybe Frankie and his cousin were moving illegal booze but not now. I'm pretty sure we're looking at a love/jealousy angle in Frankie Russo's murder."

"I hope you're right."

"By the way, thanks for having your officer meet us. It was appreciated although we didn't get very far at Haberle's. Frankie's boss couldn't add much to what we already knew except that he stayed in a rooming house nearby. He thought Park Street. Your man helped me and Jimmy check all the boarding houses but we came up empty."

"Isn't that always the way?" Fred commented.

"Are you busy right now? I was going to ask if one or two of your fellas might be able to give us a hand locating where Frankie was living."

"Why don't we trade? You get a couple of your boys to look for Tony and I'll send mine out to find your boarding house. How's that?"

"Sounds fair," Steven agreed. He pulled his notebook over and grabbed a pencil. "Give me a description of this Tony Russo."

"Average height, maybe five ten. Average build, a bit on the lean side."

"Come on, Fred. Give me something to work with."

"What can I say? The guy's nothing special."

"Even so. What else?"

"Italian looking. Dark brown hair and eyes. His wife showed me a picture. He's a good-looking fella."

"Fred, this guy could be anybody. For that matter, he could be his cousin Frankie. Well, we'll do our best." Steven put down his pencil. "Listen, I think I'd better get over to Syracuse today. I'd like to talk with Tony Russo's wife. Any objections?"

"No, I'd want to interview her myself if the tables were turned. Come to the station when you get here. We'll go over together."

In an effort to make the most of the day, Steven cancelled the morning briefing. Instead, he touched base with each of the men on his team as they arrived for work, instructing them to read the latest information on the murder board and get on with their assignments from yesterday. What he needed to do was give Chief Thompson a thorough update.

"Steven, it's been four days!" The chief was not happy. Andy Thompson, carrot-colored hair sticking out like he'd been electrocuted, sucked frosting off a finger as he popped the last bite of a pastry into his mouth then swigged a mouthful of coffee that looked like swamp mud. A cigarette burned dangerously close to a finger on his other hand but he seemed not to notice. "You're telling me you still have no idea who killed Frankie Russo?"

"The killer planned it perfectly, Chief. The whole town was at the parade on Sunday. Everybody saw everyone else but no one really paid attention. Or saw anything they realize is significant. Since our only witness ..."

"That poor kid."

"Yeah...since our only witness was killed, we have to rely on what Dickie Hughes told his pal Billy Burton. Assuming that information is correct—and our evidence backs it up so far—an unidentified woman had a picnic with Frankie Russo around noon and poisoned him with something in their lunch. Doc says it was a bread or dessert made with apples. It killed a couple of birds, too."

"I heard about that."

Steven shifted on the hard wooden visitor's chair. "Then of course, there's the motive. As far as I can see, Lucy Russo has the strongest reason to want him dead. He cheated on her for years. Before and after they were married."

"That would do it."

"Will said something though, Chief. He wondered if Lucy still loved Frankie. We've got a theory that she might have considered him more like a possession. You know, 'if I can't have him, no one can.' I'm not sure she's sorry he's dead. Her emotions have been all over the place. I can't pin her down. And she's very private which makes it worse."

"A secretive dame, huh?"

"I'm going to talk with Helen today and see if she can help me understand how Lucy thinks. A sister ought to have some insight."

"I know you like all this psychology mumbo jumbo, Steven. But don't forget good old-fashioned police work. Find some damn evidence. I want physical proof that ties *somebody* to the murder."

The chief broke off coughing. His face turned beet red. He regained control and took another swig of his coffee. "What about Adona Russo?"

Steven told him about the pantry incident.

"Makes you wonder that somebody didn't kill the bastard years ago." The chief shook his head in disgust. "Sorry, I shouldn't have said that."

"Yeah, well...we're looking at Hannah Grantham. I wasn't considering her until the other day. She lied to me."

Chief Thompson raised his bushy eyebrows. "Did she now?"

"Yes, she said her relationship with Frankie was over before he married Lucy. But I know for a fact they stepped out together several times *after* he was married. I saw them myself. They didn't look like they were two old friends having a drink. If it was innocent, why would she deny it? I'm sure they thought they were someplace safe, where no one would see them but ..."

"People are fools, Steven. Knightsbridge is a small town. There is no such thing as 'someplace safe.'" Thompson frowned.

"True. Besides, Frankie made notes in his little book about Hannah after he was married. The letter H is all over those pages. And we know H is Hannah. I'm planning on talking to Martha."

"Your cousin's wife?"

"Yeah, she and Hannah have been friends since they were kids. Maybe she'll tell me what was going on. Frankie cheated on Lucy with Hannah for years. I need to know more about that."

"I heard she got engaged to Ben Maxwell the other day. The timing seems a bit odd, doesn't it?" observed the chief.

"You mean is it a coincidence that Frankie's old flame got herself engaged two days after he was murdered? Especially after Ben had been proposing for months?" Steven's eyebrows shot up.

"Oh, he had, had he? I didn't know that," said Thompson.

"Yes, Hannah's been putting him off for some time. I heard she kept saying she wasn't ready yet."

"Maybe she carried a torch for Russo. Held out hope that something would happen with him some day."

"Well, it's not going to happen now." Steven shrugged. "I don't know, Chief, I've got to think about that. But, according to Frankie's little book, it's been two years since he was seeing Hannah. Do girls hold on to feelings that long?"

"Blackwell, you have *no* idea! I screwed up something eight months after we were married—it was stupid, not important at all—and whenever we have a fight, my wife *still* brings it up. Some people never forget." Chief Thompson coughed again and cleared his throat.

"The question we need to ask, Steven, is why now? Let's assume—although God help us, I hate to assume anything," Chief Thompson rolled his eyes. "Let's assume the motive is jealousy. Was Lucy jealous of Frankie's affairs and finally decided to take revenge? Was an old girlfriend—let's say your lying Hannah Grantham—jealous of Frankie's wife and got sick of waiting for him to leave her?"

"Don't forget, Chief, there's also the change in Frankie's behavior in 1931. And, after the first of the year—'32, I mean—there's no more H in the book." Steven stood and began to pace the small office. "I think that's the key. Will said Lucy noticed it. His boss here at the mill noticed it. We think Frankie met someone in Syracuse whose name starts with S and that new relationship changed all the old ones."

"Have you found this S yet?"

"No." Steven exhaled in deep disappointment. "Until we find the rooming house where he lived in Syracuse, we're at a dead end. None of his co-workers or supervisor at the brewery could shed any light on his private life. The only thing they knew was that he was married. There is one odd thing though. Fred Schultz called this morning. He's got a missing person by the name of Tony Russo."

"What?" Thompson exclaimed and shot forward in his chair, choking on the coffee that he'd inhaled in his surprise.

"Yeah, the fella's a cousin of Frankie Russo." Steven explained what Schultz had told him and the swap they had arranged. "I think Syracuse is going to be a non-starter because of Dickie Hughes's murder. But I've got to talk with this Tony's wife. Maybe she can tell me something. She probably met Frankie. Maybe she knows where he stayed."

"You never know. But I gotta say I don't like coincidences. The timing of this fella going missing and Frankie being murdered means something." The chief sighed. "I just don't know what. When are you going to Syracuse? Are you taking somebody with you?"

"Later this morning. No, I'll go alone." Steven gave his boss a run-down of what the men were doing today.

"We'll have a better idea of who Dickie Hughes tried to blackmail after Will's done. He's checking all the women Dickie could've talked to during those 24 hours who are Frankie's type and might have been one of his girlfriends. I think we're looking for someone who felt betrayed. *That's* the information that's going to crack this case, Chief. The same woman killed Frankie Russo and Dickie Hughes. The killer's right here in Knightsbridge, not Syracuse."

"The trail's going cold, Steven. I don't like it."

"We'll get this, Chief. Will and I were saying yesterday we think there's one more piece of the puzzle. And when we find that piece, it's all going to fall into place. You'll see."

"When you're in Syracuse, ask Tony Russo's wife if she knows who S is. Maybe Frankie brought his new girl to their house."

Chapter 32

B y the time Olivia left Steven's house, the rain had stopped and the sun was breaking through. She held her breath as she stepped off the porch. She stood on the sidewalk a minute to make sure she wasn't going to be jerked back into the 21st century. In case a curious neighbor was peeking out a window, she pretended to be looking for something in her bag. *Okay, then. Here we go.*

At first, Olivia walked slowly. She considered it a real possibility that she was protected by an invisible shield around or in the vicinity of the house, as Steven might have protected her the night they went to the pub. You never knew. She was breaking new ground today. Once again, she wondered if anyone else in the world had ever time traveled. The odds were someone probably had. Maybe even a long-lost relative of hers. Or someone in Steven's family. Maybe time travel was genetic.

By the time Olivia had reached the corner of Chiltington and Victoria, she felt more confident. Nothing had happened. *And nothing's going to happen either*, she told herself determinedly. *This is just another adventure. You've been to different places before. Yeah*, she reminded herself, *but not to a different century.*

Since she had an hour before the stores opened, Olivia decided to explore. She turned left and headed toward the western loop of the river; Knightsbridge sat nestled in a bend of the Mohawk River. She had only taken a couple of steps and was admiring the display in a flower shop window when she heard someone call her name. *What?* She looked up and saw Helen striding toward her, a teen-aged girl in tow.

"Helen! Oh, my goodness. This is a surprise."

Helen gave her a hug and said, "Olivia, this is my daughter Annie. Annie, this is Steven's friend that I told you about. The one that's doing the research project. The reporter."

"Hi, Annie. It's nice to meet you."

Olivia experienced what would be her first dizzying moment of the day. In 1934, Annie Sinclair was a high school student in ankle socks and a braid down her back. But in Olivia's time, she had been an elderly teacher with a passion for history who had volunteered at the Knightsbridge History Museum and who had recently passed away. Olivia tried not to stare as she attempted to reconcile this beautiful young girl with the nonagenarian who had just died.

"What are you doing out so early, Olivia?" Helen asked.

"Taking a walk, doing a little sightseeing. What are you up to?" Olivia immediately knew she had made a mistake. Based on the brief frown on Helen's face, she must have used an expression that didn't exist yet. She quickly corrected herself. "What about you?"

"Arranging the flowers for Frankie's funeral." Helen nodded toward Page's Flower Shop. "The police told Lucy we could make plans."

"Oh, I see." Olivia looked at Annie. "Are you off from school today, Annie?"

"No, I have a doctor's appointment this morning." Annie stuck out her thumb and pointed to a small office next to the florist.

Olivia read the sign in the window—Dr. James Summerwood, General Practitioner. *OMG. One of the doctors who delivered babies.* Never one to let an opportunity go by, Olivia quickly said, "Oh, Dr. Summerwood. I think he has a brother who lives near me in Syracuse."

"You must be thinking of someone else, Olivia," said Helen. "Both Dr. Summerwood's sisters live here in Knightsbridge. He doesn't have a brother."

Score! Dr. William Kranken it is. One down.

"My mistake."

"I'm sorry to hurry away, Olivia. But we have to order the flowers then get next door before nine fifteen. I don't want to be late."

Olivia almost said *No problem* but caught herself in time, certain the expression didn't exist yet. Instead, she said, "I'll see you soon, Helen." She stepped aside to let them pass. A tiny bell tinkled as Helen and Annie entered the shop. Olivia turned and waved goodbye.

Olivia realized there wasn't much to see in the direction she was going, so she went back to The Three Lords, turned the corner, then walked down Hickory Street. She passed one tiny shop in the short block—Sam's Tackle and Bait. Olivia would have known what Sam sold even without reading his sign, the smell of worms in the buckets outside the narrow door was a dead give-away. She swung around the next corner, heading up the Margate Road, and had to stifle a gasp as she beheld the view. Occupying a large chunk of real estate where the two streets met loomed the iconic Woolworth's five and dime. An enormous sign stretching across the width of the four-story building read F. W. Woolworth 5 and 10 Cent Store.

Towers of goods filled the huge display windows. Objects were grouped with like items. There was a stack of toiletries—razors, hair tonics, bottles of toilet water (*toilet water?*), shampoos, and soaps; a pile of spring and summer toys—tops, pails and shovels, jump ropes, jacks and balls; a family of mannequins wore warm weather clothing—the children in shorts with a bib and straps like overalls, the mother in a pale blue-and-white checked, cotton sundress, the dad in a short-sleeved shirt and trousers.

A light went on in the back of the store. Someone was getting ready for work. Olivia figured it was about nine thirty—she missed having her phone to check the time. Wanting to see what the Margate Road looked like, she wandered up the street. She passed one of her go-to places. Giovanni's Italian Restaurant looked the same as it did in her time. She came to a spectacular white stone edifice adorned with four ionic columns at the entrance. The Village Library had been constructed with funds donated by the legendary Andrew Carnegie at the turn of the 20th century. Olivia treasured memories of time spent here over the years.

As she strolled, thrilling to everything she gazed on, Olivia passed an elderly couple, a few people walking alone, a woman with a wicker basket over her arm—Olivia guessed she was heading to the market, some men who were likely going to work, and a group of little kids on their way to school. It was surreal not knowing any of these people—like being in a Dalí painting or an Ionesco play.

As Olivia approached the end of the block, she came upon the large square building that housed the offices of *The Gazette*. How had she not thought of that? To get inside and wander around would be awesome. She crossed Tulip Street and paused at the main entrance trying to come up with a plausible excuse to go in and look around.

A middle-aged man wearing wire-rimmed glasses, whose head shone like a billiard ball, skirted around her and reached for the door. As his hand gripped the handle, he exclaimed, "Oh, you must be the reporter who's staying with Steven Blackwell. Hello, I'm Sam Silverstone, the *Gazette* editor. Are you coming in?"

Unable to believe her luck, Olivia shook his outstretched hand and replied, "Olivia Watson. Yes, thank you. I'd love to see your operation."

"Sure thing. I'd be interested in hearing how our digs compare to yours. I'm proud of our paper but Knightsbridge is a small town. I know the *Syracuse Journal* is bigger." Silverstone held the door open for Olivia and followed her in.

They climbed two flights of stairs to the third floor. When they entered the news room, Olivia's senses were assaulted. They had walked into a room so full of smoke that Olivia felt like she could hold it in her hand. She coughed a couple of times and tried to breathe more shallowly. Several great ceiling fans some ten or twelve feet up moved the thick fog around but it didn't make any difference. Neither did the open windows.

All the newsrooms Olivia had ever worked in were noisy, but *The Gazette* offices were deafening beyond anything she could have imagined. People shouted. Typewriters clacked. Telephones screamed and the heavy receivers banged loudly when replaced in their cradles. On one side of the cavernous room, Olivia saw and heard a black metal box with Associated Press stamped in white letters on the front. *Oh my goodness. A Teletype machine.* She approached the clattering Teletype and watched. It reminded her of an old typewriter she'd seen years ago in the Smithsonian. A mechanism was magically typing the latest news update on a roll of paper. A newsman rushed over and tore off a long section. He scanned the contents, swore loudly, and hurried back to his desk.

Olivia was blinded by all of this noise. She began to feel dizzy. *Uh oh. This can't be good.* She turned to Sam. "Mr. Silverstone, would it be all right if I took a rain check? I just realized I can't stay right now."

"Sure. Come back any time. Any friend of Steven's is a friend of ours. Can you find your way out?"

"Yes, sir, thank you. I'll be fine."

As soon as she was out of sight, Olivia fled down the stairs and out of the building. When she hit the sidewalk, she realized she'd exited by a side door. She had run into tiny Bank Alley. A wave of dizziness hit her and she held out her hand to brace herself against the building. Before she could make contact with the rough wall, she fell to her knees. Her head was spinning, her mind so disoriented that she didn't know where she was.

It came in ripples. One minute, Olivia had the sensation of free-falling into a void. Seconds later, she floated upward, weightless and without direction. She couldn't focus. She felt sick to her stomach. Her heart beat fast and she was having trouble breathing. *Oh, my God. What's happening?* Was she being pulled back to the 21st century?

She squinted and looked up. She was able to make out what looked like a picnic table in the alley between the bank and the *Gazette* offices. Somehow she managed to get on her feet and stagger to the table as another bout of dizziness hit. She threw herself on the attached bench and tucked her head between her knees. Hoping to slow her heart rate, Olivia took slow deep breaths while holding onto the edge of the seat. If she gripped it tightly enough maybe she wouldn't be jerked back to her time, maybe she could stay here a little longer.

"Are you all right, Miss?"

Olivia gazed up into the concerned faces of two patrolmen.

"I don't know. I think so." She hoped she wasn't going to throw up. "I think it's passing."

Ralph Hiller whispered to Pete McGrath, "Is this her?"

Pete asked, "Where do you live, Miss? We'd be happy to escort you home."

"I don't live here. I'm visiting...."

"Steven Blackwell?"

"Yes, how did you know?"

"It's a small town," said the shorter of the two police officers, grimacing. He looked like a linebacker, solid and strong. "Word gets around."

Olivia stood up tentatively. She gripped the table as she exhaled. Relief flooded through her—it was over. The dizziness was gone, the shaking barely noticeable. "I think I'm okay." She smiled weakly.

"Where are you going?" asked the other man. Olivia could tell he was balding despite the policeman's cap perched on his head.

"Woolworth's." She paused. "Wait, no. I think I'll go to Bailey's. I could use a cup of coffee."

"That sounds like a swell idea," said the wiry patrolman. "By the way, I'm Pete McGrath. This here's Ralph Hiller. We work with Steven," he added unnecessarily.

"Nice to meet you. I'm Olivia Watson."

"It's our pleasure, Miss Watson," said Ralph.

"Listen, Bailey's isn't far from the station. And it's on our way. We'll walk along with you just to be sure," said Pete.

"Yeah, Steven'd have our guts for garters if we abandoned you like this," commented Ralph.

They each took an arm to support Olivia. They made small talk as they slowly walked the block and a half to Bailey's Diner. By the time they had reached their destination, Olivia felt like herself again.

"The pink's back in your cheeks," observed Ralph.

"We'll leave you here then, Miss Watson," said Pete. "You're sure you're okay?"

"Yes. I can't thank you both enough. You really came to my rescue."

Ralph and Pete beamed. Neither had failed to notice that Steven's mystery friend was a real looker.

"You just left her?" Steven bellowed. "What if it happens again?"

"Steven, she said she was fine," protested Ralph.

"She looked okay." Pete backed him up.

"When exactly was this?"

"Two minutes ago. She's at Bailey's having a cup of joe."

Steven brushed past the two bewildered policemen and rushed out the door.

Chapter 33

Steven made it to Bailey's in three minutes flat. He flew up the concrete steps and yanked the heavy glass door open. It was only when he saw her sitting on a chrome stool at the counter calmly drinking a cup of coffee that he was able to breathe. *She's okay. She looks all right.* With one goal in mind, he moved down the narrow aisle, turning to the side as an elderly couple squeezed by. Olivia looked up as he approached.

"Steven!" she exclaimed. "What are you doing here?"

"What am I doing here?" he said, aghast. "Olivia, I just saw Ralph and Pete. They told me how they found you." He slid onto the red upholstered seat next to her. "What happened?"

She made a face. "I've been sitting here trying to figure that out."

"Wait a minute. Let's go to the booth in the back. We'll have some privacy." He picked up her coffee and held her arm as she slid off the stool. They took several steps then he guided her onto the wooden bench.

"I think I had a *panic* attack," she leaned toward him and whispered, her voice sounding incredulous.

"What's that?" He nodded to the waitress who came to the table with a pot of coffee and a cup. "Thanks, Rosie."

"I've never had one but I've heard about them. I guess it's pretty much like it sounds. At first, I thought I was being pulled back to my time."

"We shouldn't have tried this. It was stupid. You could have been hurt."

"No, no, Steven, I'm okay. I don't think it had anything to do with the...," she looked around to make sure no one could hear. She whispered, "you know...travel."

"All right. So, tell me what happened."

She explained how it had started in the loud smoky press room. "I ran out of there so fast. By the time I got down to the sidewalk, I felt really strange." She shuddered. "You know how I like being in control of things. This was like I was watching myself drift away. And I couldn't do anything to stop it."

"It sounds terrifying." Steven stared at her wide-eyed. He could feel her anguish, hear it in her voice.

"I saw myself falling into a dark space, totally helpless. Thank God it didn't last long."

"It's okay, Olivia." He reached over and squeezed her hand. "It's over. You're doing fine. And I'm here."

The smile she gave him came from deep inside her. "Thank you. I admit I'm glad to see you." She turned her hand and squeezed back. "It was really awful. It felt so real, Steven. Horrible feelings kept washing over me. I remember thinking all I wanted was to feel like me again."

In the past couple of months, Steven had gotten to know Olivia well. She was independent and sure of herself. He understood this must have been a nightmare for her. He wanted to wrap his arms around her and keep her safe. He wished he could do something so she'd never have to go through that again. He realized how fond of her he was becoming.

Then, he realized he didn't mind.

Steven didn't want to let go of her hand. It seemed silly but he needed to make contact with her. He wanted to reassure himself that she was here and she was all right. "Have you been okay since you got here? You seem like yourself."

"Yeah, I am. I feel normal again. Like me." She blew out her cheeks and nodded a couple of times. "After all my adventures in other countries, I never expected something like this here. In Knightsbridge, of all places. It was like a culture shock gone wild. It really threw me."

"You're *sure* it had nothing to do with our experiment?" He raised his brows.

"Yes, I'm sure. I was fine in the pub the other night. This morning after you left, I was okay. It wasn't until I went into the *Gazette* offices."

"That place could affect anyone. Let's forget it. The important thing is that you're all right."

Steven felt the need to protect her. There was no way he was going to let her go off by herself for the rest of the day. He was sticking to her like glue. He made a quick decision. "I have an idea."

Her face lit up and her eyes sparkled. "Ooh. What is it?"

"Want to go to Syracuse with me this afternoon?"

Olivia gasped. "Really? What's going on? Is it for your case?"

Steven explained that he had to interview a woman whose husband Tony had gone missing, and who happened to be Frankie Russo's cousin. Then, he said, "You can go shopping at Woolworth's any time. Why don't we have an early lunch? It's turning into a nice day. It'll be a swell ride. Think of all the things you're going to see." He found himself getting excited for her. Maybe when this case was over, he'd be able to spend a day in her time. Now *that* was something to look forward to.

As Steven and Olivia were finishing their hamburgers, a gray-haired woman and a little boy about four years old entered the neighboring booth.

"What do you want to eat, Wilbur?"

"No, Grandma, no. Timmy. I'm Timmy," he whined.

Olivia laughed. "He sounds like Liz's husband Joe. His real name is Leonard Joseph. He hates Leonard so he uses his middle name."

Something clicked in Steven's mind. His jaw dropped and his eyes grew wide. He stared. "Olivia, what if...?"

She gasped. "Frankie!"

Steven slowly nodded. "What if Frankie's middle name is Anthony? What if the fella who's gone missing in Syracuse isn't *Tony* Russo but *Frankie* Russo? They both work at the brewery. Oh, why didn't I see it before? I've been a fool." He threw some coins on the table and slid out of the booth. "Come on."

When they arrived at the station, Steven said, "Olivia, please wait in the car. I'll only be a minute. If you're with me, all the fellas'll want to meet you. It'll slow us down."

"Sure, that's okay. I've never been in your car. I'll check it out while you're gone."

Steven escorted her to a dark green Chevy and opened the door.

"It's beautiful," she exclaimed.

Steven beamed with pride. He loved his motor car and took special care of it, washing the automobile and polishing it by hand every week.

Olivia sank onto the roomy bench seat and ran her hand over the soft tufted upholstery. The luxurious interior was a pale gray, chenille-like material. Olivia stretched out her legs and leaned back onto the seat, enjoying the moment. *Yeah, this is pretty cool.*

Moments later, Steven jumped in beside her. He had a big grin on his face. He waved a handful of papers and cried, "Listen to this—Francis *Anthony* Russo born August 20, 1906, et cetera et cetera."

"Wow! Wait a minute. How come you never saw that before? What are those papers?"

"Frankie's background information that Jimmy Bou put together.

I must have skipped over his name to what I thought was more important. And I never went back to read the whole thing. I can't believe it."

"No wonder you couldn't find Frankie's boarding house. He was using the name Tony." Olivia frowned. "Steven, maybe you shouldn't get too excited yet. A lot of Italians use the same names for their kids. They pass 'em down from generation to generation. If it's a big family, there could be two or three cousins with the same name. This could be a different Tony."

He wiggled his eyebrows at her and brandished a photograph. "I thought of that. This is our Frankie Russo. I'm sure *Tony's* wife has a photo of him. Then we'll see."

"Very good, Detective Blackwell."

As Steven depressed the clutch and started the engine, a roar filled the small parking lot.

"Yikes, don't you guys have mufflers?" Olivia exclaimed.

"Hey, this is a big improvement over the models they used to manufacture. It's not loud at all." He patted the dashboard. "She's a beauty."

Olivia chuckled. "Guys and their cars. Nothing changes."

Steven pulled out onto the bustling street. "We have one stop to make before we leave."

Olivia watched as he held the beautifully polished wooden steering wheel in his left hand while using his right to move the tall floor-mounted stick shift into first gear.

Ten minutes later, they left Father Seraphino waving goodbye at the front door of the church. Steven wouldn't tell Olivia why he'd visited the priest. She hoped it had something to do with her search for Alex. *Speaking of Alex.*

"Steven, if we have the time, do you think we could stop at a couple of Catholic churches while we're in Syracuse? I need to get serious about finding that priest for Isabel."

"Depends on how long the interview with Tony's wife takes. We'll try."

As Steven downshifted and made a right on the Embankment Road, heading out of town, Olivia cranked open the window and let the cool sweet air fill up the car.

Olivia didn't know where to look first. Steven kept his speed under forty-five so she was able to take in most of what slid past the window. She noticed numerous sidewalks but not many driveways, a lot of people walking but also more cars than she'd imagined. Most of the cars looked the same—boxy and black. She was thrilled when the occasional sleek model in a different color sped past them.

"That's a 1924 Chrysler." Steven pointed to a plain black car with skinny wheels; an extra wheel was fastened to a strap under the driver's side mirror. "That's a '31 Lincoln," he said, as a snazzy sleek coupe whizzed by.

"Ooh, chocolate and cream. That's what I'd buy."

Steven turned off Route 5 onto Route 31 heading west. They drove past long stretches of farmland being tilled by men on tractors. Cows grazed in nearby green fields. White clapboard houses dotting the landscape like dollops of cream were few and far between. An hour into their journey, they entered an area of thick swamplands, where tall cedar and tamarack reached for the sun.

"Oh my goodness, I feel like I'm in the Louisiana Bayou," Olivia exclaimed.

"This is Rattlesnake Gulch," Steven told her.

"Rattlesnake! Are there really snakes in there?"

"Yup. Hundreds." He grinned. "There's a company that uses the wood from those trees to make the barrels they pack salt in."

"I'd hate to be the guys that have to chop down the trees. Yikes!"

Shortly after passing through Rattlesnake Gulch, Steven turned south on a smooth concrete road.

"Oh, this is different," Olivia commented.

"They finished this part of Route 11 some time ago. It's actually called Plank Road because it originally was made of wood. Not a very smooth ride." He grimaced.

They drove by the Sleeth Feed Mill and Cicero State Bank. At the corner of Circle Drive sat a small wooden structure.

"That's the Lilly Gate Toll House. They used to collect money to pay for the planks."

"Nothing changes," Olivia observed. "We have toll roads, too."

It was nearly noon when they approached the Syracuse city line.

Steven said, "Listen, Olivia, I know you don't want to hear this but you're going to have to stay in the background while Fred and I interview Mrs. Russo. This is an official visit. I shouldn't even have a civilian with me."

She gave him a disgusted look. "I know you don't have women cops yet, but I'll tell you what the police do in my time. It's common to see male and female partners. If you're interviewing a woman, especially in a crisis, it can be comforting for her to have another woman nearby. A female cop can get information that a man can't."

"Actually the Syracuse police do have a couple of girls on the force—matrons they call them. But you haven't been trained, Olivia. I know you want to help. And your reporter instincts are always turned on but you could say the wrong thing or give out a piece of information that I want to hold back. You could hurt the investigation."

"How about this," she suggested, "depending on how things go, if she gets upset or stops answering your questions, give me a look. I can try to calm her down or get her to keep talking. I know loads of tricks to do that. If I don't get a sign from you, I'll be quiet as the proverbial mouse. You won't even know I'm there," she promised.

Steven parked his motor car at the curb near the corner of Clinton and Willow Streets. Together they entered the Syracuse Police Department.

"Fred, meet Olivia Watson, a friend who's been visiting me this week. Olivia, Lieutenant Fred Schultz, an old pal."

"Nice to meet you, Miss Watson."

Olivia looked him square in the eye, stuck out her hand, and gave the tall husky policeman a strong confident handshake. "Happy to meet you, Lieutenant." She hoped that her handshake told him she was more than capable of assisting them if necessary. Fred Schultz didn't look the type to put a lot of trust in what Olivia bet he'd call a *girl cop*.

"Fred, hold on to your hat," Steven said excitedly. "I think we've got something." He told Lieutenant Schultz his theory about Frankie and Tony.

"Holy mackerel! Now we're gonna get somewhere," his friend exclaimed. "Let's go!" Schultz donned his cap, completing what Olivia thought was a slick uniform: white dress shirt, light blue tie, navy straight-legged trousers and long fitted jacket that covered his hips. The stiff hat and the highly-polished badge pinned on the left side of the jacket gave the policeman a look that inspired confidence and trust. This was a man who got things done. "Come along, Olivia."

And the image crumbled.

What am I, five? Olivia bristled but forced herself to keep in mind this man didn't know any better. It wasn't personal. It was a sign of the times. This was a good reminder that she'd have to be careful of everything she said and did while Fred Schultz was with them.

Olivia eavesdropped on the conversation from the back seat of the Syracuse Police Department's black sedan. Steven and Fred were discussing what they wanted to accomplish and how they were going to do it.

"I called her after we hung up this morning, Steven. She's expecting me and a fellow officer." He slipped a glance in Olivia's direction. "You got a picture, right?"

"Yes, and I stopped by the church, too. The priest let me borrow a copy of Frankie's baptism certificate."

Fred Schultz pulled up in front of a large, two-story home with a wrap-around porch and front steps flanked by rounded columns. Dark green shutters framed long windows that Olivia knew would reach almost to the floor inside. Schultz knocked on the screen door and a voice called out, "I'm coming."

Tony Russo's wife hurried to the door, a baby on her hip. She wasn't beautiful in the classical sense, but Olivia immediately knew the attraction this woman must have held for Frankie Russo. She was petite and curvy with luxuriant auburn hair that touched her shoulders in defiance of current fashion. But, it was her eyes that did it. They were a blue so deep and so dark a man could get lost in them before he knew what was happening. Olivia bet that was exactly what had happened to Frankie. One look at this woman and he'd been a goner.

Fred said, "Mrs. Russo, this is Detective Sergeant Steven Blackwell with the Knightsbridge Police and Miss Watson."

They entered the living room where a thin man sat reading in the cozy nook of a bay window. He glanced up, murmured hello, then returned to his newspaper. A clatter of dishes and cutlery sounded from the back of the house. A thickset woman in a white uniform hurried in mumbling, "Now, where did I leave that?" She strode to the upright piano, grabbed a nurse's cap off the back, and jammed it on top of iron gray curls.

"Sir," Fred Schultz addressed the man in the rocking chair, "we need to speak with Mrs. Russo in private."

"Oh, certainly. Pardon me."

Once alone, they settled in the furniture-filled room—Mrs. Russo and Olivia on a plump sofa and the two policemen facing them in dark upholstered chairs.

"Mrs. Russo, we might have some information for you. But, we're not sure yet. Would you get that photograph of your husband that you showed me?" Lieutenant Schultz said.

"Our wedding picture? Yes, of course. It's in the bedroom."

The baby was fussing and squirming in her arms when Mrs. Russo returned. She set her on the floor whereby the little girl crawled to Olivia, hoisted herself up grabbing on to Olivia's trousers, and stood tottering, fixing big blue eyes on her.

"Aren't you a cutie? What's your name?" said Olivia.

"Charlotte," said Mrs. Russo, handing the photograph to Fred Schultz.

Steven leaned over to examine the black-and-white image. There he was—grinning like he'd won the lottery—Frankie Russo all spiffed up in a dark suit, shirt, and tie with his hair slicked back and his arm around the woman across from him.

"Mrs. Russo, what's your first name?" Steven asked.

"What a strange question, Detective." She gave him a perplexed look.

"If you wouldn't mind, ma'am."

"Stella. It's Stella."

There it was. The final clue. He'd found Frankie's S. Stella. The love of his life. His other wife.

And Lucy's real motive for murder.

Fred glanced toward the photograph and raised his eyebrows at Steven. Steven gave a short decisive nod.

"When was this taken, Mrs. Russo? When did you get married?"

Fred asked.

"September 7th, 1932. What...?"

"Where did you marry?"

"Holy Trinity. It's a couple of blocks up the street." Stella frowned. "Lieutenant Schultz, please tell me what you found out. You're making me nervous. Why all these questions about our wedding?"

"Just another minute, ma'am. Did you post the bans at church beforehand?"

"Of course we did. There was nothing irregular about our marriage. We did everything we were supposed to do."

"Did you provide the priest with identification before he married you? By the way, what's the name of your priest, Mrs. Russo?" Steven shot Olivia a conspiratorial glance.

"Father O'Brien. No," she laughed as though the question were absurd. "Father baptized me. He's known me my whole life."

"What about Tony?" asked Steven.

"Of course not. Tony's been a member of the church ever since he moved here. Father knows him. He does odd jobs in the church and rectory. What's going on?"

"Mrs. Russo, I'm sorry to have to tell you your husband was killed Sunday in Knightsbridge," Steven told her.

The color drained from her face. She gripped the arm of the sofa and fell back onto the cushion. "No! I don't believe you. I would know. I would *feel it*. Tony and I are like one person. I would have been in pain this week. Physical pain. You're wrong!"

Charlotte, sensing her mother's distress, began to cry. Olivia picked her up and walked around the room, keeping the baby in view of her mother, bouncing her on her hip, and singing a soft lullaby.

"Mrs. Russo, I'm afraid there's more bad news," Steven went on. "I don't know how else to say it so I'll be blunt. Your husband's real name was Frankie Russo. Francis Anthony Russo. And he already

235

has a wife in Knightsbridge."

Stella looked like she'd been stabbed. For several long seconds, she did nothing, said nothing. Then, she slid off the couch to the floor in a dead faint.

Olivia rushed to the kitchen. With the baby on her hip, she soaked a towel with cold water and hurried back to where Stella Russo was fluttering her eyelids.

"Mama," Charlotte wailed, throwing herself toward the other woman.

Olivia tightened her grip. Stella struggled back up on the sofa and reached for the lifeline. Olivia handed the squirming child over. Stella Russo hugged her daughter close as she sobbed into the baby-fine hair. Olivia sat next to her, pressing the cool cloth against the back of her neck.

Steven gave Stella Russo time to compose herself. After a moment, still clutching her baby and barely able to get the words out, she said, "Tell me...what happened."

"Bear with me a second, Mrs. Russo, I have a couple of questions first. Where were you this past Sunday?" he asked.

"Here," she said in a tone that indicated there could be no other answer. "I always prepare an extra nice Sunday dinner for the house."

"Tell me what you did from early morning until bedtime?"

"I took Charlotte to seven-o'clock Mass. We got home about quarter after eight. We had breakfast then I spent the rest of the morning fixing dinner. On Sundays, we eat our main meal at two o'clock. It's the only day of the week my boarders are on their own for supper. After we ate, I put the baby down for her afternoon nap. Mabel—she's one of my lodgers but she's a friend, too—she helped me do the dishes and clean up the kitchen. After that, I sat in the parlor and read the Sunday paper. Tony was supposed to be home by suppertime so I took a long bath and put a fresh dress on." She inhaled and swallowed a sob, tears leaked out again. Charlotte yelled as her mother squeezed a bit too hard. "Ooh, sorry, sweetie." She kissed her cheek then went on. "I kept thinking that any minute he'd walk through the door or call with a laugh or an explanation. In all the time we've been together, he was only late once. And that was because the bus broke down." She smoothed her daughter's hair and straightened the skirt of her little dress. "I didn't start worrying until Monday when he still wasn't home and I didn't hear anything."

"Yes, then you called us on Tuesday," said Fred Schultz. He raised his brows at Steven, who nodded again. "To answer your question, Mrs. Russo, Frankie—that is Tony—was poisoned."

"Coming back to your husband's first wife, ma'am," Steven said.

Stella Russo nailed him with fierce eyes and said, "I will *not* believe Tony was cheating on me. He wouldn't."

"But that's exactly what he did, Mrs. Russo," Steven said. "Every other Sunday he left you and returned to Knightsbridge, where he spent the week with his first and, I'm sorry to say, his *only* legal wife. Do you really expect us to believe you had no idea?"

Stella Russo hunched over and gulped huge mouthfuls of air. "This can't be true," she whispered, trembling. "You've made a terrible mistake. I *know* him. He would never do this to us. He would never do it to Charlotte."

Hearing her name, the baby began to babble.

"Mrs. Russo, I also need to ask you about Tuesday night," Steven said.

"Tuesday? What's that got to do with it?"

"If you'd just answer my question, ma'am. Where were you from seven to, say, midnight?"

"Are you kidding? I have a baby. Where do you think I would be at night?" She looked annoyed. "I put Charlotte down every evening around seven. I would *never* leave her. How can you even suggest...?"

237

"Yes, ma'am, but you have a house full of potential babysitters," Steven insisted.

Stella Russo glared at him. "I was here, Detective. Ask any of my *potential babysitters*," she said angrily. She stood up and faced the two policemen with a challenge. "I want to see him. And her. I want to meet her. I have to talk with her. I want you to prove it."

"I will let you see him, Mrs. Russo. I'll make the arrangements and have one my officers call you," Steven spoke with respect. "I don't know yet about talking with his wife. I'll have to think about that."

Stella looked as though he'd twisted the knife and drove it in deeper. She clutched the dress over her heart and winced.

"One thing at a time, ma'am," Steven finished. "And remember, we still have to find Frankie's killer."

Chapter 34

Steven and Olivia left Lieutenant Schultz at the Syracuse Police Department with a stack of paperwork and headed down Salina Street to the Assumption Church in search of Father Kranken.

"We've got the time and it's on our way home," Steven had said.

In less than five minutes, Steven pulled his Chevy to the curb in front of the massive red-brick church. Two identical towers topped with cupolas covered in a blue-gray slate and a cross at the top seemed to reach for the heavens.

"What's your plan?" asked Steven.

"I'll check the church first and if no one is there, I'll go next door to one of the other buildings. There must be an office someplace," Olivia said.

"I'll wait here for you. Good luck." He held up a pair crossed fingers.

When Olivia stepped into vast nave, a peaceful hush washed over her, reminding her that she wanted to start going to church again. Looking down the aisle to the far end, she saw a man in the traditional brown, hooded robe of a Franciscan friar on the altar. She quietly moved through the church then cleared her throat when she neared the apse. The friar turned around.

"Hello. May I help you?"

"I hope I'm not disturbing you, Father. I'm looking for a priest but

I don't know which church he's assigned to. I was hoping you might have some kind of directory."

"Yes, we do. What's the name of the priest you're looking for?"

"Father Kranken."

"I'm afraid I don't know him. Come with me to the office and we'll see." The friar led Olivia through a side door, outside, and into a plain building a few yards away. They climbed several steps and entered a small cramped office where a younger man, dressed in identical robes, was working at a wooden desk.

"Brother Peter, this lady is looking for Father Kranken. Do you have the diocese directory?"

"Yes, of course." He reached into the center drawer and extracted a thin paper booklet. "Let's see now," he said, opening it. He ran his finger down a list of names and said, "Ah! Here he is. Father Oskar Kranken, St. John the Baptist Ukrainian Catholic Church, 207 Tompkins Street." The friar looked up at Olivia. "Do you know where that is?"

"Yes, I do. Thank you so much. I can't tell you how much I appreciate your time."

Olivia practically flew down the steps, flung open the car door, and exclaimed, "I found him!"

"Wow. With only one try? That was lucky. Why doesn't that ever happen when I'm on a case?" Steven grimaced. "Where is he?"

"St. John the Baptist, on Tipperary Hill. When we get back, I'll go home and call. Maybe I can make an appointment to look at baptism records. I can't imagine they'd care after 80 years. If I can get the name of the family that adopted Alex, I can look him up online."

"With your computer."

"Yes." She grinned. "I hope I can find him. It would mean everything to Isabel."

"Do you still want to have supper together tonight?"

"Yes, I do if you do."

As Steven steered the motor car along Route 5 on the way back to Knightsbridge, their conversation turned to his case.

"At least Fred's missing persons case is solved," Steven commented. "I wish I could say the same for my two homicides." He glanced at Olivia. "*Two*, Olivia, *two*. I need to solve this before something else happens." He punched the clutch and shifted into third. "I'm getting frustrated. *And* angry." Steven glared at the road. A deep furrow appeared between his brows.

"You always say that talking about your investigation helps. Why don't you discuss it with Will before you come home? And after dinner, I'll listen as long as you want me to."

"Thanks. That's a good idea," Steven agreed.

"Hey, on the bright side, you found S," said Olivia.

"Yeah, but it sure wasn't what I expected. He *married* her, Olivia," Steven exclaimed, still sounding shocked. "I thought Frankie Russo couldn't get any lower."

"That poor woman. I can't imagine what she's going through. The love of your life goes missing. Then you find out he's been murdered. *Then* you discover he was a bigamist and he lied to you for years. And, as if that wasn't bad enough, he has a child!"

Steven knew that cheating was a sensitive issue for Olivia. She'd told him that her ex-fiancé had cheated on her and she'd been devastated when she found out. She'd insisted that she'd put it behind her and moved on. But Steven knew that raw feelings still lurked around the corner. He had witnessed how difficult it had been for her to talk about it. Olivia wasn't as tough as she pretended to be. He admired her for pushing ahead with her life but he wondered if she would ever let herself trust again.

"Do you think Stella had something to do with Frankie's murder, Steven?"

"I doubt it. I've never seen anyone pale on cue. And it's hard to fake a faint. I think she's another one of his victims."

"Do you still think the same woman who poisoned Frankie killed your witness? Because, if that's the case, Dickie Hughes would have had to know her in order to blackmail her. He wouldn't have known Stella."

"You're right, Olivia. I think the killer lives in Knightsbridge, not Syracuse."

"How does finding S help you?"

"Lucy is a stronger suspect now. Not only did Frankie cheat on her all those years, he went out and married another woman. I have to bring her in for questioning," he said sadly.

Steven dropped Olivia off at home then returned to the station. Jimmy Bou was leaning against the front desk talking up a storm with Tommy Forester when he entered. The young officer followed him to the CID room, where they found Steven's partner.

"Will, Jimmy," Steven said. "I found S. Her name is Stella. And there is no Tony Russo. It was Frankie Russo all the time."

"What?" Will and Jimmy chorused.

"Frankie used his middle name Tony and pretended to be his own cousin. The worst of it is that he married S."

"Frankie Russo was a rat!" Jimmy Bou exploded. "Of all the dirty, low-down...."

"Now, we're getting somewhere," said Will. "The big question is did Lucy know?"

"Exactly" Steven said.

"The betrayal with Stella is one more in a long list of betrayals. I wonder if years of looking the other way led to not caring anymore. I imagine she loved him at the beginning but, after everything he put her through, maybe his death is a relief," said Will.

"Grief but also a relief," Steven echoed. "You know that makes sense, Will. It would explain all the emotions Jimmy and I witnessed when we broke the news."

"So, you're saying she was sad because she used to love him. But he hurt her and humiliated her so she's glad to be rid of him. Wow!" Jimmy exhaled forcibly, his eyes big as saucers.

"And don't forget that Lucy likes to be in control." Steven told them how Lucy had spoken to Olivia when she'd stopped at his house. "You should have heard her. She does not want anyone else in her classroom with her students. Remember what Helen said about Lucy not sharing toys when they were little," he added.

"How much control could she've had in her life the way Frankie was acting?" said Will.

"Killing him would be the ultimate control, wouldn't it" Steven speculated.

"What next, Steven? Do we bring her in?" asked Jimmy Bou, hoping to be in on the interrogation.

"Yes, but I want to talk with her sister first. There's something I need to ask Helen." Steven looked at the clock. "I'll swing by on my way home. I hope she's willing to help. After all, something she says could put her sister in the electric chair."

The grim-faced policemen considered that possibility. Four people had already been electrocuted in New York State this year. Steven had always liked Lucy. He didn't want her to be number five.

"I'm still checking on Dickie Hughes, Steven," Will said. "He only went to the mill and to school Monday afternoon. Charlie and Jerry are out canvassing Lucy's neighborhood. So far, nobody saw Dickie at her house or anywhere nearby. If he was blackmailing Lucy, he must've got to her by telephone."

"Could be." Steven stood and stretched. "Where do we stand on his movements *after* school? Mrs. Sweeney said she saw him leaving the building late."

"We're working our way through interviews with all the female staff and teachers," said Will. "Ralph and Pete are there right now. Jimmy and I are going back to meet them in a few minutes. We'll have all their whereabouts by the end of today."

"I'll bring Lucy in for a formal interview tomorrow morning. It's time I put some pressure on her. We need to find out if she knew about Stella. If Lucy's sitting in an interview room here at the station, she might be more forthcoming."

"I think we should do the same with Hannah Grantham," suggested Will.

"I agree," said Steven. "When I asked her why she lied to me, she said she was embarrassed to admit she'd been stepping out with a married man. I suppose that makes sense but I didn't believe her."

Will's eyebrows shot up. "I don't buy it either. You said we were looking for someone who isn't what she pretends to be, Steven. An actress. And she *does* direct the school play every year. How much acting background does she have? Maybe we've made a mistake by not looking at her more seriously."

Steven pursed his lips. "Maybe. Although I still can't believe a failed relationship that ended two years ago would be a strong enough motive. Did you verify her alibi for Sunday?"

"I talked with Ben. He picked her up for the parade a little before two o'clock. But I haven't been able to speak with her mother yet. Mrs. Grantham went to Utica to visit her brother. Won't be back until Friday morning."

"You can't call her?"

"No, the brother doesn't have a telephone."

Helen Sinclair invited Steven to sit in the kitchen while she finished putting supper in the oven. She poured tall tumblers of lemonade and joined him at the table.

"How can I help you?" she asked, taking a drink from her own glass.

"I need to know more about Lucy's marriage, Helen. Did she love Frankie? Were they happy together?"

Helen shrugged. "Honestly, Steven, I don't know. It's funny you're asking me this. I was talking about it with your friend Olivia just the other day."

"Oh?"

"Yes, I was trying to explain how Lucy thinks. My sister and I have never been as close as I wish we were. When we were little, we didn't play together very much. She spent a lot of time alone reading." Helen looked sad.

"How did you meet up with Lucy for the parade on Sunday?"

"She came over for lunch then we all went together."

"What time was that?"

"I think she got here around twelve thirty. Something like that."

Steven made a note in his book. "How often does Lucy go to Syracuse, Helen?"

"Syracuse?" That surprised her. "Good heavens, what's that got to do with anything?"

"It's something I have to follow up. Does she go there?"

"Yes, once in a while. It depends. Oh! You think she was checking on Frankie?" Before Steven could reply, she rushed on, "No, she doesn't. She visits museums and goes to lectures at the university. Sometimes she goes to concerts. Serious stuff. She always says we don't have any *culture* in Knightsbridge." Helen rolled her eyes.

"Who does she go with?"

"Our cousin Josie. She stays at her house when the program's in the evening."

"Where does Josie live? Is it anywhere near Park Street on the North Side?"

"No, down in the Valley."

He made a note. "Does she see Frankie when she's there?"

"I'm not sure they were ever there at the same time. You'd have to ask her."

Chapter 35

Steven was beat when he got home Thursday evening. The case was swirling around in his brain so he could hardly think straight. He knew the killer must be Lucy or Hannah but for the life of him he could not nail down any proof that either woman did the deed. He felt frustrated and almost panicked, afraid he was never going to solve it. To make things worse, tomorrow was his mother's birthday.

This was another one of those firsts without her. Over the past few weeks, he'd thought he was finished grieving but at unexpected moments the sorrow rushed back, cloaking him in despair and making him want to cry. He wondered when it would be over. *If* it would ever be over. He needed a break tonight. His mother would tell him to get out of the house and enjoy himself. He could almost hear her voice. *Amuse-toi bien.* Have a good time. *T'en as besoin.* You need it.

Steven made his decision walking in the front door. He would take Olivia out and forget about the case until tomorrow.

He took the steps to the second floor two at a time and hurried down the hallway to her bedroom door. He stood at the threshold concentrating on her, willing her to appear. And she did. She was dressed in what she called 'leggings and a fitted T'. Her hair was wet. She must have taken a shower. She probably got a run in after her phone call to Syracuse. That was another big change over the eight decades separating them—she and evidently everyone else in the 21st century took showers or baths every day.

"Steven," she exclaimed. "Did you just get home?" She reached the doorway in three steps, peered up at him, and said, "You don't look so good. What's wrong? Don't tell me there's been another murder?"

"No, nothing like that." He sighed. "This case has got me crazy, Olivia. I need a break. I'm taking you out."

"Ooh. Where are we going? Is it something very 1934?" Her face lit up.

"How about fish and chips at the pub? Then...," Steven leaned over and made her wait a good five seconds.

"What? Tell me." She made a pretend-mad face.

"How would you like to watch a dance marathon?"

Her eyes sparkled. "Ooh, yes! I've been curious about those." She frowned. "Wait a minute. I thought you said you were against them. Didn't you tell me they were scams that cheated people?"

"That's true, I did. But some are legitimate. This one's on the level."

"Cool. Where is it?"

"New York Mills. It's a nice night for a drive. What do you say?"

"Let me finish drying my hair and change. I'll be ready in a couple minutes." She put on the trousers she'd worn that day and a fresh top then grabbed a sweater of Evangeline's for the cooling night air.

On the way over to the pub, Steven asked, "How did you make out with the church? Did you find out anything?"

"I think I'm almost there. I talked with the church secretary. She said all the baptism records from the twenties and thirties were boxed up in an attic. She's going to get permission from the priest to look. She's pretty sure he'll say okay because it's been so long. She thought that if Alex was still alive, he'd probably be happy to meet his sister. I'm supposed to call her back tomorrow."

"You're amazing, Olivia," Steven said, in a matter-of-fact tone. She felt her breath catch.

Walking into The Three Lords after spending a few days in 1934 was a completely different experience from their first evening. No one gaped at them. Conversations continued. People smiled and said hello to both of them. On Olivia's part, there was no staring at the pub's customers, no stomach full of butterflies. As they headed across the floor toward a booth in the back, Steven stopped at one of the tiny tables scattered throughout the pub.

"Hi, Will, Trudy." He turned to Olivia. "Olivia, this is my partner Will Taylor and his friend Trudy Evans. Olivia is visiting this week from Syracuse."

Everyone said hello. Will and Steven made small talk until a waiter arrived with the food. They wished Will and Trudy *Bon appétit* and left the couple to enjoy their meal.

Steven and Olivia had barely settled in the booth when Cooper Lewis appeared at the table like a genie popped out of a bottle. "Hello, Steven. How are you, Miss Watson?"

"Very well, Mr. Lewis. Thank you."

"We'll have two orders of fish and chips, Coop," Steven said.

"Theresa's made chicken and biscuits if you're interested. That cousin of mine sure can cook!"

"Not tonight, thanks. How is Theresa? How's that baby girl of hers?" Steven asked, raising a brow at Olivia.

She tried to disguise a smile.

"Isabel's a good baby. Never any trouble. I'll get that order up for you right away," Cooper Lewis said. "What are you drinking?"

Olivia was getting used to Steven ordering for her. She sipped her Young's Oatmeal Stout feeling at home, feeling like herself. She watched the goings-on around them. They avoided discussing the case. Instead, they had what Olivia thought of as a normal conversation. He told her more about dance marathons. She told him how she used to love going out dancing but hadn't had anyone to dance with for a while. When their food came, Olivia enjoyed every bite of the batter-fried fish and homemade French fries. By the end of the meal, she was happy to see that Steven had relaxed and was having a good time. She knew he didn't have much time for fun. He demanded a lot from himself, driving himself to catch the killer and get justice for the victim—no matter the consequences. He didn't seem to think it was important if his own life suffered.

It was after eight thirty when they entered the American Legion Hall accompanied by the mellow sounds of a waltz. Steven paid the twenty-five cent admission for each of them and took Olivia's arm as they entered the large room. Olivia read a hand-printed poster and learned that this group of people had been dancing since Sunday.

The place was crowded. Some two hundred spectators watched as a few dozen men and women moved slowly around the roped-off dance floor. The couples didn't appear to be dancing at all. They shuffled back and forth, ambling around a small space with seeming disregard for the tempo of the music. One man was slumped into the arms of his partner who kept him from slipping to the floor. Another shaved while looking into a mirror that hung around his partner's neck. A small band tucked away in a corner played Strauss's "Blue Danube" and an emcee provided a scattered commentary from the sidelines. Two men who looked like referees walked among the dancing couples occasionally tapping a slow-moving pair on the shoulder. This seemed to encourage a spurt of energy and resulted in a bit more movement on the part of the tired twosome.

Steven led Olivia to an empty table on a raised viewing platform that ringed the room.

"This isn't what I thought it would be like at all," said Olivia. "It's sad."

"It is. But remember that most of these people are probably doing it for the three squares a day and a roof over their heads. I'll bet none of these folks have a job. At least this marathon feeds them and gives them a chance at the prize money. The legitimate ones do. What burns me is that so many of them are rigged and people are cheated," he said angrily.

"I know there's a depression on, but honestly, Steven, I haven't seen that much evidence of it so far. I thought the poverty would be overwhelming. Most of the people I've come across seem to be doing okay. There are always families who are poorer than other ones. In my time, too. That hasn't changed. But, I thought I'd see men selling apples on street corners and soup lines."

"If you went to a big city, you would. We've been lucky in Knightsbridge. When President Roosevelt created the WPA last year, we benefited more than twice over. First, there's a big bridge project over on Route 5. Quite a few Knightsbridge men were hired to work on that. Then, there are all the men who aren't from here. That created a domino effect because the ones from out of town needed places to stay. Several boarding houses opened up. The landladies buy more food to feed them so the shops and farmers benefit. The men hire local women to do their washing and ironing. They buy things in our stores and spend time in the pub and Pinky's. It's been a boon for the town."

"That's fantastic. I never thought about all the repercussions one of those projects could cause."

"Ripples in a pond, Olivia," he said solemnly. "The folks at the sawmill are enjoying an advantage, too. Because of so many public building projects—schools, municipal buildings, and so forth—the lumber mill increased production. That's practically unheard of in times like this," he explained.

"Boy, you did get lucky." She turned to watch the meandering couples on the dance floor. "I still feel bad for these people though."

"I do, too. But like I said, for as long as the marathon lasts—and it could be weeks or even months—they've got a place to stay and food in their stomachs."

"Do you mind terribly if we don't stay long, Steven? I'm sorry, but it's depressing."

"Sure. But it's good that you witnessed this. It'll help your research."

"Let's go home, Steven."

Chapter 36

Friday — April 27, 1934

S teven and Olivia had finished breakfast. Olivia was getting ready to walk to school.

"Now listen to me," he cautioned. "You need to be careful today. There's still a killer loose and she has a direct connection to the high school."

The tone of Steven's warning registered—there was a real possibility of danger. Olivia's eyes widened.

"You *know* that." His eyes held hers. His face was grim. "I'm bringing Lucy in today for questioning."

"Oh, I'm sorry, Steven. I know you were hoping it wouldn't be her."

"I hope it's not but she's still our most likely suspect."

"I promise I'll be careful. I'm only talking to her classes. I'm not going to see her."

"I realize that but I know you, Olivia. The reporter in you'll be itching to come out. Before you know it, you'll be asking questions and launching your own investigation. That could put you in danger." He paused then added, "What I haven't told you is we're considering Hannah Grantham, too."

Olivia gasped. "Hannah? But I liked her. The other night at the baseball game I really enjoyed talking with her. She's more like the friends I have at home. Don't get me wrong. I like Artie's wife, too. But, we're very different. Helen seems sheltered. Hannah went away to college. She's been out in the world on her own. She's independent."

"That's all well and good, but I want you to think about how you act and what you say today. If you run into Hannah, you *have* to be careful. Remember what I told you the other night. Our killer is not who she seems to be."

The morning flew by. Olivia reveled in the experience of talking with Lucy's classes. A lot of the girls asked questions. Olivia was thrilled to tell them about all the choices they had in life. They could get married and have children. But, they could also go to college, have a career, and travel. The Depression wasn't going to last forever. There would be ways to accomplish anything they wanted to do.

"Is this seat taken?" A young woman approached the table in the faculty room where Olivia was eating her lunch.

"Hannah," she exclaimed. "No, please join me. I wondered if I'd run into you." She smiled at Steven's other suspect, finding it impossible to believe.

"How's it going with Lucy's classes?"

Olivia took a beat before she said, "Swell." She chuckled inside. *What a hoot. Look at me, all 1934.* She wished Liz and Sophie could have heard her. They'd crack up. "Isn't it awful about Lucy's husband? I can't imagine what she must be going through."

"Yes, terrible. Do the police have any ideas yet who did it?" At the look on Olivia's face, Hannah added, "Aren't you staying with Steven?" "No, a boarding house in Rome. He picks me up in the mornings so I can spend the day here. But, Hannah, he doesn't talk to me about his work." Olivia took a bite of the peanut butter and jelly on white bread that Steven had made for her this morning. "Did you know him? The man who was killed, I mean."

"We were in school together. Years ago."

While she concentrated on unwrapping her own sandwich, Hannah's mind flew back to a long-ago evening, picturing it as clearly as if it were yesterday.

She was thirteen and still struggling from the death of her adored father two years prior. She'd heard that a trench he was fighting in had been shelled. She wasn't sure what that meant. She only knew that the Great War had taken him from her. She was angry at the world and drifting.

On a Friday night in the fall of eighth grade, she and her best friend Martha went to their first dance in the school gymnasium. Her mother had bought her a new dress for the occasion. Hannah knew she looked good, but she was nervous and afraid she would be the only girl who wasn't asked to dance. She desperately did not want to be a wallflower.

Martha was invited to dance first and Hannah shrunk back closer to the wall. Please let someone ask me, she silently pleaded, balling her hands into fists at her side. And suddenly there he was. Frankie Russo stood in front of her, looking her up and down, smiling at what he saw. He didn't say a word, simply held out his hand, and led her to the dance floor. Hannah had found a new protector.

They stepped out together for the next four years. Frankie promised they would marry after graduation. Hannah had it all planned out in her mind.

Hannah forced the memory out of her consciousness and focused on Olivia. "I hadn't seen him in a long time. Actually," she wiggled her left hand, showing off a sparkling diamond ring. "I got engaged this week."

"Ooh! Congratulations! What's his name?" Olivia asked.

"Ben Maxwell. He's a construction supervisor on the bridge job. It's a very good job."

Two other women joined Olivia and Hannah at the lunch table. Hannah introduced them. "Sarah, Mrs. Sweeney, this is Olivia, Steven Blackwell's friend. She's speaking to Lucy's classes today about being a reporter." She looked at Olivia, "Sarah Hudson teaches English and Mrs. Sweeney is in my department."

Sarah Hudson was the younger of the two. Olivia remembered that she was *stepping out* with Steven's friend Gray Wilson, the photographer.

"How's the play going, Hannah?" asked Mrs. Sweeney, a short round woman with fluffy white hair. "Hannah produces and directs our school play," she told Olivia.

"It's coming along. I have some talented kids this year. Makes my job easier." She took a drink of milk. "Actually, Olivia volunteered to help."

"It'll be fun," Olivia enthused.

While the others chatted, Olivia concentrated on eating, thrilled to eavesdrop on a genuine 1934 conversation among women. She was surprised that it didn't sound much different from any of the conversations she'd had with her friends or co-workers. They talked about work. They shared local gossip. Sarah and Mrs. Sweeney grilled Hannah on her wedding plans. They speculated on the murders of Frankie Russo and Dickie Hughes. The usual stuff—except for the murders.

Steven arrived at the station Friday morning determined to get his two cases solved before another day went by. He held the shortest briefing in history, informing his team they'd likely reconvene later in the day, then, he returned to the CID room to think. He'd telephoned Lucy Russo at seven o'clock knowing that she was used to getting up early. She wasn't happy but agreed to come to the station for further questioning. While Olivia was taking Lucy's classes, Steven would tackle Lucy.

Steven thought the key to this case was the personalities of two important women in Frankie's life—his first wife and his old girlfriend. Was Lucy the kind of woman who could look the other way year after year while Frankie cheated on her and humiliated her in the eyes of the town? Or would she eventually take matters into her own hands? Was Hannah the kind of girl who would wait indefinitely for Frankie to leave Lucy and come back to her? Could she be happy with another fella after spending so much of her life with Frankie? Was she capable of a violent act?

Steven decided to organize some private notes. He pulled over a pad of ruled paper. *Look beyond what you see,* he reminded himself. *She's not what she appears. Go back to the beginning.*

Steven thought about Lucy. It made sense that her childhood and teen years had contributed to the kind of adult she'd become. He racked his memory for any details or bits of information he'd heard about Lucy when she'd been young. He recalled overhearing what had seemed like an ordinary conversation at the time.

He'd been at Artie's house for Annie's eleventh birthday party. Annie had recently been diagnosed with poor eyesight and had to wear glasses. She wasn't happy about it. It was one of the few times he had witnessed her doing a lot of pouting and frowning. Lucy had put her arm around her niece and said, "I was only ten when I started wearing glasses. The kids at school were horrible. They made fun of me all the time. They called me 'four eyes.' Of course, they were used to calling me names anyways."

Annie had asked what her aunt meant by that. Lucy replied that the other kids didn't like it that she was smart. She had loved school and the challenge of learning. She had been proud, at first, to raise her hand and answer a teacher's question. But, the incessant and cruel teasing of the other children had been unbearable. She told Annie that eventually she remained quiet.

Steven felt a moment of sadness for the bright young girl who'd hid her light under a bushel. He remembered what Mrs. Sweeney had said about the bullying Dickie Hughes had endured at the hands of thoughtless children. Steven wondered if Lucy had felt empathy for him. She would have understood what it was like.

If that were the case, could she have killed Dickie Hughes? Steven seriously doubted it. Unless she had felt pushed to the wall. Blackmail had a way of changing things. It might explain her killing him.

Steven began his notes.

LUCY

needs to be in control	independent
smart	likes to be alone
bullied as a child	quiet
private	possessive of her things

Steven remembered something else Artie had told him—Frankie Russo had been Lucy's first beau. In this day and age, that was almost unheard of. What was Lucy doing when all the other kids were stepping out, fooling around, and experimenting? Reading. Alone. The impact of that realization gave Steven a lot to consider. Lucy had been innocent and inexperienced in the ways of the world. And who shows up? Frankie Russo. What makes a smart girl pick a loser like that?

Steven added two more items to his list:

inexperienced	lonely?

He jotted down several more questions he wanted to ask. He glanced at his watch. She'd be here soon.

Next, Steven thought about Hannah. What did he know about her when she was young? Not much. He picked up the telephone and dialed his cousin Jim's house.

Martha answered. "KB32. Martha Blackwell speaking."

"Hi, Martha, It's Steven."

"Oh," she exclaimed, clearly surprised. "Jimmy's already gone to work, Steven. He won't be home until suppertime."

"It's you I want to talk with Martha. I'm sorry to do this on the telephone but I have to ask you a couple of questions about Hannah."

"I don't know, Steven. I know we're family and everything but she *is* my best friend."

"It's nothing private, Martha. I just need some background from when you were kids."

"Oh, that's all right. What do you want to know?"

"Do you remember when and how she met Frankie Russo?"

"Sure. We were in eighth grade. They met at a school dance. I was there."

"Do you remember what she said about him then or any time over the years they stepped out together?"

"As close as we've always been, Hannah's a bit secretive. I know she was crazy about him. In high school, she'd write his name all over her notebooks. She used to practice writing *Mrs. Frankie Russo* to see what it looked like. But, girls do that, Steven. It's not serious. You don't really think you're going to marry the boy you met when you were thirteen."

"Did she talk much about him?"

"In the beginning, sure. She mooned over him constantly. But, it wasn't always smooth sailing with Frankie."

"Are you saying Frankie cheated on her even back then?" asked Steven.

"I think so. He was always a ladies' man. There were times I saw him with another girl.

He'd march right up to me and give me some pathetic excuse.

He knew it would get back to her then I could serve up his stupid excuse. But, we were kids, you know? That's when you learn about relationships and how you're going to act in one."

"Do you think she knew about his cheating and put up with it? Or didn't she know?"

"She never said anything but knowing Hannah I doubt she'd put up with it."

Jimmy Bou stuck his head in the doorway. "Psst. Steven, she's here," he whispered.

Steven put up five fingers and mouthed, "Five minutes."

Jimmy gave him the thumbs up and left.

"Thanks, Martha. I've got to go. I appreciate what you told me."

"Let's keep it between ourselves, Steven. Hannah would be angry if she found out we talked about her behind her back."

"This conversation never took place."

Martha giggled. "Thanks. See you."

Steven closed his eyes and thought hard. What had he just learned?

	HANNAH
crazy about Frankie	wouldn't stand for cheating
assumes they'll marry	possessive
fierce	keeps thoughts/feelings to herself
smart (teacher)	clever (directs play)

Hannah always struck Steven as a sweet uncomplicated girl. Now, he had a new angle to consider. He reminded himself that he was looking for someone who was not who she seemed.

Before he could speak with Lucy, Steven had one more telephone call to make. He dialed Frankie's sister's house.

"Steven! Have you found out who did it?" she asked anxiously.

"Not yet, Connie. Sorry. Listen, I have kind of a strange question for you."

"All right."

"I want you to think back over the past ten years…,"

"Ten years!"

"Yes, from the time Frankie graduated from high school until last week."

"Okaaay," she dragged out the word.

"Can you think of a girl that Frankie spent time with or had a crush on whose name started with H? Somebody he was interested in or chased after?"

There was a long pause.

"Connie?" He clicked the button on the telephone base several times. "Connie?"

"Yes, I'm here. You're right, that is a strange question. Let me think a minute."

A longer pause.

"No, I can't. Obviously, you mean someone other than Hannah Grantham, right?"

"Yes, someone named Helen, Harriet, Hedda, Hailey, Hermione, Henrietta, Hope."

"I get it. I get it. Does this have to do with that little book you told me about?"

"Yes, there were notations over the years that indicate he was stepping out with someone whose name begins with H. I want to be sure Hannah is the only possibility."

"As far as I know, she is. Until the past two or three years, he couldn't stay away from her. Like I told you the other day, Steven, even after he married Lucy, he saw Hannah. She was like drink to him. It was the same for her."

"Even though he decided not to marry her?"

261

"Yes. They were addicted to each other."

Lucy Russo arrived at the station, dressed in a simple black dress and spectator pumps. Steven went to the front desk where she waited on a wooden chair.

"Good morning, Lucy. I'm sorry for the delay." He wanted her in as good a mood as possible for this interview.

"Can we get it over with, Steven? I have a lot to do today."

"Sure."

Lucy followed him down the hall, head held high, back ramrod straight. She looked neither left nor right as they marched to a small room at the back of the building. Lucy read the sign on the door—Interview 1.

"Really, Steven? I thought at least we would be in your office."

"This is an official interview, Lucy. For the record."

They sat at opposite sides of a wooden table. Lucy shifted in her seat. She stared at Steven but didn't speak.

"Would you like a glass of water, Lucy?" Steven offered.

"No, thank you." Her face was closed-off, shut-down.

"All right, let's get started then. I've known you a long time, Lucy. You're smart and this is a small town. There's one thing we have to get straight right now. You must have known Frankie was cheating on you."

"Of course, I knew. It was humiliating. We were hardly married two months when he started up with her again. He couldn't stay away from that damn Hannah Grantham."

Steven heard a lifetime of emotions packed in those few words.

"I'm sorry, Lucy. You didn't deserve that," he said quietly. He waited, knowing the silence would impel her to continue. A full half-minute passed. Lucy sighed, as her shoulders dropped.

"I suppose it all has to come out now, huh, Steven?"

He nodded. "All of it, Lucy. Every single bit of it."

"You know," she said, sounding amazed, "you read in literature about love turning into hate. And you think how could that happen in real life? Then you meet someone. You fall in love. You give them your trust and your innocence. You hand over your heart and your *life*. And they trample on it like dirt under their feet. Like it was nothing." Lucy shook her head as if to clear the memory. "When we were growing up, all the other girls talked about the boy they would marry and the children they were going to have. They went on and on about their wedding day—the dress, the flowers, the attendants, walking down the aisle, the first kiss, Mr. and Mrs. Whoever. I *never* understood.

"I dreamed about packing a suitcase—I always imagined it would be covered with stickers from all over the world." Her eyes glittered with excitement. "I would board a sleek ocean liner to Europe. I wanted to visit the most magnificent concert halls in the world. I imagined listening to the works of the greatest composers of all time played by the world's most famous orchestras." She broke off, seeming to get lost in her dream.

"And then I met Frankie. I fell in love or so I thought. You hear in songs about how someone is blinded by love. That was me. I believed what I wanted to believe. Anyway, I'll spare you the grotesque details. I knew right away I'd made a horrible mistake. The biggest mistake of my life." She swallowed hard. "I think I'll take that drink now if you don't mind."

Steven nodded. "Sure." He reached to a pitcher sitting on the table then handed her a glass of water.

Lucy took a long drink. "I'll keep this short, Steven. I can barely stand to hear myself talk about it. It sickens me when I think I actually put up with his behavior all these years." She looked devastated when she added, "What happened to my pride?" She gulped more water.

"The feelings I had for him soured quickly. I hated him for what he was doing to me. I was thrilled when he got the part-time job in Syracuse. I only had to look at his lying face every other week.

"Anyway," she sighed, "I decided I'd finally had enough. I came up with a plan. I was going to leave him. Not divorce. The Russo clan would never allow their precious Frankie to be the first one in the family to get a divorce and be excommunicated." She laughed bitterly. "No, I was leaving him. I opened a bank account that Frankie didn't know about. I've been saving every penny. And I've been looking for another teaching job. A friend from normal school teaches in Oswego. If I find a job there, I can live with her and her family until I get on my feet." Lucy took another drink. She sat up straighter, looking as though a weight had been taken off her shoulders. "I ended up hating Frankie. But, I didn't kill him, Steven. I was leaving him."

This makes sense. Steven thought. *It rings true.* They would check, of course, but at the moment he was cautiously optimistic that his best friend's sister-in-law wasn't the killer.

"All right, Lucy. I'm going to need a lot of information so we can check—names, addresses, telephone numbers." Steven pushed a pad of paper and pen across the table. "I want you to write down all the details about your plan to leave Frankie. Where's your secret bank account? I'll also need to see the passbook. A list of schools where you applied to teach. Your girlfriend's name and so forth."

"I understand, Steven. I'm happy to give it to you. I want this over. But, I don't have any telephone numbers or addresses with me. They're all at home."

"Weren't you taking a big risk that Frankie would come across things?"

She gave the first smile of the day. "No, I hid everything under the potatoes in my fruit cellar. He'd never go down there."

Steven smiled back at her. "Smart. All right, I'll drive you. We'll go to your house together. Write out everything you just told me. Leave blank spaces for the information that's at home. When you're done, we'll go get everything."

He left Lucy Russo filling page after page of detailed plans.

Steven was eager to share Lucy's story with his partner. He hurried to the CID room and found Will finishing a report. Steven told him everything.

"It's not her, Will," said Steven, feeling relieved but cautioning himself not to jump the gun.

"Not if everything checks out. There's no motive."

"Right. Why kill him if you can leave him?"

"How do you want to handle this, Steven?"

"When she's finished in there, I'll take her home," said Steven. "She can fill in the blanks. I don't see any reason why she can't stay home, do you?"

"Not right now. We'll start checking everything she told you," Will said. "So, that leaves us with Hannah."

Chapter 37

Steven was back from Lucy's by eleven o'clock. On his way down the hall, he stuck his head in the patrol room.

"Ten minutes, fellas."

He stopped in the CID room to touch base with Will.

"I updated the chief while you were gone, Steven. And I wrote up the warrant request for Hannah Grantham's house. One of the patrolmen walked it over to Judge Randolph. We should have it within the hour," his partner said.

"Thanks, Will. The sooner the better."

Steven continued to the end of the corridor where Chief Andy Thompson was holed up in his office. He was bent over his paper-strewn desk writing and mumbling. Steven couldn't make out what the chief was saying but imagined it was his usual complaint about drowning in paperwork. Thompson looked up at the sound of Steven's footsteps.

"Ah, Blackwell. You're back," said Thompson gruffly. "You got everything?"

"Yes, right where she said it would be." He indicated the large envelope he carried. "Lucy did a good job documenting her plans, Chief. There's more than enough for us to corroborate her story. She kept copies of the letters she sent to schools looking for a job." Steven sat in the visitors' chair facing Thompson. "If it all checks out, she'll be in the clear. Lucy didn't need to kill Frankie. She was leaving him. Besides, I talked with her sister. I found out Lucy was at Helen's having lunch around noon. She couldn't have been up in the field with Frankie."

"What about the other Mrs. Russo? S, I mean. Have you talked with Lucy about that yet?"

"No, we'll deal with that later. Right now, I want to verify what she told me."

"If I'm reading you right, you've settled on Hannah Grantham?"

"She's the only one left."

"But, you don't actually have any physical proof, do you?" The chief frowned. He loved hard evidence—the more the better.

"No, but we've got a lot of circumstantial evidence. I think I know what happened."

"*Think* isn't gonna put her behind bars, Steven. I hate it when you say that. Gives me the willies." He shivered. "We have to know for sure."

"We will, Chief. Don't worry. We're picking Hannah up after school. She's not going anywhere till then. She's got a full afternoon of classes. I'm going to get the whole truth out of her this time."

"You're going to get her to confess?" Chief Thompson screwed up his face.

"Yes, I am."

"I hope you're right. That's one tough cookie, although she acts like a fairytale princess."

"That's exactly the point, Chief. She's a darn good actress. She's had us all fooled."

Steven's team gathered in the patrol room. Excitement choked the air. Adrenalin skipped up and down the walls. Everyone knew this was it. They were at the end. And they all had a chance to be in on it.

Detective Sergeant Blackwell and his partner Sergeant Will Taylor entered the room together. Steven had a large envelope under his arm. It was thick and, by the way he was holding it, stuffed with important papers. Chief Thompson followed them in a few seconds later. The chief chose a spot in the back of the room and settled in to observe.

Steven cleared his throat and the room quieted. "Before I tell you about the interview I had this morning, I want to outline where we are. I realize you already know most, if not all, of what I'm going to say. But I think it's good for us to get everything organized in our minds before we take these final steps.

"Because of what Dickie Hughes told Billy Burton, we know for certain our killer is a woman. Because of the little notebook Frankie kept, we know he cheated on Lucy throughout their marriage. We've established that Frankie Russo stepped out with Hannah Grantham, in secret, long after their relationship supposedly ended. Until the fall of 1931, that is. Remember Frankie took a part-time job at Haberle's Brewery that May. For reasons we do not know, when Frankie worked and lived in Syracuse he went by the name of Tony Russo. Anthony is his middle name. Maybe he wanted a fresh start. Maybe he never liked the name Frankie. We'll probably never find out. But, what's important is that's when he met a woman named Stella. That's when his behavior changed."

"S. S. S," whispered the men on Steven's team. The mysterious S in Frankie's little book.

"In September 1932, Tony Russo—that is Frankie Russo—married Stella. We believe Frankie fell in love for the first time in his life. That would explain the change in his behavior in late '31, early '32. By the way, he also has a child with his bigamous wife—a little girl. Think about that for a minute, fellas. A child is a big commitment. It's worth noting that Frankie did not run away from that responsibility. And it would have been all too easy to do.

"You all know we've cleared the Russo relatives and Frankie's co-workers. You know everyone in town's got something with arsenic in it in their backyard shed or cellar. There have been no recent purchases. I believe we are looking for a woman who is not what she seems. Someone who's a good actress. Probably a sociopath.

"This gives us three solid persons of interest—Hannah Grantham, Lucy Russo, and Stella Russo. The three most significant women in Frankie's life. When I told Stella Russo that her Tony had been masquerading as a single man and his real name was Frankie, she blanched and fainted. I have never seen anyone faint on cue. I believe she had no idea who she married. I think when Frankie Russo met and fell in love with Stella, he changed for the better...and for good. Their marriage seems to have been a loving and devoted one. In addition, Stella Russo has solid alibis for both murders.

"So, we come to this morning's interview. *Finally...,*" Steven pronounced in an exasperated tone, "*finally,* I think I got the truth out of the very private Lucy Russo. That's what this meeting is about. Fellas," he glanced at his watch, "we have almost four hours to corroborate everything she said. Our deadline is the end of school today. That's three o'clock.

"Lucy told me she was leaving Frankie. She had a plan in place and the so-called proof is in this envelope. She opened a secret bank account and was saving money so she could walk away from her life. She started looking for a teaching job in the Oswego area because she has a friend there and a place to stay until she gets on her feet. If that's all true, Lucy had no motive to kill Frankie Russo."

A murmur had been building up as Steven spoke and now a buzz went around the room.

Steven took a beat and let their emotions rise. He wanted every man on his team energized and focused on the tasks he was about to assign.

"All right then. We've got a two-pronged attack this after-noon—Lucy Russo and Hannah Grantham. We're going to *carefully* examine the information Lucy gave us. I'm talking a fine-toothed comb here, men. If everything checks out, Lucy Russo has no motive.

"I'm going to tackle her secret bank account. Ray and Jerry, you're going to Oswego to interview Lucy's college friend. I want you to talk with her face to face." He handed Ray a piece of paper. "Here's the name and address of the school where she teaches. Her name's Doris Fellows. Her home address and telephone number are on here, too." He explained what he wanted them to find out. "Ray, take one of the department cars."

"You got it, Steven," Ray exclaimed. "We'll leave right now. We'll get back as fast as we can."

"If it takes longer than we think, call me with your results before two o'clock," Steven instructed.

Steven opened the envelope and extracted a sheaf of papers. "Charlie, you're making phone inquiries. These are copies of the letters Lucy said she sent to schools where she was looking for a teaching job. I want you to call the high schools in Oswego, Fulton, and Mexico. Verify that she actually sent the letters. Find out if she filed an application and gave them whatever other information they asked for. We need to be sure the job search was real."

Charlie reached over Ray's shoulder and took the papers from Steven.

"You'll have to call the operator to get the telephone numbers. Use Will's desk. It'll be quiet in the CID room," Steven suggested.

"Now, as for Hannah Grantham. I've already caught her in one lie. It may or may not be significant. But, we all know that once someone starts lying, it's hard to stop. Her mother was supposed to get back this morning so we can finally check Hannah's alibi for Sunday and Tuesday night. Will and Jimmy are going to Hannah's house to talk with Mrs. Grantham and search for evidence that the poisoned food was prepared there."

Tommy Forester entered the room, a paper in his hand. "Excuse me, Detective Blackwell. Your warrant." He handed it to Steven.

"Thanks, Tommy. Good timing," Steven said, passing it to Will.

"Hey, Steven, what about us?" Ralph's voice boomed from the side of the room.

Everyone laughed.

"Don't worry, Ralph. I haven't forgotten you and Pete. I saved the tricky job until last."

Ralph and Pete made eyes at each other. "Ooh."

"We have to find out if Hannah knew about Stella. What if she was still in love with Frankie? What if she thought he'd leave Lucy some day and marry her?" Steven paused dramatically. "What if Hannah discovered a second wife? How would she feel then?" He took a breath. "So, Ralph and Pete, your job is to find out if Hannah Grantham went to Syracuse some time in the past couple of months. She doesn't drive so you'll need to check the bus and train."

"Phew!" Pete exclaimed. "You weren't kidding, Steven. That *is* tricky. You're counting on someone remembering her?"

"Hoping, Pete. I'm hoping we catch a break today."

Chairs scraped across the rough floor as the meeting broke up and Steven's team tackled their assignments. Less than four hours to prove Lucy Russo's innocence. And make a solid case for Hannah Grantham's guilt.

Chapter 38

Olivia's day had flown by. And it had been *swell*. She grinned to herself as she strolled down School Hill Road Friday afternoon. The students in Lucy's classes seemed genuinely interested in what she had to say. Every class ended in a lively question-and-answer session and several girls—led by Annie Sinclair—surprised her with a visit after the final class. They asked more questions and, when she told them about her project, pleaded with her to participate. Olivia accepted their offer and made arrangements to meet them at the soda fountain after school. Her head was buzzing with ideas for discussion with the girls. She couldn't remember the last time she was so excited about her work.

Olivia was especially thrilled about meeting one girl in particular. When they had introduced themselves, her whole body registered shock. In a few decades, Molly Silverstone would become Sophie's grandmother. For the first time since she'd traveled to 1934, she desperately wanted her phone. This was a text she was dying to send.

Olivia reached the corner and craned her neck to see the clock hanging off the wall of the bank. *I need to buy a watch.* Plenty of time. She continued down Victoria toward Bailey's. Tucked in between the diner and Mo's Barber Shop was the third item on her 1934 bucket list—Sal's News. Maybe she wouldn't have a chance to shop at Woolworth's this week, but she could sure buy some newspapers and magazines.

Sal's was a narrow little shop that was deceiving from the sidewalk. Two long aisles were packed with newspapers and magazines. Olivia checked the prices. The magazines ranged from ten to thirty-five cents, *Vogue* being the most expensive, and newspapers were (*What?*) two cents for *The New York Times* and a penny for the local papers. (*I love 1934!*) She calculated that she could buy both newspapers and an armful of magazines and have plenty of money left from Steven's five dollars to buy ice cream for the girls. Olivia read the headlines. The hunt for John Dillinger was still the big story of the day. She noted articles on Roosevelt's New Deal, Japan's policy with China, price controls on milk, Gloria Swanson getting her fourth divorce, and coal and glove strikes being settled. She was tingling with excitement; she couldn't wait to read every single word.

Thinking of her girls' night with Liz and Sophie, Olivia picked up the latest issues of *Vogue*, *Vanity Fair* with Katharine Hepburn on the cover, *McCall's*, *The Ladies' Home Journal*, *Motion Picture*, and a cool-looking fashion magazine called *The Delineator*. Ever the reporter, she also grabbed the current issue of *Time* at fifteen cents. She paid the man at the cash register and returned three dollars and change to Evangeline's purse.

If she'd had any prior doubts, walking into the Village Drugstore confirmed that Olivia was in the past. Why hadn't they preserved this fantastic place? The drugstore in her time was positively boring in comparison.

To begin with, the name was misleading. Certainly all the products she expected to see filled the wooden shelves—aspirin, toothpaste, lipstick, tissues—but the star of the show was the soda fountain tucked away in the back. Behind the dark green-and-white marbled countertop, the mirrored wall reflected a shiny silver cash register with keys that had to be pushed, spigots for pressurized soda water, and machines for whipping up milk shakes and other delights. Sundae glasses and banana split boats hung upside down by their pedestals in a mirrored nook. A board held slips of paper informing customers of the dozen or so different kinds of ice cream served—some with colorful, mouth-watering illustrations. A large red circle advertising *Coca Cola* took up the center of a round clock hanging above a storage cupboard.

As Olivia approached the booths, the oaken floor creaked and shifted beneath her feet. *Maybe it's a good thing this place didn't make the trip across time. I'd want to come here every day. That'd be the end of my skinny jeans.* The girls were already there—Annie Sinclair, blue-eyed and freckled; Lilly Coffin, with her baby-fine hair and big hazel eyes; and Molly Silverstone, tall and slender with hair the color of fine whisky. The three friends sat sipping water through straws and chatting up a storm in a booth on the right.

Annie waved to her excitedly. "Olivia, here we are!"

Olivia slid onto the seat next to her, tucked her purchases between them, and set her notebook on the table. "Hi, girls. Thanks for meeting me. I'm really excited you want to help with my project."

"Are we going to be in a magazine?" asked Molly. "Which one?"

"Will you put our names in the article?" said Lilly.

"I'm going to sell it to a magazine but I don't know which one yet," Olivia replied. "I'm not sure about printing your names. Maybe just first names. Something like *fourteen-year-old Annie S. hopes to be a history teacher one day.*"

"How did you know that?"

"Your mom told me."

The waitress appeared and Olivia ordered four ice cream sundaes, cherry on top and all the trimmings. "My treat," she said.

"Oooh!" they chorused, eyes bright with anticipation.

While they waited for the waitress to bring their sundaes, Olivia asked the girls if they had known Dickie Hughes. "That must have been terribly upsetting for all the kids," she said.

"Yeah," said Lilly "but he was older. We didn't really know him."

"He was nice, though," said Annie.

"I wonder if Miss Grantham is upset," commented Molly.

"Why do you say that?" asked Olivia.

"I think he was going to help with the play. I saw them talking after class the other day. I heard her say she'd see him later. Play practice is after school. So, he was probably going to join the crew. Miss Grantham has been trying to get some of the boys to help." Molly's face fell and she pouted. "I want to paint scenery but my grades are too low. I *hope* I passed the test this week."

"We've been working really hard on the play but it's fun," said Annie.

"Yeah, I think Mrs. Russo was helping the other day, too," said Lilly. "I saw her at the end of rehearsal."

"You did?" said Annie.

"Yeah, I forgot my English book and went upstairs to get it. Mrs. Russo was coming out of the Home Ec. room. I think she was getting some props for Miss Grantham."

"She's nice. I like her," said Molly.

As Olivia and the girls swirled hot fudge sauce through the rich vanilla ice cream, mixing in whipped cream and nuts so they'd get a little bit of everything in each bite, the girls talked about school, their lives, and what they wanted for their futures. Annie and Lilly teased Molly about a boy who had been paying attention to her lately.

"Who's this guy?" Olivia asked, leaning forward to catch some chocolate dripping off her spoon.

"His name's George. George Talbot," Annie told her.

Olivia nearly choked.

"Molly thinks she's too good for him," Lilly kidded with a slight jab of her elbow in her friend's ribs.

"Ouch! No, I don't. That's not it at all. I don't want to get my hopes up. George Talbot steps out with a different girl every five minutes. I want someone who'll last longer than that."

Olivia had never found it harder to keep quiet. Molly and George were Sophie's grandparents. Little did she know, Molly was going to get exactly what she wanted—sixty-four years with George Talbot.

The girls chattered while they enjoyed their sundaes. Annie was passionate about history and her scrapbooks which she filled with movie star clippings from fan magazines and newspapers. Lilly was eager to grow up and see the world outside of Knightsbridge. She showered Olivia with questions about big cities and nearly swooned when Olivia said that she'd traveled in Europe. Molly was confused about wanting a husband and a career. Did Olivia think it was possible to have both?

Olivia turned the conversation to famous women of the time and discovered they couldn't have cared less about Mrs. Roosevelt. *She needs to get to a beauty shop!* They'd never heard of Georgia O'Keefe. *Who?* And they thought Amelia Earhart was brave but not fashionable. *Look at her clothes!* Instead, they swooned over Jean Harlow, Carole Lombard, Fay Wray, and Myrna Loy.

"We go to the pictures every Saturday," Annie informed her.

"I wanted to see *Hell's Angels* but my mom said I was too young. I love Jean Harlow!" sighed Lilly.

"Olivia, did you see *King Kong* last year?" Annie asked.

Olivia gave a short low scream and pretended to struggle in the ape's fist.

The girls giggled.

"Good one," said Molly. "My favorite is Carole Lombard." Then her face fell. "She got divorced from William Powell last year. Gee, if *she* can't do both...," she groaned, as though this were the answer to her own struggle.

"Molly, believe me when I tell you this. You *can* do both. Trust me. You *will* figure it out," Olivia reassured her.

Molly reached across the table and squeezed Olivia's hand. "Thank you." She looked deep into Olivia's eyes. "I believe you."

So, this was where it started, Olivia thought. *I always wondered about the connection I had with Sophie's grandmother. It began here over ice cream sundaes.* She smiled warmly at the girl who would become a life-long friend.

"Mmm! Those look good," said a voice over Olivia's shoulder.

"Hi, Miss Grantham," said Molly.

"We're helping Olivia with her research," Lilly said excitedly.

Olivia twisted around and saw Hannah standing there. "Hi, Hannah. Come join us."

"I'd love to, thanks, but I can't. I only stopped in for a minute to pick up something. I have to go back to school."

Olivia noticed the clock and frowned. "So late?"

"Actually, I'm on my way back from Utica. I went to get some props from a special store. I want to get them set up for rehearsal tomorrow."

"Do you need some help? We're just about finished. I'd better send these girls home before their parents start to worry. It's nearly suppertime."

"My mom knows I'm here. She won't worry," said Annie.

"Supper," groaned Molly.

"I'm stuffed," added Lilly.

"Nevertheless," said Olivia.

"Did we give you enough to write about, Olivia?" asked Annie. "If you need more, you can always come over to my house. Have Steven bring you."

Two months ago, Olivia had discovered that Annie had a massive crush on Steven. She thanked her and turned back to Hannah.

"What do you say? I've got about twenty minutes before I have to get back."

"That's nice of you, Olivia, thanks. But, it won't take long. Then I'm meeting Ben. To be honest, I could use the help tomorrow morning if you're free."

"Sure, I'd be happy to. What time?"

"How about ten? In the auditorium?" Hannah glanced around the table. "And, Molly, I'll see *you* at rehearsal."

"I passed?" she gasped. She jumped out of the booth and hugged her teacher. "Thank you."

"Yes, you did. You're officially a member of the crew." Hannah grinned. "Wear old clothes. It's dirty back stage."

Olivia hugged all three girls on leaving the soda fountain and said she'd see them at rehearsal in the morning. Checking the clock that hung in the drugstore's front window, she realized she'd better get going if she wanted to catch the secretary at St. John's before the woman closed the office for the weekend. How did time manage to get eaten up like that? It's a good thing Hannah had said tomorrow instead.

Chapter 39

S teven quickly filled in the request for a warrant for Lucy's bank account. To save precious time, he drove to the judge's office. Judge Hal Randolph was Steven's father's closest friend. The judge and his wife treated him like the son they never had.

"You're in luck," said Randolph's secretary. "He just got back. He doesn't have to be in court for another hour and a half." She knocked on the door frame and led Steven into the book-filled office.

"Steven, my boy," Judge Randolph exclaimed, as he rose and enveloped Steven in a big hug. "Where have you been keeping yourself? Margaret said the other day that it seems like ages since we've seen you." He sat down and motioned Steven to do the same. "I suspect you're not here to chit chat. I approved a warrant for you a while ago."

"Thanks, Judge. I need another one." Steven explained why he needed to check the bank records.

"Looks like your case is heating up. I have to admit I was surprised not to hear from you much this past week." The judge reached for a pack of Camel cigarettes—*Smoke a fresh cigarette. Every package now a humidor.* He blew a thick cloud up toward the stained ceiling. "I take it this has been a tough case?"

"You said it. I'll tell you all about it when it's over."

"All right. Now, let's see what we have here." Judge Randolph stuck a pair of glasses on his long slender nose and peered down at the warrant request. He reached the end and pronounced, "Makes sense." He grabbed an expensive-looking fountain pen and signed with a blue flourish. "Here you go."

Steven's stomach growled as he threw his motor car in gear and sped to the bank. No time for lunch today. He parked in front of the historic building, sliding his '29 Chevy between a Plymouth 30U and a bright red Ford Cabriolet. He took the steps two at a time and flew through the entrance.

A hush greeted him as he entered the bank lobby. Cherubs floated amongst clouds painted on the high ceiling and crystal chandeliers softly lit the vast space. Steven crossed the marble floor negotiating his way around Doric columns and skirting the brass-legged, glass-topped tables with their pigeon holes full of deposit and withdrawal slips. He spied his old friend Marty Carpenter in his office. As Steven approached, Marty looked up and waved him in.

"Steven," the recently-appointed bank manager exclaimed. "Haven't seen you in a while. How are you?"

"Fine, Marty. You?"

"Still getting used to the new job."

"That's right. Congratulations. You sure deserved it. You've worked hard."

"Thanks for saying that, Steven. What brings you here?"

Steven took the warrant from his jacket pocket and handed it across the desk. "I need to access a bank account belonging to Lucy Russo."

"Frankie's account is frozen, Steven. Standard procedure in the case of a murder."

"Not Frankie's, Marty. A private account that Lucy opened some time ago."

"Oh, I see," the manager exclaimed as he reached for the paper.

Steven watched his friend unfold the warrant and read its contents.

Carpenter was a smallish, rawboned man with bowed legs. Steven had never gotten used to seeing him dressed in a suit and tie. He'd always thought Marty looked like he should be wearing dungarees and a cowboy hat. But now that he'd been promoted, curiously, it all seemed to fit.

"You look good in this office, Marty. It suits you."

Carpenter grinned. "I have to admit I really like this job. Okay, Steven. Let's go see what we've got."

It took less than a minute for Steven to realize Lucy had been telling the truth. He was amazed at the amount she had been able to save. She must have been putting the majority of her teaching salary into this account. He wondered if she would actually leave now that Frankie was out of her life.

Officer Ray Monroe pulled the police sedan into a parking area in front of Oswego High School, a three-story, honey-colored brick building. He and Jerry entered the main office and presented their identification and badges to the secretary at the counter.

"Do you have a teacher here called Doris Fellows?" Ray asked.

"Yes. Her room's right across the hall and...," the woman glanced up at a clock, "she's probably in there by herself right now. She doesn't have a class this period. I'll walk you over."

After the secretary had introduced the two policemen and left the room, Ray got right to the point. "I'm sure you have a lot of work to do, Miss, so we'll be quick. We need to know if you have a friend by the name of Lucy Russo."

"Yes, we've known each other for years." Although the woman was surely in her late twenties, she could have been one of the students. She had light-brown hair that had a mind of its own, an innocent-looking face, and a trusting smile.

"We understand you offered to let Lucy stay with you if she finds a

281

teaching job in the area," said Jerry.

"No." A puzzled look appeared on her face.

"No? You didn't tell Lucy Russo she could live at your house until she got on her feet?" asked Ray.

"Why would she need to stay with my family? Did something happen to her husband?"

Ray and Jerry looked at each other. They had not expected this.

"When's the last time you spoke with Lucy?"

"We don't talk very often, long distance is too expensive. The last time I saw her was before she got married." She paused. "That would have been maybe five years ago."

They asked a couple more questions then left the teacher to her work.

"Wow," exclaimed Jerry, once they had closed the classroom door and were standing in the hallway.

"We'd better call Steven," said Ray. "Let's see if we can use a telephone in the office."

After Steven had left with the envelope of papers, Lucy stood at the kitchen window thinking and wondering. *Would the police check everything?* The bank account would hold up. She knew that for sure since she had actually toyed with the idea of leaving Frankie. Not for Oswego, though. More like Boston or New York. There was enough money in her secret account to convince even someone as dogged as Steven Blackwell. *But, what about Doris? Would they call her? Would Steven send someone all the way to Oswego to talk with her in person?* That was going to be the problem.

Lucy still found it impossible to believe that she had done it. Damn that Hannah Grantham! It was all her fault—and the timing. The timing had been lousy. If only she had gone to the ladies' room ten minutes later.

Lucy hurried down the hall to the ladies' room. She still had some work to catch up because of yesterday's snow day and she couldn't wait until she got home. She pulled open the outside door, took two steps, and pushed the second door. She stopped. Somebody was in one of the stalls sobbing as though someone had died.

"Hello. Can I help you?" she said.

Nothing.

"Is there something I can do? Who is this?" She knocked gently on the door. She heard the lock click. And out staggered Hannah Grantham.

"Hannah!"

"So, here we are," Hannah looked destroyed. Her creamy complexion was blotchy, her eyes swollen and red.

"What's wrong? Is it your mother?"

"It's your damn husband," Hannah managed to purse her lips amid choking on her tears.

"Yeah, you'd know about Frankie, wouldn't you?" Lucy turned to leave. She sure wasn't going to help Hannah Grantham. Not on your life.

"We're in the same boat now, Lucy."

Lucy spun around. "What are you talking about?"

"I went to Syracuse yesterday."

"So?"

"You don't know, do you?"

"Spit it out, Hannah, I've got work to do."

"Frankie has another wife and a baby girl." A malicious smile snuck onto her face.

Lucy stared. "What? You're lying!"

And Hannah told her about Stella and Charlotte.

Then, she told her about her plan.

"He has to be punished, Lucy. He can't get away with it. He's ruined both of our lives. The bastard needs to die."

"You're insane. I'm going to pretend I never heard any of this."

"Let me know when you change your mind, Lucy." Hannah dried her face, brushed past Lucy, and walked out the door.

It had taken Lucy less than a month to change her mind.

Ralph and Pete decided to check the bus depot first. Because of everything that had been going on, they hadn't been able to get there yet to check on Frankie's movements Sunday. This would be a chance to kill two birds with one stone.

A large blue-and-white box on wheels sat with its motor idling in front of the terminal. On the side of the motor coach roof a sign read Greyhound Lines, the words chased by the outline of a sleek greyhound. The police officers elbowed through a swinging door into a small, shabby waiting room. A bored-looking man sat on a stool in the ticket window.

"Hi, Nate," said Ralph. "How're you doing?"

"Hey, Ralphie. You're a sight for sore eyes. Pete, how's tricks?"

"We're here on police business," Ralph told the clerk.

"You here for Frankie Russo's suitcase? I got it in the back."

"That's swell, Nate. Do you remember what time he got here last Sunday?"

"It was late morning, I can tell you that. Not sure of the time. But I remember asking him why he was so early. His bus didn't leave until one thirty."

"What did he say," Pete asked.

"Just said he had some stuff to do and would I keep his suitcase for him until he came back."

"Did he buy a ticket? Ralph asked.

"No, said he'd get one when he got back but he never came back. So, do you want the suitcase?"

"Yeah, in a minute. We're here for something else, too," said Ralph.

"Don't tell me we got another murder?"

284

"We need to find out if Hannah Grantham took a bus to Syracuse some time in the past two months or so," said Ralph.

"Jeez. You don't ask much, do ya?" He hopped off the stool and disappeared as he bent to retrieve something. He popped up with a ledger in his hand. "Lucky for you, everybody has to sign this when they buy a ticket." He pushed the register across the counter. "Go ahead and look all you want."

Ralph grabbed it and opened it at random. He went back to the end of February. He trailed his finger down through the names on page after page until he reached the final entry. Pete looked over his shoulder and read along.

When they got to today's date and read 7 a.m. Charlie Finch, they realized that if Hannah had gone to Syracuse she had not traveled by bus. Ralph and Pete thanked the Greyhound clerk, took Frankie's suitcase, and left.

A few minutes later, Ralph pushed open another swinging door into second waiting area, this one in need of a cleaning and some fresh paint. They made for the DL & W Railroad ticket counter. One window was shuttered. The other open, but empty. Pete leaned across the counter and yelled, "Hellooo. Anybody here?"

A high squeaky voice drifted out from a back room. "Hold yer horses. I'm comin'."

A skinny white-haired man shuffled up to the window. His name tag said Stuart Ferguson. "What can I do fer ya?"

Both officers showed their identification and repeated their question. "Mr. Ferguson, we need to know if Hannah Grantham took a train to Syracuse some time in the past two months."

"Yep," the man said with certainty.

"How do you know?" asked Pete, amazed. "You didn't even look anything up."

"Don't need to. It was the day of the blizzard last month. Don't remember the date," said Ferguson.

"I remember. It was March 13th," said Ralph.

"How the heck do you know that?" asked Pete.

"My grandma's birthday. We had to change her party until a few days later."

"Sounds about right," said the rail clerk.

"Mr. Ferguson, can you start from when she came in and tell us everything you remember?" Ralph took out his notebook.

"Sure, she blew in around eight thirty in the morning. Wanted to buy a round-trip ticket to Syracuse on the nine-o'clock train. She asked me if she could leave the return open because she didn't know when she'd be back. Probably late, she said. I told her okay. I asked her what she was doing out in the storm. She said school was closed and she was going to visit a friend. Surprise him. That's about it."

"She said 'him'? Her friend was a fella?" asked Ralph.

"Yup."

"Did you notice when she came back?" asked Pete.

"It was early. Around two. I was surprised when I saw her get off the train 'cause she said she was gonna to stay in Syracuse all day. When she came through the station, I yelled did she have a good time. She threw me a miserable look and kept walking."

"Describe how she looked." Ralph said.

"Upset…no…mad. Really mad. I guess her surprise didn't go like she planned."

Chapter 40

As Hannah made the short walk back to school, the memory assaulted her. The last time she'd stood alongside a booth in an eatery, her life had changed in a flash. The future she had been so sure of imploded, leaving her staring into an abyss filled with despair and heartbreaking sorrow. She would never forget the day—Tuesday, March 13th. There had been a blizzard the night before and school was cancelled.

She hadn't planned it. The idea simply entered her mind and she went.

Hannah had been worried about Frankie's behavior for some time—three years ago May as a matter of fact—ever since he got the job at Haberle's. Once he'd started spending a week here and a week in Syracuse, he had changed. At first, she thought he was just tired from holding down two jobs and doing all that traveling back and forth. Then, she noticed little things.

For years, they'd been meeting in back of the stage at school. Since Hannah was the play director, she had a master key to the building. They couldn't go to his house because of Lucy or hers because of her mother, and of course a hotel was out of the question. The school was the perfect choice. It was empty by seven most evenings and on the weekends. Given its isolated location, they were able to sneak in and out through the basement door at the rear of the building. Nobody was ever the wiser. One year,

Hannah had selected a play requiring a couch as one of the props. Some generous soul had donated one and it had never left. That was where they met.

The most difficult time in all the years of being with Frankie was when he first married Lucy. He wouldn't see Hannah for two whole months. During those grueling, painful weeks Hannah thought she would go mad or die. But naturally, he couldn't stay away from her— his real soul mate, the true love of his life. And they had started up again.

Then, he got that stupid job at the brewery and all of a sudden he didn't want to see her as often. She was sure it would blow over like before, but it got worse. By the end of 1931, Frankie refused to see her at all. He said it was over between them. He was done cheating.

The two years without him passed in a blur. She attempted suicide once, swallowing half a bottle of pills. Instead of dying, she threw up and suffered stomach cramps for three days. She called in sick to work, moped around the house in her pajamas, and lost herself reading soppy love serials in The Ladies' Home Journal. *Since her mother didn't know Hannah had been spending time with Frankie, she had no idea what was wrong with her. But she recognized the signs of a love-sick girl. She put her foot down and told her daughter to "get on with it." Having lost her own husband during the Great War, Mrs. Grantham knew you had to put one foot in front of the other—every single day.*

Martha's husband Jim introduced Hannah to Ben Maxwell and they began stepping out together. Often when she was with Ben, Hannah's mind drifted and she found herself day-dreaming of Frankie. Sometimes she even pretended it was Frankie kissing her. Ben Maxwell was nice but he couldn't hold a candle to Frankie Russo.

Thus, on that snow-filled day in March, a little over a month ago, Hannah Grantham fought her way through six-foot high drifts, in a howling wind, to the DL & W train station where she bought a ticket to Syracuse. She meant to confront Frankie, to have it out with him, and find out what had changed. She intended to get him back. What she discovered was a knife through her heart.

It was nearly noon when she arrived at the Haberle Congress Brewing Company in Syracuse. Not sure exactly how to start, Hannah paused a moment at the corner across from the main entrance. While she debated her options, a young woman holding a baby, all bundled up against the fierce cold, climbed the steps and went in the door.

As Hannah was about to cross the street, the door opened again and Frankie came out. With the woman. With the baby.

Her breath caught in her throat. Acting on instinct, she followed them. The woman handed the baby to Frankie and tucked her hand through his arm. It was a comfortable gesture. More than that, it was an intimate one. The couple walked quickly in the biting air to an eatery a block away.

Luckily for Hannah the place was long and crowded. Frankie and the woman disappeared into a booth across from the far-end of the counter. Frankie sat with his back to the door and to her. Hannah threw caution to the winds and slipped into the seat directly behind him. She could slide down and hide her face if Frankie turned around for some reason. During that lunch—the worst moments of her life—Hannah's food sat untouched, growing cold on the plate in front of her. To this day she had no recollection of what she had ordered. After about forty minutes, Hannah felt the back of the seat shudder as Frankie rose. She prepared to face the wall and hide behind her scarf but he headed toward the back to the men's room.

On impulse, Hannah took a risk. She got up and pretended to be going to the restroom as well. As she passed their booth, she dropped a glove. She moved slowly on purpose and heard the woman say, "Oh, Miss. You dropped this."

Hannah turned around and the woman handed her the glove. As her left hand moved, a beautiful diamond ring caught the light. It sat nestled next to a gold wedding band. Hannah eyes popped and she stopped breathing. She willed herself not to be sick. The baby cooed and waved her chubby hands as she gave Hannah a grin, three tiny teeth peeked out. I will not be sick. I cannot fall apart. *Her lower jaw trembled.*

"*Are you all right?*" *inquired the woman.*

"*Yes, thank you. Something I ate. What a beautiful ring and such an adorable baby,*" *Hannah forced herself to be polite when what she really wanted was to claw the woman's eyes out.*

"*Oh, how nice you are. Yes, we'll be married two years in the fall.*" *She glowed with happiness.*

The baby grabbed a spoon and banged the teacup.

"*No, no, Charlotte. Here, take your bunny.*"

The little girl gave the stuffed rabbit a big sloppy kiss and began a babbling conversation in earnest.

Hannah nodded to Charlotte's mother and spun around. She threw some coins on her table and fled the diner.

She slipped and nearly fell twice on patches of ice, but made it to the corner of Salina Street. She was panting, gasping for breath, freezing and sweating all at the same time.

Oh, my God. Oh, God. What am I going to do? *She thought of taking off her outer gear—heavy coat, wool hat and scarf, gloves, and boots—and curling up in a doorway on an isolated side street where no one would find her as she froze to death. She thought of waiting until a bus or big truck came barreling down the street then running out in front of it. Maybe she should go over to one of the streets where the train tracks ran and fling herself in front of a locomotive.*

Then, across the street, she noticed a bar. Two hours later, Hannah staggered out the door with a plan.

Chapter 41

Sergeant Will Taylor, accompanied by Jimmy Bou, rang the bell at 105 Second Street. Hannah Grantham's mother answered the door.

"Police, Mrs. Grantham," said Will, as he introduced himself and Jimmy.

"Oh, my goodness," she said. "What is it?" She nervously fingered the bib on her apron.

"We have some questions for you and also a warrant to search your house."

"Oh, my goodness," she repeated, growing more flustered.

"May we come in, please?"

"Yes, yes, of course." Shuffling in her slippered feet, she led them into the living room.

Inside, Will handed her the warrant. "You can read it if you wish. Officer Bourgogne is going to start while you and I talk." He chose a comfortable-looking side chair and gestured for Mrs. Grantham to sit across from him in a second upholstered chair. He took out his notebook. "Now, Mrs. Grantham, there's no need to be nervous. I only have a couple of routine questions. First of all, I need you to tell me about last Sunday."

"Sunday?" she said vaguely.

Will could see her struggle to recall the previous weekend. He'd heard she was becoming absent-minded, senile someone had said.

"Yes, ma'am. Do you know where you were Sunday from about nine o'clock in the morning until bedtime?"

"Probably here." She gazed off into the distance. Then, her eyes widened and a happy expression settled on her lined face. "Oh, Sunday. Hannah and I have breakfast on Sundays. I finish my ironing and fold the clothes for the boarding house men. I think Hannah helped me fold." She squeezed her eyes shut. "I can't remember too good lately."

"That's all right. You're doing fine." Will gently encouraged her. "Did you and your daughter have lunch together?"

"That I remember." Another smile lit up her face. "My sister invited us for lunch. She lives next door. Hannah didn't want to go but I did."

"What time was that, Mrs. Grantham?"

"I went in the morning for a nice long day. I like being in my sister's house. I don't know the time. Hannah can tell you."

Will made a note. "How long did you stay at your sister's?"

"All day. We sat and talked and had left-overs for supper. I helped her with the dishes."

"Was Hannah home when you got back?"

"No, later, I think. We listen to the radio on Sunday night." She looked confused. "Why are you asking *me* these questions?"

"It'll help our investigation." Will hoped a simple explanation would satisfy her. It did.

She nodded absently and fidgeted again with the edge of her apron.

"We're almost done, Mrs. Grantham."

She began smoothing the skirt of her housedress, in short repetitive movements.

"Only one last question. Were you home Tuesday night?" Will asked.

"Tuesday? Um, I don't know?" It sounded like a question. A deep furrow appeared between her brows. "When was that?"

Will could see she'd had enough. "That's all right, Mrs. Grantham. You did great. Thank you for helping." As he stood, Jimmy Bou re-entered the room. The young officer gave a slight shake of his head. "We'll get out of your way and let you unpack." He indicated the small overnight case near the doorway. "Did you have a good visit with your brother in Utica?"

"Mmm. Yes. Goodbye." She held the front door open. A glazed look had appeared in her beautiful eyes.

When Will and Jimmy Bou entered the CID room, Charlie was hanging up the telephone on Will's desk and Steven was updating the murder board. Under *SUSPECTS*, he wrote *Bank acct. verified* next to Lucy Russo's name.

"Steven," Charlie called over, "Lucy never sent in any of the job applications."

"What? None of them?"

"Nope. I talked with the principal at each of the schools. She sent the letters but never followed up with the applications."

Steven added: *job letters—yes applications—no.*

Will jumped in. "Steven, Hannah's alibi for Sunday doesn't hold up."

"Well, that's something. Finally!"

"Hannah's mother spent the day at her sister's house next door."

"I checked with Mrs. Eastwood," said Jimmy Bou. "Mrs. Grantham was at her house from around a quarter to eleven in the morning until about seven in the evening."

"That's another lie Hannah told. She said she fixed lunch for her and her mother," Steven said. "Now, we're getting somewhere. What about Tuesday?"

"Mrs. Grantham didn't know. After a few minutes of answering questions, she got flustered. It was painful to see her struggling to remember, Steven. I told her it was okay. We talked with Ben again.

He did have coffee with Hannah and her mother after supper on Tuesday but he went home earlier than she led us to believe."

"What was it he said about Sunday?" Steven ran his finger over the notes on the murder board.

"He didn't pick her up until two, Steven," said Jimmy Bou, excited to be a part of this important conversation.

"So, we have no idea where Hannah was or what she was doing from eleven to two on Sunday," Steven said.

He turned back to the board and wrote next to Hannah's name *Alibi/Sunday? No.*

Tommy hurried into the room. "Steven, Ray just called. Long distance from Oswego," he added, sounding impressed. "Mrs. Russo's friend Doris said no."

"What?" Steven, Will, and Jimmy all yelled at the same time.

"Yeah. Ray says the last time Doris talked to Mrs. Russo was five years ago. She had no idea what they were talking about. Mrs. Russo is not going to live with her."

"Now what?" said Jimmy Bou, gaping at Steven and Will.

"They're *both* lying." Steven turned to his partner. "We've got to pick her up again, Will."

Ralph and Pete rushed in, bursting with news.

"She *knew!*" Ralph shouted. "Hannah took a train to Syracuse on March 13th."

"That was the day of the blizzard and everything was closed," said Pete. "Remember?"

Ralph went on. "She told old Mr. Ferguson she was making a surprise visit to somebody. She said *he*. So, it must'a been a fella. I'd bet a hundred bucks it was Frankie."

"There's more, Steven," Pete said. "When Hannah got back, she wouldn't even talk to Ferguson. He said she stormed through the station. She was really upset."

Ralph read from his notebook. "He said, 'Upset...no...mad. Really mad. I guess her surprise didn't go like she planned.'"

"We think she found out about Stella," said Pete.

"What do we do now, Steven?" asked Jimmy Bou, eager for the next step. "Are we gonna get her in, too?"

"Too?" said Ralph. He and Pete looked at each other. What had they missed in the past couple of hours?

"Lucy lied about the arrangements in Oswego. Her friend didn't know anything about Lucy moving in with her. They haven't talked in five years," Steven explained. "Lucy didn't send in the job applications either."

"And Hannah doesn't have an alibi for Frankie's murder. She lied, too," said Jimmy Bou.

Will had been quiet. When he spoke, it was like an electric current snapped across the room. "Steven, listen to what you just said: Hannah and Lucy both lied."

"No, Will. They *hate* each other."

"Hannah and Lucy were both betrayed by Frankie. Hannah and Lucy work together. What if Hannah did find out about Stella and she told Lucy?"

"I still can't imagine the circumstances where they would possibly agree to do something together. Especially something as big as murder," Steven exclaimed. "I've known Lucy a long time. I can't see her killing anyone, with or without Hannah."

"What if something horrible happened that tipped her over the edge?" said Pete.

It hit Steven and Will at the same time. They stared at each other and whispered together, "Adona."

"That day in the pantry," exclaimed Pete.

"When Frankie forced himself on Adona," said Ralph.

"I bet that would do it," said Will.

295

"Lucy was able to look the other way all those years when Frankie cheated on her. But, forcing a girl would be too much for her to take. Yes, that would do it," Steven said sadly.

"Steven, you said you can't see Lucy as a killer," said Jimmy Bou. "If they were in it together, she wouldn't have to be the one who *gave* Frankie the poisoned food. What if she made it and *Hannah* gave it to him? What if they each did a part?"

"The two of them together makes sense," said Will. "It answers every question. And I do think that somewhere along the way Hannah told Lucy about Stella."

"I agree. And I'd be willing to bet it was Hannah who killed both Frankie and Dickie Hughes. All right, we bring 'em both in. Right now."

Ralph and Pete drove to Lucy's. Will and Jimmy Bou hurried to the high school.

"Mrs. Stoner, we need to see Hannah Grantham," said Will. "When's this class over?"

"Hannah isn't here, Will," said the plump secretary. "Mr. Kennington gave her a couple of hours off this afternoon. For the play."

Jimmy Bou looked aghast. Standing next to the strong reliable Sergeant Will Taylor, he looked even skinnier and more vulnerable than usual. "What?" he gasped.

"Do you know where she went?" Will asked.

"Utica. She had to get some props. She said today was the only time she could get a ride when the place is open. Anyway, Mr. Kennington told her to go. One of the other teachers is sitting with her last class."

"I need the name of the store, please," Will said.

Back in the police sedan, Jimmy Bou was clearly dismayed. "Will, what do we do?"

"When we get back to the station, I'll call to make sure she really did go there. Then we come back here and wait for her."

"Let's hope Lucy hasn't disappeared, too," Jimmy Bou grumbled with an uncharacteristic note of pessimism.

Steven rapped on the frame of the open door. "Chief, we got a break."

"Finally! What happened?" He put down his pen.

"Lucy Russo and Hannah Grantham have *both* been lying to us." He dropped onto the visitors' chair. "Lucy tried to make me think she didn't have a motive for killing Frankie because she was leaving him. But, only half her story was true. She's got the money but nowhere to go."

Chief Thompson leaned forward in his chair and whistled. "No kidding."

"Yes, a secret bank account that she's been filling up for a couple of years. But, something happened a few weeks ago that we think tipped her over the edge—whether she was seriously thinking of leaving or not."

"What?"

"Frankie tried to force himself on Adona Russo. Lucy saw them."

The chief looked like there was a nasty smell under his nose. "That makes me sick."

"It's disgusting all right. We think after that Lucy couldn't look the other way any more. Frankie crossed a line."

"So, how'd Lucy and Hannah get together? There's no love lost between those dames. They've hated each other for years," the chief said.

"We don't know yet. I'll find out when I question them."

"What did Hannah lie about?"

"Her alibi for Sunday," said Steven. "She said she was home with her mother but Mrs. Grantham was next door at her sister's house all day."

"I'll never figure out why smart people think they can get away with telling dumb lies." The chief frowned and drew his bushy brows together. "What's your plan? Do we have them in custody?"

"We're picking them up now," said Steven, rising from the hard wooden chair.

Ralph stuck his head in the doorway. "We got Lucy Russo. Where do you want her, Steven?'

"You did like I told you? You didn't say anything about why she's here?"

"Not a word."

"Good. Take her to Interview 1 and stay with her. Tell her I'll be right there," Steven instructed. "But, Ralph, I'm actually going to wait an hour. I want her in a position where she'll want to talk to me."

As Ralph was turning to go, Will slipped into the office around him. Steven knew by the look on Will's face it wasn't good news.

"What happened?" he asked anxiously.

"Hannah wasn't at school. The principal gave her the afternoon off to go to Utica to get props for the play. I called the store. The owner said she'd just left. Jimmy and I are going back to the school now. We'll be waiting when she gets there."

"I'll be here." Steven sat back down and faced his boss. "I don't like this business with Hannah, Chief."

"Don't worry about Hannah," Chief Thompson said. "She's got no idea you're on to her, right?"

"No, we weren't seriously considering her. Her affair with Frankie was years ago." He stood again and paced back and forth in front of the desk. "She's got her play next week. You know how dedicated she is to that. I don't think she'll go anywhere until that's done."

"I agree. She's got no reason to think about taking off." Thompson lit a cigarette. "It's a good idea leaving Lucy Russo alone to stew."

"I figure that after waiting a while, not knowing what's going on, with no idea how much we know, and no clue what's going to happen to her, she'll want to tell me everything. At least I hope so. This is going to be hard for her. That hour's going to seem like a long time. Lucy is used to being in control."

Chapter 42

Friday — Present Day

Olivia turned left out the door of the Village Drugstore and reached the tiny park on the corner of Hickory Street. She was about to turn up Chiltington when she ran into Jean Bigelow, the school librarian. Olivia had spent a free period browsing the book shelves that morning and the two women had enjoyed a long conversation on literature and favorite authors.

"Hi, Olivia. What a nice surprise. Where are you headed?"

Olivia told her about treating the girls to ice cream in exchange for information on her project.

"Oh, I heard about your research. It sounds fascinating. I'm happy to say I've noticed a subtle change in magazines recently. Editors are starting to understand that not every woman is a housewife and mother. Don't misunderstand me, I'm not knocking it. But, I think you and I know not everyone wants the same things. *Cosmopolitan* has begun publishing some good fiction. And my copy of *Good Housekeeping* this month printed an article written by Frances Perkins—you know, the Secretary of Labor—about the problems of economic recovery."

"Things are changing. That's for sure," agreed Olivia. "Would you like to get together for a cup of coffee sometime? I'd love to get your opinion on some issues for my research."

"Sure, sounds like fun. What about breakfast tomorrow morning?"

"That's perfect. Where? Bailey's?"

"Is there any other place?" the librarian laughed. "How's eight o'clock?"

"Swell. See you then."

Moments later, Olivia arrived at Steven's house. Wishing she could text him, she took the time to write a note longhand. She laid it on his kitchen table and hurried up the stairs. She left the hydrangea hallway behind her as she stepped over the threshold, easily sliding back into her time.

Once in her bedroom, Olivia grabbed her phone and dialed the number for St. John the Baptist Ukrainian Catholic Church on Tipperary Hill, in Syracuse. The secretary picked up on the first ring. Olivia identified herself then listened.

"Oh, that's great...Yes, I imagine it must have been very dusty...Oh, wow. You did?...What? Oh my goodness! You're kidding!...I can't believe it...When?...Under what name?...Mrs. O'Sullivan, I can't thank you enough. And thank Father for me as well. This is wonderful news."

Olivia knew that Liz would be in the chapel putting up decorations for the ceremony tomorrow and Sophie was taking Isabel to get her cast off. Now, if one more detail would fall into place, they'd have a lot more than the renewal of Liz's vows to celebrate tonight.

Although Olivia enjoyed wearing Evangeline's beautiful wardrobe, it felt good to get back into her own clothes. She pulled on a favorite pair of jeans, ran her fingers through the layers in her new haircut, swiped on some mascara, eye liner, and blush, and puckered for a fresh coat of lipstick. She grabbed the purse she'd thought to fill last night and locked the front door behind her.

Five minutes later saw Olivia parking her blue Toyota next to Liz's silver SUV in St. Joe's parking lot. She pulled open the heavy, carved oak door tucked away in the back below the main church. A hush enveloped her as she stepped into her favorite part of the church. Built in the late 1800s, in the style of the Assumption Church in Syracuse, St. Joseph's underground chapel also featured a grotto with a tiny waterfall. The builder had used stones from Lourdes, France to construct the walls and form the water feature. The sound of trickling water near the statue of the pieta washed all cares from one's soul. Olivia understood why Liz and Joe had chosen the grotto for the renewal of their wedding vows. The space was solemn yet gentle, thrilling but peaceful.

When Olivia entered, she saw Liz attaching the final flower arrangement to the end of a pew along the center aisle. Looking like they'd been plucked from nature, the bouquets suited the space perfectly. At the far end of the chapel, a nun was cleaning the small altar. Robed in an ankle-length gray dress and white veil, her back was to the grotto.

"Who's that?" Olivia whispered.

"She just got transferred from someplace. Father told me she offered to help but I got it done."

"She's the new transfer? What till you hear what I found out," said Olivia excitedly. She whispered the results of the phone conversation she'd just had.

Liz gasped. "No! Is that her?" she said, pointing to the nun on the altar.

"Let's find out," Olivia answered.

The sister finished her tasks on the altar and turned to step down. A beam of soft light fell on her face.

Olivia's jaw dropped and her eyes popped. She gasped. "Oh, my

God."

"Holy cow!" Liz gaped.

Up on the altar, Isabel's face peeked out from the white veil.

Olivia slowly approached the sister.

"Alex?" she whispered. "Alex Lewis Williams?"

Clearly upset, the nun tucked her hands inside the sleeves of her gown and frowned. Olivia noticed a slight tremble around her mouth. "What do you mean? I'm Sister Mary Grace."

"But, you used to be Alex, didn't you? Before you took your vows," Olivia insisted, still stunned. Alex wasn't a brother. She was a sister. An identical twin sister. There was no doubt about it. This woman was the mirror image of Isabel. "I'm sorry, Sister. I don't mean to be disrespectful. It's just that I've been looking for you."

Sister Mary Grace relaxed but still regarded Olivia warily. "What do you mean? Why would you be looking for me?"

"Because your twin sister Isabel asked me to." *Oh, no!* Olivia silently panicked. *What if Alex's adoptive parents had never told her?*

The nun's face lit up with joy. Tears filled her eyes and her lip quivered. "You know Isabel? You know my sister?" Her face crumbled. She stood on the altar quietly weeping. "Oh, my heavens. I'd almost given up hope." She pulled a handkerchief from her sleeve, wiped her eyes, and blew her nose.

"Yes, we're very close. By the way, I'm Olivia. I live next door to your sister."

The nun was visibly trembling. Reminding herself that this was an eighty-year old woman and she had no idea what condition her health was in, Olivia stepped onto the altar so she was within catching distance. "Do you want to sit down? I imagine this has been a shock. Can I help you?"

"Yes, thank you." Sister Mary Grace allowed Olivia to guide her to the first pew. She dropped onto the wooden bench. "Where is Isabel?

Can I see her?"

"Absolutely. She lives here in Knightsbridge," Olivia said.

The nun gasped. "Right here? After all those years of wondering about her, God dropped me in her back yard. I never should have doubted." She crossed herself then shook her head, evidently admonishing herself for the human failing.

"This is Liz," Olivia said, as her friend joined them. "She cares about Isabel, too. Your sister was our first-grade teacher. We've been like family ever since."

"We'll make sure Isabel's back from the doctor's," Liz said. Then, seeing the concern on Alex's face, she hurried on, "It's nothing serious. She broke her arm a few weeks ago. She's getting the cast off this afternoon. Then, we'll take you over to her house."

"Thank you," the nun whispered.

"I'll text Sophie," Olivia said.

A minute later her phone buzzed. Olivia read Sophie's answer and said, "We're good. They just got back. I'll tell her to stay there and tell Isabel to brace herself for a surprise."

Olivia's heart was pounding. She couldn't imagine how Alex was feeling. The nun sat silently in the front seat, mumbling. Olivia thought she was probably saying a prayer. She pulled into her driveway and said, "This is my house. That's Isabel's." She pointed to the left. Liz came up to the passenger door and helped the sister out of the car. Together, she and Olivia led her across the lawn. A wind blew the veil into the nun's face and picked up the bottom of her gown, whipping it around her legs. Sister Mary Grace pushed the white cloth back and bent over slightly to straighten the skirt. Olivia could see Isabel's sister still trembled.

The front door house opened and Isabel stood there in shocked silence, her mouth agape and her eyes wide. She swayed. Sophie caught her from behind and put an arm around her to steady her. Isabel whispered, "Alex?"

The two sisters stumbled toward each other. They stood inches apart and stared. Both were sobbing. Isabel reached for her twin and pulled her into a fierce hug. Alex wrapped her arms around Isabel. They stood weeping and clinging to each other for a long time. Isabel broke the hug first. She leaned back and put her hands gently on her sister's wrinkled cheeks. "I thought you were a brother. Mom only said 'Alex'. She never said you were a girl. No wonder I couldn't find you."

Olivia, Liz, and Sophie waited, joyful tears washing their faces. All three loved Isabel.

Isabel grabbed Alex's gnarled hand and led her into the house. She turned to Olivia and pulled her into a tight hug. "I will never be able to thank you for this. Never."

"It's okay," Olivia whispered. "I'm so happy for you."

"We'll let you two get know each other," Liz said. "C'mon girls. Let's go to the pub. I could use a big glass of wine."

"Oh, yeah," said Olivia.

"Me, too," Sophie exclaimed.

They hugged Isabel and Alex one more time and left the twins to a long evening together.

Chapter 43

Friday — April 27, 1934

At three thirty, Steven entered Interview 1. He thanked Ralph for waiting with Lucy Russo and closed the door behind the patrolman. Steven sat across from her at the same table they had occupied less than twelve hours ago.

Earlier today, Lucy had been her usual meticulous self. Now, the smooth, put-together appearance had vanished. Her hair was tangled, as if she'd been napping and not bothered to comb it after rising. Steven noticed shadows under her eyes and her pale complexion. She seemed wary but also annoyed.

"What's this about, Steven?" she asked. "I need to get things ready for the wake tomorrow and Frankie's funeral on Saturday. I already told you everything this morning."

"Not quite everything, Lucy." He waited. "You know we had to verify what you told me."

"I have the money to leave. Did you go to the bank? Did you check?"

"Yes, I was impressed when the manager showed me your account. It must have taken years to save that much."

"Yes, it did." she relaxed a bit. "Frankie was such a hot shot bookkeeper and he didn't suspect a thing."

"Clever. But, I'm confused about the job applications," Steven said.

"Did you call the schools? I sent every letter I told you about."

"But, you didn't follow up. Each principal we talked with said they were impressed with your qualifications and mailed you the job application right away. But they never got the applications back. Why didn't you complete the process?"

"I was thinking of changing my mind and applying to schools in Syracuse. It's a bigger city. There are museums and concerts. I have a cousin there that I'm close with. I could stay with her."

"And if I called your cousin? What would she tell me?"

"I didn't ask her yet. I'm still thinking about it."

"I see. Well, we did talk with your friend Doris in Oswego. She said she hadn't seen you in years. She didn't know anything about your plans. She was quite surprised to learn you might be moving in with her."

"Like I said, Steven, I thought I might change my mind and apply in Syracuse. There was no point asking Doris until I was sure."

Steven slowly nodded his head. "You seem to have an answer for everything."

"Well, it's the truth,"

"No, it isn't."

"I don't know what you want me to say, Steven," she smiled at him. It was the smile that did it.

Fine, he thought, *keep lying to me. Two can play this game.*

"Lucy, we have Hannah in custody. She's already talking."

"She's lying. Hannah always was a liar," Lucy said.

Steven thought he heard a bit less conviction in her voice. "I haven't even told you yet what she's saying," he countered.

"Doesn't matter. That's Hannah. That's who she is."

"She said she gave the poisoned food to Frankie."

"That's right! She did."

"And how would you know that, Lucy?"

Lucy's mouth opened but nothing came out.

"You and Hannah aren't friends. Given her history with Frankie, that's hardly surprising. Why would she tell you, of all people, that she poisoned your husband?" Steven could see her casting about for something to say. "You know what I think, Lucy? I think Hannah's hoping to get a deal if she tells the truth. And so far it's working, she's doing a good job cooperating." He paused. "By the way, she told me you made the poisoned food."

"Like I said, Steven, she's a liar. I don't know what you're talking about."

"Lucy, we know everything. We have the evidence. We have Hannah's confession. You're only making it worse for yourself." He gave her some time to consider. "Lucy, I can see you're torn right now. Think of how much better you're going to feel when you get it all out."

"If I tell you everything, will I get a deal?"

"That'll be up to the DA. But, you'll be a lot better off than what you're doing now."

Lucy sat and thought for what seemed like a long time. Steven knew she was weighing the few options she possessed. He also knew she was smart enough to recognize and accept that they'd reached the end.

She sighed heavily. "I want to get this over with."

"No lies this time. No half-truths."

She slowly nodded.

"Start from the beginning, Lucy," he said.

"What I told you this morning was true—or mostly true. I had decided to leave Frankie. I was saving money. I really did send those letters to the schools. But, before I had a chance to fill out the applications or write to Doris, I ran into Hannah."

"Tell me about that meeting."

"It was the day after the blizzard in March. I stayed after school to catch up on some work because we'd had a snow day. I went into the ladies' room and Hannah was there sobbing like somebody had died. I asked her what was wrong and...she told me she found out Frankie was married to another woman in Syracuse. Hannah was going to surprise him the day school was closed and she saw them together. She managed to talk with the woman so she was positive. And...and...," she began to cry. "They have a baby." She looked at him through glistening lashes. "I never thought I wanted a baby until I heard he had a little girl."

Steven could almost see the knife enter her heart. He handed her his handkerchief.

"Then, what did Hannah say?" he asked.

"She said Frankie needed to die. I told her she was crazy. I was going to pretend I never heard her say that."

"So, what changed?" Steven softened his voice for his next question. "Was it when you caught him with Adona in the pantry?"

"You know about that?" she gasped.

"Yes. Nothing happened, Lucy. Adona fought him off," Steven told her.

"What difference does that make? He tried, Steven, he tried. And Adona of all people." Lucy dried her eyes and wiped her face. She leaned forward and said earnestly, "Steven, Adona is a lovely girl. She's sweet and innocent. She adores Nico. Frankie was going to destroy her."

For a moment, Steven saw the Lucy he had always known.

"You need to understand," she pleaded. "That bastard forced himself on his cousin's wife while the whole family was in the next room. He was like a dog that had to be put down." She slumped back in her chair. "He had to be stopped."

"So, you told Hannah you'd help her?"

"Yes. She already had the plan to poison him. I told her I didn't want to know anything. When or where or how. Nothing. I said I'd make Frankie's favorite muffins. That was it. I baked them in the Home Ec. room after school and she picked them up after her play practice."

"Then, you threw out the bowl and pan and utensils in the trash behind the school." Steven said with certainty.

"Of course. I couldn't take a chance. What if I didn't wash all the residue out. Some poor student could die."

"Speaking of students," Steven began.

Lucy's face crumbled and she moaned. "That poor boy. I had *nothing* to do with Dickie Hughes," she said, wrenching the words out. "That was Hannah's idea. She didn't tell me she was going to do it. I don't know anything about that. You *have* to believe me."

Steven pushed a pad of paper and pen across the table.

"Write it down, Lucy. All of it. Don't leave out a single detail," Steven instructed.

"What's going to happen, Steven?"

Steven stood and sadly looked down at her. "Lucy Russo, I am officially charging you with murder. You'll remain here for now."

Steven felt drained after the interview with Lucy. He wondered how he was going to tell Artie that he had arrested his sister-in-law for murder. *I can't think about that right now.* He entered Chief Thompson's office. The chief looked up from his paperwork.

"How'd it go? Did she talk? Were you right?"

"Yes, she's in there writing it all down. I've got one of the patrolmen standing by the door. Did Will bring in Hannah?"

"Not yet. Listen, Steven, you look lousy. Go home. You need to be in good shape for tomorrow. Put your feet up. Have a beer. Forget about it. There's nothing more you can do tonight. We've got Lucy.

By morning, we'll have Hannah. Get some rest. You've got another tricky interview to get through."

"But, Chief…,"

"Hannah's in Will's capable hands. Don't worry. He'll bring her in."

Will and Jimmy Bou returned with the bad news as Steven was walking out the door.

"Hannah never went back to school," Will said.

"What?" His voice was strained.

"When I called earlier, the store owner told me she left his place in Utica around three. She should have been back before three thirty. Even if she stopped for another errand, it only takes fifteen minutes."

"I asked around the school," Jimmy Bou said. "Nobody saw her come back."

"We waited until almost five, Steven," Will added.

Steven organized a search. He grabbed every available officer before they had a chance to leave for the night. He sent them out to all parts of town, instructing them to ask everyone they ran into if they had seen Hannah Grantham in the past few hours. He updated the chief then returned to his desk to telephone every place he could think of and everyone who was important in Hannah's life. He called her mother, her aunt, her best friend, Ben's house, and no less than ten restaurants within driving distance.

Everywhere he called and everywhere the police went, Hannah Grantham wasn't there.

By nine o'clock, Chief Thompson told everyone to go home. "Wherever she's gone," the chief said, "she's hunkered down for the night. We'll grab her in the morning when she goes to her play practice."

Steven grumbled to himself all the way home Friday night. Half a case was no case at all. He had Lucy locked up, but Hannah had disappeared. He was furious. He should have thought of the possibility of Hannah not being at school in the middle of the afternoon. But then, why would he? She had a job to do, a classroom full of students to teach. She should have been there. A voice in his brain piped up: a good cop always considers every possible outcome and plans for it. He banged his hand against the steering wheel and let out a frustrated yell.

After Chief Thompson had convinced him he could do no more tonight, Steven forced himself to put thoughts of the case aside. He needed to get rid of the pounding headache and the knot in his chest. He had to get some rest. It was imperative that he be clear-headed for his interview with Hannah in the morning.

Steven thought about what he wanted to do with Olivia tonight. *With what's left of tonight.* He pulled his motor car into the drive and, after setting the parking brake, got out. It was beginning to rain, a light misty drizzle. The cool water felt good on his face. He decided to copy Olivia and take a shower before supper. She was always bathing. Maybe she did it because it felt good and not just because she needed it.

When Steven set his lunch box on the porcelain countertop of his cupboard unit, something caught his eye. He took a step toward the kitchen table and saw the note.

> *Dear Steven,*
>
> *I want to remind you that I won't be home until late tonight. Liz, Sophie, and I are getting together before Liz's ceremony tomorrow. Remember she and Joe are renewing their wedding vows? I hope you'll still be able to come with me. I hope your case won't keep you at work. Fingers crossed!!*
>
> *Can you come and get me before you go to the station*

in the morning? I'll make sure I'm up and ready by
6.30 so I don't hold you up. I made plans to meet the
HS librarian for breakfast at 8. Thank you.
Hope you had a good day. Mine was "swell"!! haha
See you in the morning.
Olivia

Steven was disappointed, then he reminded himself he had a real date with Olivia tomorrow in the 21st century. He was going to see what the future looked like outside the house. He might as well enjoy his night off. Steven threw the note on the table and saw more writing on the back.

BTW, (*What the heck is that?* he thought, and kept on reading.)
I don't know if this is important but I have 2
things to tell you from my adventures today.
I saw Hannah at the soda fountain after school. I
still think she's nice. It can't be her.
One of the girls I was with said she saw Lucy coming
out of the Home Ec. room the other night after play
practice. Don't know if that means anything or not.

Steven shuddered at the thought of Olivia being anywhere near Hannah. What was Hannah doing in the soda fountain? What time had that been? That might explain why she wasn't at school when Will and Jimmy Bou were waiting for her to get back. It eased Steven's fears. It didn't sound like she was running away. But, even so, where had she gone after that?

When Steven reread the line about Lucy, a big smile appeared on his face. *Olivia, you've done it again. It looks like Lucy did tell me the truth.*

Relaxed and confident, Steven jumped in the shower then changed into his pajamas. He got a nice cold Jenny out of the icebox and heated up leftovers on the stove. He turned on the radio and settled himself on the couch, legs stretched out and feet up on the footstool. He'd missed his favorite program earlier this week but the network was re-broadcasting it tonight.

A deep voice boomed out from the set. *Good evening, Crime Club members and fans. Relax, settle in, and join Spencer Dean—Manhunter as he tackles crime and puts the world right.*

Maybe it wasn't such a bad day after all.

Chapter 44

Saturday — April 28, 1934

A s Steven prepared coffee and set out the breakfast things, he went over the plan to bring in Hannah Grantham.

Will was taking Ralph, Pete, and Jimmy Bou to Hannah's house. They would arrive no later than eight. They would caution her as to the seriousness of the visit and take her to the station for the interrogation. In the meantime, he'd send two of his men to the high school to go through the trash looking for the murder weapon—the dishes Lucy used to make the poisoned food. Later, he'd send one of the patrolmen to the school to cancel the rehearsal and send the kids home.

Steven glanced at his watch. Time to get Olivia. He climbed the stairs and walked to the end of the hall. As he got closer, Steven watched his mother's elegant Art Deco boudoir fade away, revealing Olivia standing on the other side of the doorway in her cozy room.

"Good morning," Steven gave her a smile that reached deep into his eyes. He liked starting out the day with her.

"Steven! Good morning. You found my note," she said. "Did you wrap up the case yesterday?"

"Almost. I think we will this morning."

She gave him an encouraging smile. "Hang in there."

Steven laughed. "That expression always gets me." He reached over the threshold and held out his hand. "Are you ready?"

Olivia set her phone on the charger and grabbed Evangeline's bag. She glanced inside to be sure she had her notebook, pen, and several well-sharpened pencils. She stepped to the doorway and took his hand. Steven took three slow steps back and once again Olivia found herself in the midst of a hydrangea-filled bower.

In the kitchen, Steven poured their coffee then ate his Wheaties while Olivia told him about finding Alex.

"Steven, I've never been so stunned in my whole life. First of all, the secretary tells me Isabel doesn't have a twin brother, she has a twin *sister*. Then, I find out the sister is a nun. No wonder Isabel couldn't find anything online. Then, beyond all coincidences, the nun is transferred to Knightsbridge. Of all places! It was one shock after another." Olivia took a drink of her coffee. "So, I decided to go over to the chapel and finish helping Liz with the decorations then go to the rectory and try to find this nun. I get to the church and there's a nun on the altar. She turns around and *boom!* a dead ringer for Isabel. I couldn't believe it. Luckily, her adoptive parents, the Williams, had told her about her twin sister and the family history. It made it a lot easier for me to convince her that I wasn't crazy and she could trust me to drive her over to Isabel's house. When we got there, we were all crying. It was unbelievable." Olivia caught her breath. "By the way, did you have a chance to try on the clothes I got you for tonight?"

"They fit fine. But, Olivia, are you sure about them? There's no suit jacket. And you forgot a hat." He looked flabbergasted.

"Don't worry. I got you the right stuff." She laughed. "The women'll probably be more dressed up but all the guys'll be wearing the same thing as you. Men don't wear hats like they do in your time. But, Steven, the big thing is…make sure you wash all that stuff out of your hair. Fix it like I showed you. The hair style would definitely stand out."

"And we don't want that." He heaved a sigh. "Okay. It feels strange but I trust you."

Olivia reached across the table and squeezed his hand. "I'd *never* put you in an awkward position. You know that."

"Yes, I do. So, what's our plan? I'm working all day. I hope I can finish by four."

"Like I told you in the note, I'm meeting Jean for breakfast. I'm really looking forward to it." Olivia had decided she didn't want to worry Steven on such an important day in his investigation. The last thing he needed was a distraction. If she told him she had promised to help Hannah with play practice, he would be distracted so she said nothing. "I'll have plenty of time before I need to get back to my time."

"Don't you have a lot of last-minute things to do? I'm surprised you arranged an engagement for today."

"Liz has everything in hand. The chapel's decorated. The tent's being delivered and set up this morning. Joe's meeting those guys. The caterers are coming around five thirty. They'll take care of the food and the bar. That's it. I just have to show up." Olivia studied him for a moment. "I wish your case was settled and you could spend the day being excited about tonight. I feel like you're being cheated out of all the anticipation."

Steven laughed. "Only you would think of something like that. Don't worry. I'm not going to let myself be cheated. I'll wrap things up today and tonight will be a celebration for me, too."

"That sounds good. I'll meet you upstairs at six. That gives us time to get to the chapel. The ceremony will be short. Then, we'll come back here and have fun all night long."

Olivia looked so childlike and determined that Steven burst out laughing for a third time that morning.

At twenty minutes to eight Saturday morning, Will threw the motor car into second gear. The police sedan careened out of the parking lot, spitting gravel. Next to him on the bench seat, Jimmy Bou was thrown toward the middle. Holding onto his hat, he righted himself while in the back Ralph and Pete grabbed for the leather straps above the windows.

"Jeez, Will," said Ralph, "let's get there alive, huh?"

Will ignored him as he sped south on Hickory, crossed First Street—narrowly missing two pedestrians as they jaywalked to the First Methodist Church on the corner. The gears screeched as Will downshifted and flew around the corner at Second Street.

The heavy black automobile skidded to a stop in front of Hannah Grantham's house. Ralph and Pete hurried around to the back door. Will and Jimmy Bou ran up the steps to the front landing. Will pounded on the wooden door and rang the bell simultaneously.

"Look in the windows, Jimmy."

Jimmy Bou cupped his hands around his eyes and peered in the window. "She's coming."

The door slowly opened. Hannah's mother looked vaguely from one officer to the other. Her deep-set eyes were not quite focused. "Yes?"

"Police, ma'am. We need to see your daughter Hannah."

Mrs. Grantham sucked in her already sunken cheeks and mumbled, "She's not here."

Jimmy Bou failed to stifle a groan.

"Has she already gone over to the school for her play practice?" asked Will.

"I don't know."

Will wondered how bad her condition was and if it could worsen within days. "Did you see Hannah this morning?"

She nodded. "Before Ben came."

"Oh," Will exclaimed. "Ben picked her up?"

"I think so."

"Thank you, Mrs. Grantham. We won't trouble you any more." Will smiled gently.

Ralph and Pete returned from the back of the house. The four men got in the motor car.

"Where to now, Will?" asked Jimmy Bou. He turned to the back seat and told Ralph and Pete, "Hannah's not here. Ben picked her up this morning. We don't know where they went."

Will angled in his seat to address all three officers. "I think we'd better split up. Ralph and Pete, you fellas get over to the high school. At least we know she'll be there for her rehearsal at nine thirty. Patrol the area. Stay out of sight so you don't spook her."

"Yeah, we don't want her making a run for it. That's for sure," said Ralph.

"Where do you think they'd go on a Saturday morning, Will?" asked Pete.

"I'd say a fella might take his girl out to breakfast."

"Yeah, good idea," enthused Jimmy Bou. "Bailey's? Or maybe Mother's?"

"We'll check both," answered Will. He addressed Ralph and Pete. "We'll either meet you at the school or I'll get word to you that we've got her at the station."

As Olivia walked to the high school to meet Hannah and the kids for play practice later that morning, her brain was buzzing from the conversation she'd had at breakfast. Of all the women she'd met so far during her time in 1934, she shared the most interests with the school librarian. Jean was as passionate as Olivia was about *knowing things*. They'd started discussing Jane Austen then moved on to architecture and archeology. Suddenly, Jean had started to giggle.

319

Olivia looked at her curiously and said, "What's so funny about a dig in the Sahara?"

"Look at the way our conversation is going. Jane *Austen*. Architecture. Archeology. Is Austria next?"

Olivia joined in the laughter. "Right! Then, we do birds, Belgium, botany, and Balzac."

"Hey, we could form a club. The ABC Breakfast Club."

"You know what that reminds me of? One night when I was in grad school, my best friend and I opened a bottle of wine and toasted every letter of the alphabet."

The librarian burst out laughing again. "I wish I had been there. That sounds like fun."

"Let's do this again," Olivia said when they parted out on the sidewalk in front of Bailey's. "I'll get ready to talk about 'B' things."

"Yes, and don't forget J. M. Barrie, L. Frank Baum, and the Bronte sisters."

"And Boston, Bangkok, and Barcelona."

Olivia had heard her laughing all the way to the corner.

The cast members watching the scene from the auditorium applauded and cheered their friends. Hannah Grantham rose from her directorial seat in the first row and climbed the wooden access stairs on the far right of the stage.

"Good job, kids," she said to the cast of *Little Women*. "Next, we're going to rehearse our big scene." She consulted her watch. "Why don't we take a ten-minute break first?"

Hannah walked across the apron and hopped off the low stage to join Olivia who had quietly pulled down an upholstered seat at the end of the fourth row.

"You've got a talented bunch, Hannah. They're doing a great job."

"Thanks. Olivia, could you do me a favor? Go backstage and find

Manny—he's the red-haired kid. Ask him when they're going to finish painting the proscenium so we can put it up."

"So, you're putting me to work already, huh?" Olivia joked.

Hannah laughed. "You said it. Anyone who walks into this auditorium is fair game. Nobody escapes."

Olivia pushed the heavy, burgundy-colored curtains aside and wove her way among the boxes, crates, step-ladders, racks of clothes, and assorted props that filled the back of the stage. She found a bunch of kids painting scenery and got Hannah's answer. She stopped to talk with Molly who was happily painting a window on a backdrop destined to become a living room wall.

On her way back to the orchestra pit, where she heard Hannah discussing a scene with a group of girls—the March sisters?—Olivia paused to look at the jumble of props and furniture. A rickety table and three wooden chairs, one with a hole in the woven seat. A colorful braided rug rolled up and lying on a twin bed. Mismatched dishes, pots, and pans stacked on the floor. And, thrown across an upholstered chair with some of the stuffing peeking out, a wool blanket in red-and-blue plaid. Olivia froze. Red-and-blue wool. What was it about red-and-blue wool? Why did that hit a chord? Before she could pinpoint the memory, Lilly ran over and grabbed the blanket.

"Oh, Olivia, hi. Would you give this to Miss Grantham, please? They need it for Beth's death scene."

Olivia gave her a warm smile and took the blanket. "Sure."

Hannah was studying her copy of the script, oblivious to the activity around her and unaware of Olivia's approach. A wave of blonde hair fell across her face. She absently tucked the loose strands behind her ear as she penciled a note in the margin.

"Hannah," Olivia called to get her attention. "Manny said the paint just has to dry and the proscenium'll be ready to hang. And one of the kids gave me this for you. Where do you want it?" She held up a red-and-blue plaid bundle of wool.

Hannah froze inside. She stared at the blanket in Olivia's hand. *The* blanket. Her eyes bore into Olivia's. What was going on? Was this a trick? Had Steven put her up to it?

Who was Olivia anyway? Why had she suddenly come to visit Steven? Hannah had a panicky thought. What if Olivia was really a matron with the Syracuse Police Department? What if she was sent here to *pretend* she was a friend of Steven's family? What if her mission had been to get to know Hannah and befriend her? This could be a trap. There could be police officers hiding in the auditorium waiting to arrest her then lock her away. She glanced around surreptitiously. If so, Hannah was sure the police would wait until the kids were gone. She had time. She'd be ready. She knew it had been a good idea keeping it here. All she had to do was get it without Olivia seeing her.

As casually as she could manage, Hannah smiled and said, "Oh, thanks, Olivia. Just set it on the couch. Beth wraps up in it just before she dies."

Why is she looking at me like that? Olivia thought. *Something's not right.*

Then it dawned on her. Red-and-blue fibers at the scene of the crime. The killer and Frankie sitting on a blanket. *Oh, my God! It's Hannah.*

Once the realization struck, clues flooded Olivia's mind. Hannah putting Ben off every time he asked her to marry him. Until Frankie was dead. Until there was no longer a possible future with her old boyfriend. The look Hannah had given her when Olivia had asked yesterday at lunch if she'd known Frankie. She'd *said* he was only a high school boyfriend. But how many times had Olivia heard about old flames never dying? Steven's comment about someone not being what they seem to be. Now, here was Hannah on a stage, surrounded by props, directing a play, in a theater. An actress, Steven had said. It all fit.

It had been right in front of their eyes all the time.

"Olivia, I'm going to let the kids go. But, if you have the time, I'd really like to hear your thoughts on the scene," said Hannah Grantham.

Olivia felt trapped but, for once in her life, she couldn't think of anything to say without giving it away that she knew. She decided to play along then leave in a few minutes. After all, what could Hannah do here in the school?

"Sure, I've got a few minutes but then I have to leave."

Hannah ushered the cast and crew out the back of the auditorium. The heavy double-doors banged shut behind them. The theater was silent.

Chapter 45

At the police station, Steven checked his watch. Going on nine already. Will should be bringing in Hannah any minute now. He rubbed his forehead where a headache threatened. He needed to organize his notes and get ready for the interrogation.

Steven spread out the affidavits, forensic results, and two autopsy reports over the surface of his desk, pushing aside his coffee and a stack of file folders. He cleared his mind and focused. Now that he knew who had killed Frankie Russo and Dickie Hughes, it was so obvious he couldn't believe he hadn't seen it sooner. He might have saved that poor boy. He shook himself. No time for emotion. He heard movement in the hall. Will and Jimmy Bou hurried in.

"She wasn't home, Steven." Jimmy Bou said breathlessly.

Steven's heart thudded to the floor.

"Her mother said Ben picked her up this morning," said Will. "I thought maybe he took her out to breakfast. We checked Bailey's and Mother's. They weren't at either place. I sent Ralph and Pete to stake out the school."

"Damn!" Steven reached for the phone. "Hi, Martha? It's Steven …Fine, thanks. You?…Listen, do you know what Hannah was doing this morning before play practice?…Oh, swell. Thanks."

He set the receiver in the cradle. "Ben was taking her for fry cakes and coffee at Buttercup Bakery. Hannah wanted to get to rehearsal early. She's probably on her way there now." Steven began to cross the room then froze. Somewhere in the back of his mind, he remembered over-hearing a snatch of conversation between Olivia and Hannah at the baseball game the other night. Something about Olivia helping with play practice. His blood chilled. *No, not today. Not before tonight's ceremony. She wouldn't have time. Would she?*

"Listen, Will, I just remembered something." Steven told him. "Olivia and I ran into Hannah at the Little League game a couple of days ago. I heard her talking with Hannah about helping with the play. She's meeting Jean Bigelow for breakfast this morning. I'm going to see if they're still at Bailey's. If not, I'll run over to my house and see if she's there. I need to be sure she doesn't go to the school today."

"Go! Ralph and Pete should be there by now. I'll take Jimmy. We'll meet you at the high school in a few minutes."

The screaming of metal on metal hurt his ears when Steven shifted before his foot had fully depressed the clutch. He winced, slammed the clutch all the way to the floor, and flew out of the parking lot.

Olivia wasn't at the diner.

Steven rushed back out, dove into his Chevy, and peeled away from the curb. Moments later, he threw open his front door, knowing he was about to discover an empty house. He went in just the same. He called for her as he passed through the front parlor and hallway, as he climbed the stairs and poked his head in his mother's room. He was on his way through the kitchen to check the back porch and yard and almost missed it. As he crossed the floor, a paper fluttered from the table. He bent to pick it up.

Steven,
In case you're looking for me, I'm meeting
Hannah for play practice at the high school. I

probably should have told you this morning. I
didn't say anything because I didn't want
you to worry. DON'T WORRY! I'll be fine. See you later.
Olivia

His entire body chilled and he broke out in a sweat. He ran to the telephone and dialed the station.

"Tommy, quick, get Will." Steven tapped his foot. *Come on, come on.*

"Hello."

"Will, Olivia's at the high school." Steven swallowed hard. "With Hannah."

"We're on our way!"

Steven didn't wait for the receiver to slam down in his ear. He fled the house.

Laughter filled the air as George Talbot, egged on by his pals Manny and Teddy, tried to snag a kiss from Molly Silverstone,

"Look out, Molly!" Lilly tried to warn her friend, as she blew smoke rings up into the sky with an imagined air of sophistication.

Play practice had finished. Miss Grantham had kicked them all out of the school. The kids lounged on the front steps of the building chatting, flirting, and smoking.

"Aw, go on, George. You can tell she wants you to," leered Manny.

"Lay one on her, Georgie boy," smirked Teddy, slipping his arm around Lilly.

Molly stood and ran her hands down the skirt of her dress, smoothing it out. She tossed her hair back and grabbed Lilly's hand. "Come on, let's go. We don't need these cretins drooling all over us."

"We certainly do not!" Lilly tried to appear worldly as she mimicked Molly.

Steven braked at the curb and jumped out of the dark green sedan.

Before he could say a word, a black police vehicle screeched to a halt next to him and two officers spilled out. At the same moment, two more policemen came running around the school from the back. The kids' jaws dropped and their eyes bugged out.

"Has everyone left?" Steven shouted at the group on the school steps.

George found his voice first. He blinked hard and his jaw trembled slightly. "Yeah, all the kids are gone. There's just us."

"What about Miss Grantham and Miss Watson?"

"They're still inside," said Molly. "Going over director's notes. You know, play stuff."

Steven rushed up the stairs.

"It's locked," said Lilly. "Miss Grantham locked it behind us."

"Spread out, fellas," Steven instructed the police officers. "We have to find a way in."

Teddy elbowed George and whispered, "Tell him."

"No, shut up," George muttered through gritted teeth.

Jimmy Bou had ears like a bat. "Tell him what?" He swooped down on the boys.

A guilty expression took over George's reddening face. He said, "Eh...I...um...."

Steven grabbed his shoulders and fixed him with a glare that allowed no holding back. "This isn't a joke. Miss Watson's life could be in danger. Tell me!"

"I wanted to spend some time with Molly...um...alone. I left the stage door open. I taped over the lock so we could get back in."

"You kids stay here." Steven drilled them with a look. "Do *not* move."

Steven and his team ran to the back of the school. Carefully, Steven inched open the door. In the pitch black backstage, you'd never know it was a bright sunny day outside. The police officers took a moment for their eyes to adjust. Steven whispered instructions to Jimmy Bou,

Ralph, and Pete. "Fan out," he whispered. "Be careful." The men split up. Tall shadowy stacks of unidentifiable items teetered as they brushed by. Objects were scattered everywhere. Thick ropes hung in groups along the sides and the heavy stage curtains hung behind the proscenium.

Jimmy Bou eased along the back wall behind a piece of painted scenery and disappeared into the wings, stage left. Ralph and Pete crept along the opposite side, slowly making their way toward the front of the stage. Steven and Will carefully made their way across the old oaken boards, hoping not to step on any loose ones. They noticed light near the front of the stage and headed for it, moving in zigzag fashion. They passed thick draping curtains, avoiding the heaps of fabric puddled on the floor. They slid among pieces of scenery propped up against step ladders. It was a mine field.

Suddenly, Olivia's voice broke the silence.

"Put the gun down, Hannah. That's not going to get you anywhere."

"Did you tell him? Did you tell Steven it was me?" Hannah's voice sounded higher than usual.

"No. How could I? I didn't realize it until five minutes ago."

"You're lying!"

"No, I'm not. I only figured it out when I saw the blanket."

"I don't believe you."

"It was when I was standing here and you were looking at me so funny. It hit me." Olivia took a tentative step toward Hannah. "Come on, Hannah, you don't want to do this."

"Stop! I won't hesitate, Olivia. You mean nothing to me."

Olivia reached out, palms down, and gently moved her hands up and down as she tried to calm Hannah. "Okay, okay. I'm just standing here. I'm not going to do anything." She took a half-step back. "But, Hannah, why? I thought you loved Frankie."

"What would you know about it?" Hannah sneered then stepped

into the circle of light that shone down on Olivia.

Jimmy Bou reached the main curtain which was pulled back to the side. Light from the auditorium carried onto the front of the stage making it easy to see Hannah and Olivia. Hidden from view barely three feet away, Jimmy Bou watched. He was going to sneak around to the proscenium and tackle Hannah from behind. He took a step. His boot caught in a piece of loose rope that had slid off a pulley. He tripped and grabbed the heavy drape to break his fall.

Hannah caught the movement in the corner of her eye and shot out with lightening speed. She grabbed him as he struggled to untangle himself. She pulled him into the light and shoved the gun against his head.

"Come out, come out, wherever you are," she taunted. "I'm sure this idiot didn't come alone."

Four police officers slowly emerged from several directions. Steven and Will had their weapons drawn and pointed at Hannah. She looked around wildly. "So," she glared at Steven, "the great Detective Blackwell got here in the end. And believe me, this *will* be the end."

Hannah backed up dragging Jimmy Bou with her. She quickly glanced to the side to see how far she was from the stairs. When she did, the hand holding the gun moved away from the police officer's head. That was all Olivia needed.

Two years of kickboxing training made the moves second nature. Olivia coiled and sprang in the air. She brought her knee up high and close to her body. Her leg shot out straight from her hip. Her foot kicked the gun out of Hannah's hand. Hannah stared, paralyzed for a second.

"Holy shit!" yelled Jimmy Bou, flinging himself away.

Steven, Will, Ralph, and Pete froze open-mouthed. But, there was no time to be amazed. Hannah was livid. She quickly recovered and rushed at Olivia. Olivia spun around and landed a sharp elbow square on the side of her head. Hannah dropped like a stone. She let out a savage cry, shook her head, and blinked furiously. She got up on her hands and knees and scrabbled crab-like across the stage floor to seize the weapon. Steven was faster and kicked it away. The gun sailed across the stage. Ralph bent, picked it up, and trained it on her.

Will lunged and pushed Hannah to the floor. He shoved his knee in the center of her spine and pinned her arms behind her back. Steven pulled out a pair of hand cuffs and secured her wrists together. The two of them hauled her to her feet.

"Hannah Grantham, I am arresting you for the murders of Frankie Russo and Dickie Hughes, for assault-with-a-deadly-weapon on Olivia Watson, and for the attempted murder of Officer Jimmy Bourgogne."

Will and Jimmy Bou escorted her out, closely followed by Ralph and Pete. They marched her to the police vehicle in full view of the stunned students still waiting on the school's front steps.

Steven rushed to Olivia, who had fallen back on a chair after hitting Hannah. He knelt in front of her.

"You're shaking," he said. He reached out and rubbed her arms.

"I could have killed her," she said slowly. "Oh, Steven. What if my elbow had hit her in the temple? I never should have done that."

"I take it this is what you mean by kickboxing?" He rubbed her arms again and said, "No, Olivia, you probably saved Jimmy's life. When a killer is armed and the weapon is pointing at someone, we take any measure—do *anything*—to stop them." He leaned in closely. "You did the right thing."

"I want to go home."

Steven drove as if he had a car full of eggs. He kept glancing over to look at Olivia, checking that her color was back and her trembling had stopped.

"Steven, I'm okay. Stop worrying. I bounce back fast." Olivia reached over and patted his arm. "Hey, by the way, what ever happened to that suitcase of Frankie Russo's that you were going crazy looking for?"

Steven laughed. "It ended up not being important. Ralph and Pete found it but they were able to track Frankie's movements anyway."

When they arrived at their house, Olivia assured Steven one last time that she felt fine. "Listen, I really am okay. I just needed a few minutes to process everything. I don't want you to think about me this afternoon. You need to concentrate on what you're doing."

He studied her. "All right. You do look like yourself again."

"I'm going for a run," Olivia said. "There's nothing like a long hard run to set things right."

Steven checked his watch. "I shouldn't have any trouble getting back here in time to get cleaned up and changed for tonight." The thought of their evening plans rushed through him in a thrilling flood of emotion. "Wow, Olivia! I'm going to the future tonight. I can't wait."

"Me, too." She got out of the car then leaned in the window. "See you at six."

Will, Jimmy Bou, and the rest of his team were gathered in the CID room when Steven returned. Jimmy, Ralph, and Pete were falling all over themselves, each wanting to be the first to tell Charlie, Jerry, and Ray every detail about Olivia's amazing feat.

"You should have seen her," Jimmy Bou exclaimed. "It was like something in the pictures!"

"Steven, is Olivia okay?" asked Will.

"Yes, she's a bit shaken but she'll be fine."

"What *was* that?" asked Ralph.

"Yeah, where'd she learn how to do that?" Pete asked in wonder.

"It's a sport she practices. It's called kickboxing."

"Never heard of it," Ralph and Pete chorused.

"Where is she?" asked Steven. "Hannah, I mean."

"We've got her in a cell. She's not going anywhere," said Will.

Steven nodded. "I'll let the chief know what's going on. You fellas start your reports while everything's fresh in your minds. This one's going to be tricky so take your time. Get it right."

On his return to his desk, Steven said, "Will, would you watch from the other side of the mirror? We don't know what we're dealing with yet. She was pretty erratic back there."

"Sure, I can do that."

"Good. I'm going to let her sit awhile. The longer she waits, the more she's going to want to talk."

An hour later, Will stationed himself at the other side of the new two-way mirror, where he could observe and listen to the interrogation without Hannah even suspecting he was there.

Steven entered the room and sat across the table from her. He stared at Hannah for a good few minutes while she shifted uncomfortably in her chair.

"Come on. What's the hold up, Steven?" she said defiantly.

Steven noticed that her chin trembled slightly and she held her hands in tight fists. He saw the white knuckles and marveled at her composure.

"Hannah, we have you dead to rights. Lucy already told us everything. I guarantee you'll be convicted for the murders of Frankie Russo and Dickie Hughes."

He gave her a minute for that to sink in.

"But, you can make it easy on yourself. If you talk to me, you might be able to work out a deal with the DA. Cooperate and maybe you can trade the electric chair for a prison sentence. It's your choice."

She glared at him but said nothing.

"Or you might be hanged. Did you know there have been eight hangings so far this year? Hanging's cheaper than using all that electricity. New York State might decide to save the taxpayers some money and just hang you."

Her upper lip curled and her eyes narrowed. "You think this little history lesson scares me?"

"I'd be scared if it were me." He heard the fear beneath the bravado. "Come on, Hannah. You're smart. You know how this is going to go."

Hannah sighed. "Fine. I know when I've lost. The game's up, as they say."

"Good decision." Steven nodded and gave her a friendly smile. "So, the first question is why, Hannah? I know you loved Frankie at one time."

"He ruined my life."

"Tell me about it."

She unclenched her fists and placed her hands flat on the table. Her voice was unnaturally calm. "Ten years I waited for him. He promised we'd be together. He swore he was going to leave Lucy. Then, it would be my turn. He said marrying Lucy was a mistake. He never loved her. I was his real love. His one true love. And I believed him. I went along with it for all those years."

"Then, you found out about Stella," Steven whispered.

That surprised her.

"Oh! Yes, I did. I guess you're a better cop than I thought you were."

Steven didn't blink and his eyes never left hers.

"It was an accident really. I *never* expected to find another wife...and a family." Hannah looked for a moment like she was going to cry. She took a deep breath and told him about the snow day, taking the train to Syracuse, and seeing Frankie with Stella. She told him about talking with Stella and discovering they'd been married for a couple of years. A feverish tone took over the calm demeanor of a moment ago.

"An affair I could have dealt with. But he *married* her! I realized he never intended to marry me. Ever. I wasted all those years. He was only stringing me along, lying to me, using me.

"And if all that wasn't enough, there was this beautiful little girl. *I* was supposed to have his children." She laughed bitterly—the hurt, the betrayal, the devastation evident on her face. "It was the baby that did it. A daughter. It was obvious he adored her. I'd never seen him like that. He was a different person."

She hung her head and swallowed hard several times. Steven poured a glass of water and passed it to her. She took it with a shaking hand. She drank greedily and wiped her mouth.

"I spent half my life waiting for him. Now, it's gone." The look she threw at Steven dared him to contradict her. "He took my life. So, I took his. And I'm not sorry."

"How did you convince him to meet you for the picnic?"

"I told him I had gotten engaged and was going to marry Ben. I said let's get together one last time for old time's sake."

"And he went for it. Just like that?" Steven's brows rose.

"Sure," she said, as if it were the most natural thing in the world.

Steven allowed several seconds to pass.

"And what about Dickie Hughes, Hannah. What did he ever do to you?"

"Little delinquent tried to blackmail me. He was in the woods on Sunday. He saw me do it." She laughed hysterically. "No loss. He had a crummy life anyways." She gazed out in the distance. When she turned back, she looked deflated. "Yeah, that was a shame. I felt kind of bad afterwards."

Chapter 46

Saturday — Present Day

Steven took his time getting ready but still had a half hour to kill. Nervous energy buzzed inside him. He was about to spend the evening eighty years in the future. For the very first time, he was going to see what the 21st century looked like in person, not just on Olivia's television. He was going to talk to real people. He felt his heart racing. *Slow down*, he told himself. *Relax or you'll make a fool of yourself.* That was the most important thing tonight. He didn't want to say or do anything to embarrass himself or Olivia.

He went down into the kitchen and drank a glass of water. He prowled the living room, climbed the stairs again, and surveyed himself in the mirror for the fourth time. The clothes weren't too hard to get used to. The dark grey pants weren't as roomy—that felt strange—and he had never imagined that he'd wear a shirt with pale pink stripes in it. But, the tie and vest were familiar enough and he'd been able to wear his own shoes.

At last, it was time to meet Olivia. Steven took a deep breath and walked down the hall toward the bedroom.

Steven's jaw dropped when Olivia faded into view. "Holy mackerel, Olivia. Wow!"

Olivia was wearing a simple black silk top. What made his eyes pop was her skirt. The short black skirt was covered in what looked like feathers and something sparkly. Her high heels were red leather.

"Thanks. You look perfect, Steven. Good job with your hair. Are you ready?" She held out her hand.

"I think so." Her hand felt soft and warm.

"Are you nervous?" she asked.

"A little. Promise you'll let me know if I do something wrong."

"I will. Don't worry, I've got your back. But, you're going to be fine. Liz and Sophie, and Joe, already know who you are. And who cares about anyone else?"

Olivia took a couple of slow backward steps into her room, bringing Steven into the 21st century. They turned a small half-circle then returned to the door and stepped over the threshold. Together they strolled down her hall and out of her house.

On the front porch, Steven paused. "Let me adjust to the future for a minute." He grinned at her. He didn't speak as he scanned the neighborhood. Motor cars of every color whizzed by. A fella with indecently short shorts and a skimpy sleeveless undershirt ran past. A girl walked by holding something to her ear, talking loudly and gesturing with her other hand.

"Oh," he whispered then let out a deep breath. "All right. I'm as ready as I'll ever be."

As they stepped off the porch, Olivia pointed something at her dark blue automobile. Steven heard a faint click.

"What are you doing?"

"Unlocking the car."

When Steven slid into the bucket seat, he didn't know where to look first. "Separate seats. And they're leather, huh?"

"Yeah, they're heated, too."

"Heated? That must be something in the winter. I hate waiting for the engine to warm up. I'd sure go for these."

Olivia laughed. "Yeah, they're great in the cold weather."

He looked up. "What's that?"

Olivia touched the push button starter then the button for the moonroof. The panel slid back and the car was flooded with sunlight.

"Oh, my goodness." His mouth was hanging open. "What else have you got here?"

Olivia pointed out the control features on the steering wheel, explained the Bluetooth system, and demonstrated the power windows, locks, and seats.

"You need to put on your seatbelt, Steven." She showed him.

"What's this for? It's awfully restricting." He clicked the end in place.

"Safety. They save lives. People drive fast these days."

As Olivia was backing the car out into the street, Steven said, "Tell me what to expect tonight."

"Liz and Joe got married ten years ago. Their priest will repeat the vows they made that day and they'll promise all over again to be faithful and true."

"That's nice. I like them already."

"That'll take around a half hour or so. I think there're some prayers, too. Then, we'll come back here for dinner and the rest of the evening. We've got music set up and we cleared off the patio so people can dance if they want to."

"It sounds swell. Oops. No, it sounds *awesome*." He broke out laughing. "*Awesome*. What an expression."

"I'll tell you what else is awesome." Olivia laughed along with him. "Sophie made French pastries for dessert."

Together they *mmm*ed.

Olivia drove slowly so Steven could get a good look at everything. His head swiveled like a bird of prey as he gaped out his window then leaned over Olivia to look out the other side. He stared out the front, his eyes raking the road ahead.

"I don't know where to look first. It's noisy." He wrinkled his nose. "The air smells different. Oh, look at that!" He turned to Olivia as she negotiated a turn. "Olivia, nothing is the same. I see why you had the panic attack the other day. It's like being on another planet."

They approached the next corner.

"Holy mackerel! What is *that*?" His jaw dropped and his eyes popped.

Across the intersection, at a four-way stop, sat a red Corvette.

"That's a Chevy." She grinned.

"I want to live long enough to buy one of *those*." He fell back in the seat shaking his head, his mouth still open.

Olivia parallel parked behind a black Jeep Cherokee in front of St. Joseph's. Steven stared at the SUV. When she locked the car with the remote and it beeped, he jumped. Everything had changed, even a simple car key. He said a silent prayer that he wouldn't put his foot in his mouth tonight in front of all her friends.

Father O'Brien's voice rang out. "Liz and Joe, we mark the ten-year anniversary of your wedding day. On that beautiful spring day, you made a pledge and exchanged rings to symbolize the never-ending love you have for each other. I am privileged to witness your vows once again and to bless your union for the next ten...or twenty...or...." The congregation laughed.

"Elizabeth Magdela Smithson, do you promise to love this man, to honor and care for him, to be faithful to him for as long as you both shall live?"

"I do."

"Leonard Joseph Smithson, do you promise to love this woman, to honor and care for her, to be faithful to her for as long as you both shall live?"

"I do."

"In the presence of God, in the company of family and friends, we celebrate the loving commitment of these two young people." He smiled at Joe. "You may kiss the bride."

Applause and cheers rang out as Liz and Joe held on to each other for several moments before stepping apart.

"Olivia!" A young woman with luscious red curls and midnight blue eyes hurried toward them across Olivia's back yard.

"Hi!" She stuck out her hand and stared at Steven. "I'm Sophie."

"I'm pleased to meet you, Sophie." Steven's deep voice filled the space between them.

"Me too! Finally." She snuck a look around them making sure no one was eavesdropping. "What do you think so far, Steven?"

"Where do I start!?"

Liz and Joe came over and Olivia performed the introductions.

"Steven," Joe put his arm around Steven's shoulders, led him a few steps away, and said conspiratorially, "I'd like to ask you a favor if I could. I've got this awesome collection of baseball cards. But I'm missing some from the thirties. I was wondering if maybe you could help me out. And listen, I want you to know I'm not trying to score something valuable. I just want to fill in a few gaps."

Steven was so happy to be on solid ground—you could always rely on baseball—that he didn't even mind the questionable proposition. He chuckled. "Sure, Joe. I'm a baseball fan, too. I'd be glad to."

The evening passed in a whirlwind for Steven. He ate fancy dishes he'd never had before, tasted drinks he'd never heard of, listened to conversations that he understood only parts of, and tried to block out loud noise that was supposed to be music. As the party drew to a close, the music changed to a soft slow song. *This I can do,* Steven thought. He stood up from the table, gave Olivia a little bow, and held out his hand.

As they came together on the dance floor, Steven and Olivia were thinking the same thing.

I could get used to this.

Not the End

Acknowledgements

My heartfelt thanks to the following people . . .

To Beta Readers Mickey Hunter, Karen Lasher, John M, Marylou Murry, Risa Rispoli, and Sue Scheeren Watchko for taking their time and giving me valuable feedback.

To Dr. Francisco Gomez for his help on poisons. (Any errors are my own.), Anna Cotter for checking my Italian, and Belinda King for her advice on whiskey.

To Shawn Reilly Simmons for her enthusiasm for this project and her insightful comments which helped me add an extra layer to the book.

To Everyone at Level Best Books for their work on behalf of Steven and Olivia, and for giving them a home.

To my Friends and Family who encouraged me, listened to me, and enthusiastically supported me throughout this process. Much love and thanks for always being there.

A very special thank you to G.M. for his help with police procedure and for making this a better book. (Any errors are mine.)

And last but not least, to all the readers who fell in love with Steven and Olivia in *Doorway to Murder* and have stuck by me through this long wait for the follow-up. I truly appreciate your support!!

A Note from the Author

Threshold of Deceit is a work of fiction. All characters and events are the product of the author's imagination. Any resemblance to a real person or persons is coincidental. While the Mohawk River and Adirondack Mountains certainly do exist, geographic liberties have been taken for the sake of the story. The town of Knightsbridge exists only in this novel.

Threshold of Deceit - A DISCUSSION GUIDE

RELATIONSHIPS

1. In the two months since they first saw each other (*Doorway to Murder*), Steven and Olivia have gotten to be good friends. They've spent nearly every evening together in either his or her kitchen and know each other well. Discuss the challenges they would face if their relationship turned romantic.

2. When Olivia visits Steven in 1934, he is hosting her as a guest but she is on an adventure. Discuss the differences in how they react to each other while she's in his time.

3. There were 4 significant women in Frankie Russo's life: Hannah, Lucy, Adona, and Stella. Discuss how these women are different and also how they are alike.

4. Why do you think Hannah, Lucy, and Stella were attracted to Frankie? Discuss the circumstances in their lives that brought them to him.

5. Often we hear of strong independent women being attracted to abusive men. Why do you think Lucy married Frankie?

6. Olivia, Liz, and Sophie agree that their lives would never be the same without one of the three. Many of us understand how important it is to have women friends. (To the men in the group, change this to "men friends.") Share your feelings about having a support system made up of friends. Why do you think this is so important?

THE CRIMES

7. Did you guess the killer? When? What were the clues?

8. Steven and his fellow cops solve crimes without 21st-century technology like DNA testing, cell phones, GPS tracking, and computers. What advantages and disadvantages are there in working without these tools?

TIME TRAVEL

9. Olivia spends several days in 1934 and interacts with people of that time. Discuss the challenges and pitfalls she faces in attempting to blend in so as not to reveal her and Steven's secret. How could she be easily tripped up?

10. Before the inventions of Thomas Edison, Alexander Graham Bell, and the Wright Brothers, the world was a different place. Electric lights, speaking with someone miles away, or soaring above the earth was the stuff of science fiction—or magic. Before smart phones, computers, and software applications like Skype, it was hard to imagine talking on the phone and *seeing* the person on the other end. Today, the idea of time travel is inconceivable.

- If we could time-travel some day, how might it affect our everyday

life?
- How might people use the ability? How could they abuse it?

11. Olivia travels 80 years into the past, from 2014 to 1934. A former journalist, she's interested in seeing newspapers and listening to the news on the radio.

If you could time-travel into the past . . .

- What year would you visit? What would you want to see?
- Would you like to spend time and talk with someone famous? Who? What would you ask or say to that person?
- Would you want to meet your parents or grandparents? At what point in their lives?
- What would you talk about with them?
- Would you want to find your younger self? What would you say? Would you try to change something in your life or warn yourself about something?

12. Steven travels 80 years into the future. He's excited to see the cars of the 21st century and to experience the technology that Olivia shows him, like the large, flat-screen TV and her laptop. He wants to know how the police solve crimes. However, he does **not** want to know *his* future.

If you could time travel into the future . . .

- What year would you visit and what or whom would you want to see? Why?

- Would you want to see yourself at a future time? If so, what year and why did you choose that year?
- Would you want to know about your future? Your death?

THE BOOK

13. What was your favorite scene and why?

About the Author

A Francophile at age 11, Carol Pouliot dreamed of going to Paris. After obtaining her MA in French at Stony Brook University, she headed to France for her first teaching job. She taught French and Spanish for over 30 years in Upstate New York. She also founded and operated an agency that provided translations in some 24 languages. Carol is the author of The Blackwell and Watson Time-Travel Mystery series, which includes *Doorway to Murder* (Book 1) and *Threshold of Deceit* (Book 2). When not writing, Carol can be found reaching for her passport and packing a suitcase for her next adventure.

Find Carol at http://www.carolpouliot.com

CPSIA information can be obtained
at www.ICGtesting.com
Printed in the USA
LVHW111046280820
664156LV00001B/165